THE SHIP WITH NO NAME

The deck heaved beneath him, and there was a *whoosh* of flame and smoke. He threw himself from the cockpit only a second before his own plane exploded, and rolled towards the promising shelter of the island, surrounded by burning and exploding gasoline, exploding bullets and, now, detonating bombs ... The after part of the ship was a blazing inferno; his entire squadron had disappeared in flame and smoke. *Akagi* was sinking.

He sat up, and looked around at the magnificent fleet which had been steaming so majestically towards victory only half an hour earlier. Now it was scattered like a herd of sheep attacked by a wolf. And *Akagi* was not the only ship sinking.

THE SHIP WITH NO NAME

Christopher Nicole

**THE SHERIDAN
BOOK COMPANY**

This edition published in 1995 by
The Sheridan Book Company

Arrow edition 1987
Random House, 20 Vauxhall Bridge Road, London SW1V 2SA

© F. Beermann BV 1987

Printed and bound in Great Britain by
Cox & Wyman Ltd, Reading, Berkshire

ISBN 1-85501-673-7

To my son Jack; for his considerable assistance in the researching of this book.

CONTENTS

On 18 April 1942, sixteen B-25 Mitchell Bombers of the United States Army Air Force, led by Lieutenant-General James H. Doolittle, took off from the United States carrier *Hornet* and flew eight hundred miles to bomb Tokyo.

PROLOGUE

April 1942

As the sun peeped above the eastern horizon, the airmen saw Japan. They had flown the eight hundred miles from the heaving, cluttered flight deck of the *USS Hornet* in darkness, low over the calm Pacific to avoid reconnaissance patrols. Now, all their months of training were to come to a culmination in a matter of seconds.

The sixteen bombers, the largest in the world, were silhouetted against the sunrise as they flew towards the sandy beaches and low green hills of the island empire, taking their course from the immense, snow-capped peak of Mount Fuji away to their south-west, from which the brilliant rays of the rising sun reflected like a beacon. Fishermen hauling their nets just offshore looked up without surprise. If it was only five months since their government, by attacking the American naval base at Pearl Harbor in Hawaii, had launched them into a global conflict, war itself was nothing new to the Japanese. They had been officially at war with China for nearly five years now, and they had been unofficially at war with both China and Russia for longer than that. Aeroplanes roaring out of the dawn were quite usual to these fishermen; the Japanese air forces, army and navy, never ceased their training, their preparation for the next battle.

The fishermen stood up in their boats – each craft painted a bright red and yellow, with huge black and white eyes in the bows to make sure they would always be able to find their way home – and waved their flat hats at the airmen. Then one of them frowned. He had never seen planes like these before, strangely squat about the front section, and yet far larger than anything possessed by the Japanese Air Force. And now the suddenly frightened men could make out the markings on the wings of each machine, as the bombers flew only a hundred feet above their heads: red, white and blue stars, where there should have been the glowing red sun of Japan. Before they could understand what this meant, the planes were gone, rising to pass over the low hills which surrounded Tokyo Bay. And already the watchers could hear the dull impact of the exploding bombs.

Keiko, as usual, was up before dawn to do his exercises. And, again as usual, Yoshino Hatatsune was there to watch him, with proud sorrow.

Keiko bent and stretched, extended his legs and leaned forward to place his hands flat on the ground, brought his legs back together and jogged on the spot for several minutes, raising his knees higher and higher, while sweat gleamed from his shoulders and face. He was above average height for a Japanese, and in singlet and shorts his superb physique was almost beautiful. He had possessed that physique even as a youth, and Yoshino had always been proud of it, as she was of his handsome face, his liquid black eyes, the intensity of his character, and, since manhood, his uniform as a navy pilot. Yet now she hardly wished to look at him. She remembered too well how he had been brought home after the attack on Pearl Harbor. There had been broken ribs, and broken bones in his legs as well, where the American bullets had ripped through the body of his machine to find the body of the man. She had screamed in horror, and torn her hair. Not even the reassurance of Admiral Yamamoto himself had been able to ease her throbbing misery.

'Your son is a hero, honourable Mrs Hatatsune,' Yamamoto had said. 'All those who flew to Hawaii are heroes, but Keiko is a breed apart. He was attacked by two American fighters.' Yamamoto gave one of his grim smiles. 'They were two of the very few American fighters to reach the skies that day. One of those planes he shot down, even while being hit by the other. And he would undoubtedly have shot down that as well, had the American not turned tail and fled. And then, his aircraft badly damaged and he himself losing blood all the time and in great pain, he not only regained his carrier, but made a perfect landing before he fainted. His behaviour will be an inspiration to millions of Japanese. And the Emperor himself will decorate him, when he is well again.'

That was four months ago. And, remarkably, Keiko had not died. He was not even left a cripple, forever deprived of the use of his legs, which had indeed been her greater fear. He had instead made such a good recovery that the investiture took place last month, when she and her husband actually stood in the same room as His Majesty, and watched the Lord of all Japan shake their son by the hand. She supposed that had been the proudest moment of her life. Yet it had been but a moment. And now . . .

Keiko was grinning at her as he towelled himself. 'Not a twinge. Not a hesitation, honourable mother. They will have to pass me as fit for combat at my next examination.'

'And you will go back to sea, and to war, and to death,' Yoshino said sadly.

'Is that not a man's privilege, honourable mother? Besides – ' he gave one of his famous smiles: the picture of his smiling face had been reproduced in every Japanese newspaper, the portrait of a hero – 'there is no death any more. The Americans are pulling out of the Pacific far faster than we can ever hope to catch them up.' He pulled on his kimono. 'I will bathe, and then. . . .' He frowned, as he heard the drone of the engines.

Yoshino sighed. 'Your comrades do not even allow us to sleep,' she said.

'Yes, but those are not Japanese engines!' Keiko ran from the shelter of the trees to stare into the slowly lightening sky, and listened to the first *crump* of an exploding bomb. He gazed at the immense shape silhouetted against the light, and recognised it immediately from his hours of study of all the world's aircraft. 'B-25s,' he muttered.

His father stood beside him, still rubbing sleep from his eyes. Masawa Hatatsune had fought against the Russians in 1905, and regarded all wars since as mere skirmishes. Yet he too stared at the aircraft swooping low over Tokyo; there had been no aircraft above Mukden and Port Arthur. 'What can they be?' he wondered.

'They are American bombers!' Keiko spat the words.

Yoshino had hurried to join them. 'Americans? But how can that be? No American plane can reach Tokyo. The Emperor has said so.'

Keiko gave her an impatient glance. The navy had said so – that was what mattered now. His navy, from which he was separated, and at such a time. There were no Japanese planes to be seen, and the city's anti-aircraft defences, sparse enough, were just coming to life; they had all been taken completely by surprise. Meanwhile, the enemy planes wheeled and swooped, and dropped their bombs; already pillars of smoke were rising into the air . . . and one of the huge machines was flying a path straight at them, or so it seemed.

'Down!' he bawled, throwing his arms round his parents' shoulders to hurl them to the ground. He heard

14

the whistle of the bombs, and then the *whoosh* of the impact. Yet there was no blast. He sat up and gazed at his father's house, suddenly glowing. The Americans were using incendiaries, knowing that those would cause the most damage amidst the cardboard-walled houses of the Japanese capital.

'Fire!' Yoshino screamed, also sitting up, her face incongruously stained with leaves and earth; like all Japanese women, she was normally totally immaculate in her dress and cleanliness.

Keiko scrambled to his feet and ran towards the blaze. His mother shouted after him to be careful, but the raid was already over; the American planes had gone. Neighbours clustered around with pitiful buckets of water to throw on the flames, and in the distance he could hear the clanging of a fire-engine bell. But it too would be useless; the Hatatsune house was blazing like the stiff paper which was all it was.

'It cannot have happened,' someone said. 'We must be dreaming. The gods would not allow it.'

'They were devils from hell,' swore another.

As we were being devils to them, Keiko thought, when we swooped above Pearl Harbor, and Manila, and Singapore. That knowledge did not assuage his anger; rather it increased it, because now it was tinged with apprehension. He was well aware that the whole world, with the exception of Japan's allies – Nazi Germany and Fascist Italy – had condemned the surprise attack on Pearl Harbor as an infamous act. This was not a point of view he was prepared to concede. As a serving officer, his duty was to obey orders, not worry about their implications. Besides, to attack without warning had always been the Japanese way – such an attack, on the Russian naval base of Port Arthur in 1904, had led to Japan's greatest triumph, at least up to now. The whole conflict with the United States had been undertaken on the premise that by launching a

15

surprise attack – not only to knock out the American Pacific Fleet for a period of at least six months, but also to seize a far-flung perimeter of islands and gain the precious oil of the Dutch East Indies and the tin and rubber of Malaya – Japan would establish an impregnable empire, so as to enable the Japanese people to take their proper place in the sun as the arbitrators of Asia. And the plan had worked. Pearl Harbor had been bombed. Hong Kong and Malaya and Sumatra and the Philippines had been overrun. Even the mighty fortress of Singapore had surrendered to the irresistible *élan* of the Japanese armed forces. Only a handful of Americans still held out on the island fortress of Corregidor in Manila Bay, and they were expected to surrender any day now – no soldiers could fight forever without hope of success.

Only the one aspect of the operation had not gone entirely to plan: the three aircraft-carriers of the American Pacific Fleet had been absent from Hawaiian waters on the day of the raid. That had simply been bad luck. It had not been regarded as of vital importance. Three aircraft-carriers, unsupported by battleships, did not make a fleet, especially when opposed to the massive navy commanded by Admiral Yamamoto, which included six aircraft-carriers and several battleships, among them the largest in the world, the *Yamato*, displacing nearly seventy thousand tons. Yet here was sudden and alarming proof that the Americans were not as shattered as had been supposed, that they were even willing to risk at least one of their carriers in a desperate counter-attack. And those planes *had* to have come from a carrier – there was no American-held territory within aircraft range of Tokyo. But to use such a precious ship for carrying out a bombing raid on the Japanese mainland . . . she would have had to penetrate to within a thousand miles of Tokyo, through all the submarines and reconnaissance aircraft which patrolled

16

those waters without cessation. And B-25s: Those were not naval aircraft. They were huge, lumbering, land-based bombers. To carry them at all was a remarkable concept, much less to ask their pilots to take off from the tiny, heaving flight-deck of a carrier . . .

'Your medals,' Yoshino wailed.

And his uniform. And his honour. Except that of course honour was already avenged. Those planes had nowhere to go, save down into the sea or the earth. The carrier would undoubtedly have been found and sunk by now. It was a raid — a gesture of defiance by a proud people who had been outwitted and outfought at every turn. It could be treated with contempt.

'They will give me other medals, honourable mother,' he said. 'And another uniform.'

'Your father, honourable Commander,' someone gasped.

The old man lay on his back, his face mottled, his breathing stertorous.

'It is a heart attack,' someone else said. 'Send for an ambulance.'

Keiko knelt beside his father and cradled him in his arms. 'Help is coming, honourable father,' he promised.

'But . . . the enemy,' Masawa Hatatsune panted.

'They have gone,' Keiko told him. 'They will be punished. There can be no doubt of this. Oh, they will be punished.' He looked above his father's head at his mother. 'Akiko!'

'You must go to her, honourable son,' Yoshino said. 'And make sure she is safe. You will come to me at the hospital, when you have seen Akiko, and tell me she is well.' Yoshino gazed at the ashes of her home. 'We have much to discuss.'

That Keiko Hatatsune, the most famous Japanese air ace yet to emerge from this brief war, should be striding through the streets of Tokyo wearing a kimono instead

17

of his uniform, occasioned little comment on this day; the people of the city were too stunned by the events of the morning to feel additional surprise. They stood around in clusters, pointing and talking to each other, every so often looking to the east, as if expecting yet another wave of bombers to come winging over the hills.

In some ways Keiko was reminded of that unforgettable, terrifying day, 1 September 1923, when the great earthquake had struck. He had been ten years old then, and he could clearly remember the academy shaking as if caught in a giant wind, the floors moving beneath his feet as, with his fellow students, he had run out into the yard. Then there had been clouds of smoke, and screams, and silence. Tokyo had soon been rebuilt, despite the almost incomprehensible violence of nature which had killed a hundred and fifty thousand people in the space of seconds, and destroyed over six hundred thousand homes. For eighteen years after that, the city had been inviolate.

Now there was again smoke in the sky, drifting across the morning. But how little. How puny and ineffective had been the Americans' attempt to avenge Pearl Harbor. In physical terms. It was the people who had been affected more than the houses. In 1923 there had been terror, and horror, but also a stoic determination to resume their shattered lives. The gods had willed the earthquake: blessed be the gods.

But the bombers this morning had not been piloted by gods; they had been piloted by men, men whose lives, now and for the forseeable future, were dedicated to the destruction of Japan. The people were frightened by that realisation. It was seven hundred years since any men had actively sought the destruction of Japan, and then the Mongol hordes, painfully propelling themselves across the sea from China, had been scattered and destroyed by a typhoon – ever since called the

18

Kamikaze, or Divine Wind – which had swept out of the Pacific. Today, the wind had been absent.

Saigo Tarawa's house stood undamaged, in an undamaged street. Yet here too the crowds were gathered, chattering and fearful. Keiko shouldered his way through them, and was met by his future father-in-law. 'Honourable Commander,' Tarawa said. 'You are safe.'

Keiko bowed, and then clasped the older man's hand. 'As are you, honourable sir. And Akiko?'

'She waits for you. She is concerned.'

Keiko kicked off his sandals and went into the house. Akiko and her mother knelt before him, their hands raised to their lips. Keiko bowed to Mrs Tarawa, and then to the girl who would be his wife. 'Akiko,' he said.

'Honourable Commander.' She gave him her hands and allowed him to raise her to her feet, which he did as easily as if she had been a feather. Akiko Tarawa was barely five feet tall, and a slender young girl. Her black hair was neatly coiled on the nape of her neck and secured with an ivory pin: her body was totally concealed by her pale yellow kimono; and her obi – the broad sash which secured the garment at the waist – was a darker shade of the same colour. Her black eyes shone. She was the proudest girl in Japan, to be betrothed to Keiko Hatatsune.

But even her fingers were tight with anxiety. 'We have heard rumours,' she said. 'Your house?'

'Is destroyed,' Keiko told her.

'May the gods curse the Americans and all their works,' Mrs Tarawa said.

'The gods use men to carry out their will, honourable mother,' Keiko said. 'They will, I hope, use me.'

He smiled at Akiko. 'As soon as I can have a new uniform made.'

'To fly . . .' she shuddered.

'To avenge this insult.' He turned as there was a banging on the door.

19

Saigo Tarawa opened it, and stepped aside as a man burst in. 'Commander Hatatsune,' the man shouted.

Keiko frowned, and released Akiko.

'Your father, honourable Commander . . .'

'Well? What is it?' But instinctively he knew.

'He had another heart attack on reaching the hospital. Honourable Commander, your father is dead.'

The uniformed secretary stood to attention. 'Admiral Yamamoto is in conference, honourable Commander.'

Keiko nodded. 'I will wait. It is most urgent that I speak with him.'

The secretary gazed at him. There was no trace of grief to be seen in Keiko's features; only the fact that he wore a white mourning band on the sleeve of his ill-fitting and obviously borrowed uniform indicated that he had just scattered his father's ashes. But his face was set and angry. 'If you would take a seat, honourable Commander . . .' The secretary picked up his house phone.

Keiko chose a straight chair and sat down, back stiff, body erect. He stared at the desk, and at the man on the telephone, but without really seeing him. Remarkably, he did not see his father, either, although he knew this was remiss of him. But now was not the time to think of Father, only of the way he had died. Thus he thought about the airmen flying those B-25s.

He wondered what they were like. In particular, he wondered what Clive Wharton was like. It was a name he knew well; the only name of an American flyer he knew at all. They had met, in the air, over Honolulu, last 7 December.

Like most ambitious young Japanese officers, Keiko had taken the trouble to learn English. Thus he had understood much of the chatter over the air as he wheeled above Hickam Field. He had been attacked by two navy fighters. One he had shot down almost

20

immediately, and the pilot, apparently unable to release his cockpit cover and thus use his parachute, had shouted into his mike, 'Get him, Wharton, get him for me.'

Wharton had all but succeeded, as Keiko's three months in bed and five months' incapacity for duty had proved. Wharton *would* have shot him down, Keiko knew . . . but as the American had closed in for the kill, his guns had jammed. That was why he had broken off the combat – not cowardice, as Admiral Yamamoto claimed. Wharton had proved himself a pilot every bit as good as Keiko himself; as determined, and as courageous. Keiko even knew what he looked like. Then, he had caught but a glimpse of an oxygen-masked and flying-helmeted head, but since then he had been given a copy of an American newspaper picked up in Manila, and on the front page was the photograph of an American pilot. 'Lieutenant Clive Wharton,' the caption read, 'one of the heroes of Pearl Harbor'. The story had gone on to relate how Wharton and his companion had attacked the cloud of Japanese planes above Hickam Field, and how Wharton alone had survived.

Keiko had studied the man, his big chin and his thrusting nose, his crooked, embarrassed grin and his big white teeth. Not handsome, but suggestive of a friendly bear. When he wished to be friendly.

He would not be friendly again, until this business was settled. He would not, of course, have been one of yesterday's marauders; those had been army personnel, and Wharton, like Keiko himself, was in the navy. But if the Americans did mean to make a fight of it, Wharton would be around. As he himself would be around, Keiko mused. He hoped they would meet again, when he would prove himself to be the better man. Only on Wharton, the name and the face he knew, could he centre his desire to avenge his father's death.

21

The secretary replaced the phone and looked up. 'You are to go in, honourable Commander.'

Keiko stood up in surprise. 'To the conference?'

'That is correct, honourable Commander.'

Keiko hesitated, for the first time concerned about his uniform. Then he squared his shoulders, tucked his cap under his arm and followed the secretary down the corridor to the conference room, and stepped inside as the secretary announced him, giving a deep bow.

'Commander!' Isoroku Yamamoto rose from his chair at the head of the table to take the young man's hands. 'Keiko! My heart bleeds for you.'

Keiko stood straight, looking into the eyes of the man who controlled the lives of every other man in the Japanese Navy. Yamamoto was slightly the shorter, but was more heavily built. He gave the impression of immense strength, not only in the formidable shoulders, the barrel chest and the obvious physical power which underlay every movement, but also in the strong jaw and prominent nose, the flatness of the lips, the depths behind the black eyes.

'I seek only to avenge my father's death, honourable Admiral,' Keiko said in a low voice.

'I had expected nothing less.' Yamamoto escorted him to the long, polished table. 'Gentlemen. You know Commander Hatatsune? There is no finer pilot in the navy.'

The other admirals nodded their assent. They were all faces very familiar to Keiko, even if he had never before encountered them all together and at such close quarters. Now he looked from the almost square, determined face of Vice-Admiral Chuichi Nagumo to the pessimistically downturned features of Admiral Takeo Kurita, to the proud, angry stare of Vice-Admiral Jisaburo Ozawa.

'I must apologise for my uniform, honourable Admirals,' Keiko said. 'Mine was destroyed with my home.'

'We understand, Commander,' Yamamoto said, gesturing him to a chair. 'Your home will be rebuilt. That will be the navy's charge. But tell me, when will you be fit for duty?'

'I am fit for duty now, honourable Admiral.'

'You have seen the doctors?'

'No, honourable Admiral. I see them tomorrow. But they will pronounce me fit for service. I seek an immediate posting, in order to strike back at the Americans.' He glanced from face to face. 'We do mean to strike back at the Americans?'

'I am afraid it is necessary,' Yamamoto agreed. 'Although not logical, at this time. We all know that the raid has been the most abject failure. A few houses burned, casualties of no consequence, in exchange for the destruction of sixteen of America's best bombers and the loss of their crews . . .'

'We do not know they are all lost,' Nagumo growled.

'We may safely assume it,' Yamamoto insisted. 'There is no possibility of those planes carrying sufficient fuel to return to any carrier which might be waiting for them, or of such planes as B-25s being able to !and on the flight-deck of a carrier. Those aircraft and their crews are undoubtedly lost. Indeed, one crashed just outside the city; the crew is already in the hands of the Kempai.' He paused reflectively. He was a sailor, and a gentleman. He detested the very thought of the secret police, much less their methods. But those methods, which dictated that a prisoner was an object worthy only of contemptuous treatment and ignominious death, were approved by the generals who ruled Japan. He raised his head and looked from face to face. 'So the raid, I say again, was in tactical terms a failure. Unfortunately, it is the psychological factor which matters, and must be overcome. The people are disturbed, afraid. We have been foolish enough to make the boast that no enemy bombs would ever fall on Japan, and even more foolishly, we allowed His Majesty to quote us. We must now make it plain to the people, to the whole world, that those who do seek to violate our territory will be punished a thousandfold.'

'Let us take our carrier fleet across the Pacific and blast San Francisco to rubble,' Ozawa said.

'That is a senseless idea,' Nagumo objected. 'To take our carrier strike-force within range of the American shore-based bombers would be suicide.'

'In any event,' Kurita pointed out quietly, 'what is San Francisco? Or Los Angeles? Or both together? Great cities, like Nagasaki and Shimonoseki. But of no more importance. The Americans have not bombed Nagasaki or Shimonoseki. They have bombed Tokyo. To retaliate on a lesser target would but compound the loss of face we have suffered today.'

Ozawa gave a snort of contempt. 'So you would bomb Washington or New York? What is our first step, honourable Admiral – to ask permission of the Americans to take our fleet through the Panama Canal?'

'Those are all dreams,' Nagumo said.

'Not necessarily so, honourable Admiral,' Keiko ventured, and then paused, aghast at his own temerity, but with his heart pounding. The concept of retaliating against the mainland United States had already been occupying his mind; he had spent the past five months lying on his back and studying every navy and every air force in the world, in so far as he could obtain information on them.

The admirals were all looking at him. 'Say what you have in mind, Commander Hatatsune,' Yamamoto invited.

Keiko drew a long breath. 'I think you, honourable Admiral,' he said, 'will be able to confirm my understanding that the Nazi government, our allies, have a modern aircraft-carrier lying ninety per cent completed in the harbour of Kiel.'

24

'Why, that is perfectly true,' Yamamoto agreed. 'Work has been stopped on the vessel in order to build up the U-boat fleet.'

'Yet the ship could be completed within a few weeks,' Keiko said. 'If we can obtain the use of that German carrier for a single sortie, honourable Admiral, we can achieve our objective and regain all the face we have lost by yesterday's raid.'

'You mean we will be seen to have employed our allies to avenge us,' Nagumo said distastefully.

'Not so, honourable Admiral. The carrier may be German, but the planes and aircrew will be Japanese.'

'And how is this to be accomplished? Do you suppose the Russians will let us fly a squadron of our bombers across their territory to link up with the Germans, whom they are fighting?' Ozawa asked.

'We will buy the aircraft off the Germans, honourable Admiral, and repaint them with Japanese markings. As for transporting the aircrews, do not Spanish and Portuguese, Swedish and French vessels enter and leave our ports all the time?'

'An interesting conjecture,' Kurita observed. 'But you have not considered one most vital point, Commander. The Germans have no plane which can be compared with the B-25. Their Heinkels and Junkers are altogether smaller planes, with a correspondingly shorter range. You would have to get them within five hundred miles of their target at the very least.'

'I believe that by using the weather, and in total secrecy, a single carrier, unescorted, could reach as far as the Grand Banks of Newfoundland before being detected, honourable Admiral,' Keiko said. 'That would permit its strike force to reach New York. Washington, alas, is not possible, I agree. But New York is the greatest city in the United States. It is the city everyone thinks of when America is mentioned.'

'That is true,' Nagumo agreed. 'But the range is still

the decisive factor. The American planes appear to have been trying to reach those portions of north China still under the control of Chiang Kai-shek, thus even if the planes will probably be lost, there is every chance that the crews will survive, and may even regain America to fight again. That is simply not practical with regard to New York. There is *no* friendly country within another three thousand miles.'

'I took those factors into account, honourable Admiral,' Keiko declared.

Nagumo stared at him. 'You are proposing a suicide mission, Commander?'

'You say there is a chance that some of the Americans may get home, honourable Admiral. A chance. But they must have accepted the fact that theirs was a suicide mission. Are we to suppose there are less dedicated men in the Japanese Navy?'

Ozawa gave a brief laugh. 'You would create a latterday Divine Wind, Commander.'

'I would, honourable Admiral,' Keiko said angrily. 'And I will lead it myself.'

'You?' Yamamoto asked. 'My dear Keiko, you are our leading ace. We need you. And your father has just died. Your mother needs you. And you are soon to be married.'

'I but crave the right of every son, to avenge his father. My mother, and my betrothed, will understand this.'

Yamamoto gazed at him for several seconds, then nodded. 'I do not doubt either your courage, Commander Hatatsune, or your devotion to duty, or your ability to carry out such a raid. However, there is one last factor you may have overlooked: the Nazis. Why should they devote their only aircraft-carrier to such a cause, with the consequent possibility of destruction?'

'Because, honourable Admiral, they do not yet have

an aircraft-carrier. They have failed to complete her. Supposing we proposed to them that we assist in the completion of this vessel, with materials and, more important, with our expertise, gained in actual combat – would they not be grateful? Then, there is less chance of her being lost than the *Hornet*. I know that a year ago the British caught and sank *Bismarck* as she emerged from the Denmark Strait. But that was because they knew she was coming, and because *Bismarck* maintained radio contact with Germany. Honourable Admiral, you took our combined fleets to within a few hundred miles of the Hawaiian Islands without detection simply by the maintenance of proper security. And is it not a fact that, even since the loss of *Bismarck*, German surface raiders, such as the heavy cruisers *Scheer* and *Deutschland*, and even more, armed merchant cruisers, some as large as fifteen thousand tons, have passed through the Denmark Strait with great regularity, escaping the British patrols and reaching as far as the South Atlantic and the Indian Ocean? Has not *Scheer* just returned from a year's cruise, in which she virtually reached Australia?'

'That is what the Germans are claiming, certainly,' Yamamoto said.

'And we are not asking the carrier to undertake such a voyage,' Keiko emphasised. 'All she has to do is launch our planes and then run for home, before anyone knows where to start looking for her. And yet, after the raid, the Nazis will be able to trumpet their share in a great and signal victory.'

Yamamoto gave a slight cough. 'It is a bold and dramatic concept; one which, if successfully carried out, would certainly yield an enormous amount of prestige.' He leaned forward, his hands clasped on the table in front of him. 'However, gentlemen, wars are not won by brilliant and dramatic strokes. Wars are won by relentlessly pursuing strategical objectives. Our strategical objectives last December were twofold. First, to secure for ourselves an unchallengeable source of the raw materials we need for the survival of our country – the oil of the East Indies, the rubber and tin of Malaya and the rice of Indo-China. Second, to protect this new Japanese Empire by a defensive perimeter which would be unbreachable. To achieve this, it was necessary to eliminate the United States Navy as a factor until our perimeter could be achieved and fortified. In this last aim we failed. We may have supposed we succeeded, thanks to the apparent victory at Pearl Harbor, but the events of yesterday have illuminated our mistake. Our failure to destroy the three American carriers at Pearl Harbor was the cause of the raid on Tokyo. Equally at fault was our failure to envisage a perimeter even larger than we had originally planned.

'Now, gentlemen, my intention, and it is supported by General Tojo, is to rectify those two errors. Our perimeter will be enlarged by several hundred miles, thus making a raid such as yesterday's quite impossible in the future. This operation has already commenced, with the dispatch of a task force to seize New Guinea and the Solomons as advance bastions. We will continue that line round in a vast semi-circle which we will anchor on the island of Midway. Now, as you know, Midway is currently an American base. But as you also know, once we take it, our land-based bombers will be within range of Hawaii. Therefore the Americans, whatever they do about the Solomons and New Guinea, will have no option as regards Midway; they must either fight, or withdraw their carriers and indeed their entire fleet to the West Coast of America. Whichever decision they make, we will still have reached our goal. But if they do decide to fight, what are they going to fight with? Only those three carriers. At Midway, gentlemen, we shall bar the door to the Japanese Empire, and if we are given the opportunity, we shall destroy what

28

remains of the American battle fleet.' He leaned back in his chair. 'We will also regain all the face we lost yesterday.' He gazed down the table at Keiko. 'Do not be disappointed, Keiko. Your plan was brilliant, and well thought out. But Midway will bring you greater rewards, because you will lead the assault, honourable Commander.'

'You are sad, my Keiko,' observed Akiko Tarawa.

They walked together in the garden of her father's home, aware that Mrs Tarawa was seated by the back door, overlooking them. They would have had it no other way. Theirs was a relatively modern relationship, in that, once the betrothal had been announced, they had been encouraged to get to know each other – unlike traditional Japanese engagements, where the future husband and wife never even saw each other until the day of the wedding. But to walk together and talk together was as far as either of them wished to go at this time. They were too well-born ever to dream of holding hands; time enough for that, in the privacy of their own home, when they were married.

Yet she loved him dearly, he knew, and would weep if she knew how carelessly he had offered to repudiate her before the admirals. Then was he not relieved that his offer had been rejected? He wasn't sure. He wasn't sure if Yamamoto, his idol as a man and an airman and a commander, had merely been being kind when he had pretended interest and even admiration for his project. Certainly, he had dismissed it with devastating logic, and equally certainly, he was right; to destroy the remnants of the American fleet was of far more value than dropping a few bombs on New York. And he had been given tactical command of the air strike force. He should be the proudest man in Japan, and would be, when it had all sunk in. But for the moment, having made the offer, he was aware of a tremendous sense of

29

inbalance, as if he were not really walking in this delightful garden with this most delightful of women, enjoying the April sunshine, but was already committed to a covenant with death.

'Should a man not look sad, my Akiko,' he asked, 'when he has just lost his father?'

She bowed her head. 'I understand, my Keiko, and I apologise. And now you are to go to sea again.'

Keiko smiled. 'Briefly.'

Her head turned sharply. 'There is to be another attack on the Americans?'

'That is what we are fighting this war for,' Keiko pointed out. 'But it will be like catching fish from a barrel. They are too few; we are too many. Nor do I think they really understand what modern war is all about. I shall get no medals for this one. But when I return, your father has agreed that we shall be married immediately.'

'When you return, my Keiko,' she said, suddenly and uncharacteristically squeezing his hand. 'Oh, when you return.'

'I wish you to write a letter to Grand Admiral Raeder,' Isoroku Yamamoto said, leaning back in his chair.

His secretary raised his head in surprise.

'I wish you to convey to the grand admiral my regrets that he has so far found it impractical to complete the fitting out of the German Navy's new aircraft carrier – I believe it has been named the *Graf Zeppelin*, which is entirely appropriate: Zeppelin was the man who designed the first military aircraft. You could say that it is thanks to his genius we are where we are now. I wish you to tell the grand admiral that here in Japan, our experiences have taught us that aircraft-carriers are truly the most vital factors in sea warfare today, and that the addition of such a vessel to his new battleship *Tirpitz*, when supported by his battle-cruisers

Gneisenau and *Scharnhorst*, will give him a force quite capable of facing the British Home Fleet with every prospect of victory. In this regard, you will further convey to the grand admiral that it is Japan's earnest desire to see the question of British refusal to concede defeat settled as rapidly as possible, and so we should be pleased to assist him in any way he may require with the completion of the *Graf Zeppelin*.'

Kato waited, but when it became obvious that his superior was finished, he raised his head; he was of course familiar with what had been discussed at the meeting of the admirals, for it was Yamamoto's habit every evening to dictate notes of everything brought to his attention during the day. 'With respect, honourable Admiral,' the young man said. 'But do you intend to implement the suggestion of Commander Hatatsune?'

Yamamoto smiled. 'It is a bold project, is it not, Kato? Because he is a bold and brilliant man. No, I do not intend to implement it. It would merely be sending sixty of our best fliers to their deaths for no true gain. No one will talk to us of loss of face when we have sunk those three American carriers. But' – he got up and went to the door – 'I should be a poor commander, did I not keep open every possibility, every alternative means of striking at the enemy. Write that letter, Kato, and let us as least discover if the Germans are interested in cooperation.'

PART ONE

Summer 1942

CHAPTER 1

The Project

The signal rating placed the neatly typewritten decoded message on the desk and stood to attention. 'From Pearl, Commander,' he said.

Jennifer Rhodes frowned at the words. The man behind her had allowed no intonation to creep into his voice, no suggestion of surprise or concern. She remembered from her own days as a decoding clerk that the content of a message had never penetrated her brain until the transcript was complete. It was a matter of training that one should never try to anticipate what word might be coming next – there was too much room for error.

'Thank you, sailor,' she said, pushed back her chair, and got up. Heads in the office stirred and turned. Male heads. These signalmen might have been working here for several months, but when Jennie Rhodes moved, male heads always twitched. And a few female ones as well. She was somewhat tall, a good five feet ten inches in her stockinged feet – and how every man in this room would like to see her in stockinged feet. Wearing regulation low-heeled shoes, she headed the six-foot mark. She was thin, from the solar plexus down; but not even the heavy blue uniform jacket could conceal the fact that she had large breasts. The combination of swelling flesh above and the almost boyish hips, from which extended unusually slender legs, made the most blasé of men start to think. Not even the insignia of a commander in the Waves which marked the jacket could stop them from looking.

Above all of that were the classically beautiful features of a woman who should, had she been so inclined, have been earning a fortune in Hollywood instead of propping up a desk in Washington. These features were surrounded by the glow of pale golden hair. In the office, which was the only place any of these men had ever seen her, Jennie wore her hair in a fashionable and correct wartime bun on the nape of her neck. But a glance could tell that it would be like silk to touch, straight, and very long. Most of these men had only seen Veronica Lake at the movies, but they could look at Jennie Rhodes in the flesh every day, and Jennie had the height the film star was reputed to lack. As Chief Petty Officer Markham had once remarked, 'Jesus! Think of those legs wrapped around you, man, while you're lying on those tits, bouncin' up and down.'

His tone had been the more wistful because she was inviolable. She would have been anyway, to an enlisted man, but she had never been known to date any officers, either. Her rank had something to do with this; she had climbed too far too fast, and it was difficult to have a good time with a date who had to call you 'ma'am'. But then there was her job. As the highest-ranking woman in Naval Intelligence, Jennie Rhodes was a woman of secrets, personal as well as national.

Yet here was an occasion, considered Signalman Brown, when the barriers could come down. 'Looks like a showdown,' he remarked.

Jennie Rhodes looked at him, and he hastily came to attention. 'Ma'am.'

'Yes,' Jennie said. 'It does look that way.'

She crossed the office in a few strides, knocked, waited three seconds with her hand on the latch of the door, then entered. Behind her, a faint sigh hung on the air.

She placed the sheet of paper on the admiral's desk and stood to attention. The admiral was a stickler for protocol – in others. Washington at the end of May could be a very warm place, and while she wore jacket and properly buttoned blouse, and sweated, he had slipped his tie knot down far enough to unfasten the top two buttons of his shirt, and had removed his jacket; the breeze swirling off the Potomac almost made him look cool.

But the admiral was never cool. He was actually the only man in this entire vast building who had seen her in her stockinged feet. Once. Jennie had gone along with the idea because she had just been promoted, on his recommendation; because he had been trying to get her between the sheets for some time; and because she had been feeling even more desperately lonely and unsure of herself than usual. Being beautiful – a recent achievement after a somewhat pimply and brace-toothed adolescence – was not an entirely satisfactory compensation for having been left at the altar.

It had been a disaster, sexually, and even more because in his emotional explosion, knowing that she was his very own aide, the admiral had wished to talk about many things, most of which she already knew and regarded as shop. But then he had mentioned something she had not known before. Learning then, in such circumstances, lying naked on her back sharing a cigarette with a man old enough to be her father who had been no great shakes as a lover, after nearly four years, just why she had been abandoned, had left her feeling as cheap as dirt.

As for the admiral . . . Jennie reckoned once had been enough for him because she was a girl who indulged in outsize climaxes, even with flaccid admirals. He was now afraid of her, despite the fact that he lived on his own in Washington; his estranged wife preferred Palm

Beach. But he certainly still wanted her, from time to time – she could read it in his eyes.

'God *damn*,' the admiral said. 'So Nimitz is opting for Midway. Christ, I hope he's right. Or we could have the whole damned Jap Navy turning up right there in San Francisco Bay.'

'I think Admiral Nimitz has made a correct appraisal of the situation, sir,' Jennie said. 'It is logical for Midway to be Admiral Yamamoto's next objective. And surely Midway has more strategical importance than a hit and run raid on San Francisco.'

'Well, I hope you're right too, Commander. All I can say is, being able to break the other guy's code isn't worth a piss in hell if you make the wrong interpretation. Christ, what would I give to be there. You ever been to Hawaii, Commander?'

'Yes,' Jennie said, reflecting that her boss's near panic was why he wasn't there now, and Chester W. Nimitz was. 'Before the war.'

The admiral's eyes dropped shut. No doubt he was imagining her on the beach at Waikiki.

'I should've been there last year,' he sighed. 'Those fucking bastards wouldn't have caught me napping. And now, to be taking on those yellow shits face to face . . . you know anyone with the fleet?'

'I think so, sir.'

The admiral grinned. 'One in particular, eh, Jen?'

She hated being called Jen. The admiral, of course, was oblivious of what he had let slip that night in bed. And yet, even if Johnnie, who should have been there, wasn't, Clive Wharton was particular, she supposed. They had been good friends, once. They had been the three caballeros, even down to guitars. Clive, and Jennie . . . and Johnnie Anderson. That she had slept with Johnnie instead of Clive hadn't been important to their relationship. Clive had been Johnnie's best friend, and everyone had known that Jennie and Johnnie were

38

going to get married, one day. But, in the summer of 1938, war had not seemed a possibility, except to Johnnie. Johnnie had known, even then, just as he had known he would stand her up, because there were more important things to do. If only he had told her. But how could he have done that?

'Well,' the admiral said, having read the message again. 'This is it, Commander. One way or the other, this is *it*. If we lose this one, we're up the creek swimming in shit. You ever swum in shit, Commander?'

'Yes, sir,' Jennie said. With you, she thought. 'Perhaps the second time may be more interesting, sir.'

She saluted, and returned to her desk. Another signalman was standing there, waiting with another message. From Europe. Her heartbeat quickened, even if today wasn't the day. Like every operative the navy maintained, Agent Seven-Twenty-One reported once a week, save in emergencies, and pray God there was no emergency affecting Agent Seven-Twenty-One. In any event, this was from Greece, not Sweden. Oh, Johnnie, she thought, if only you could have told me. Or if only things had been different.

But if things had been different, Johnnie might be with Clive, on board *Yorktown*, steaming for Midway. And a showdown.

Huge plumes of smoke, dust, metal and men spurted upwards from the little atoll. Gasoline installations crumbled and erupted into flame, houses disintegrated. 'The Divine Wind,' Lieutenant Tomonaga shouted into his intercom. 'The Divine Wind.'

Keiko was more interested in the runways. The runways were all that separated Midway Island from any other of the coral-surrounded sandbanks which dotted the Pacific. From those runways twenty-six gallant fighter planes had risen into the dawn sky only minutes before, to contest the day with the hundred and

39

eight fighter bombers under his command. They had been destroyed, although he reckoned he had lost about a third of his force. And the runways were still not sufficiently damaged to prevent their use by the huge, sinister B-26 bombers he could see parked in their sand bays, safe from anything save a direct hit. It was already a victory, of course, but not yet a decisive one.

He spoke into the intercom. 'Lieutenant Tomonaga,' he said. 'Make to all planes, return to base. Then make to flagship, second strike considered necessary.'

He pulled his own machine out of its slow downwards spiral through the smoke and the puffy white clouds, and turned its nose up, towards the blue horizon and the still rising sun. The Rising Sun of Japan, he thought. That was of far more importance than any Divine Wind. Tomonaga was a romantic. He looked at his watch: the time was ten minutes to seven. In only ten minutes the final Japanese objective had virtually been achieved. Now it was simply a matter of occupation and fortification.

Once those B-26s were rendered ineffective.

He banked the machine due west, while listening to Tomonaga's excited chatter over the radio. The Americans would be listening to that, too. But it was unimportant – the only thing they could do about it would be either to launch their bombers on a suicide run into the teeth of the Japanese fighters, as high-altitude bombing was too inaccurate to bother the battle fleet . . . or send the great planes scuttling back to Hawaii. And even further.

Not an American carrier, the only possibility of a viable counter-attack, had been seen or heard of since the fleet had left Japan several days before. They had either fallen for the baited trap Yamamoto had set by sending, with total openness, a task force north to assault the Aleutian Islands; or they had decided not to risk their carriers after all, and had withdrawn them

40

too to the security of American home waters. From all reports, they had already suffered serious damage – and perhaps lost one of their precious ships – in their attempt to stop the New Guinea invasion fleet from penetrating the Coral Sea north of Australia. That attempt had actually been successful; the invasion force had turned back rather than risk unacceptable losses. But either way, Midway had been left as a sitting duck.

He looked left and right; his planes were back in formation, flying west. The pilots were jubilant. Apart from their repartee over the radio, they were waggling their wings and gunning their engines. He could not blame them, although he hoped none of the fools ran out of gas before they regained the fleet.

'Carriers in sight, honourable Commander.'

Keiko's gloved hands tightened on the controls as he looked down. No matter how often he saw this sight, his heartbeat still quickened. The four great carriers, *Akagi, Kaga, Hiryu* and *Soryu,* steamed in box formation, two abreast, with the two huge battleships immediately outside them, surrounded by their guarding cruisers and destroyers. There could be no finer fleet in the world, he knew; and when he thought that there were two more fleets behind, commanded by Yamamoto himself, and including no less than five more battleships – amongst them the mighty *Yamato* – his whole being swelled, to consider himself a part of such splendid force and power.

'Message from flagship for you, honourable Commander.'

'Hatatsune,' Keiko said into the mike.

'Commander Hatatsune,' the voice said. 'This is Admiral Nagumo speaking. I wish your planes to land as rapidly as possible.'

'Immediately, honourable Admiral,' Keiko said, frowning. No congratulations? And it was very unusual for the admiral himself to issue such instructions.

'Haste is most imperative,' Nagumo said. 'Out.'

The first plane was already dipping towards the flight-deck of the lead carrier. The empty deck, Keiko observed, his frown deepening. When they had left, nearly three hours before, the after end of those decks had been crowded with fighters and torpedo bombers waiting to attack any American naval force which might be in the vicinity. That they had been sent down to the hangars had to mean there *were* no American ships about . . . but if that were so, why the urgency in Nagumo's voice?

He began to circle, watching his fuel gauge. As leader of the strike force he would be the last to land, but he did not think there would be a gas problem; their course and speed, to and from Midway, had been too carefully calculated. He watched plane after plane go in with marvellous speed and precision. The first had touched down at thirty-five minutes past eight, and they were now landing one every thirty seconds, while the four carriers and their escorts continued to steam majestically into the wind. He looked right and left. The skies were empty; so were the seas, beyond the carrier task force. Nagumo was merely being anxious; of course a carrier was most vulnerable when waiting to recover aircraft, because of the necessity of maintaining a certain course and speed. Presumably there had been a report of American submarines in the vicinity.

'It is time, honourable Commander,' Tomonaga said.

Keiko began his descent, circling behind the carrier, maintaining speed just above the stalling mark as he dropped towards the flight-deck. It was, indeed, a simple landing today; the seas were calm. His wheels touched, the wires attached and the throttle was pulled right back. The aircraft slid to a halt and was immediately surrounded by mechanics and officers. 'Commander Hatatsune to the bridge,' said one of them.

Keiko nodded, saluted the superstructure and hurried

for the ladders. As he did so, the carrier heeled as she made a sudden ninety-degree turn to port. Keiko looked round in surprise. The entire vast task force was performing the same manoeuvre, turning away from the wind. And away from Midway.

He grasped the iron rails and climbed upwards, emerged on to the fighting bridge, bowed and saluted.

'Keiko,' Nagumo said, hurrying towards him. 'My congratulations. What is the situation on Midway?'

'One more strike will make the island indefensible, honourable Admiral.'

Nagumo nodded. 'Well, re-arm your planes as rapidly as possible. When I got your message, I ordered my other machines below, to exchange their torpedoes for bombs. It has now become necessary to countermand that order and have them re-armed with torpedoes as quickly as possible, so your squadrons will have to carry out the second attack as well. But I want you airborne in an hour. I need that flight-deck.'

'There is an enemy, honourable Admiral?'

'Yes, Commander. There is an enemy.' Nagumo flung out his arm, pointing to the north-east. 'Out there. An aircraft-carrier. At least one. There has been faulty reconnaissance. That *anything* was out there was only discovered half an hour ago, after the decks had been cleared, when an American scout plane was sighted and followed. But what was I to do, even when the enemy carrier was confirmed? Bring up my torpedo planes for launching, while you and your boys ran out of fuel and crashed into the sea? I have already informed the commander-in-chief of the situation. We have time. We were only spotted by a single plane, and our alteration of course will have thrown them off the scent. But haste is still imperative, because they will certainly find us again.' The admiral was clearly in a state of high nervous apprehension.

'Haste, honourable Admiral.' Keiko saluted, ran for

the ladder, and checked, as a voice said quietly down the intercom from the observation platform immediately above the bridge: 'Enemy planes in sight.'

'They have found us, after all,' Nagumo commented.

Everyone moved to the port wing, staring into the morning. It was by now bright, and a rising but still gentle breeze threw up one or two whitecaps.

'There,' said the captain of the *Akagi*, and the fifteen little dots became visible, dropping down through the thin clouds almost to water level.

'Torpedo aircraft,' said the flag lieutenant.

Keiko's heart constricted.

'Helm hard to starboard,' said the captain.

'Haste, honourable Commander,' Nagumo said quietly, visibly relaxing now the crisis was actually upon him. 'Clear my flight-deck.'

Keiko slid down the ladders, still watching the approaching aircraft. There should be a screen of fighters up there to bring down the attacking planes before they could get within torpedo-launching range, which was hardly more than two thousand yards. And, as he looked, fighters did rise from one of the other carriers, where refuelling had been completed, and swarmed towards the Americans. The sky became a mosaic of tracer patterns, plumes of smoke, screaming engines. He reached the flight-deck, where Lieutenant Tomonaga waited for him. Together they gazed at one machine, which had broken through the fighter ring and seemed to be heading straight at them. Keiko remembered that April day in the garden of his house, staring at approaching death. But this would come from underneath rather than above. Even as he watched, the long silver-painted fish dropped from the fusilage of the bomber and hit the surface, immediately forming a deadly white streak.

Alarm bells jangled, and the carrier altered course again, this time to port, while every anti-aircraft gun on board *Akagi* was now chattering and booming, the huge ship almost seeming to move beneath the recoils.

Yet they waited for the explosion beneath them, and heard nothing; the torpedo had missed. Even as Keiko watched, the enemy plane just disintegrated into a thousand pieces, falling into the sea, sending a huge cloud of smoke and steam pluming upwards.

'All gone,' Tomonaga said. 'Just like that.'

Fifteen planes, Keiko thought. Destroyed in seconds. Truly, these Americans did not know how to wage war, except with senseless *élan*. He watched the fighters sweeping low over the surface of the sea, seeking survivors, giving victory rolls and filling the air with their cries of triumph. 'Come on,' he snapped. 'Let's get airborne before any more Americans arrive.' He ran towards his men. There were forty aircraft now on *Akagi*'s deck being re-armed and fuelled. But the first ten were ready, including his own. He got behind the controls, listened to Tomonaga settling himself in the seat behind him and heard the engines of *Akagi* increase speed even as the whole ship swung back to starboard. 'Damnation,' he muttered. There was no possibility of taking off while the ship was being thrown about like this.

Then he heard the loudspeaker. 'Enemy dive-bombers. Enemy dive-bombers. Shoot on sight.'

He looked up through his perspex hood and saw them, angels of death, peeling off to come down on to the Japanese carriers. They had to be stopped. He looked at the fighters, still wheeling close by the sea. They had got the message too, and were hastily pulling into a climb. But they would never get there in time. The American torpedo plane attack, however seemingly futile and indeed disastrous, had yet done its job – those thirty aircrew had sacrificed themselves to divert the Japanese defences.

His brain seemed to solidify, even as his stomach

turned to liquid. He switched on his intercom to speak to Tomonaga and all his other ready pilots above the enormous chatter of the machine-guns and the pompoms, the roaring of the engines beneath him, and heard a voice say, in English, 'The flagship is yours, Clive. Make it good.'

He tilted his head back and watched the planes screaming downwards. Darts of destruction. Headed by Clive. Clive who? Clive was a common name in America. But it wasn't common enough.

The deck heaved beneath him, and there was a *whoosh* of flame and smoke. He threw himself from the cockpit only a second before his own plane exploded, and rolled towards the promising shelter of the island, surrounded by burning and exploding gasoline, exploding bullets and, now, detonating bombs. He reached his feet and was hurled down again, then found himself on the outside of the flight-deck, only prevented from going overboard by a steel stanchion. But he was going overboard anyway, he realised. The deck was tilting away from him as *Akagi* listed; at least one of the bombs had penetrated past the elevator and exploded in the fuel store. The after part of the ship was a blazing inferno; his entire squadron had disappeared in flame and smoke. As with that morning in April, he had a sense of unreality. But it was happening. The pain from his burned hands and face, from his injured back, told him that. *Akagi* was sinking.

He sat up, and looked around at the magnificent fleet which had been steaming so majestically towards victory only half an hour earlier. Now it was scattered like a herd of sheep attacked by a wolf. And *Akagi* was not the only ship sinking.

'Message from Admiral Nagumo, honourable Admiral,' said the flag lieutenant.

Isoroku Yamamoto, peering out through the bridge

46

screens high above the massive eighteen-inch guns of *Yamato*, half turned his head. 'Yes?'

' "Fleet subject to air attack from at least two carriers," ' the lieutenant read. ' "I have to report heavy casualties . . ." ' the lieutenant's voice faltered.

'Continue,' Yamamoto snapped.

' "Carriers *Akagi*, *Soryu* and *Kaga* are sunk." '

There was a gasp, and every head on the bridge turned. Yamamoto did not speak for a moment. His brain was trying to grasp the significance of what he had just been told. Half of Japan's entire carrier force had been lost, in minutes. 'Go on,' he muttered.

' "Have transferred flag," ' the lieutenant read. ' "Will press home attack with *Hiryu*." '

'Brave man,' Yamamoto said. 'Oh, brave man. Increase speed, Captain. We must support Admiral Nagumo, and turn this into a victory. They have sunk three of ours. Why then, we must sink three of theirs. That will still leave us with a superiority, eh?' He went back to the bridge windows, pounding his right fist into his left hand. 'Speed. Speed. We must support *Hiryu*.'

There was a sudden shuffle of feet behind him, and he turned to look at the lieutenant, who had been joined by another, also carrying a piece of paper, his face altogether tragic. 'Speak,' Yamamoto commanded, his throat dry.

The young man cleared his throat. ' "*Hiryu* under attack and sinking. Regret to inform honourable Commander-in-Chief that my carrier force has been destroyed. Awaiting your orders. Nagumo." '

Yamamoto stared at the lieutenant, while everyone on the bridge stared at the admiral. Yamamoto licked his lips. 'Instruct Admiral Nagumo to steam west and save the remainder of his force,' he said. 'Captain, bring this fleet about and also steam west. Signal Admiral Ozawa to do the same.'

'Aye, aye, honourable Admiral.' The captain gave

47

the necessary orders, and the huge ship began to turn, accompanied by all the other battleships and cruisers and destroyer screens. The captain moved to stand beside his commander-in-chief. 'How could this have happened, honourable Admiral?' he asked in a low voice.

Yamamoto gazed at the sea, sparkling blue in the morning sunlight. Those peaceful, almost beckoning waves had sucked four of the finest ships in the world into their eternal embrace. 'Who knows?' he replied. 'Faulty intelligence? Faulty reconnaissance? Or someone's mistake. That is not important now. We have lost a battle.' His voice nearly broke. The Imperial Japanese Navy had not lost a battle since it had been formed, nearly seventy years before.

'What will the people say?' the captain wondered.

Yamamoto glanced at him, then went down to his day cabin and sat in the chair before his desk. What would the people say? They would simply not be told that the Japanese fleet had, in one morning, been destroyed as an offensive force. He knew he could not take his battleships into action without air cover. Midway had been going to be the decisive battle of the war, the great atonement for the Tokyo raid, the centrepiece of his career.

Well, he thought bitterly, it might well turn out to have been the decisive battle of the war, at any rate.

What would the people say? And what would the Navy do, in the person of its commander-in-chief?

He sat straight. It would cease looking over its shoulder, for a start. He had been defeated. Instead of falling into his trap, the Americans had laid one of their own, into which Nagumo had steered. *His* first decision had to be whether or not the defeat was of such a magnitude as to require his atonement by seppuku, the performance of ritual suicide with which a Japanese gentleman expiated all his sins.

Yamamoto's brow puckered. He was not afraid of death, even so painful and unpleasant a death as cutting open his own belly. As a Japanese officer, he had known from his days as a cadet that such a sacrifice might be demanded of him at any moment in his career; certainly it would have to be done in preference to surrendering to an enemy. But as commander-in-chief, he had wider responsibilities. He knew he was the only man in Japan with a proper understanding of the strategical requirements of this war. He had made a mistake today. Perhaps the past six months had been too easy. He had suffered grievous casualties; but aircraft-carriers could be built, and there were sufficient men in Japan eager to serve in them. He had not lost his fleet; he was now sitting on board the mightiest battleship in the world, and her sister ship, *Mushashi*, was already working up. He had lost a battle, but not the war – providing he remained in direction of affairs.

He could not afford to die, for the sake of the nation.

But there remained that senseless raid on Tokyo. The people had been promised massive revenge. He had anticipated being on the radio by this time to announce a great victory. Now he could say nothing; if he dared not admit such a defeat, he equally dared not risk claiming it as a victory – too many men had gone down with the four carriers. The ups and downs of warfare were one thing; people could understand that. But the raid on Tokyo remained unavenged – and now could not be avenged for the foreseeable future. Lacking aircraft-carriers, Japan would be forced on the defensive for at least a year, until adequate replacements could be built.

So the Americans would crow their triumph, and the people of Japan would writhe in resentful impotence. He drummed his fingers on his desk, then pressed his intercom. A moment later his flag lieutenant appeared, bowing. 'Honourable admiral?'

'I wish a list of survivors picked up from *Akagi*.'

'Immediately, honourable Admiral. Is there anyone in particular you wish to know of?'

'Yes,' Yamamoto said. 'I am anxious to learn if Commander Hatatsune survived the loss of his ship.'

The room was crowded with seated figures squatting on cushions on the tatami mats which occupied every square inch of the large floor. Both sexes wore the kimono, exquisitely neat and tidy. It was a scene of peace and happiness, a peculiarly Japanese scene in its simple beauty, from the variegated robes of the people to the flawlessly arranged vases of flowers in the corners.

The spectators gazed at the low dais in the centre of the room, where the bride and bridegroom sat together. The earlier part of the wedding ceremony had been completed; Keiko Hatatsune's manhood and valour had been praised to the skies, as had Akiko Tarawa's beauty and virtue. The tea-tasting ceremony was finished, and now there were the last small cups of sake to be drunk. They were man and wife, and only now did Akiko throw back her veil. This was etiquette: her husband could not look upon her face until he *was* her husband. But, earlier, she had been grateful for the protection, as even now she was grateful for the thick white ceremonial paint which covered her face. She loved this man, and she had thought she knew him as well as she knew anyone, even her own brothers. But since his return from his last campaign, she had not known him at all.

She did not know what had happened. No one knew that, and no one dared ask. She did know that Keiko had either been shot down, or his ship had been sunk; when she had hurried to the hospital, distraught with anxiety, after the fleet had docked, she discovered he was being treated at once for burns, fortunately superficial, and also for prolonged exposure; he had spent several hours in the sea.

He had made a very rapid recovery, because of his superb strength and fitness. And he had sought but one thing, his marriage. Yet there was very little happiness in those eyes which had been so capable of sparkling. Those eyes had looked upon something too terrible to be forgotten.

But he had wanted to marry her, despite his personal tragedy. That was reassuring. And the ceremony was over; Keiko was offering her his arm to leave the dais and speak to their guests. They were man and wife, and her husband was Commander Keiko Hatatsune.

There was still a great deal to be done. Keiko had to bid farewell to his mother- and father-in-law, and she had to accompany her mother-in-law – who was, in law, now her mother – to the Hatatsune house. A new house, this, rebuilt in a matter of weeks, as there was very little labour involved in building a Japanese house.

She had washed her face clean of the paint and released her hair, and now the two women sat together and sipped tea. Then Yoshino said, 'It will not be long now, my daughter.'

Akiko bowed before the older woman, and went into Keiko's bedroom. Here the mattress was arranged on the tatami mats, and beside it, the washbasin and heated towels. It was a room prepared for lovemaking, and it would be a unique experience for her. This neither disturbed nor frightened her; in her culture there was nothing mystical or secret or obscene about the thought of sex. It was necessary for the procreation of children, but the gods had so arranged it that both men and women found it an enjoyable pastime – otherwise there would be no children, and no human race.

Behind the basin, there was a little shrine to the household gods of the Hatatsune, and after Akiko had

51

again washed her face and then her body clean of all impurities, she knelt before the shrine and prayed. She was a Hatatsune now. This family's joys were her joys, and its sorrows were her sorrows. Above all, that applied to her husband.

The door behind her slid open, and then closed again. She remained kneeling, her back to him, for the first time uncertain. At this moment she was shrouded in her hair; he would see nothing but a faint suggestion of pale shoulder, pale thigh. When she turned, he would see all of her. She wanted him to look at her – but only if she was sure that he would like, that he would love, what he would see.

So she waited, and he knelt beside her. He still wore his kimono, but the sash had been loosed. She allowed herself a sideways glance, and a tentative smile. For several seconds there was no response, because he too was praying. Then his hand moved, just to brush her flesh. 'You are beautiful, my Akiko,' he said.

She inhaled in relief, and turned on her knees, raising her shoulders, using one hand to flick stray strands of hair away from her breasts. He leaned forward, and touched one nipple with his tongue. She gave a little shiver of the purest delight. She had never felt anything like that before. Breasts, nipples, were certainly areas of sensation. Whenever she had bathed with her friends and they had soaped each other, they had giggled at the feelings they had thereby induced, and sometimes they had used the ivory balls to complete the spiral. But this touch, so gentle, was unlike anything she had ever known.

His kimono was open, and she could look down his chest and belly to his groin. Again, in the baths, at the far side of the room beyond the partition, she had seen sufficient naked men, and when *they* had soaped each other she had often watched a penis harden and rise. Keiko's penis was flaccid, like a man's before the

52

soaping began. She did not know what to do, for a moment. He had kissed her nipple. That was a sexual gesture. Had he not found it so? Because she was becoming increasingly aware of a rising excitement in her belly, a great want in her groin.

'Shall I wash you my Keiko?' she asked softly.

He raised his head. If only he would smile, she thought. Then without a word he took off his kimono and lay on his back, gazing at her. Face serious but heart pounding, she laid the washcloth on him, gently grasped the flesh beneath and moved the cloth to and fro. For how long she had wanted to do this. But the flesh would not rise.

'Do I not please you, Keiko?' she asked.

He sighed. 'I should not be here.'

She turned her head to look at him, frowning.

'I should be dead,' he said. 'I led my men to death. Tomonaga . . . all of them. It was on my recommendation that Nagumo cleared his decks. Mine. And then, Wharton . . .' His voice had become almost a snarl.

Akiko licked her lips.

'But I was forbidden,' Keiko muttered. 'Forbidden because I must lead other men to death. And you,' he said, his tone at last softening. 'Oh, my dearest Akiko . . .'

At last, a response. Akiko stretched herself on her belly on the mattress, legs spread as lasciviously as she knew how, and buried her face in the penis, using lips as well as hands, cuddling and kissing, stroking and fingering shaft and testicles. And feeling him too, as he sat up, and his hands slid down the sheen of her back, reached the soft mounds of her buttocks and slipped between. She shivered with delight, and rose to her knees, to sit on him. Now he was hard. She held him in both hands, and introduced him into herself. For a moment the pain surprised her, took her breath away; it was far sharper than she had imagined it would be.

But even through the pain the sensation persisted, the suggestion of ultimate pleasures far greater than any provided by the ivory balls. And now, too, he was happy, moving against her, jerking against her and into her, filling her with damp warmth. At last she was a wife. Keiko Hatatsune's wife. She was the proudest woman in Japan.

'Sit down, Keiko,' Yamamoto invited. 'You look fully recovered. A honeymoon is the best therapy in the world, I always think.' He smiled. 'Providing a man does not make it his life's work.'

'I feel like a criminal, honourable Admiral.' Keiko sat down before the desk.

'For deceiving your wife? That is necessary in every man's marriage, at some time or other.'

'For marrying her at all, honourable Admiral, and thus causing her so much grief.'

'You have done her a kindness, Keiko. Consider this: had you simply gone off, could she ever have married another man? And if she had, could she ever have been happy with him? You would have lain on her mattress like a bolster between them. But now she is your wife. She may even be bearing your child, to perpetuate your name. And be sure that she will be a charge on the state, at the highest level, forever. Besides, she will be a comfort to your mother,' he added, watching his protégé very closely.

'I accept these things with gratitude, honourable admiral,' Keiko said. 'And yet . . .'

'Having tasted the joys of your Akiko's arms, you wish to taste them again,' Yamamoto suggested gently.

Keiko's head came up. 'I will lead the mission, honourable Admiral. I have sworn this.'

'Very good. Then listen to me very carefully. You have three weeks to recruit your men. They must know nothing of the mission until the very last moment. You are taking them to Germany to study the methods of the Luftwaffe. Nothing more. But they must be made aware that this is a highly dangerous exercise, that no man who volunteers can expect to return to Japan.'

'Understood, honourable Admiral.'

Yamamoto looked at the sheet of paper on his desk. 'You will sail from Nagasaki on the Spanish vessel *Jaime Jorge*, on 28 July. Your destination will be Cadiz. The voyage is expected to take three weeks. In Cadiz you will be met by German officials, and they will see you safely through Spain and France into Germany. In Germany, the *Graf Zeppelin* will be waiting for you. The Nazis are being most cooperative. They intend to provide you with a hand-picked crew and with their best captain: Hjalmar Koenig. Have you heard of this man?'

'No, honourable Admiral. What is he best at?'

'It appears that he, of all German commanders, is most experienced at penetrating the Denmark Strait and evading British and American patrols. He has now done so three times, made his way into the South Atlantic and the Indian Ocean, and has sunk more than a hundred thousand tons of allied shipping. That is a considerable achievement for an armed merchant cruiser.'

'You mean, this man does not even command a warship?'

'He is an officer in the German Navy, Keiko, and is highly thought of. Besides, armed merchant cruisers are warships, at least of a type. Handling them, evading detection by the enemy, evading recognition by their victims until it is too late, calls for a high degree of nerve and seamanship. Now, you understand that you will have to train your aircrews from scratch once you get there, both in the basic handling of their Junkers machines and in taking off from a flight-deck in those essentially land-based planes. You will also have to study the weather conditions you may expect to find in the North Atlantic. You can hardly be ready before the end of the year, and by then, from my information, the weather off Greenland is the worst in the world. This will of course provide you with the maximum protection from discovery. But it will also make the actual mechanics of your task more difficult.'

'I understand these things, honourable Admiral. But if there is indeed a carrier waiting for me, and a competent crew, and I can reach Germany by the end of August, I will be ready by the end of October.'

'Hm.' Yamamoto got up, went to the window and looked down at the garden below. 'I think you will need another month, Keiko.'

'Not so, honourable Admiral.'

'I think so.' Yamamoto turned to face him. 'I have been giving this matter some thought. We have again failed to achieve our objectives. And now, I realise, our ultimate perimeter will have to wait until I can build new carriers to replace those lost at Midway. The Americans will be cock-a-hoop at this time. But they will also know that they are in no position to bring the war to us at this time. Both sides, therefore, are in a position of rebuilding, for next year. In 1943 the war will begin in earnest, and all we have seen so far will seem mere skirmishes. Therefore, let us bring this fact home to the Americans. It is my wish that you bomb New York on an especially symbolic date, one that will make them aware that they have not defeated us: they have merely checked our advance.'

Keiko's eyes shone. '7 December, honourable Admiral.'

'Good.' Yamamoto returned behind his desk and sat down. 'There remains but one detail left to be settled. Our friends the Germans are very keen on the use of code words. They talk in terms of Codes White and Black and Brown, and Sea Lions and Barbarossas and absurdities like that. They wish this operation also designated by a word, which will of course have meaning only to the very few people who will be absolutely in the know.'

Keiko was frowning. 'Our allies *are* aware, honourable Admiral, that should there be the most minuscule leakage of what we intend, either to London or Washington, our chances of success are halved?'

'Your chances of success would be exactly nil, Keiko. This operation can only succeed if we take the Americans entirely by surprise. I have impressed this upon Grand Admiral Raeder, and he entirely agrees. However, they still wish a name. Choose a name, Keiko, which might appeal to our friends.'

Keiko thought for a moment. New York! He would be leading his men and their bombers over the most spectacular city in the world. They would circle the Empire State Building, and watch that mighty edifice come crumbling to the ground. He laughed, as memory went back to a movie he had seen some years before. An American movie, which had caught the imagination of the world.

'Commander?' Yamamoto raised his eyebrows.

'Kong, honourable Admiral. We shall name this, Operation Kong.'

Yamamoto gazed at him for some seconds, then he too understood the connotation. 'Kong,' he said. 'That is good. Kong.' He too began to laugh.

CHAPTER 2

The Lovers

Signalman Brown placed the typewritten message on Commander Rhodes' desk and stood to attention. Jennie glanced at the words, and felt a slow warmth begin to seep through her system. There had been no communication from Sweden last Friday. Or the Friday before. Two whole weeks. There had been missed Fridays before, but every miss left her nerves just a little more raw and ready to scream.

'Thank you, sailor,' she said, and got up.

The admiral had put on his jacket; he was ready to go home for the weekend.

'That delayed message from Stockholm has finally come in, sir.' Jennie placed it on his desk.

'Well, what do you know. I was beginning to think that guy had bought it.' He picked the paper up, read it aloud. ' "AMC *COLOSSUS* RETURNED SAFELY CLAIMING FIFTEEN THOUSAND TONS SHIPPING DESTROYED STOP AMC *ATLAS* STILL AT SEA EXPECTED RETURN TWO WEEKS STOP POCKET BATTLESHIP *SCHEER* IN DRY DOCK FOR TEMPORARY REPAIR AFTER AIR RAID WORK ESTIMATED MINOR STOP WORK RECOMMENCED *GRAF ZEPPELIN* STOP UNABLE TO ESTIMATE COMPLETION DATE AT THIS TIME STOP SEVEN TWENTY ONE STOP". Big deal. One armed merchant cruiser back after a successful raid, another still out there, causing havoc. Who's that fellow commanding *Atlas* again?'

'Hjalmar Koenig, sir.'

'How the hell do you remember all those Kraut names, Jen?'

'It's my job, sir.'

'Well, isn't he the son of a bitch who's now made three sorties, each a killer? What the God-damned hell does the British Navy *do* out there? And what the hell is this *Graf Zeppelin?*'

'That is the aircraft-carrier the Germans have had under construction for some time, sir,' Jennie explained.

'Oh, Jesus Christ, we can forget *that*. The Germans don't know one end of a flat-top from the other. You know, I sometimes wonder why we maintain Seven-Twenty-One. He's never given us one God-damned bit of information worth a piss in hell.'

Jennie drew a long breath. 'I think you are probably right, sir. Why don't we bring him home?'

'Oh, for Christ's sake, we can't do that. His cover is immaculate. Don't you realise this guy actually was born in Sweden? He might come up with something, one day. And with this North African thing on the way . . .' He flushed, as he met her gaze. They weren't supposed to mention Operation Torch, even to each other. 'Just let him stay, until the Gestapo pick him up. That'll shake the bastard.' He handed her the paper, but did not notice the coldness of her expression. 'File that. And say . . . how about a drink tonight?'

'I'm sorry, sir. I have a date.'

He frowned. 'You don't ever get confidential between the sheets, or talk in your sleep, or anything like that?'

'Only to myself, sir. I'll check in tomorrow. Have a good weekend.'

'You're a great girl, Jen.' He followed her to the door. 'I don't know what I'd do without you.'

'Get yourself another girl . . . sir,' Jennie suggested,

and opened the door. The office stood to attention as the admiral walked through.

The outer door closed behind him. 'That's it, sailors,' Jennie said. 'Liberty men, stand down.' She picked up her handbag, took out her mirror and added a perfunctory dab of powder to her nose. She looked exactly as she felt, that she needed a bath. And a bottle. She always felt that way after a Seven-Twenty-One came through, which was why she had lied to the admiral. She would have lied to him anyway, even if his stupid remark about the Gestapo hadn't made her feel like kicking him in the balls. But on a Seven-Twenty-One night she *did* have a date, with herself and a memory, with a hot bath and a bottle of champagne, which she would drink sitting up in bed, before falling asleep.

She wondered what John Anderson would say if he knew how the strange currents of war had blown her into the position of being virtually his mother.

She took the elevator, jammed in with another twenty uniformed men and women, emerged into the downstairs lobby, nodded to various acquaintances, all of whom regarded her merely as some super secretary, went towards the street door and the warm July evening, and stopped. A man had just emerged from a door to her left, and had also stopped, on seeing her. 'Holy Jesus up the mountain!' the man remarked. 'Jennie Rhodes!' He looked at her more closely. '*Commander?*'

'They're nice to us girls here on the East Coast, Clive,' she explained.

He hadn't changed much. He still resembled the man in the moon out for lunch, all chin and nose and crooked smile. But for him to appear, tonight!

'You going to introduce me, Clive?' asked his companion, also wearing the uniform of a navy pilot.

'Nope,' Wharton said. 'I'm going to say piss off, old chum.'

The man shrugged, and left without showing offence.

'That wasn't nice,' Jennie remarked.

'Seeing you is, though. And I'm not about to share with *anyone*. How about dinner?'

She intended to get drunk tonight; her brain was firmly committed to that single objective. But she had firmly rejected the idea of getting drunk with the admiral, because of what might be involved afterwards. But Clive was an old friend. And getting drunk by oneself was a boring business. 'Why not,' she said. 'After I've had a chance to bathe and change.'

'I'll go along with that,' Wharton agreed. 'Say, can you recommend me a good hotel?'

She realised that the briefcase he was carrying in his left hand was actually a valise.

'I only got in this morning. And I've been locked up in here all day, listening to a load of bullshit.'

'You won't find an empty hotel room in this town. You'd better try the Y.'

'Great. Well . . . what time shall I pick you up?'

Jennie hesitated. With Clive, it might well be a case of getting involved *before* getting drunk. But he was her second oldest male friend. And she was so very lonely. 'Or, you could try my place,' she suggested.

They walked, because the apartment building wasn't far. On the other side of the river, Washington bathed in the evening sunlight, the dome of the capitol gleaming like a beacon. 'So what brings you to town?' she asked. 'Or is it top secret?'

'Secret? I told you, it's a load of bullshit.'

'So shoot.' It always surprised her how, while she knew so much about the navies of every other nation of the world, she only knew about her own navy when things were about to happen.

Wharton shrugged. 'Too many missions. They say. They've given me another stripe and a kick in the ass.

Still,' he grinned, 'if I hadn't got that extra stripe, I'd be calling you ma'am.'

'Where are you being kicked?'

'Wait for it: Goose Bay. Goose Bay! Christ, it even sounds like a joke.'

'It's in Labrador,' she told him.

'I just found that out. And that isn't a joke. I've spent the last few years in Hawaii, remember.'

'I remember,' she said quietly.

He glanced at her, then made a face. 'So guys drop out. What the hell. I felt so bad about that. And not only for you, Jennie. He was my buddy. But if you don't know it all, you don't know nothing. You sure as hell don't pass judgement. Not on a buddy.'

Christ, she thought, I have *boobed*. If he mentions Johnnie one more time he'll have to go. And the evening, having promised *something*, would be more lonely than ever. 'It's a walk-up,' she said, and took her latchkey from her handbag.

'That figures. I'm on the same pay scale, you know.' He took the key from her hand to open the door.

She climbed the stairs ahead of him, and could feel his gaze on her calves; the silk seemed to be melting. 'How was Midway?'

'Ups and downs. Mainly ups, for us. Say, how'd you know I was there? What do you *do*, anyway? I never knew dames got to be commander.'

'It can happen. We need the other key.'

He opened this door as well, only slightly out of breath.

'Home,' she said, and opened the curtains.

Wharton stood in the centre of the small living room, hands on hips, and looked at the evening sunlight being absorbed into the chintz cushions on the sofa. There was a small dining table, through the door on the right he could see the kitchenette, and the door on the left led to the bedroom.

'It came fully furnished,' she apologised.

'Looks great to me.'

'Bags the bathroom first.'

'It's your john. Where's the gin?'

'There's scotch in the cupboard.' She went into the bedroom, took off her cap and jacket, and wrinkled her nose at the sweat-soaked blouse beneath.

'Ah, hell,' Clive said. 'Didn't anybody ever tell you I shake the best martini in the Pacific?'

'So pour the best highball in Washington. It's Chivas Regal.' She took off her blouse, dropped the rest of her clothes on top of it and ran the water. Even on a hot July evening, she enjoyed a soak in a hot tub. Besides, tonight she wanted to be clean all over. She took off the snood, allowed her hair to cascade on to her shoulders and then beyond.

'I guess we'll manage,' Clive said. 'You decent?'

'No,' she said, sinking beneath the water.

He pushed the door open, placed her glass on the end of the bath where she'd have to sit up to reach it and looked down at her. 'Now there is a sight I'd never hoped to see again.'

'Again?'

'Sure. You forgotten that stream below Mauna Loa?'

She hadn't forgotten the stream, or bathing there: she'd simply forgotten Clive had also been along. 'Seems a hell of a long time ago,' she said, and stretched out the legs she had drawn up protectively. Then, very deliberately, she sat up and reached for her drink, swallowed, and lay back again.

'You can say that again,' Clive remarked. 'It's been growing again, I see.'

She assumed he was referring to her hair, which was floating around her like a fish net. 'It does.'

He sat on the toilet, legs crossed, glass dangling from two fingers. Mainly he looked at her face as she soaped, but when he looked elsewhere, he wasn't embarrassed

63

about it. She found that reassuring. Then he spoiled everything. 'You ever hear from him?'

'Here from who?' Jennie stood up to soap her pubes. Maybe he'd be distracted.

But flying aces who kept alive couldn't ever afford to be distracted. 'Johnnie, of course.'

'No,' Jennie said, and sat down again.

'You mind if I smoke?'

'Yes,' she told him, and shampooed her hair.

He lit a cigar, adding to the steam gathering in the little room. 'You know, it's strange how you just never know anybody. I grew up with that shit. Well, virtually.' He blew smoke at the ceiling. 'I must have known him as well as I knew myself. We shared everything. We even shared you, in the beginning. We both fell in love with you the same day. That was the day we first saw you. We went back to the station and looked at each other, and then we agreed that whichever one of us you smiled at first next day . . . we were taking you out to lunch at that little crab house by the beach, remember?' He sighed. 'So you smiled at Johnnie. I won't pretend I wasn't disappointed. But I was happy, too. Couldn't have happened to a nicer guy, I thought. And we'd always be friends – you, me and him. I'd be his best man, so I'd at least get to kiss you. Hell, I could see it all, white uniforms, raised swords . . . and then, *pffft*. What was it? Booze or drugs, you reckon? He sure kept it a secret. And you know what? I nearly came calling, that same day. Then I said, that's not the way to do it. So I came three days later, and you'd gone.' His shoulders heaved.

Jennie stood up and stepped out of the bath, dripping water. She took the cigar from his mouth, plunged it into the water, pulled it out again, and stuck it back between his teeth. It drooped, and brown water stained his shirt front. 'Johnnie Anderson is not a shit,' she said, and went into the bedroom.

Clive removed the cigar from his mouth, looked at it for several seconds, then dropped it into the trash can. He stood in the doorway, watching her towel. She did that, as she did everything, vigorously.

'I didn't mean to get you all burned up.' he said. 'But Christ, you're not still carrying a torch for that guy? He left you virtually on the day before your wedding, quit the navy . . .'

'Which of those bothers you the most?'

'Well, hell,' he sighed.

He was making a habit of sighing, she thought, maybe to win her sympathy. The odd thing was, he wasn't doing too badly. Not by sighing, but by what he had just said: that he had wanted to come to comfort her. She'd always wondered why he hadn't done that.

'You know what?' he asked. 'I came up here to ram you tonight. I thought to myself, this is *it*, buddy boy. What you've been waiting for, for four years. You reckon I've blown it?'

She wrapped her wet hair in a towel, herself in a dressing gown, and turned round to face him. 'Could be. Why don't you have a bath and I'll see what I can find in the kitchen?'

She opened the icebox, took out one of the bottles of champagne, opened it, filled two glasses and went back into the bathroom. He sat in her soapy water, soaping. She presumed that was symbolic. 'Hell.' He took the stem. 'You mean I'm forgiven?'

'No. But you might just be if you drink a toast to Johnnie Anderson.'

Some of the bubbles might have got up his nose.

'Johnnie didn't drop out,' she told him. 'He wasn't on beer or Scotch or gin or even snow. He had a job to do. A job he was told to do. And a job that was bigger than being a pilot. Bigger even than being married to me.'

Clive frowned. 'You *know* this?'

65

She'd gone too far as it was. 'No,' she lied. 'It's what I believe. It's what I'm going to go on believing. You drinking that toast?'

She scrambled eggs, added a liberal dose of red pepper; she liked her food spicy.

'I thought I was taking you out,' Clive complained.

'I don't go out, Friday nights. So cross yourself and take a chance.'

He sat opposite her across the little table, wearing a towel. Their bare toes touched.

'Tell me about Midway. About Pearl. About everything,' she said.

'Why?'

She shrugged, 'I guess I want to know. I sit here in Washington, and I file reports, and I transmit orders, and I see names . . .'

'My name?'

'Sure. Sometimes. But a name is just a name, on paper. You have to stop and think that those are people who breathe and feel, and can die. You have to understand that because some admiral has read the piece of paper I have just finished typing up, those people, those names, are going to find themselves shooting at other people, and being shot at themselves. That's a kind of heavy responsibility, at two o'clock in the morning.'

'You don't make the decisions.'

'I still like to know.'

He emptied the champagne bottle.

'There's another,' she said.

He got it, and returned. 'If it's any comfort to you, we don't think. Oh, sure, we think before, and we think afterwards, but not during. I guess we're too busy doing.'

'You're wearing a star. Tell me about it.'

'Oh, that. I got airborne at Pearl. Big deal. So did Sandy Scott. Sandy bought it. I got a Kate.'

'What's a Kate?'

'A Japanese fighter-bomber. And then I should've had another. That would have been something. But my fucking guns jammed. Would you believe it? And then I was dead lucky. That Hatatsune character was so shot up he couldn't do anything about it.'

Jennie frowned. 'Hatatsune? You don't mean you knew the man you were fighting with?'

'Nope. Not then. And you never do, really. But I read about him after. Seems he was their number one ace, over Pearl. He claimed three of ours, including one of a pair of navy planes. He was hit by the other, but escaped because the navy plane's guns jammed. That just has to be me. And then he covered himself with glory by getting his busted machine back to his carrier. Keiko Hatatsune: that's not a name I'm likely to forget in a hurry. But brother, if those guns had held up . . .'

'Do you hate him?' Jennie asked curiously.

Clive frowned at her for several seconds, drank some champagne and ate the last of his eggs. 'You know, I never thought about that, before now. I guess in some ways I do. He killed Sandy. But in other ways I kind of admire the guy. It was one hell of a feat, getting that plane back. I often wonder if he was at Midway. Everyone else was.'

'In which case, he's probably dead.'

'Yeah.' His face was again serious.

'You got the air force cross for that, didn't you?'

Clive grinned. 'Sure. I'm as big a hero as old Hatatsune, now. For what? Those torpedo boys should've got all the medals going at Midway. They did the work, and got killed for it. All I had was the biggest target I've ever seen in my life, one great big juicy flat-top sitting there like a jellyfish on a beach. She wasn't just unprotected: she had forty planes stacked on the flight-deck taking on fuel. I reckon I could've sunk that ship with a hand grenade. But I just happened to have a five-hundred-pound bomb on me at the time. So I'm a fucking hero. God-*damn*.' He gazed at his empty plate.

'There's ice cream,' she told him. 'Not for me.'

He brought back two dishes and set one before her. 'You dieting or something? You don't want to do that. You're as skinny as a rake, most places. Say, what do those things measure, anyway?'

'I hate to disappoint you, but only thirty-six at the last count. They look bigger than they are.'

He sat down and gazed at her across the table. 'You know something, babe? I *love* you.'

'You'll get over it when you've had your screw.'

'You mean I'm going to get it? Spite all?'

She got up, walked to the sofa, sat down. 'It could happen.'

He ate her ice cream as well, then came to sit beside her. 'I have a forty-eight-hour pass before I head for the Arctic. Goose Bay! Christalmighty! The very name makes you shiver.'

'Why are you going?'

'I'm to train green pilots. Me! I don't know how the hell a machine flies, or what you do when you get a Zeke in your sights. I just do what comes naturally. How the hell am I gonna tell other guys what to do?'

'You'll learn. But no combat?'

'Hell, there's a carrot. There always is. Seems we fly training patrols over the Grand Banks and even as far as South Greenland. The bottom end of the Denmark Strait, right? They tell me the route's used by the odd surface raider from time to time. I didn't know they had any.'

'Their heavy cruisers use the Denmark Strait quite often.'

'Is that a fact? Well, I hope to God you're right. Oh, they've also promised us the odd U-boat. Big deal.'

'Then there are the others,' she said. 'Keep your eye open for *Atlas*.'

'*Atlas?*'

God-damn, she thought, I'm saying things I shouldn't.

Two bottles of champagne was one and a half bottles too many. But she couldn't make him suspicious by an abrupt change of subject. 'It's a name I read on some report. She's an AMC, you know.'

'AMC?'

'Armed merchant cruiser. She looks like a liner or a large freighter and she flies the Spanish or Swedish flag, and she trundles along until she finds herself in an empty piece of ocean close to a British or American ship, then she uncovers a couple of six-inch guns.'

'Sounds real Nazi.'

'We use them too.'

'Really? And this *Atlas* is their best?'

'Well . . . she's been their most successful, so far. Her captain has a big reputation. Character named Koenig. That's German for king, you know.'

'Yeah? Say, how come you know all this stuff?'

'I read books. I even have an English-German dictionary.'

'I meant about these ships. This *Atlas?*'

Jennie shrugged. 'Ships are my business, Clive.'

'Sounds real exciting,' he commented without conviction. 'Now, say, about marrying me . . .'

She flipped up his towel to look at him. 'I don't reckon you can wait that 1ong.'

'*Jesus!* You mean you really want to fuck? Me?'

'That's one hell of a question coming from someone who's just asked me to marry him.'

Hesitantly he opened her dressing gown, touched her breasts. He was a fighting machine who had recently sent God alone knew how many men to their deaths, but he was a gentleman and he was scared of her. All men were scared of her. Except Johnnie Anderson.

He had wanted to touch those breasts for so long. She didn't stop him, because she liked to touch them herself: the admiral was six months ago, thank God. But tonight she had a man. She played with him as their lips met, and his hands left her breasts to slide down her stomach to her groin, and gently part the hair, and then go between, and while there, lift her from her seat and bring her on to his lap.

'You *are* in a hurry,' she remarked as he entered.

'I don't want to be.'

'So relax.' She got off him, went to the kitchen, took an ice cube from the refrigerator, came back and rubbed it gently over his glans.

'Jesus!' He stared at himself.

'Kind of numbs sensation for a while,' she said.

'How do you *know* these things?'

'I told you, I read books.'

'I gotta get the name of your librarian. Now what?'

'We leave him alone, for five minutes. But there's no need to neglect me.'

He knelt between her legs. His hands roamed over her buttocks while he kissed her slit; then he played with her breasts, and every so often he came up to kiss her mouth. It was four years since anyone had made love to her like that. But then, in four years, only one man had made love to her at all. And that hadn't been love, but mutual frustration. She shook the towel from her head. Her hair was still wet, but the hell with the cushions.

'Christ,' he said. 'Oh, Jennie, Jennie. You . . . when I get like this . . .'

She didn't think even ice was going to cause much of a postponement now. 'You'd better come inside.' She allowed herself to sink sideways on to the sofa.

He entered slowly this time, lovingly, reaching as far as he could, staring at her. Now she surprised him. When she was finished, he was more exhausted than she.

'*Jesus!*' he said. 'Jennie, you gotta marry me. *Please.*'

70

'No,' she said.

'Ah, shit.' He got off her.

'There's tissues in the bedroom.'

He went in there, holding his penis in his left hand, returned suitably wrapped up and sat beside her. 'You *are* still carrying a torch for Anderson.'

'Fuck Anderson!' she shouted in a sudden fury. 'And fuck you too, you bastard!'

She went into the bathroom and sat on the toilet. He stood in the doorway, the pink tissue fig leaf fluttering in the breeze they had stirred, watching the tears rolling down her cheeks. 'I didn't mean to upset you,' he said.

'Well, you did. Sometimes I feel like screwing the whole human race. I mean, *screw*.'

She dried herself and got up. 'You just remember, Clive Wharton, when you're in here with me, it's me, and it's you. Not another God-damned shit.'

'Okay.' He trailed behind her into the lounge.

She flung herself on to the sofa. 'You got a cigarette?'

'I didn't know you smoked.'

'Only right afterwards.'

He gave her the packet, found his lighter and flicked it for her. She inhaled, coughed and sat up. He took the cigarette from her lips and smoked it himself. 'I just want to marry you,' he said.

'Forget it. I'm not the marrying kind.'

He got up. 'I guess you want me to go.'

'What for? This is the only place in Washington or Arlington you're likely to get a bed. I thought you had a pass until Monday morning?'

'I do. Oh, babe ... but you won't marry me.'

'If you say that again, Clive Wharton, I am going to bite it right off.'

'Okay. Okay.' He sat down again and put his arm round her shoulders. 'But oh, babe, I am so glad we met up tonight. Even Goose Bay could be bearable now.'

She kissed him on the mouth. 'Just be sure you come back,' she said. 'From time to time.'

CHAPTER 3

The Action

'Monday morning blues,' Clive Wharton remarked, playing with the last of his egg.

'You've had too many eggs.' Jennie poured him a second cup of coffee. 'What time's your flight?'

'Quarter after nine.'

'Then you'd better hurry.'

'Yeah.' He drank, put down the cup and gazed at her. 'Did you mean what you said, Friday night? About coming back, some time?'

She considered him. She had never in her life before let herself go quite the way she had let herself go this weekend. If this morning she was again smartly and correctly dressed, if her hair was confined in its neat bun, and if her face was carefully lipsticked and powdered, she was still sure anyone looking at her – and especially the admiral – would know that she'd taken quite a tumble. The whole world could have come to an end, and she wouldn't have known about it. She had given herself a weekend pass to match his, and she had let her hair down and kept it down. For sixty hours, until in fact half an hour ago, she had worn not a stitch of clothing. She had made love, and bathed, and made love, and cooked – eggs, because she had nothing else in the apartment save canned soup – and made love, and eaten, and made love, and bathed, and made love, and slept in his arms, and then made love again before recommencing the cycle. In those sixty hours she had made up for all the past four lonely years of frustration, of midnight fears, of messageless Fridays.

She had never known anything like that with Johnnie Anderson — which was ironic, but not difficult to explain. Four years ago she had been a different human being, a bubbling twenty-three-year-old Vassar graduate who had had an unhappy love affair and been packed off to stay with an aunt in Oahu for a summer while she thought about things. No one doubted she would do that: she had always been sophisticated, on the surface. Her upbringing had made her so. Successful stockbroking had paid for Daddy's big house in Connecticut and the ski lodge in Vermont, as it had paid for the trip to Europe and the Lincoln Continental, as it continued to pay for the French champagne and claret, the charge accounts at Saks and Bloomingdales.

The love affair from which she had been supposed to recover had hardly been that, she now knew. At the time it had seemed like the end of the world. He had played basketball and was even taller than she; he had come from a Texas oil mine, or at least, the bank which financed it; he had also been to Europe and he also could tell a grand cru from a vin du pays by sniffing the cork. The marriage could have been fashioned in heaven, as the song went. And heaven was probably the only place it could have worked, she had realised as they got to know each other. There was no sex in heaven.

Her enthusiastic approach to the subject had frightened him. Well, sometimes it frightened herself. She had been a virgin, and had not been prepared to yield that important asset to anyone save her future husband. However, having discovered a future husband she had seen no reason why she should wait any longer. He had not been a virgin, or so he boasted. But whatever his experiences, they had not penetrated his mind. Their lovemaking had been a disaster, not least because he

74

had just not fitted her idea of a man, much less a basketball letterman.

So she had fled to Honolulu, unsure whether to be ashamed of herself or him, certainly not intending to risk intimacy with anyone else for an awfully long time – and run full tilt into two recently commissioned navy fliers. And found that one of them, at least, was definitely her idea of a man; she hadn't got around to noticing the other, then. Johnnie Anderson didn't come from any Texas bank, or any commuter belt, either. His father, having Anglicised the Swedish Anderssen, sold real estate in Florida, but somehow always managed to miss the best properties. Johnnie was the family hero, because he had done so very well. She had fallen in love with him, but because of all those factors, she had not really let herself go, as she had during the past sixty hours. How she regretted that, now.

But she regretted so many things. The despair the Anderson family in Miami – she had never met them but they had been going to come to the wedding in Hawaii – must have felt, because to them, too, Johnnie had been a drop-out; after they had scrimped and saved to put him through Annapolis he had just thrown up the whole thing and disappeared. If they thought of him at all, it would be lying on a street in the Bowery.

Then she regretted the quarrel with her own family. They hadn't much liked the idea of Johnnie at all, and they had been offended that she had wanted to be married right there in Pearl instead of having a big splash on the East Coast. When it hadn't worked out, Ma had been unable to resist an I-told-you-so. So she had pushed off and done the only thing that made any sense to her at that time: she had joined the navy herself.

On the surface, that had been a smart move. She had got in on the ground floor, when the Waves were just coming back to life as the threat of war approached. Thus her background, added to her natural intelligence and ability, had sent her up and up. But it had also left her at the mercy of the admiral, and because of that, it had taught her the truth about Johnnie.

So, did she regret this weekend? Since Johnnie, she had once again been a virgin, save for the admiral. Now this great hulk . . . she didn't really know anything about him. Except that while he had always presented an exterior of totally violent masculinity, he could be as gentle as a kitten; and while he had always faced life with a fuck-you attitude, he had been genuinely upset at the thought he might have hurt her; and while he had become a highly decorated war ace, he could still admire rather than hate his enemies. She had once supposed she knew everything worth knowing about John Anderson. Then she had supposed she knew nothing, in never suspecting that any man could let her, and himself, down so very badly. Now she knew, thanks to a drunken admiral, that she had known even less than nothing, in never suspecting that in reality Johnnie had had the character of a Roman hero, willing to ruin his career and his life, and risk that life, because the navy wanted him to. She didn't know if he would ever come back, and what sort of a human being he would be when he did. Or what sort of human being she would be, either. And waiting, knowing what he was doing and risking, was turning her into a zombie.

'Sure I meant it,' she said.

'But you won't marry me.'

'No,' she said, and reached across the table to squeeze his hand. 'Not right now, Clive.'

'Could be some sparks flying off Portugal,' remarked Leading Signalman Brown, who seemed to have appointed himself her personal assistant.

There were a whole stack of messages, accumulated from agents all over the world. Most of them she should have seen already – had she come in over the weekend, as she usually did. Signalman Brown was looking both censorious and interested; he could tell she hadn't spent her weekend in bed with *Gone with the Wind*.

'The boss in yet?' she asked.

'Monday morning? No, ma'am. But he'll be tickled by that one.'

It bore a four as its initial number. Four was Portugal. Jennie's interest evaporated, and then returned as she scanned the words: 'BRITISH STEAM SHIP *MOMBASA* REPORTED UNDER ATTACK FROM GERMAN RAIDER STOP RAIDER POSSIBLY *ATLAS* STOP UNDERSTAND RN DESTROYER *EREBUS* DETACHED FOR RESCUE POSSIBLE INTERCEPTION STOP WILL CONFIRM LATER STOP FOUR THREE ONE'.

Jennie reached out to the books in front of her, pulled back her personal code book and flipped it open, Four-Three-One was stationed in Lisbon, but as Portugal was neutral he really had the run of the country – and she knew he had some close friends in the Portuguese Navy. His information was usually gilt-edged. Possibly *Atlas*! If the unhappy *Mombasa* had got off her distress call in time, *Atlas*'s career might just have come to an end. And with her, of course, the career of Captain Hjalmar Koenig. She wondered why she felt that was important. Like everyone else she dealt with, he was only a name and a number. She had never faced him in combat, the way Clive Wharton had faced the Japanese – what was his name, Hatatsune? – in combat. And Clive respected Hatatsune, while she felt an almost personal antagonism towards this Koenig. That was creepy. She supposed it had something to do with the female mothering instinct. If she dealt only in pieces of paper and names of ships as well as men, if she had to look on the whole thing as a gigantic game of blindfold chess, she still had a personal interest in using *her* pieces to the best of her ability, and of caring for them until they simply had to be sacrificed, while Hjalmar Koenig's interest was in destroying them as rapidly as he could – and he was very good at it.

It all depended, of course, on this ship *Erebus*. She reached across her desk again, picked up her Royal Navy reference book and gave a grunt of displeasure as she found the name she wanted. *Erebus* was an E-class destroyer, two thousand tons displacement, armed with four four-point-seven-inch guns; *Atlas* had six six-inch, and displaced fifteen thousand tons. Yet the Royal Navy apparently considered *Erebus* equipped for the task. She flipped the pages. The captain of Erebus was Rodney Bowen, Lieutenant-Commander, RN, DSC.

She supposed it all boiled down to whether or not this Rodney Bowen was man enough for the job. But a Distinguished Service Cross had to count for something.

Go to it, Rodney Bowen, she thought. Blast the bugger right out of the ocean. She gave a little shiver.

She had never become so personally involved before. It had something to do with the weekend with Clive, having one of her pieces of paper suddenly come alive and into her arms.

She wasn't sure she enjoyed the sensation, or what it was apparently doing to her character.

'Position,' Lieutenant-Commander Bowen said quietly.

'Thirty-six degrees fifty minutes north latitude, fourteen degrees eight minutes west longitude, sir,' replied the navigating lieutenant. 'I make it fifty miles to the casualty.'

'Anything on the box?'

'Nothing in sight, sir,' said the radar rating.

'Let me have a fuel report, please, Mr Winder.'

'Aye aye, sir,' Winder said, and picked up the intercom. His voice was immediately lost beneath the scream of the engines, the swish of the water racing past the destroyer's sides. The twin-shaft Parsons geared-turbines were pushing the ship at her maximum speed of thirty-six knots; even the brain inside Rod Bowen's head seemed to be vibrating. And he had a great many thoughts trying to occupy that brain, amongst which fuel was the most important.

But none of them really mattered, supposing the raider was *Atlas*.

He raised his binoculars and swept the horizon. It was three o'clock in the afternoon, and the sea was utterly calm, with a light south-westerly wind and a high, oily swell which portended bad weather some time in the next twenty-four hours. Bowen remembered that the Battle of Trafalgar had been fought on a day like this, according to the history books – and indeed Cape Trafalgar on the Spanish mainland was only three hundred odd miles behind them now, although they were steering away from it, crashing to the west.

Rod Bowen liked to think in historical terms; the Royal Navy was his life. He was tall and slim; he played sufficient squash, when ashore, to keep his waistline as trim as a midshipman's, and he was thirty-five years old. He also liked to think of himself as a totally civilised man, when off duty. He kept a photograph of his wife and his two young daughters and his Labrador dog on his desk in his cabin, a book on the propagation of roses beside the well-thumbed copy of Mahan's *Sea Power* on the shelf above his bunk. He genuinely enjoyed returning to his Buckinghamshire home, about as far away from the sea as it was possible to get, in England. But he never made the mistake of wishing to be civilised at sea in a war. Then he was a professional killer.

He had now commanded *Erebus* for more than a year, and loved every inch of her three hundred and eighteen feet of sleek length, every pound of her nineteen hundred tons deep-load displacement. He couldn't say that he loved every man of her hundred and forty-five complement, but he knew every one, and knew his capabilities, too. He had not volunteered for this mission, simply because he had been trained to await orders, and then to carry them out to the best of his ability. But when the distress signal was received by the flotilla captain, he had none the less hoped a response would be made, and that his would be the ship to be detailed, fuel situation or no; *Erebus* was not the only escort in the Gibraltar convoy to be short of fuel, after a long Atlantic crossing.

And perhaps to have another crack at *Atlas*! He picked up the message from the flotilla captain and looked at it for the fiftieth time in the past three hours. '*EREBUS* STOP *MOMBASA* UNDER ATTACK AND SINKING ON GIVEN COORDINATES STOP I MAKE THAT FOUR HOURS STEAMING STOP WORTH A LOOK STOP YOU WILL AID CREW BUT IF SITUATION WARRANTS ENGAGE ENEMY AND DESTROY STOP REALISE ODDS UNDERSTAND *EREBUS* NOT TO BE HAZARDED STOP REPEAT ACTION ONLY IN FAVOURABLE CIRCUM-STANCES STOP AM ALERTING OTHER UNITS STOP HE WILL NOT ESCAPE THIS TIME STOP HARDY'.

That was a sop: action only in favourable circum-stances. Where was he supposed to find that, unless *Atlas* was doing, or had done, something very silly. And *Atlas*, he knew, was not given to doing silly things.

They had met before. Just a year ago, in fact, and just after he had assumed command of *Erebus*. He had then been detailed for patrol duty at the southern end of the Denmark Strait, because that was a place about which the British had become most sensitive. Only a couple of months before *Erebus* had gone on station, the mighty *Bismarck* had come slipping through those fog-shrouded waters, to sink *Hood*, Britain's finest capital ship, and turn the North Atlantic into a turmoil before she was finally hunted down. But every commander in the Royal Navy was well aware that *Bismarck* had merely been the biggest, not the only, German warship to exit through that strait, and that very few of the others had ever been caught.

And then he had seen *Atlas*, first of all as an unidentifiable blip on the radar screen, and then, emerging through the mist, as a large freighter, clearly Swedish from the blue flag with the yellow cross which stood away from her masthead. His orders called for the inspection of all neutral cargoes, and so he had signalled the big ship to heave to and receive a boarding party, whereupon the apparent neutral had suddenly uncovered six six-inch guns, cunningly built into her upper decks so as to be totally concealed from anyone who didn't know exactly where to look, and begun to fire with extraordinary accuracy. Bowen never denied that he had been taken utterly by surprise. The six-inch guns had of course outweighed his own four-point-sevens, but as he was also armed with eight twenty-one-inch torpedo tubes, deadly weapons at close range and as long as the torpedoes actually worked – which did not always happen – he had tried to close the range as rapidly as possible.

He had not succeeded. A six-inch shell had burst just forward of the bridge, knocking out both his forward gun turrets, and slashing the thin glass and metal with a million flying steel slivers which had killed or wounded everyone within reach. He had been one of the lucky ones and escaped with just a few splinters in his back, but it was not a moment he would ever forget. Even less would he forget how that shell had wrecked his steering gear and left the destroyer aimlessly steaming round in circles, until the auxiliary steering right aft could be brought into use, and until he himself had recovered sufficiently from pain and shock to resume command. In that half an hour *Atlas* could probably have sunk him, and he knew it. But the German undoubtedly had her orders, which, as an armed merchant cruiser, would certainly have been not to engage any British warship except for purposes of escape. She would also have been aware that *Erebus* had put out a call, giving position and time, before her aerials had been shot away. There were undoubtedly British units on the way, and *Atlas* had not risked waiting for them. She had steamed into the mist, making for the broad, sunlit and unpatrolled wastes of the South Atlantic. But her captain had sent a message, which had been picked up by the reserve radio receiver, deep in the bowels of Erebus: 'BETTER LUCK NEXT TIME BRITISHER STOP KOENIG'. That had smacked almost of the age of chivalry.

Of course, Koenig would not have supposed there would ever be a next time. Bowen had doubted it himself, during the long weeks in hospital, and the even longer months waiting for *Erebus* to be ready for sea again. This was in fact only his second convoy duty since returning to sea. In the interim he had been awarded the Distinguished Service Cross. For losing a battle through his own complacency. The citation said, for bringing his stricken vessel safely to port after engaging a superior enemy.

But the chance of ever meeting *Atlas* again had been remote in the extreme. Until today. Because Koenig had already done a silly thing. He had attacked a freighter within five hundred miles of the Portuguese coast. Perhaps he had thought he was safe. He could not have known there was a fully escorted convoy off that coast at that very minute. But it had still been a rash thing to do.

Lieutenant Winder was back. 'Fifty-three tons of fuel left, sir.' He did not look terribly happy about it.

Bowen allowed his eyes to droop half shut as he did some rapid calculation. *Erebus* had left Plymouth a

82

fortnight before with her full fuel load of four hundred and fifty tons. At a reasonable cruising speed of fifteen knots, she burned one ton an hour; that gave her a range of better than six thousand nautical miles, or Plymouth to Halifax and back to Plymouth without refuelling. And, in fact, the flotilla had not gone as far as Halifax; they had picked up the convoy on schedule from the Americans just off the Grand Banks. Convoys did not steam at fifteen knots. Mostly they steamed in the area of ten knots, the speed of the slowest merchant ship, which was fine; save that for the escorts there were several daily dashes of full speed, up and down and round about, chasing false alarms, and on two occasions on this last voyage, actually depth-charging enemy submarines – all of which burned fuel like water. That had not been important, as the fleet was intended to refuel in Gibraltar before proceeding to Malta – and was probably doing so now. Save for *Erebus*.

At full speed, fuel consumption was tripled. When he had left the convoy, two hundred miles off Cape St Vincent, he was down to just over sixty tons, good enough for nine hundred miles at cruising speed – but he had been instructed to reach the scene of the casualty as quickly as possible, and thus steamed flat out for more than three hours. And he still needed to get back to Gibraltar. Even at cruising speed, that five-hundred-mile journey was going to need thirty-seven tons, and that was supposing he encountered no bad weather – such as was obviously coming. He also had about another hour's fast steaming, consuming a further three tons, before he could reach the position of the attack on *Mombasa*. That would leave him just four hours at high speed available, maximum – because if he chased the enemy into the Atlantic, every mile he followed her meant a mile to return.

Of course he realised Captain Hardy had been perfectly aware of these things, hence his insistence upon action only under favourable circumstances; having been identified and pin-pointed, *Atlas* could be left to other forces.

Bowen picked up the other message. *Mombasa* had transmitted her distress in clear English: 'ABANDONING SHIP ON COMMAND OF LARGE DISGUISED ARMED MERCHANT CRUISER STOP NO NAME DISCERNIBLE STOP ESTIMATED TONNAGE FIFTEEN LENGTH FIVE HUNDRED STOP'. Then the coordinates. He gazed at the empty afternoon, the slowly drooping sun, the shimmering sea, while all manner of thoughts and calculations drifted through his mind. The description fitted. *Atlas* had broken through the northern cordon some five months ago, and since then only vague reports of her sightings had come in. These had occurred in the Indian and South Atlantic Oceans. Therefore she had to be on her way home. After five months, it was tempting to suppose that she too might have fuel problems, although of course her engines were diesels, not turbines. This prevented her achieving any startling speeds, but also kept her consumption very low.

'Blips bearing two-one-four, sir,' the radar rating said.

Bowen sat up. 'How many?'

'One, two, three, sir.'

'Those will be the boats. Reduce speed, Mr Winder.' He left his chair, and went out on to the bridge wing. It was just four in the afternoon, and actually, apart from the eye-searing glare, visibility was very good. Now he knew in which direction to look, he levelled his binoculars and made out three lifeboats, rising and falling on the swell, each crammed with men. Someone was signalling with a lamp.

'Large blip bearing two-four-zero degrees,' said the radar rating.

Bowen straightened, his heart giving a curious thump. 'Distance?'

'Range thirty-five miles and gaining. Speed estimated sixteen knots.'

That was far beyond visual range, of course. Bowen snapped his fingers. 'Trumpet,' he said. The destroyer was now very close to the boats; he could even make out the faces of the men. A seaman pressed the speaking trumpet into his hand. 'Ahoy!' Bowen called. 'Any casualties?'

A man in the last lifeboat stood up. He wore a blue uniform jacket with braid on the sleeve. 'All present and correct.'

'Did you identify the raider?'

'No. His name was blacked out. But he was here until just over two hours ago,' the *Mombasa*'s captain said. 'Made us come alongside so that he could check for casualties himself, gave us food and water to reach Porto Santo.' That was the northernmost of the Madeira group, and was some two hundred miles to the south.

'And he gave us time to abandon ship, although he must've known we'd sent a distress call. You've a gentleman there, captain.'

Bowen did some more thinking. He would never find more favourable circumstances than this – if only he possessed another ten tons of fuel. 'Can you manage for a few hours yet?'

'We can manage into Madeira,' the shipmaster said. He could tell what Bowen wanted to do, and he knew that for the destroyer to wait to take on all the seamen from each lifeboat would waste another precious hour, while the presence of an extra fifty people on board could only hamper the navy in the coming fight.

'There's weather on the way,' Bowen told him. 'We'll be back for you by dusk. I'll put up a white flare when we spot you on radar.'

'Aye aye, and good luck,' the master said.

'Course is three-two-zero, Mr Winder,' Bowen said,

returning inside the bridge. 'If we push him anywhere, it's going to be north. And I want maximum speed.'

'Think we can do it, sir?' Winder rang the engine telegraph, and the turbines began to growl. The merchant seamen raised a cheer as the destroyer moved off.

'He doesn't make more than sixteen knots, flat out. We'll haul him down in a couple of hours.'

'Have we got that long, sir?'

Bowen glanced at the first officer. But Winder had made a very good point. With a start of, say, forty miles, it would take at least two hours to get within range of the German, and then two hours to get back to the lifeboats – quite apart from fighting the action. To allow his ship to run out of fuel on the high seas would be the most utter dereliction of duty. And in these latitudes, even in July, it would be dark in two hours. 'When we're down to forty-five tons, Mr Winder,' he said, 'we'll break off the action.'

He sat down again, watching the bow wave curling away from the destroyer as she worked up to full speed. Koenig, he thought. A German sea captain. And a good one. He had to be, or he would have been sunk months ago. And also a gentleman? He supposed the two were not incompatible. They had indeed been synonymous in British eyes at the beginning of World War I. But that had been before all German seamen had become tainted with the hideous blemish of unrestricted submarine warfare, to which could now be added the hideous taint of Nazism. But here was a man who preserved the old traditions of the sea. The merchantman had been British, and was therefore an enemy; it had to be destroyed. But her crew had been non-combatants, and therefore should not be wantonly slain. Indeed, should be helped to survive, as far as possible – even if it meant endangering his command.

Hjalmar Koenig. Bowen rested his chin on his hand

as he stared at the empty horizon. He wondered what his adversary looked like.

'Smoke dead ahead,' Lieutenant Winder said. 'She must be able to see us as well.' He cast an anxious glance at the sun, now lower than ever, hanging immediately above the western horizon like a huge red ball. When it went, it would go like a snap of the fingers, and the world would be plummeted into darkness.

'Range?'

'Eighteen miles and closing,' the radar rating replied.

'Book.'

The reference book was opened in front of him. He already knew what he was about to read; he had memorised it after that first action. But it was never wrong to refresh one's memory. His book told him that the guns mounted on *Atlas* were old secondary armaments, taken from scrapped German pre-Dreadnoughts. That indicated a maximum range of about fifteen thousand yards, or just over seven nautical miles; his new four-point-sevens actually had an equal range – the difference was that the larger German gun would be firing a shell weighing just over a hundred pounds, while his calibres could deliver only half of that. Therefore, relying on gunfire alone, he would have to hit the enemy twice at least for every shot he took in return. Speed was the essence here. Speed, and manoeuvrability, and then, if he could get close enough, his torpedoes. Each silver fish carried eight hundred pounds of explosive, or four times the punch he could deliver with a broadside of all four of his guns . . . but the torpedoes were only effective up to about two and a half miles. That was very close.

'Calculation,' he said.

Winder had been working on it. 'Based on sixteen knots for the enemy, and thirty-six for us, sir, and

87

present range, we can close to firing range in one hour and twenty minutes. Just on sunset sir,'

'Which can't be bad,' Bowen mused. The German would be silhouetted against the afterglow, at least for a few minutes, while the destroyer was every moment fading into the purpling night horizon. Not that visibility was very important in these days of radar-directed fire, but there was a psychological value in being able to see one's target. 'Pipe hands to action stations.'

The ship began to seethe. Bells jangled, pipes whistled. Men donned their tin helmets, and took their places in the gun turrets. Below decks, Bowen knew, all inflammable material would be being soaked and stowed, while the four-point-seven-inch shells would be riding their conveyor belt upwards. Surgeon-Lieutenant Pratt would be laying out his instruments in the ward-room, which doubled as a sick bay in action, and the cooks would be swearing as they contemplated their half-cooked dinners. But dinner need not actually be delayed; everything would be settled by eight o'clock.

He studied the horizon through his binoculars. Now the superstructure of the other vessel could be seen, a black outline against the crimson glow of the sunset. 'Transmit,' he said to the signalman artificer standing at his elbow. ' "From HMS *Erebus* to unidentified vessel bearing three-two-zero, distance seventeen miles, stop Heave to and await boarding party." '

'Aye aye, sir.' The man hurried off.

'Ship's company at action stations, sir,' Winder reported.

He won't catch us napping this time, Bowen thought, still watching the silhouette. The sun seemed to be dropping even faster than usual tonight.

'If he heaves to,' Winder said thoughtfully, 'and waits for us to stop to put down a boat . . .'

'He could probably blow us out of the water,' Bowen agreed. 'But it'd be suicide for him as well, because he'd

88

be under our torpedoes.' Yet there was a good deal of point to Winder's apprehensions. The German would be manned by the cream of the navy, every man a volunteer, every man an expert. That would go for her gunlayers, too. 'See what's keeping sparks.' he said.

Sub-Lieutenant Packe, panting with eagerness – this would be his first ship-to-ship action, as he had joined *Erebus* after the last meeting with *Atlas* – saluted and hurried for the wireless room, to return a moment later. 'He's still sending, sir, but the enemy isn't replying.'

Bowen nodded, and looked out at the very last glow of the day, as the sun hovered, its lower edge already cutting the line of the horizon and seeming to spread and form a base for the remainder of the incandescent ball. 'Range?' he asked.

'Ten miles and closing, sir,' said the radar rating, his face lost in the visor for the screen.

'Load "A" turret with one blank round, Mr Winder,' Bowen said. 'All other guns to be loaded with live.'

The raider was gone, as was everything else. As the destroyer was carrying no lights, the darkness was utter; only the glow from the binnacle, reflected from the half-obscured radar screen, glinted from the cap badges of the officers on the bridge. Looking forward, the white bow wave could still be seen, hanging in clouds of phosphorescence.

'Nine miles and closing,' said the radar rating.

'Will *Atlas* have radar, sir?' Winder asked. He was as nervous as a kitten.

'Yes,' Bowen said. 'But German radar isn't supposed to be all that accurate.'

'Eight miles and closing.'

Bowen sensed rather than heard that another man had joined them on the bridge. 'Well, chief?'

'I think you should know, captain, that we're down to forty-seven tons.'

'Thank you,' Bowen said. He could spare one more hour.

'Seven miles and closing.'

Koenig would certainly know where they were, and he would also know he could not allow them to get within torpedo range.

'Target altering course two-six-zero,' said the radar rating.

He was turning up. To escape? Or shoot? 'Fire your blank round, Mr Winder,' Bowen said. 'And then stand by to open fire.'

'Aye aye, sir.'

The forward turret exploded in a flash of light.

'Alter course three points to port,' Bowen said.

The coxswain spun the wheel, his stand-by stepping forward to help him, and the destroyer turned the opposite way to the raider. Just in time, for almost immediately there was a flash of light in the darkness, and seconds later huge plumes of water rose from where they had been moments before. 'Oh, good shot,' Lieutenant Winder acknowledged, and then bit his lip in embarrassment.

'Target now steering three-zero-zero,' said the radar rating.

'Prepare to shoot, Mr Winder,' Bowen said.

'Range?' Winder asked.

'Six and one half miles, red one hundred and ten.' The rating gave the bearing off the ship's bow.

That meant all four of the guns could bear. 'Range six and one half miles,' Winder said into his intercom. 'Red one-one-zero. Shoot.'

The entire ship became bathed in flame and smoke, and the slender hull rolled violently to port. Bowen levelled his binoculars, but at that distance and in the darkness it was impossible to tell if they had even come close. Yet the German had also fired at extreme range, and her shooting had been distinctly accurate.

'Steer three-two-zero,' he said.

Erebus swung violently to starboard, now making even farther north of west than the enemy, while the guns were swung to port. Once again his evasive action had been just in time; there was another flash out of the darkness, but this time the German salvo pitched further astern.

'Six miles and closing,' said the radar rating. 'Enemy now steering three-four-zero.'

Bowen and Winder looked at each other with raised eyebrows. If Koenig was coming even more to starboard, he was actually endeavouring to close the range. 'Steer three-six-zero,' Bowen said.

Erebus came up to due north, steering a converging course. 'Hold your fire, Mr Winder,' Bowen said. He did not know what was on Koenig's mind, or even if he might have suspected a problem, such as a malfunctioning radar. He did know that torpedo range was coming closer by the second.

'Five miles and closing.'

Flame belched from the horizon, and there was an enormous *whoosh* of water spouting out of the sea, hurling solid green right over the destroyer, splattering even on the bridge screens. The little ship heeled and then came upright again.

'Damnation,' Bowen said. Once again he had underestimated his enemy. Koenig had been suffering no malfunctions and had made no mistakes; he had closed the range with deliberate nerve in order to shoot more accurately. 'Get below and make a damage report, Mr Packe,' he said. 'Fire as you bear, Mr Winder.'

'Range four and one half miles,' chanted the radar rating. 'Green zero-five-zero degrees.'

'Shoot,' Winder said.

As the destroyer's guns exploded there was another flash of red from the horizon. But these fell into the sea some two hundred yards astern. And Winder had hit.

Bowen stared through his glasses, watched red flame belch upwards rather than outwards and almost thought he could see the outline of the freighter's super-structure for a moment, silhouetted now against her own fires.

A cheer rang out from the foredeck.

'Good shooting, Mr Winder,' Bowen said. 'Hit him again. Steer three-five-zero, cox.' Straight for the blighter, he thought.

'Target now steering two-seven-zero,' said the radar rating.

Koenig had thrown his ship right around, and now there came another salvo. Neither his guns, nor his manoeuvrability, had been impaired. But he had been hit.

'Two seams sprung on the port side, sir,' Sub-Lieutenant Packe reported.

'Thank you, Mr Packe. Start the pumps, and I wish another report in half an hour. Yes, chief?' As if he didn't know what the engineer would say.

'Forty-five tons, sir.'

The forward guns exploded again, but this time there was no answering gush of flame out of the blackness; Bowen realised he was not going to outgun the German, even if he had scored a hit. He could finish the job only with torpedoes. And with *Atlas* zigzagging and shooting with remarkable accuracy, there could be several hours' chase in front of him. His eyes strayed to the message on the chart table: UNDERSTAND EREBUS NOT TO BE HAZARDED. Even if he could close in an hour and sank Koenig with his first torpedo, and it was a very big if, he still had to return and find the lifeboats before the weather got up, which might involve another search. 'Shitting cunts and fucking arse-holes,' he remarked in the quiet voice he usually reserved for commands.

Winder raised his eyebrows. Unlike their compatriots

in the RAF, the navy's officers were not supposed to swear on duty.

'Send off one more salvo, Mr Winder,' Bowen said. 'Coxswain, alter course zero-nine-zero.'

There was a moment's hesitation, then the coxswain repeated. 'Zero-nine-zero, sir.'

The destroyer began to turn away.

'Range six miles,' said the radar rating, 'and gaining.'

The after guns exploded, but to no obvious avail.

'At least we hit the bastard,' Winder said. 'He could be in trouble.'

'Yes,' Bowen said. He went outside, leaned on the bridge rail and stared into the darkness.

'Range eight miles and gaining,' chanted the radar rating; the two ships were now travelling in opposite directions.

'Cease firing, Mr Winder.' Bowen stepped back into the bridge. 'Mr Packe, make to Gibraltar. Give them identity of enemy, position and estimated speed and course of target at termination of action. Report some damage caused, but insufficient to reduce speed or manoeuvrability.' He sighed. 'And then stand the crew down. Pipe all hands to dinner, Mr Winder.'

CHAPTER 4

The Raider

'Well, for Christ's sake,' the admiral remarked. 'These Limeys give me the shits. They have this guy Koenig within six miles, they score a hit, and then they let him get away.'

'There is a fuel problem, sir,' Jennie said.

'Balls to that.'

'Also the weather is deteriorating rapidly, and Commander Bowen has the lifeboat crews to pick up. What would you have done in those circumstances, sir?'

He glared at her.

'And *Atlas* was positively identified, in a fixed position, sir,' Jennie went on. 'Half the British and American navies will be waiting for her off Greenland. He won't get through.'

'He'd better fucking well not,' the admiral growled. 'If he does, that guy Koenig is going to be some kind of super-hero. That's bad propaganda. Next thing, this character is going to be given command of something real big. Suppose they were to give him *Tirpitz*? And then send him out into the Atlantic? Just about the time Torch begins. Christ, it's enough to drive a man to drink.'

'Supposing he gets back this time, sir,' Jennie said. 'And supposing anyone in Germany knows anything about Torch, yet.'

The admiral ignored the implied reproach, and leaned back in his chair, staring at her. But she knew he wasn't really seeing her. He might be the biggest asshole who ever got scrambled egg on a cap, but she knew that was at least partly because he had always wanted to see action, and had never been given the opportunity. Now he was clearly dreaming of the North Atlantic, of being on the bridge of a ship in that fog and rain, seeking the enemy. 'I want to *know* about Koenig,' he said. 'Tell Stockholm to contact Seven-Twenty-One and give him something to do, for a change.'

Jennie closed the door behind her and sat at her desk. She didn't know enough about the emotions involved, that was the trouble. This man Bowen was claiming a hit. Even if he didn't claim it was crippling, the smallest shell hit was a serious matter, she knew, not only to the ship, but to the men who had sailed together for six months. It meant death and injuries to shipmates. Hjalmar Koenig would be coping with all that, in steadily deteriorating weather, and also with the certainty that he was being hunted, and very much in British home waters. His only chance was that he had got away at night. But no matter how he used the night, at some time he still had to turn north for the Denmark Strait, and home. Then he would even come under surveillance from Goose Bay. Technically, he shouldn't come under any surveillance from Clive Wharton: Clive would only have got there yesterday. But Clive would surely get airborne the moment he heard *Atlas* was in the vicinity.

She allowed her imagination to roam over the mists and rainsqualls of the North Atlantic, seeing in her mind's eye the ship below, listening to the drone of the aircraft above, waiting for the crash of bombs which would indicate that she had been sighted. And then she saw the aircraft, could almost hear the pilots cursing as they couldn't see through the cloud, debating on their radios about the possibility of continuing the search just a moment or two longer, while their fuel gauges dropped steadily towards zero. Clive would search until he was flying on air, literally. And then he would go in, to the ice-cold North Atlantic.

She realised she had snapped her pencil. But this was ridiculous. If she was going to get het up about Clive as well as Johnnie, she might as well resign now and head for the nearest nuthouse. But how did one not get het up about a man in whose arms one had spent sixty hours? Simply by telling oneself that he didn't matter, she decided. He had been a chance encounter on a Seven-Twenty-One night, when all things were possible.

Far better to think about Koenig. If he did make it back to Germany, he might indeed be worth keeping an eye on. By Johnnie, she wondered? But that was his job, whatever the dangers.

She wrote out the message quickly and crisply in her big, determined, legible hand, before she could brood on it any more. 'Seven-Seven-Four (that was the Swedish control) for Seven-Twenty-One Stop Wish evaluation present and future status . . .' She opened the appropriate book. All German ships, and their commanders, had their individual numbers and letters. 'A plus Ninety-Three,' she wrote. But could not help adding, 'If applicable.'

'Sailor,' she said.

Signalman Brown stood at her elbow.

'Have that coded and transmitted to Stockholm,' she told him. 'Top priority.'

'Damage report,' Hjalmar Koenig said.

First Officer Wiedermayer saluted. 'Fifteen feet of deck plating torn open just aft of number one hold, sir. Two men killed, seven injured from number three gun. The gun is out of action, but this will only be temporary.' He gazed into his captain's suddenly stricken eyes. 'The gun commander is only slightly wounded, sir.'

Koenig's eyes flickered. 'Thank you, Wiedermayer. Continue.'

'The deck will have to be repaired before we can accept any real weather, Herr Captain, and the wind is rising. But I will need deck lights.'

Koenig peered out at the darkness. No wind penetrated the bridge screens, but he could hear it start to moan. The seas remained calm, but in a few hours they too would start to rise – already *Atlas* was giving an occasional tremble. 'We will have to leave it for a while,' he said. 'Range?' he asked the radar operator.

'Fifteen miles, and rising, Herr Captain.'

'Strange, that he should turn away like that,' Wiedermayer commented. 'Do you think we scored a hit?'

Koenig shook his head. 'I saw nothing to indicate that. She will be short of juice. She has just completed a trans-Atlantic convoy.'

The radio operator came on to the bridge and saluted. 'Enemy is signalling Gibraltar, Herr Captain.'

'Can you decipher any of it?' Wiedermayer asked.

'No, sir. Save for the ship's name. *Erebus*.'

'*Erebus*,' Koenig said thoughtfully. And then laughed. He was a short man, inclined to stoutness, with a round, chubby face and head, clean shaven and prematurely bald. In repose he was inclined to look like a cuddly teddy bear, and he laughed easily, whatever the circumstances, and always with genuine humour. 'We have encountered *Erebus* before, Wiedermayer. Last year, in the Denmark Strait. Do you remember?'

Wiedermayer, who was tall and ~~lugubrious~~ in appearance, apparently did n~~ot~~ know what she is sending . . .'

'Oh, that is simple to deduce,' is calling up everything within r~~ange~~ cannot show any deck lights for ~~fear of~~ a Sunderland overhead at any m~~oment~~

Wiedermayer snapped his fin~~gers~~

97

was too great. With respect, Herr Captain, I told you so.'

'I know you did, Wiedermayer,' Koenig said, somewhat wearily. 'However, we have been hunted before. What is your present course and speed?'

'We are steering two-six-zero, herr captain, and making sixteen knots.'

'Then you will maintain your speed, but alter course two-two-zero.'

'But, Herr Captain, that will take us even farther away from the strait . . .'

'It will also take us away from the enemy flying boats.' Koenig reminded him. 'You will steer two-two-zero for eight hours. Then we will turn north and run for home.' He looked at his watch. 'Call me at zero-four-zero-zero. And Wiedermayer, remember, no lights until then. Spread canvas over the hole and tar it. We will work on it tomorrow at first light.'

Wiedermayer came to attention. 'Yes, Herr Captain. Heil Hitler.'

'Of course,' Koenig agreed, and left the bridge.

Albing, Koenig's personal steward, was waiting in his day cabin with dinner: hashed canned meat, borscht – made from reconstituted cabbage – and a bottle of hock. The meals were becoming repetitive as the voyage drew to a close, but at least the hock was genuine. He had shipped twelve cases of fifteen before leaving Wilhelmshaven five months before, and he was going to have just sufficient to see him home, at the rate of one per night, even if the constant vibration was causing a certain amount of additional fermentation.

Koenig sat behind the table, and Albing poured the wine. Koenig nodded, and the steward clicked his heels, ed and withdrew. Albing had served with Hjalmar for two years now, and understood that his was a silent man who enjoyed his own

98

company as well as anyone's, save perhaps for that of his son. Especially towards the end of a voyage.

Hjalmar Koenig wondered if Albing understood why that was so. Why, indeed, he, and perhaps all the ship's company, grew increasingly morose with every passing day. The reasons were interconnected. The life of a commerce destroyer was essentially lacking in redeeming features. This awareness was perhaps tempered, when a mission began, by an almost manic feeling of exhilaration. The voyage they were commencing might well be their last, but they were in the mood for confrontation and sudden death.

But there had as usual been no confrontation, until this evening, due to the skill of their captain. Instead, having evaded the Allied patrols, there had been an escape into the convoyless tropics, day after day of patient steaming, at hardly more than two or three knots to conserve fuel. In the equatorial region, the steel of the deck was too hot to touch, and the sun was a glowing ball of flame apparently perched at the top of the radio aerial, and the only relief was the almost daily thunderstorm, which arrived about noon and had disappeared by two in the afternoon. This was a world devoid of submarines – it was far beyond the range of any U-boat – and also of patrol craft and aircraft. It was an empty world, so empty that those ships with legitimate reasons for being in such waters – whether they were carrying meat from Argentina, nitrates from Chile, gold from South Africa, or troops and munitions to South Africa and India – could afford to dispense with escorts. To meet an enemy in such wastes was a chance in a thousand.

Except where the enemy, like *Atlas*, carried aircraft. The seaplane would fly high, drifting in and out of the clouds, spotted only by the keenest of eyes, and was able to return to the mother ship and report that there was a British freighter two hundred miles away, steering such and such a course, speed calculated to be such and such. Interception, after that, was simply a matter of mathematics.

It was a difficult world in which to sustain moods of suicidal valour. Instead, it was a world of a fox in a huge, unprotected chicken run. The chickens merely had to be spotted to be consumed. Cruising in such circumstances gave men a sense of immortality. The sea was odd, that way. The endless reaches, the rising sun which cut the horizon in the morning, the setting sun which did the same thing in the evening, the days of perfect calm, the other days of homicidal violence when the winds determined to blow, could not but help fill a man at once with a sense of his own finite irrelevance, when set against nature on so vast a scale, but equally with an awareness that he was part of this unceasing progression of nature through the ages.

Koenig lit a cigar. These too were rationed, one to a night. And these too would see him home to Wilhelmshaven, God willing. But was he dealing with God?

Because he believed he was, that all human beings had to, he had always tried to preserve the essentials of humanity. Not all agreed with such a point of view. Wiedermayer, for one. Wiedermayer, contrary to his public image, was by no means a fervent Nazi. He was, absurdly in such a society as that of Germany in 1942, a fervent democrat, as well as a fervent German. Into the hows and whys of the Nazis achieving power he was not prepared to look. He accepted that they were *there*, and in charge of the Fatherland. That was sufficient for Wiedermayer. He gave the government his unswerving support, and if the rest of the world, as he had been taught to believe, was out to crush Germany into the ground and leave her a third-rate power walled in by France and Russia and liable to insult by Poland and Czechoslovakia, he was prepared to take the rest of the world on with all his strength and power. In many ways Koenig envied Wiedermayer his simplistic approach to life and duty. The lieutenant was only thirty years of age, and had known nothing but the disappointments of the Weimar days, the horrors of the Nazi-Communist street battles, and then the clear-cut vision of the victors. The problem was, there were too many Germans of his age, at least mentally.

Koenig was forty-six. As a very young lieutenant in 1916 he had served on *Seydlitz* at Jutland. *Seydlitz* had survived that epic battle, just; Koenig could well remember the struggle to get the stricken ship back to Wilhelmshaven with several thousand tons of water inside her hull. Yet it had been a triumphant day and night. No one in Germany had doubted they had won a tactical victory.

But nothing more. Strategically they had accomplished nothing. It did not matter that they had sunk three battle-cruisers to the loss of one; the British had battle-cruisers, and even battleships, emerging from their builders' yards every month. And Germany had been ruled by generals, not admirals. The German fleet had not destroyed the British fleet, therefore the German fleet had failed. Koenig had also been on board *Moltke* when she had steamed into Scapa Flow to surrender.

There was a knock on the cabin door, and Koenig immediately leaned forward to pour the glass of wine he had been saving. 'Come in,' he called.

The young man wearing the insignia of a third officer in the merchant navy entered, saluted, and closed the door. 'The range is now twenty-five miles, Herr Captain,' he said formally.

He remained at attention, gazing at the wall above Koenig's head. His left arm was bandaged and in a sling. His face, round and inclined to chubbiness, was cold. He could not understand why his father had not gone rushing down to the sick-bay to discover how he was. He would never understand just how much will-power and self-instilled discipline had been required to stop his father from doing that, from treating him differently to any other member of the crew. But Koenig had made this rule from the beginning; except for a precious half an hour every night after dinner.

'Sit down.' He pointed. 'How is the arm?'

'It is not serious, sir.' But the young man's face twisted, briefly, as the arm touched the table.

'But it hurts like hell, eh?' Koenig asked. 'It is bad luck, to be hit in your very first action. It is good that the wound is not serious.'

Kurt Koenig flushed at the implied suggestion that he was making too much of it. He was very like his father in more than just the shape of his face, but he was a couple of inches taller. That was inherited from the mother he had never known. Hesitantly he sipped the wine.

'What did it feel like?' Koenig asked. 'The first time.'

'I would have liked to sink the Britisher.'

'They would have liked us to try. We won. Every time we survive to fight another day, we win.' The philosophy of Jutland, no more understood by the present regime than it had been by the Kaiser or Ludendorff. Yet he served this new government, and was pleased his son served it too. There was nothing political about that. Kurt was all he had. His only pleasure was having the boy sailing with him. It was dangerous, but if they had to go, they would go together.

He had felt that way about Kurt's mother, but she died of starvation. The word was not, of course, entered on her death certificate. She had died of pneumonia aggravated by malnutrition – precisely, starvation – while he was enjoying Scottish sunsets and thick oatmeal porridge.

He had not realised that things in Germany had

become so bad in the few months he was away. His sister also died, but not until after his return. The baby boy she had been nursing was his. Koenig had not expected either of them to survive very long, in 1922; there was suddenly no navy, and not even a merchant navy worth speaking of. His Iron Cross became an object of contempt. He had peddled trash, and lived – once one of the wheelbarrowfuls of trash contained nothing but mark notes. That had not been worth anything, but the realisation that money could be worthless helped him to survive. And in time there had come a job, on a coaler between Rostock and Tallinn. He had hidden his Iron Cross in his hip pocket.

Then came 1933. He had thought Nazism ugly, and had not changed his mind in nine years. But the Nazis wanted good men, and once they were in power they had access to the navy files, and thus had known where to look. He had not been able to resist the temptation to rejoin the navy, with his old rank and the promise of speedy promotion. Besides, he could again wear his Iron Cross at his neck.

The future suddenly became limitless. He was invited to Berlin, sat down with Grand Admiral Raeder, even had an audience with the Führer. There was talk of new ships, talk to make the mouth water. How would he like to command *Graf Spee*? There was a dream. The Western Press had coined the phrase 'pocket battleship'. *Graf Spee* and her sisters were actually very heavy cruisers, revolutionary in design if only because of their diesel engines, which gave them, if no great speed, virtually round-the-world capacity without refuelling. *Atlas* was fitted with diesels.

Graf Spee! The idea had almost made everything else worthwhile. It could never had atoned for Brigitte, and it could never have atoned for the brave comrades who had fallen by the wayside. But he could have commanded her in the spirit of their memory. Yet it had not happened. There had been interviews, containing what he now knew were trick questions, not all of which he had understood in time. The odd thing was that Langsdorff, who had got the command, was no more a Nazi than himself. Langsdorff had merely answered the questions more carefully. And where had it got him? A famous battle, and then a lonely room in Montevideo, a loaded pistol, a single shot.

Koenig has been given *Atlas*. His Nazi masters were too shrewd to waste so much talent. They had, in fact, offered him a U-boat. He had declined. He had never been a submariner, and suffered vaguely from claustrophobia. But the real reason, as his masters had understood, was, that such warfare contained too great an element of the treacherous assassin to appeal to him. In disgust they had given him an armed merchant cruiser. And unwittingly, also given him an opportunity for far greater fame than even Langsdorff. And he was still alive. When he returned to Wilhelmshaven this time he would have completed four successsful voyages. After his last return, Hitler had personally decorated him with the oak leaves to add to his cross. He wondered what the Führer would think of giving him this time.

'Will we make it, father?' Kurt asked. He had drunk half his glass of wine, and was beginning to relax.

'Of course. If the weather is bad, we will make it without difficulty. If it is good.' He gave one of his impish grins. 'We will float about out here until it becomes bad.'

Koenig lay in his bunk and listened to the throb of the MAN diesels far below him. There was no more reassuring sound in the world, because there was no more reliable engine in the world. Diesel engines needed only a clean supply of fuel, sufficient water for cooling and sufficient air for compression. They depended on no uncertain sources of energy such as electric sparks, or even batteries, once started.

The ship lurched, and the single screw raced for a moment, before once again biting into the sea. Now he could hear the howling of the wind. The gale was upon them, and soon hundreds of tons of water would be pouring over the foredeck. Nothing to cause the slightest concern to *Atlas*, normally. But tonight a part of every wave would find its way below, and the pumps would be clacking away. Yet he dared not show a light, and he dared not heave to, until he was beyond the range of searching Sunderland flying-boats.

He had made a mistake – not in sinking the Britisher the moment his radio had begun to flash, but in attacking *Mombasa* at all. It had been a combination of many factors. Boredom, certainly. Situation, certainly; he had been flying the Spanish flag and approaching the European continent as if on course for Cadiz. And a death wish? That too could be blamed on boredom, on self-disgust at the task which had been set him. Put him in the same few thousand square yards as an unarmed merchantman, and he was monarch of all he surveyed. Add even a destroyer to those few thousand square yards of ocean, and he must run for his life – as he was now doing, for the second time, from *Erebus*. His whole being had been screaming at him to chance the torpedoes and stay and fight it out, pitting his superior guns, and gunnery, he was sure, against the Britisher's speed. But that would have been a direct contravention of orders, and so he had fled, and was now fleeing further and further. Flight, and stealthy destruction, were his reasons for being. He could never be proud of that.

He slept fitfully, and awoke when the whistle came down the intercom from the bridge. He pulled on his clothes and climbed the ladder. He gazed at the wind-torn waves dissolving into spumes of flying spray, and at the bow, plunging into the dark waters and coming up again to throw green seas over its shoulders on to the already punctured well-deck, and listened to the whine of the wind.

Predictably, Wiedermayer was also on the bridge. Koenig did not suppose his first officer had turned in for a moment. 'There are three feet of water in the hold, Herr Captain,' he reported.

Koenig nodded. 'Wind direction and speed?'

'South-south-west, thirty-five, gusting forty knots.'

'Anything on radar?'

'No, Herr Captain,' said the rating on watch.

'Very good. Reduce speed to seven knots, and alter course to north-north-east.'

Thankfully, *Atlas* swung away from the wind and the seas, rolled heavily for several minutes, and then settled on her new course downwind, travelling with the elements instead of against them, rising and falling with a rhythmic pattern which every so often changed to a lurch as she entered a larger than usual trough, but with almost no water coming on board now. 'Rig deck lights and get to work, Mr Wiedermayer,' Koenig said. 'And have those bilges pumped dry.'

'Aye aye, Herr Captain,' Wiedermayer said enthusiastically, sliding down the ladder.

Koenig turned his head as Dr Schenck emerged on to the bridge. They were old friends, and Koenig had asked specifically for Schenck to serve with him from the beginning.

'Congratulations,' Schenck remarked.

Koenig grinned. 'We were lucky.'

'As usual. There comes a time when a man ceases to believe in luck, and knows that it is skill that matters.'

'Tell me about Kurt.'

'It is a good, clean wound. I removed the steel splinter, dressed it, gave him an anti-tetanus injection . . . with fortune, there should be no problem.'

'With fortune?'

Schenck shrugged. 'The tendon may have been cut. It is difficult to say without X-ray apparatus.'

'And what would that mean, to Kurt?'

'Time, and discomfort. But for a naval officer, no permanent disability, in my opinion. You do not have to rush around firing revolvers and waving swords.' The doctor peered at the low grey clouds, obvious even in the darkness as there was not a star to be seen. 'Is this weather going to last?'

'It is a deep depression, certainly. It may last for two days.'

'As I said, congratulations,' Schenck repeated. 'My other subjects are ready, by the way.'

Koenig sighed, and nodded. 'We will bury them at sunrise,' he said. 'And then run for home.'

There was a brass band blaring across the harbour and the estuary of the River Jade beyond. There was a flotilla of small boats. There had been an escort, indeed, ever since *Atlas* had rounded the Roter Sand Light Tower, twenty miles offshore, where the great rivers Jade and Weser and Elbe swirled past their protective sandbanks to debouch into the North Sea. And now, with the island of Mellum falling astern and the rooftops of Wilhelmshaven already visible in the distance, there was an official admiral's barge nosing alongside.

'Stand by to receive the admiral,' came the call, and the guard of honour, armed with rifles and wearing their full-dress shore-going uniforms, fell in on the well-deck. The boatswain coo-eed, and Koenig and Wiedermayer descended the ladder from the bridge.

Wiedermayer was trembling with excitement. To have an admiral wishing to come on board ... and not merely an admiral, but *the* admiral, the supreme commander of the German Navy ...

Koenig gave his first officer a wink, and took his

position at the top of the gangway; speed had been reduced to just steerage-way, enabling the ship to breast the current while the ornate barge came alongside, varnish and brightwork gleaming in the morning sunlight. The life-saving mist and wind had been left behind in the Atlantic.

Grand Admiral Raeder gripped the rails of the accommodation ladder and came up with the practised ease of the seaman he was. He stood in the gangway and saluted the bridge. Then he flung his arm upwards in another salute. 'Heil Hitler!'

'Heil Hitler!' echoed both Koenig and Wiedermayer.

'Koenig.' Raeder shook hands. 'My congratulations! Once again you have confounded the enemy. Your name is a tonic to the German people.'

'Thank you, Herr Admiral. You have met my first officer, Hans Wiedermayer?'

Wiedermayer saluted, face crimson. Koenig thought he might burst into tears when Raeder shook his hand as well. 'Wiedermayer,' the admiral said. 'A name to remember. I have something for you, Wiedermayer. Germany knows how to reward her heroes, eh?'

'Herr Admiral,' Wiedermayer gasped.

Raeder stepped past him. 'Fine men,' he said, walking down the ranks of the guard of honour. 'You are . . . ?' He paused before the officer. 'Sub-Lieutenant Kurt Koenig, Herr Admiral.' Kurt stood stiffly to attention, sword held rigidly upright in his white-gloved right hand; his left arm remained in a sling.

'Koenig?' Raeder glanced at Hjalmar in feigned suprise. 'But you are wounded.'

'Only a scratch, Herr Admiral,' Kurt protested.

'Well said, Herr Lieutenant. Well said. Now, stand your men down.' Raeder walked across the deck and gazed at the very obvious, but equally entirely waterproof patch on the deck. 'Splendid work.'

'Lieutenant Wiedermayer's work, Herr Admiral,' Koenig said.

'Well, then, why should we wait?' Raeder asked. 'Assemble all your men who can be spared, Captain.'

'Of course, Herr Admiral.' Koenig nodded to the boatswain, who coo-eed his whistle again. Men appeared from fore and aft to assemble on the deck.

'Lieutenant Hans Wiedermayer,' Grand Admiral Raeder said, 'by the authority invested in me by Adolf Hitler, our beloved Führer, I hereby place around your neck the insignia of the Iron Cross, Second Class. Heil Hitler!'

'Heil Hitler!' shouted the assembled crew.

'And three cheers for the navy,' Raeder added, removing his cap to reveal his curiously shaven head; hair grew thickly to either side of a central swathe which extended from forehead to crown.

The cheers rose skywards, scattering the seabirds and drawing answering applause from the small craft which surrounded the big merchantman.

'And now, Koenig, shall we go up?' Raeder asked.

Koenig gestured to the ladder. He was aware of a curiously empty feeling in his stomach, a sort of floating in space, waiting. . . . The commander-in-chief of the German Navy would not have come out to meet one of his surface raiders simply to pin a medal on the breast of the first officer.

Raeder went into the captain's day cabin and flicked open the log book, which Koenig, having been alerted by radio of this impending visit, had placed on the table. The grand admiral sat down and turned page after page quickly, appearing to be lost in the narrative which was unfolding before his eyes, and undoubtedly also in his imagination. But actually, Koenig knew, he was seeking only the salient factors, the wind speeds and directions, the tonnage of the ships encountered, the timing and importance of each of the hundred and one decisions required to a master during a voyage of this nature.

'I see you know how to use the weather as well as always,' he commented at last.

'I was lucky, Herr Admiral.'

'Lucky? You mean you are supremely competent, Koenig. But a little over-confident sometimes. As with *Mombasa*, eh?'

Koenig smiled. 'I am entitled to say that there I was unlucky. I could not use the Albatross because I had run out of fuel for it. Thus I was unaware that there was a British convoy only a hundred miles away.'

'I was thinking of the amount of time you gave the crew to abandon ship,' Raeder remarked.

'There was clearly bad weather coming, Herr Admiral. I could not leave them to drown.'

'Were these men not the enemies of Germany?'

'They were seamen, Herr Admiral. Like ourselves.'

Raeder gazed at him for several seconds. Then he too smiled. 'And being Hjalmar Koenig, you got away with it. Just. Do you know how many ships were out looking for you? And aircraft?'

'I heard them talking,' Koenig said. 'And flying overhead. But with the cloud ceiling never more than four hundred feet, and the wind never less than thirty knots, and the seas never smaller than eight feet . . .' He grinned.

'It was still a great feat,' the grand admiral said. 'And now, two hundred tons of shipping sunk . . .'

'Ah, no, with respect, Herr Admiral. One hundred and eighty-nine thousand.'

'Bah. It is probably two hundred thousand. You cannot be positive of the exact tonnage of every ship you have sent to the bottom. It is two hundred thousand. We have announced it to the world as such. We released the figure as soon as you were reported off the Horn Reef. You are a national hero, Hjalmar.'

Koenig waited. Grand Admiral Raeder had never addressed him by his Christian name before.

'So now, I think, we must find you employment more in keeping with your talents,' Raeder went on, leaning back in his chair.

'It will be my privilege to serve wherever I am needed,' Koenig said, heart now pounding. Could he be going to be given a real warship at last?

'I have never doubted that. And it so happens that circumstances have arisen which enables us to make the maximum use of those talents. The moment we dock in Wilhelmshaven, I wish you to accompany me to Berlin. The Führer himself wishes to speak with you. It is his province to discuss the project we have in mind. But I feel it is my duty to acquaint you with the main points, because make no mistake, this is no simple task we wish you to undertake. It will involve, primarily, another venture into the North Atlantic.'

'Of course, Herr Admiral.' He could only wait. He knew Raeder's delight in tantalising his officers.

'However, you will be given command, for this mission, of a much larger ship than any you have hitherto had. I hope that will please you.'

'It pleases me very much.'

'The ship, however, is not yet completed.'

Koenig frowned.

'So you will personally supervise the final stages, in the light of the mission. This is important. Ask, and you will receive, if it is possible.'

'I understand, Herr Admiral.'

'I must also impress upon you' – Raeder stared at him – 'that this is a fighting mission, and that there can be no question of magnanimity to any enemy. I have to be very sure that you understand *this*.'

Koenig returned his gaze. 'I will do my duty, Herr Admiral, no matter what may be entailed.'

'I was sure of it. Well then, Captain Koenig, resume

command of your vessel and let us make all possible haste for Wilhelmshaven and then Berlin.'

Koenig stood up, hesitating. 'May I ask who will succeed to the command of *Atlas*?'

Raeder stroked his chin. 'If you were to recommend Wiedermayer, I should be happy to consent.'

Koenig frowned. But did not Wiedermayer deserve to command? He was experienced, capable, courageous . . . and he would seek only to destroy, without warning, wherever possible, and always without pity.

'I would wish to recommend Lieutenant Wiedermayer, Herr Admiral,' he said.

'Good. That is settled, then.'

'But I would like to take certain members of my crew with me to my new command, Herr Admiral.'

Raeder shook his head. 'I'm afraid that will not be possible.'

'May I ask why?'

'You are thinking of your son, I imagine.'

'Amongst others, Herr Admiral, I was also thinking of Dr Schenck.'

'I sympathise with your feelings. But it still cannot be done, Hjalmar. This assignment is secret to the very highest degree. Nothing can be allowed to raise even the slightest comment that what is taking place is not a routine matter. Thus, you have now commanded *Atlas* for four very successful voyages. It is entirely reasonable for you to be promoted to other duties, and it is routine that your first officer, who has undoubtedly absorbed your brilliantly successful technique, should take over command of *Atlas*. It is also routine that the crew should remain with their new commander. It would be highly suspicious for you to leave for a new berth and take with you the third officer and the ship's doctor. You may take your personal servant.'

Koenig bowed his head. 'I apologise, Herr Admiral.'

Raeder got up and threw his arm round Koenig's

shoulders. 'I know it is hard to leave a son. But he will earn his spurs, perhaps more easily with Wiedermayer than under the critical eye of his father. As for you, Hjalmar, Operation Kong is going to earn you immortality. Nothing can be allowed to interfere with that.'

Operation Kong, Koenig thought. Am I being sent to Africa? Or Japan?

CHAPTER 5

The Spy

'Any word from Stockholm yet?' asked the admiral. 'Christ, did you read the official release from Berlin this morning: Koenig home in triumph. Two hundred thousand tons of Allied shipping destroyed. National hero. Jesus. What the hell is that character Seven-Twenty-One *doing*?'

'I am sure that Agent Seven-Twenty-One will very soon have the information you wish, sir,' Jennie said coldly. 'Whatever the risk involved.'

The admiral raised an eyebrow. 'Who's riled, then? One would almost think Seven-Twenty-One was a friend.'

'I regard all our people as my friends, sir.'

'Okay, okay. You've a period, right?'

Jennie glared at him. She wished she had. It would give her an excuse to be bad-tempered – and besides, sixty hours with Clive Wharton, now they were behind her, were beginning to raise some doubts.

The admiral returned to signing letters. She left the office, and sat at her desk. She was fuming. And that was senseless and silly. It was just that ever since she had sent that message to Stockholm she had been growing more and more aware that this was the first time they had ever asked Seven-Twenty-One for specific information. He was an observer, not a spy; there was a difference – even if, as an American naval officer masquerading as a Swedish journalist he would be

114

treated as a spy by the Germans, were he ever found out. But now he had been asked to hunt, rather than observe, for no reason at all other than some hunch of the admiral's. How could it possibly be important what honours Hjalmar Koenig now received? Suppose they gave him *Tirpitz:* that was as high as he could go. Suppose they sent him against the Torch invasion fleet? If they were going to risk their only remaining battleship against Torch, would it really matter who was in command?

And that presumed the Germans had even an inkling that the Americans intended to invade French North Africa, and there was no suggestion of that as yet.

The band blared even louder as *Atlas* moved slowly in to the dock, herded now by three tugs. The crowds cheered. Most of the crew had homes in Wilhelmshaven, and wives and daughters, sons and sweethearts, were there to greet them, to scream their joy in the hysterical fashion which went with all emotions in this new, hysterical Germany. Inspired by the political agents, and the handouts which had been scattered amongst the crowd, they chanted, 'Koenig! Koenig! Koenig!' as the ship came alongside.

Newsreel cameras clacked away. Ships like *Atlas* invariably left Wilhelmshaven in the utmost secrecy, at night – try as he might Jan Anderssen had only once or twice succeeded in obtaining prior information about such departures, and those had been pure luck; he was not here to risk his neck, because it would be a waste of his carefully set up situation, and because it was no part of his plan to become an unsung hero by pressing too hard. But when ships like *Atlas* came home, he – and everyone else – was always invited to cheer and photograph, and boost, another Nazi triumph.

The warps were secured, the gangway was swung open, the boarding ramp run ashore. The crowd surged forward, to be checked by the coal-scuttle-helmeted policemen. The Press corps came first. The six men made their way up the ramp, greeted by a guard of honour on the well-deck, and hurried forward as Grand Admiral Raeder descended the ladder, followed by Captain Koenig and First Officer Wiedermayer. Notebooks and cameras were poised, questions rippled across the afternoon.

Jan Anderssen remained at the back of the throng. He could afford to. He towered above his fellows, and Hjalmar Koenig had already noticed him and given him a nod. Jan Anderssen looked more like a member of the Aryan master race than any German present, with his six foot two inches of muscular height, his shock of brilliant yellow hair, his ice-blue eyes. And so far as anyone was aware, he was probably more of a Nazi supporter than anyone present. Thus he was popular, and with Grand Admiral Raeder most of all. Jan Anderssen was the naval correspondent of a leading Swedish daily, and his reports and vivid descriptions of sea battles at which he had never been present had helped to create the legends which surrounded men like Hjalmar Koenig.

As Koenig himself was well aware. 'Jan.' He shook hands.

'Congratulations,' Jan said. 'Perhaps you will tell me just how much they are in order.' He glanced at the admiral.

Koenig wrinkled his nose. 'You will have to ask him, my dear fellow. Me, I'm off to Berlin for a rest.'

'I'd say you deserve it,' Jan agreed. 'I understand you stopped a shell.'

'A single hit.' Koenig pointed. 'Easily repaired. We lost the use of one gun.'

'And the Britisher?'

Koenig grinned. 'We scored no hits.'

'So you broke off the action?'

116

Koenig continued to smile; he had no doubts that Jan Anderssen was on his side. 'He had friends in the vicinity. I did not.'

'Captain Koenig behaved with his usual impeccable judgement and resourcefulness, added to his courage, Jan,' Raeder said, joining them. 'Be sure you report that.'

'I intend to, Grand Admiral.' Jan scribbled vigorously. 'And now?'

'Captain Koenig is going to have a spell ashore,' Raeder said. 'He has served his country as well as any man, and is too valuable to be risked. I think we can better employ him in teaching other men how to do as well as he. Be sure you put that in your newspaper, Jan. Now we must hurry, Hjalmar. There is a train waiting.'

Koenig winked at Anderssen, and went off with the admiral, while Wiedermayer gave orders, obviously now commander of the ship. Liberty men fell in, smiling for the cameras, while the reporters wandered over to inspect the damage repair. Jan Anderssen left them and went to the bridge ladder, where Third Officer Kurt Koenig stood, somewhat forlornly, watching his father get into a waiting Mercedes.

'Tell me about your wound.'

'A shell splinter. Nothing serious.'

'You must be very proud of your father.'

'I am, Mr Anderssen.'

'As he must be proud of you.'

'My father is proud of every member of his ship's company, Mr Anderssen.'

'Oh, quite,' Jan agreed. 'What is the plan now? Are you joining your father in Berlin?'

'No,' Kurt said.

He was being unusually terse. 'You are wounded. You must be due for a furlough.'

'I have not yet thought of it.'

'Well, if you're ever at a loss for an evening, stop by

117

and have a drink,' Jan invited. 'You know my place.' He slapped the boy on the good shoulder and turned away. Hjalmar Koenig and Grand Admiral Raeder had already left the dock.

Jan Anderssen walked back through the streets of Wilhelmshaven towards his apartment. He was a man who seldom hurried. Ambling through life at a gentle pace was a part of his image. It went with his size, with his Swedish stolidity, with his neutralism, his disengagement from the ferocious passions which had been unleashed by this war. It was an attitude he had cultivated not only as an image, but because it was good for the nerves. Impatience and haste could only breed carelessness – and disaster.

He often wondered about his superiors – that strange set of beings whose business it was not only to think about the possibilities of war in a country dedicated to peace, but about all the possible ramifications and requirements of war, should it come – and what had made them decide *he* was the man they wanted for this job. Of course there were strong physical and family reasons. He had actually been born in Sweden; his father had not followed the example of an elder brother and emigrated until after the end of the First World War. Jan had lived in Stockholm for the first seven years of his life and still spoke the language like a native. He still had relatives scattered about the place who remembered him and were prepared to welcome him back – and who could be checked out by any zealous German spycatcher. Additionally, he spoke German fluently.

On top of all that, he had spent two years as a cub reporter before qualifying for Annapolis. But even that would stand up. To any investigator, he had gone to the United States simply because that had been the decision of his father. He had tried hard to fit into the

118

new life, but obviously must have failed. No doubt at the bullying of his father, who possessed all the excessive patriotism of an immigrant, he had even attended naval college, passed out, and become a flier ... and then had resigned his commission because he could not stand the covert American opposition to everything he claimed to believe in. He had assumed his old name, returned to Sweden and become a journalist again. The break with his past had been so complete he had not even told his family where he was going and what he was doing.

As a journalist on a very right-wing Swedish newspaper, and as a drop-out from the United States Navy, he had been sent to Germany as naval correspondent for the paper. Those were all logical and easily checkable incidents in a man's life. And once in Germany, he had been able to give public utterance to Nazi sympathies, his belief that the new order erected by Hitler was the only hope for the world. He said so on every opportunity, and no one reading his column could doubt where his sympathies lay. Of course he had no doubt at all that as he was an alien and had lived in America, and as the Gestapo was composed of suspicious men, he was watched, but watching him was as far as they were prepared to go. He was popular with the German Navy, and he did them proud in every searing article which praised the Reich and heaped damnation on its enemies. If the Gestapo ever felt that some of the officers he cultivated so assiduously in his search for material were speaking out of turn, that was between the Gestapo and the officers in question. Besides, what could they do to Jan Anderssen, save deport him to Sweden?

This was the scenario outlined to him by the men who had talked to him that day in Washington. It had been impeccably thought out, impeccably implemented. It had required the cooperation of only one man not in that room, his editor, Sven Horstrup. But Sven Horstrup already bore the title of Seven-Seven-Four, and had apparently been garnering information for the United States' Stockholm embassy for several years. As a newspaper editor he was in a good position to do so. It was Horstrup who had suggested implanting a man into Germany itself, as the war clouds gathered.

But how had they known he would go for it? He hadn't, of course. Not at first. His reaction had been sheer amazement; the sacrifice they were demanding had been so far above and beyond the call of duty as to be almost surrealistic. They had known that. And yet they had not been in possession of the vital piece of information which caused him to accept, and thus they would never know how lucky they were.

The admiral had said, leaning across his desk, 'John, boy, I want you to know that we understand just what we're asking you to do. We're asking you to become a failure and a write-off in the eyes of the world. We're asking you to risk your life. And' – he had given one of his disarming smiles – 'we're asking you to give up flying for a little while. Just a little while, John, boy. But we have to know what's going on inside Nazi Germany. I mean, behind the propaganda and the refugees' horror stories. We have to know if they do mean war, and what kind of a war. Especially, we have to know what they mean to do with that navy of theirs. We know they're building like mad, but we don't know what, how, or when. We have to find that out, because every day makes it look more and more likely that some time we are going to have to take those bastards on.' He had leaned back. 'You'd be serving your country far better than by flying planes, and when you come home, boy, there'll be an extra stripe waiting for you. At least one. And remember, it's only for a while.'

John Anderson had not been such a fool as to accept any of that at face value, especially when he had asked if he could tell his family, and been refused: he just had to drop out and run. Then he had nearly told them to forget it. But the admiral had forestalled him with another disarming smile. 'We don't expect you to make a decision this minute, John, boy. You go home and think about it. To yourself, mind. Come and see us again Monday morning.'

He climbed the stairs, and smiled and blew a kiss to his landlady, who lived on the ground floor and dissolved into giggles whenever she encountered her most handsome tenant.

He unlocked the door of his apartment, took off his hat and jacket, poured himself a Dortmunder lager from the tiny icebox and sat at his desk. He took the cover off his portable typewriter, inserted a piece of paper and got to work. Words poured from his mind through his fingers and then the keys on to the paper. He dealt in hyperbole; phrases like 'magnificent achievement', 'greatest of German naval heroes', 'terror to the British', 'another blow to Churchill's waning prestige', bounded across the page, while his thoughts went in other directions.

Some of his reasons for saying yes that Monday morning had been straightforward and worth believing, even if he found them difficult to accept himself. They were the reasons which had obviously attracted the admiral, and which the admiral had felt would entirely govern his decision: his Swedish background: and the fact that he was not an American born, but the United States had taken him in, together with his family, made that country the greatest force yet to enter his life. On the other hand, his ancestors had been French, and from them he had inherited a love of adventure, of chancing his arm – if he had never been attracted to dice or cards or horses, it had been because he preferred to gamble with life itself. And there could be no greater challenge than living a lie for the sake of one's country. All of

121

these aspects of his personality had undoubtedly been observed by his superiors and entered on his record. They had been the admiral's secret weapons, he thought. And they were the considerations which had kept him awake that unforgettable weekend – and kept him sane in the four years which had elapsed since.

He had spent several months training in secret to become a spy. That had been the most difficult part of the whole assignment. Not the training – that had been simple enough for a man who had qualified as a navy pilot – but being there, knowing he could still change his mind, knowing that Jennie was at the end of a telephone . . .

He had returned to Sweden in the autumn of 1939, just before the big bang. Even then he had been promised a couple of years, no more. But too much had happened between the autumn of 1939 and the autumn of 1942. Everything had escalated, and his information – particularly in respect of such German giants as *Bismarck* and *Tirpitz*, greater warships than any possessed by Great Britain or the United States – had become too valuable. It had not been convenient to withdraw him when his two years expired.

Spying! There was another reason for what he was doing: the romance of it. Actually, there was very little romance connected with his work. He was a journalist, pure and simple. He wore no cloak, and he carried no dagger, not even a penknife; he certainly did not possess a gun. But still the idea had carried a certain glamour, and in addition there had been the freedom from rules and regulations, the ability – indeed, the necessity – to cultivate a totally non-navy image. And all at virtually no risk, up to this morning, together with the security of knowing that everything was waiting for him when they finally took him home.

He extracted the sheet of paper from the typewriter and studied it. It was good, solid, poor-quality, hysterically one-sided journalism – not only to keep the Germans happy, but because his choice of words had to be outlandishly simple. Now he must choose the words which mattered. When that was done, the key was simple; he always not only dated his dispatches, but added the time of completion. No one knew, or cared, exactly when he composed his copy, so the time was his to play with – he used the twenty-four-hour notation, which was all Sven Horstrup needed. Seventeen-twenty-six would mean, to the casual eye, that the dispatch had been completed at twenty-six minutes past five in the afternoon; Sven would know that if he took the seventeenth word of the copy, then went back two words, then forward six, and then began again, moving forward seventeen, back two, forward six, and so on, he would extract a brief, succint and pointed message for relaying to the US Naval Attaché in Stockholm, and thence, by yet another cipher, to the Office of Naval Intelligence in Washington, where some girl who wouldn't have a clue what she was doing would carefully decode it and place it before the admiral, who would, hopefully, be able to make something of it. The system was not only utterly simple, which was the secret of all workable systems, but almost foolproof. He even had to clear all of his dispatches with the local Gestapo office; they had never censored one.

But of course, he thought, as he began composing his message – the time would be selected and the necessary word adjustment made afterwards – if he ran no risks whatever in Germany, he ran enormous risks back home. When he returned, he had been promised, he would be a hero, and the secret of what he had been doing for his country would be released to the world. Presumably that could only happen after the Allies had won the war. But were the Allies going to win? It didn't look quite so certain, from where he sat, exposed only to German newscasts.

And even if they did, and he was hailed as a hero by the admiral, and presumably by all the other admirals, what about his peers? What about someone like Clive Wharton, who had once upon a time been his best friend? Clive was not the man ever to understand the intricacies of spying, or the forces which might lead a man to take up such an occupation. Clive carried his manhood up front, in every way. Clive would have been at Pearl Harbor when the Japanese attacked. He might even have been killed there. Or, if not there, somewhere else. News was scanty. There had been some big air and sea battles since last December. All won by the Japanese, of course – at least according to the Germans. Clive had undoubtedly bought it by now.

But just supposing he hadn't, he and all his other buddies; they would have spent a year, two years, three years, four years – God alone knew how many years – flying their machines in actual combat, killing and being killed, staring at their enemies down the barrels of their machine-guns and their cannon, allowing only hatred and valour and courage and patriotism to dominate their minds. They could never re-accept a man who had rubbed shoulders with those same enemies, drunk with them, smiled with them and praised them to the skies. Even if they could believe that he had been doing a job of work intended to bring their eventual victory that much closer, it would still not have been their work. He had never looked at an enemy in cold, killing anger.

Perhaps it was beginning to bother him at last, because he actually found himself liking some of those enemies. Men like Hjalmar Koenig.

He had found the pattern he wanted, now, and wrote rapidly on his pad, making changes where necessary on the draft of his report. Both pad and draft would of course be burned when the message was complete. He had been taught the importance of total security.

Those thoughts, those considerations of the future,

124

had been imponderables four years ago, although he had known, at least subconsciously, that he could never truly go back. That gut feeling had nearly led him to refuse, because he would be even further apart from Jennie. But then, he had accepted the assignment simply because of Jennie – to save her from herself. There was a nice heroic thought. It had also been to save him from himself. And the admiral had never suspected by how narrow a margin he had gained an acceptance. Or had the admiral known all along, even if the engagement had never been officially announced?

But the admiral had never given a sign that he even knew of the existence of a young woman named Jennie Rhodes. And John Anderson had never told him, never seized that obvious out. There was the biggest "why" of all.

Jennie could have walked straight out of the pages of a Norse legend. She could easily have walked in from any Stockholm street. but she hadn't; that was the trouble. There was no Swedish in Jennie's background: she came of half-Irish and half-Scottish stock, firmly planted in that original centre of America – New England. When he had first spoken with her, on the beach at Waikiki, she had been a blonde sun goddess in a tantalising one-piece bathing suit and an even more fantastic all-over suntan. Blonde sun goddesses with good tans were not all that rare on Waikiki, and this one had seemed no different to any other, wearing no jewellery, hair magnificently long and fine. He hadn't known enough, then, to be able to guess the cost of that swimsuit. She *could* have been a Swedish girl, that day, who had come across third-class on a shoestring, as the Anderssens had done twelve years before. It had only slowly dawned on him that she hadn't. He often wondered if Clive had known just what she was, at that first meeting. The pair of them, when they returned to Pearl and looked at each other, had said, almost with one voice, 'Christ, did you ever see such tits. And the legs!' And they had agreed that when they took her out next day, as arranged, the one she smiled at first got the green light from the other.

Then, there had been nothing but sex on his mind. His dream had been of getting between those long legs and coming to rest on those magnificent breasts. And he had been surprised, because there was nothing on her mind but sex, either. Or so it had seemed. She had been hesitant: she had known what she was doing, but she hadn't been sure she liked it. By then he was already realising she was a lady, and was beginning to feel a little hesitant himself. But she had seemed to like doing it with him. It was only after he was invited back to the home of the aunt she was staying with, and had taken in the verandahs and the acres of land and the view, and discovered that the cutlery was solid silver and the china came from Limoges and the wine was Château something or other 1932, and realised further that these people ate and drank on this scale every day and thought nothing of it, that he understood just what he had got himself into.

He had wanted to turn and run, then. But Clive had talked him out of it. Clive was a fifth-generation American. 'We don't have class here,' Clive had said. And winked. 'Or we don't let it stop us, anyhow. So what if her folks came across on the *Mayflower* or have an oil well in the backyard? She loves you, Johnnie boy. It just pops out of her eyes every time she looks at you. Pass this one up and you'll regret it for the rest of your fucking life.'

But how could a man carry on a careless affair with a girl like Jennie Rhodes? She had said, yes to his proposal of marriage, without hesitation, joyously and happily and excitedly, and then started to make plans. Stamford, Connecticut. The cathedral. Seven hundred and fifty people . . . her euphoria had slowly died as she watched his dismay. If he had drawn some conclusions about her, she had certainly drawn some conclusions about him. She thought they didn't matter, but she hadn't taken them far enough. She hadn't thought about dear old mom and dad, who still had trouble deciding which end of a sentence to put the verb, in the midst of seven hundred and fifty refugees from the *Mayflower*. But Jennie was a girl of quick decisions. She had laughed. 'Oh, bugger that nonsense,' she had declared. 'I can think of nothing more horrible. I want to be married in the chapel right here at Pearl. I want raised swords and white gloves and just family.'

He hadn't believed her. But she had been convincing, and had stayed convincing, even though he could tell she was getting hell from New England. He was getting a fair amount of hell from Florida, even if the two situations had been so far apart as to be laughable. 'Are you sure this is a *good* girl?' Papa had written.

All of that was why it was possible to imagine that perhaps a string or two had been pulled, behind his back; that he had been singled out for the assignment by the admiral, less because of his qualifications than because someone in Connecticut had telephoned someone in Washington who probably belonged to the same country club and said, 'Get that asshole out of there before he marries my daughter!'

That was possible. But irrelevant. The only relevant fact was that when he had been given a choice between marrying Jennie and proceeding slowly on his way towards admiral himself, by moving entirely into her world and forsaking his own; or not marrying Jennie, by just disappearing from the face of the earth – he had opted for the disappearing trick.

Because she was the most beautiful girl he had ever known? Because every time he touched her – and she did like to be touched – he felt he was defiling a materialisation of Freya? Because every time he took her out

127

for a meal he curled up and died at his own inadequacy in not knowing exactly how every dish was going to be cooked and which year was bad for claret? Because she had only ever spent three days in Stockholm and they had been at the Grand, a hotel he had never actually entered, even since his return as a journalist? Because the only cabin she had ever been in on a ship had been first class? Because she wore silk underwear? Because her cocktail watch was a gold Rolex? For day wear she wore a chunky gold Omega. If only she had worn a watch that day on the beach, and given him an inkling.

Or because she had never suggested, when he had got a furlough, that they go back to Connecticut so that he could meet her parents? That had taken some figuring out, and the answers had all been bad. Either she and her folks had definitely split over him, or her folks had definitely asked her not to bring him home, or she had realised only too well that he would be a disaster in a New England mansion. 'I'd rather holiday right here on the beach,' she had said. 'They can meet you when they come out for the wedding.'

But then she confessed they weren't coming out at all, that they had actually forbidden the marriage, because the idea of Jennifer Margaret de Courcey Rhodes marrying the son of a penniless Swedish clerk in a real estate office, even if he was an officer and therefore by definition presumably a gentleman, was too absurd to be considered.

'Screw them,' Jennie had said. 'I'm twenty-three. If they don't want to come to our wedding, they don't have to.'

When he had run, he told himself he was really doing her a favour.

So going back would necessarily be to nothing. Even if Jennie wasn't married and three times a mother by now, she wasn't ever going to forgive a man who had walked out of her life just a week before the wedding, without even saying goodbye. Just a note, an apology, and silence. He had wept that night. But by then he had been on a plane to his secret training camp, and again, silence.

Then why was he suddenly scared? No one, least of all himself, gave a damn whether he lived or died. So what if the admiral had suddenly emerged from three years of silent contentment with the quality of his information and demanded something specific? What he wanted was neither difficult nor dangerous. For the life of him, John Anderson could not think why he wanted to know about Hjalmar Koenig. Hjalmar was certainly a hero – to Nazi Germany. But despite the present trumpetings, John could not believe he was widely known to the rest of the world, simply because he operated so much of the time in secret. It was possible that the admiral was simply over-reacting to German propaganda, and it was tempting merely to forward the information that Koenig had been retired from active service to a desk job in Berlin, and would therefore be of no further interest to anybody.

Save for the fact that sea captains who are being retired to desk jobs are very seldom met on board their own ships by commanders-in-chief. Therefore the admiral was clearly in possession of information which he needed to have confirmed. Thus the job would have to be done properly. He had already completed his message to Sven Holstrup with the words, "Other matter in hand". But what did he mean by that? Koenig had certainly been taken to Berlin, and there was only one source in Berlin which was available to him. It was a source on which he had turned his back six months ago because, even as a spy, he retained certain of the handicaps of an officer and a gentleman. But it was a source which would have to be reactivated, if he was going to get the information the admiral wanted, without sticking his neck out.

*

One of the most remarkable aspects of Germany at war, John Anderson thought as his train pulled into the Tiergarten station, was the way the war had not yet actually affected the country. It was very important to include that 'yet' in such a thought, if the Allies *were* actually going to win. But while there was bomb damage in several of the major cities of the Ruhr, and there was even bomb damage to be seen in Berlin itself, it appeared in no way to have disrupted the ordinary lives of the German people.

From time to time, on the railway journey from the west, he had seen large numbers of soldiers either entraining or detraining, but they could all have been going on holiday. There was no decent coffee to be had for love or money, and a bottle of good Scotch whisky, such as he had in his case, was worth its weight in gold. But there had been no mobilisation of German women as a labour force, as, he was told, had happened in Britain and Russia. And there was no anxiety. Why should there be? If Leningrad and Moscow had not yet fallen, and the casualty lists from the Eastern Front were frightening, this was still regarded as a temporary situation: the Russians were holding on by their boot-straps. Equally the British were clearly holding on by their bootlaces in Egypt, a bare sixty miles from Alexandria. In the Atlantic, too, the British, even with the support of the Americans, were only just keeping their heads above water, with the U-boat wolf packs sinking up to half of every convoy that left North America, and men like Hjalmar Koenig accounting for a large proportion of those coming from elsewhere.

John did not actually have any doubts that the enormous industrial power of the United States would triumph in the end, nor did he have any doubts that with American support Great Britain would remain thrust as a salient into the side of Fortress Europe ...

but in terms of victory he equally had no doubts but that he was looking a long way into the future.

Which meant that future was becoming increasingly bleak for him. So why not enjoy life just a little – especially when he could do so and pretend to be doing his job at the same time? Simply because his conscience was still acting the fool?

He sat on his bed in his hotel room – having been greeted with much pleasure by the staff, as he always used this hotel when visiting Berlin – and asked for a number. There was no hesitation in connecting him; he wondered what would happen if he sat in a bedroom at, say, the Dorchester in London, and simply dialled the Admiralty.

'Admiralty.'

'I'd like to speak with Fräulein Staffel, please.'

'One moment please.'

Clicks and thumps.

'Admiral Doenitz's office.' The voice was quiet, controlled, brusque and entirely impersonal.

'Helga,' John said, making his own voice as seductive as he could.

There was a moment's hesitation, then she said, 'Who is this, please?' Her voice became much more attractive when she was interested.

'Jan Anderssen. Who else?'

'Jan?' The voice became more attractive than ever. Hurdle number one had been successfully leapt. 'How good to hear from you. Are you in town?'

'At the Albert.'

'As usual,' she said. 'Perhaps we could have a drink some time.' Some of the initial coldness was returning as she started to remember. But she *had* been pleased to hear his voice.

'That's why I'm ringing,' he told her. 'How about this evening? There's a bottle of Grant's Standfast standing on this table beside me.'

131

'Have you never been told that it is a criminal offence to attempt to bribe a serving officer in the German Navy?' Helga Staffel asked him. But her voice was again relaxed.

'Perhaps I could come to your apartment.'

This time the hesitation was longer. He could tell exactly what was going through her mind, and he was beginning to know that unpleasant feeling of being an utter heel. She would want him to go round to her apartment, because of what had happened six months ago. But she would have to make up her mind whether she could afford to risk his walking out on her again.

Helga Staffel was an unusual girl, in every way. Far from being a typical Aryan beauty, she was a Bavarian, small and dark, with silky black hair. She was in the strongest possible contrast to Jennie Rhodes physically, and he had actually been attracted to her because of her job. Helga was one of the few German women who had allowed the war to affect her directly. But that was because she was Helga Staffel. Her father was Hans-Jurgen Staffel, the toy-store king, and if there were perhaps more important things to be made in Germany in 1942 than toys, he remained a wealthy and important man. He was a personal friend of Hitler's, and had supported the party with money even in the bad days when the Nazis were a poor joke. Helga did not wear her faith in the party and its leader as a flaming torch, as did so many others, but she was deeply committed to everything Nazism stood for, especially its role as the only effective bulwark in the world against international communism. Thus once the die had been cast, she had enthusiastically abandoned her role as a bored young socialite who was hostess at her widowed father's parties, and applied for a uniform. As she was Hans-Jurgen Staffel's daughter her request had immediately been granted, and as she was Hans-Jurgen Staffel's daughter she had begun life at the top. Admiral Doenitz had taken her on as one of his personal secretaries; he too was a friend of her father's.

The amazing thing was that whereas he had been put off, and indeed frightened, by the aura of wealth and position that surrounded Jennie Rhodes, the aura of wealth and position that surrounded Helga Staffel had not frightened him at all. Because she was an enemy, to be exploited wherever possible? He had certainly tried to tell himself that. She might have been made to order. She had access to top-secret navy material, she was young and extremely pretty, she had taken an immediate shine to the handsome Swedish reporter . . . and she possessed the utter amorality of the typical Nazi.

Yet it had been that amorality which *had* frightened him off. Observing her interest in him at a succession of parties, and deciding that there were after all perks in this job, he had decided to allow himself to be seduced. He had not expected her to sit beside him, on the occasion of their fourth meeting, dangling a half-empty champagne glass from one hand while he tried not to look down her cleavage, and remark, in the most casual of tones, 'I have been thinking of you, Mr Anderssen. Do you think I could call you Jan?'

'I'd be flattered, Fräulein Staffel.'

'Then you must call me Helga. I would like to have a baby by you.'

The dropping of his champagne glass had been accepted as Swedish gaucheness. 'You Swedes,' Helga had remarked with one of her quiet smiles. 'You live such sheltered lives, up there in your Arctic forests. But it is the duty of every German girl to bear at least one child for the Reich. I have not yet done so, simply because I have never seen a man I would wish to share a bed, or my body, with. Until you.' She had allowed her gaze to drift up and down. 'I think you would give me a magnificent child.'

133

'You wouldn't by any chance be proposing marriage?' he had asked, desperately trying to surface.

Her frown had been genuine bewilderment. 'Good Lord, no. Do you want to be married?'

'No, as a matter of fact. I can't afford it.'

'I do not wish to be married either,' she confided. 'Marriage is such a bourgeois habit. Are you afraid to sleep with a woman unless you are married to her?'

Contempt had lingered. But not for long – on her part, at least. On his, self-contempt had come rushing in too quickly. She had, incredibly, been a virgin. That didn't bother him. Her collapse into love for him had. What more could he ask for, he kept telling himself. This girl has fallen in love with you, just as Jennie Rhodes fell in love with you. There were differences, of course: Jennie had been on the rebound from the Texan basketball player.

Once again he had cut and run, but for a different reason. He might be living an artificial and despicable life, which could only end when he had milked Germany dry, and every German who could be used to accomplish that end . . . but he could not bring himself to be such a heel as to milk this girl dry. Besides, he had reasoned, she could even be dangerous. Suppose he was to make the mistake of falling in love with her too? He had supposed he could never love anyone other than Jennie Rhodes. But Helga Staffel could be a powerful second best. Wilhelmshaven had suddenly seemed a very safe place to be.

That was several months ago. She had written him a couple of letters, and made a couple of telephone calls, then she had got the message. But now he was back. What she was debating was whether she still wanted him, after he had stood her up so badly. But now she had decided. 'Why, yes,' she said. 'I think that would be rather a nice idea. Come round at seven tonight and I will cook you supper.'

She hung up. He wondered if her heart was pounding for joy. His was certainly pounding. It had been a long six months.

Helga Staffel wore a midnight blue housecoat, which encased her from her neck to her ankles; matching high-heeled mules gave her a much needed extra three inches. Her black hair was cut very short and upswept, isolating the sharp but quiet contours of her face; she had high cheekbones and a small mouth, a pointed nose and chin, and reflective grey eyes. In repose her face, while pretty, had a certain air of discontent. When she smiled, her mouth was elongated and her eyes glowed, and she was almost beautiful.

She was only half smiling as she opened the door. 'I was surprised to hear from you.'

'Well, I was in town, so . . .'

'You thought we should try again?' Now she did smile. 'With more success, perhaps.' She stood aside, and he entered the apartment. Presumably apartments reflected the character of their occupant. This place, with its deep crimson curtains and purple rugs, its indirect lighting and leather upholstery, always made him think of an antechamber in hell.

'I did try to explain . . .'

She closed the door and shot the bolt. 'That you are not worthy of me, simply because you do not have enough money? That is a very old-fashioned point of view.'

'I'm afraid I'm an old-fashioned man.'

'So I understand. Did you bring the bottle? The glasses are over there.'

He poured. 'Water?'

'Why spoil it?'

He brushed the glasses together and gave her one. 'It is good to see you again.'

'Why did you not let me know you were coming?'

'I didn't know myself, until yesterday. Anyway, I didn't know what sort of a reception I'd get. I thought that perhaps by now . . .' His gaze drifted to her stomach.

She smiled. 'I am not pregnant. I could not possibly be. I have not tried again.'

He frowned at her. 'That's hard to believe.'

'No man has entered this apartment since the day you left it, Jan. So, aren't you going to kiss me?'

She set her glass on the table, put both arms around his neck and seemed to climb up his body. He kissed her mouth, tasting the whisky on her tongue. Then she was slipping, and had to be supported. He grasped her buttocks to keep her up to his mouth, and felt nothing under the housecoat save flesh — flesh which moved under his hands as she squirmed against him. 'Oh, Jan,' she said. 'Jan, I have missed you so.'

He realised she was weeping. He wanted to hurl himself through the door and out into the night and find the first available whore and screw her until his eyes popped out. But Helga went with the job. And screwing Helga was going to be one million light years sweeter than screwing any whore. The difference was that he couldn't possibly hurt the whore — mentally.

She slipped down his front and kept on going, to sit on the leather-upholstered settee. The housecoat had fallen back from one very white leg. For all her dark hair she had the whitest skin he had ever known.

He knelt beside her and sent his hands under the coat, sliding up her flesh. As he had estimated, she wore nothing underneath. She shivered when he reached her thighs, but it was a shiver of joy. She preferred masturbation to entry, at least to begin with. He had barely touched her when she was away. Her orgasms were small, quiet things, in keeping with the rest of her, but no one could doubt they were total. Her head sagged back on the cushions, the flesh around her lips was wet with sweat, her tongue lolled and her eyes glazed. He unbuttoned the housecoat and found the rest of her – small and hard and anxious. But so was he, save for the small.

He held himself off her. He liked to watch her, as she recovered from the first climax and began to float in the direction of another. Her lips moved, although her eyes had shut. Sometimes her mouth twisted. The first time he had observed that he had withdrawn for fear he was hurting her. Now he knew it was a twist of pleasure. That she didn't get pregnant was unbelievable. But maybe she would, this time.

He lit a cigarette and finished his whisky while she cleaned up, him as well. Then she refilled their glasses, took a drag from his cigarette and stuck it back in his mouth. She wasn't a habitual smoker, but now she was most certainly exuding happiness. Therefore, so must he. He caught her round the thighs to kiss her and fondle her again. But she could tell his heart was no longer in it. 'I have sausage.' She winked. 'Only seventy-five per cent bread. And cabbage. And turnips. After we have eaten, we will make love again, and you can fart all you wish.'

'Sounds right.' He had to wait for a cue. He finished his drink, poured another. Part of the expertise required for this job was to be able to drink any ordinary human being under the table while retaining his own mental control and, most importantly, his memory.

'So what brings you to Berlin?' Helga asked, busy in the kitchen. 'If not to see me?'

He got up and went to the doorway to watch her. She had not bothered with the housecoat, moving from stove to cupboard to table to sink in a series of white-tinted portraits. 'I did come to see you. Didn't I call the moment I reached the hotel? But I had to have an excuse for coming up. I'm hunting a story.'

'What story?' she asked.

137

'One with which you might be able to help.'

She gave him one of her quick, shrewd glances. 'You know I cannot give you any information, Jan.'

'Sure you can. The admirals will pat you on the back. I want to do a feature on Hjalmar Koenig.'

'The hero,' she remarked disparagingly. While she would cheerfully die for her beloved Führer, he knew, she would wish it to be in uniform, surrounded by other men and women in uniform. Disguised raiders did not appeal to her.

'Well, doll, let's face it, he has got to be the most famous German sea captain of this war.'

'That is simply because he is still alive,' Helga pointed out, grilling frankfurters.

'That's as good a reason as any, I suppose. But the fact remains that he's someone people want to know about. The Swedish people, anyway. I'm going to do a big spread on him.'

'I look forward to reading it.'

'But I need an ending.' John wandered back into the lounge. 'It's going to be a bit downbeat if his career is over.'

'Is it over?'

'Well, I spoke with Raeder in Wilhelmshaven, and with Koenig himself. They gave me the impression that he's not going to sea any more.'

'They probably feel his nerve is gone. That often happens, after too many missions.' She placed the plates on the table, handed him a bottle of hock to uncork and sat down, flicking her napkin open.

'I don't believe Koenig has any nerves.' He poured, tasted, nodded. 'Good.'

'From father's cellars. You must meet father, one day.'

'I'd like that.' He filled her glass. 'I'd like to know what job Koenig is going to next.'

'Oh?'

138

'Well, hell, doll . . .' He sat opposite her; the table was very small, and their bare knees touched. 'I can't end a story with, now the great hero's been brought ashore because his nerve has gone. That won't please anybody. Least of all Raeder. I have to say, now he's being promoted to do, well, whatever it is he's going to do.' He raised his glass. 'I adore you.'

'In other words, you wish me to find out confidential information and give it to you.'

'For God's sake, what can be confidential about Hjalmar Koenig's next job, if he's not going to sea?'

'It has to be confidential, or Raeder would have told you what it was. You're one of his favourite people. He's told me so.'

'Favourite or not, keeping people on a string is the way Raeder gets his kicks. Listen, Helga, find out for me where Koenig is going next, and I'll screw you every night for a month.' He was being crude, but he suspected that was what she really wanted. 'And if you're not pregnant then, well . . .'

'You will have to be sterile,' she observed. 'That has to be the lowest form of bribery. I do like the idea, only it would be treason.'

'Oh, rubbish. What can be treasonable about it? Anyway, listen: whatever he's going to do, he's going to be doing it within the next month. I won't have my story ready for a month. But if I have all the information, and can release my story the day Raeder announces Koenig's new appointment, well . . .'

'Everyone will know you have a source.'

'So they're going to take Hans-Jurgen Staffel's daughter and put her up against a wall?'

She made a moue. 'Uncle Adolf wouldn't let them.'

'Do you actually call him uncle?'

'Of course. He dandled me on his knee as a baby.' She finished her meal, got up, carrying her glass of hock, sat on the settee and crossed her legs.

'So how about it?' he asked.

She shrugged. 'I do not suppose it is very important, if you promise not to use it until it is made public. Are you going to move in here?'

'I'm paying for a hotel room.'

'You can't screw me every night for a month from a hotel room, Jan. Move your things in here tomorrow.'

'But . . . I can't stay in Berlin a month, either.'

'So it was another of your lying promises.'

'Hell, no,' he lied. 'But I have a job of work to do.'

'All right.' She gave another of her entrancing shrugs. 'Just so long as you come and stay in this apartment whenever you're in town. And just so long as you come to town at least once a week.'

'Sounds great.' He seemed to have jumped with both feet into a quicksand. 'When are you going to get that information for me?'

'Are we bargaining or making love, my darling?'

He hesitated. But he dared not push it. The admiral would just have to wait a day or two. 'I'd prefer to make love.' He went towards her, then checked as he saw the book on the table by the settee. 'What in the name of God is that?'

'A Japanese phrase-book. Do you speak Japanese?'

'No. Don't tell me you're going to Japan?'

'Don't be silly. Japan is coming to Germany.'

He sat beside her, brain ticking. 'Tell me.'

'It is very hush-hush. That you *can't* use.'

'Then I won't. But I'm intrigued.'

'Apparently there is a party of Japanese fliers coming here. They are due any day now. And we navy secretaries have been told to entertain them.' She gave one of her little shivers. 'The whole idea is repulsive. I hate Orientals.'

He took her in his arms. 'What on earth are the Japanese coming to Germany for?'

'It's some sort of mutual training programme.

Presumably our boys are on their way to Japan. I only know about it because these are navy fliers.'

'But if they're just coming to train, why is it so secret?'

'God knows. Everything is secret nowadays.' She kissed him on the mouth. 'You're not going to be jealous of a few Japanese? All we have to do is have a drink with them and take them to a nightclub, and that sort of thing.'

'It's what happens after the nightclub that bothers me. I think I'm going to have to meet these characters.'

She moved her head away to gaze at him. 'I told you, you can't use it.'

'So let's forget it.' He held her close. 'When did you say you wanted me to move in?' he whispered in her ear.

PART TWO

Autumn 1942

CHAPTER 6

The Disappointment

'Oh, Christ!' the admiral remarked, studying the message. 'He's gone mad. I guess we just left him there too long.'

'I'm afraid I don't see how you figure that, sir,' Jennie said coldly.

'It's that, or he's hitting the bottle. Little yellow men? Jesus. They'll be green men next, and he'll have seen space ships landing on the Unter den Linden.'

'With respect, sir,' Jennie explained, keeping her temper with difficulty, 'I think Seven-Twenty-One is referring to the Japanese.'

'Oh, for Christ's sake. If he meant Japanese, why didn't he fucking well say so?'

'Because of the code he uses, sir. It is taken from his normal weekly dispatches to his paper in Stockholm, and must be completely above suspicion. He can certainly find a legitimate reason for using words like "little" and "yellow" and "men" at various places in his dispatch, but obviously he cannot use the word Japanese when recording events in Germany, especially if these people's presence there is confidential.'

'I guess you've a point. But hell, Japanese airmen in Germany? It doesn't make any God-damned sense. And not a fucking word about Koenig.'

Jennie gathered up the messages. 'Well, sir, I think this could be a very important piece of information.'

'Yeah? So tell me what it means.'

'I have no idea, sir. But it must mean something.'

'Something,' the admiral growled, and snapped his fingers. 'Torch! God-damn it! I just knew it. They're meaning to hit the Torch armada. Christalmighty!'

'Excuse me, sir, but what are they going to hit Torch with?' Jennie asked, genuinely interested.

'That carrier, of course. *Graf Zeppelin*.'

'Seven-Twenty-One's last report on *Graf Zeppelin* indicated that the ship was not yet completed, sir.'

'Sure. But only a week ago he reported work on her had been resumed, right?'

Jennie frowned. She had forgotten that the admiral, whose assets at least equalled his faults – which was why he was an admiral – had a memory like an elephant.

'It's beginning to tie in, Jennie. By God it is.'

'Save that there is no evidence whatsoever, sir, that the Germans know anything at all about Torch.'

'Sure. Well, if they do know something, they're not going to shout it to the world, now are they? They must be sitting over there with saliva dripping out of their mouths. If they could catch the North African invasion fleet with a strike from a carrier . . . and that's why they need those Japs, don't you see? The Krauts have no experience at flying off carriers. And of course Koenig is the man to captain the carrier. If there's anyone can take her out into the North Atlantic, he can. Now, you listen to me, Jen. You draft a message for Seven-Seven-Four to relay to Seven-Twenty-One and mark it most urgent. I want to know about these Japs, and about Koenig, and about *Graf Zeppelin*. I want to know the *hour* that ship is putting to sea.'

'With respect, sir,' Jennie said. 'But you are asking me to tell Seven-Twenty-One to start probing one whole hell of a lot deeper than he's ever had to in the past.'

'He knew the risks when he took the job. Maybe he's

forgotten them. He's just had it too good these last three years. Get on with it.'

She glared at him, but he had already lowered his head and was consulting the next item on his agenda. He was a God-damned workaholic, she thought. And he didn't give a damn about people's lives.

Slowly she closed the door and returned to her desk, sat down and stared at the blank forms in front of her. What a fool she was. If only she'd gone along with his idea that Seven-Twenty-One had hit the bottle or gone crazy, Johnnie could have been on his way home by now; far better for him to be honourably discharged for ... she supposed it would be called combat fatigue ... than to be picked up by the Gestapo for asking too many questions. Oh, Jesus Christ, she thought.

'This one's personal, ma'am,' remarked Signalman Brown, standing at her elbow.

Jennie scanned the sheet of paper. 'WEEKEND PASS AVAILABLE FIRST SEPTEMBER STOP MEET YOU NEW YORK STOP ROOM BOOKED PLAZA MR AND MRS WHARTON STOP I LOVE YOU STOP CLIVE'.

Oh, Christ, she thought again.

'Shall I acknowledge, Commander?' Signalman Brown asked. 'Sounds like a fun trip.'

'Why don't you fuck off, sailor,' Jennie suggested.

'Heil Hitler!' The words, emanating from several throats at the same time, seemed to fill the room. Keiko Hatatsune was deafened. These people were so very loud in everything they did. But he composed his features into the proper arrangement, representing at once pleasure and awe, as the somewhat short man advanced into the room. This man was, after all, apparently some sort of god to his followers, even if he possessed no pedigree whatsoever.

147

'Commander Hatatsune.' Hitler beamed; he did not appear to have any doubt that Keiko would speak German, and in fact Keiko had spent the three weeks at sea studying the language sufficiently to make himself understood. 'I would like to shake your hand.'

'It is my great privilege, honourable Führer,' Keiko said, giving a quick bow as his hand was squeezed.

'Oh, the privilege is ours,' Hitler insisted. 'To have so famous an airman in our midst. Eh, Herr Reichsmarschall?' He glanced, smiling, at the huge figure beside him. But Reichsmarschall Goering, dressed in the most spectacular uniform – all white and gold – that Keiko had ever seen, did not look amused. 'And your project,' the Führer went on. 'So imaginative. So simple. So devastating, if it works.'

'I intend that it should do so, honourable Führer. And I wish to express the great gratitude of my government, and my people, that you should be so willing to cooperate as to grant us the use of your only aircraft-carrier for this mission.'

'Ah,' Hitler said. 'Yes. It has been a great pleasure meeting you, Commander Hatatsune. And I wish your mission every success. I will leave you now, so that you may get down to details with Admiral Raeder and Admiral Doenitz and Reichsmarschall Goering.'

The officers stood to attention. 'Heil Hitler!'

Hitler returned the salute with a flap of his right hand, and left the room.

'The chair is yours, Reichsmarschall,' Raeder invited.

'No, no. I can only spare a few minutes,' Goering said. 'You may chair the meeting, Grand Admiral.'

'Well, then,' Raeder said. 'Will you please be seated, gentlemen.'

The officers sat round the table. There were eight men present, six wearing the uniforms of German naval officers; Goering and Keiko sat together at the foot. Keiko had not brought along any of his men; only his immediate deputy had as yet any idea of the purpose of the visit to Germany.

'Perhaps, as you have another appointment, Reichsmarschall, you will deal with your business first,' Raeder said.

'I merely wish to know Commander Hatatsune's requirements in aircraft,' Goering said.

'Twenty Junkers 88 bombers, honourable Reichsmarschall.'

'Have any of your men ever flown a Junkers before?'

'No, sir. I intend to implement, starting tomorrow morning, a period of intensive training.'

'You also intend that these machines should be flown from the deck of an aircraft-carrier,' Goering pointed out. 'They were never designed for that purpose.'

'Neither were the B-25s the Americans used to bomb Tokyo, honourable Reichsmarschall.'

'So I am being asked to write off at least twenty-five machines,' Goering complained. 'Your people will undoubtedly lose one or two in training.'

'That is possible, honourable Reichsmarschall.'

'I will allot you twenty-five machines,' Goering said. 'I will also allot you the necessary mechanics. But do not come back to me for more. We have other commitments, you understand.'

'I do understand, honourable Reichsmarschall. And once again, I am deeply grateful for your cooperation.'

Goering pushed back his chair and stood up. 'I consider the entire project madness, Commander,' he announced. 'Were the Führer not interested, because these gentlemen' – he swept the naval officers with a co. .nptuous gaze – 'have assured him that your plan can work, I should have nothing to do with it. Twenty-five machines,' he snorted, and left the room.

No one spoke until the door had closed behind the Reichsmarschall, then Doenitz commented, 'There speaks the man who threw away more than nine hundred machines over England in a couple of weeks.'

'He is learning thrift now,' Raeder remarked. 'However, there is some point to his remarks. Your people do understand the difficulty in taking off from a flight-deck with a fully laden bomber, Commander Hatatsune?'

'My people are all experienced flyers, sir.'

'Oh, I accept that. However . . . you also understand that because of the short range of the Junkers 88, as compared with the B-25, it will be necessary to manoeuvre the launching vessel to within a few hundred miles of New York?'

'I understood that these matters had been considered and resolved before I left Japan.'

'They were. However, we have never doubted the hazardous nature of the enterprise. I must tell you that I cannot accept the risk probable in providing you with a suitable escort.' He gazed at Keiko. 'Or in providing an escort at all.'

'I have never asked for an escort, honourable Admiral. The whole concept is based on the premise that one ship can penetrate a blockade where a squadron is certain of detection.'

'It is not quite as simple as that,' Raeder pointed out. 'We are talking about three days at sea, each way. Do not misunderstand me. We have in Germany many men who would willingly commit themselves to such a mission, and have done so. However, it is not our intention to squander our hard-earned resources on a mission of doubtful strategical or tactical value, whatever it may mean in propaganda terms. I must tell you, Commander Hatatsune, that in view of the impossibility of providing an escort, or of guaranteeing the safe return of the vessel, it has been the Führer's decision that the *Graf Zeppelin* cannot be risked on such an adventure.'

Keiko stared at him in consternation.

'However,' Raeder hurried on, 'the ship will be available for your men to train from.'

Keiko continued to stare at him. 'Then what do we actually fly from?' he asked.

Raeder smiled at him. 'As it is naturally our intention to stand by our promises to our esteemed ally, we are prepared to make a second carrier available.'

'A second carrier?' Keiko cried.

'A sister ship to *Graf Zeppelin*. Or she was intended to be. Her keel was laid in 1939, and she is almost ready for launching . . .'

'Almost ready for launching?' Keiko gasped, knowing that a ship, after being launched, needed at least a year's work to be ready for sea.

'She will enter the water next week.'

'Honourable Admiral, my mission must be completed by the end of this year.'

'The date I have been given is 7 December. However, I can see no reason why your ship should not be ready to go to sea by 30 November. She is not, after all, being completed with a view to taking her place in a task force, or even for an extended voyage. She is being prepared for a six-day dash. If she is discovered, she will in any event be sunk, so arming her or indeed armouring her is a waste of time. So it is simply a matter of making her watertight and sending her to sea.'

For a moment Keiko could not speak, he was so angry. 'Because you *expect* her to be sunk,' he said at last.

'As a matter of fact, I do not expect her to be sunk, Commander,' Raeder said. 'Because a ship is only as good as the men who sail her and, above all, the man who commands her. We are giving you Hjalmar Koenig as your captain.'

'Hjalmar Koenig?' Keiko looked down the table at the other officers.

'Oh, Koenig is not here,' Raeder said. 'He is already

in Kiel, preparing your ship. He is a real go-getter, Koenig. Once he heard about the project, there was no holding him. He means to have the ship ready for sea by 30 November. He is our leading naval hero, at the moment, and he is also an expert in the art of evading Allied patrols and harassing their shipping. If any man can get you to Newfoundland, and get his ship back, it will be Koenig.'

'Even if he is commanding some hulk?' Keiko snapped, quite forgetting his manners.

'Your ship will have two very powerful engines, Commander,' Raeder told him. 'She will be watertight. She will have a flight-deck. And she will have an expert master. What more can you ask of us?'

'With respect, honourable Admiral, we were promised the use of *Graf Zeppelin*, a fully equipped aircraft-carrier.'

'I think that if you consult the correspondence between Admiral Yamamoto and myself, Commander, you will discover you are mistaken. When this joint venture was first proposed, Admiral Yamamoto suggested that you be given the use of *Graf Zeppelin*. Perhaps he mistakenly led you to believe that we had agreed to that proposal. But our promise to Admiral Yamamoto was to deliver you and your strike force to within a reasonable range of New York. This promise we will keep.'

Keiko gazed at him for several seconds. But he knew there was no use in arguing with these people, who seemed to have absolutely no concept of honour. He must either refuse to continue with the mission, and return to Japan in disgrace, or make it a success, with whatever collection of junk the Germans landed him with. He bowed his head. 'I accept your interpretation of the agreement between our two navies, honourable Admiral. As I accept with gratitude the use of this . . .

unfinished aircraft-carrier. May I ask where she is lying?'

'At the Germaniawerft yard, in Kiel harbour.'

'*Graf Zeppelin* is also there?'

'No,' Raeder said. '*Graf Zeppelin* is already at a secret destination in Norway, awaiting your men.'

'Then I wish my men taken to her tomorrow, honourable Admiral. My second in command, Lieutenant-Commander Takanawa, can begin their training, but the sooner this commences the better. However, I wish to go to this shipyard in Kiel first, to see this unlaunched vessel.'

'I quite understand your anxiety. And I know Captain Koenig is keen to meet you. You will go to Kiel tomorrow.'

'Is it not possible to go there this afternoon, honourable Admiral?'

'Why, of course. But do you not wish to sample some of the pleasures Berlin has to offer? Especially after your long and dangerous, and' – he smiled – 'shall I say, sterile journey?'

'Pleasures?' Keiko demanded. 'I did not travel twelve thousand miles for pleasure, sir.'

Raeder got up, and the other officers rose with him. He walked the length of the table and threw his arm round Keiko's shoulders. 'If you are engaged upon a suicide mission, it would be foolish not to enjoy certain pleasures before you depart this earth.' He laughed. 'It is by no means guaranteed that you will find them on the other side, eh?'

'Honourable Commander is angry?' inquired Lieutenant-Commander Takanawa.

'Angry,' Keiko grunted, gazing at himself in the full-length mirror. He had just finished inspecting the other thirty-eight members of his party – they were all officers – making sure their dark blue uniforms, their white

153

gloves and scarves, their sword hilts and their cap badges, were flawless; if the Germans insisted upon entertaining them, they had at least to match their hosts in splendour. 'These must be the most dishonest people I have ever encountered, Tadatune.'

'Is it to do with the mission?' Takanawa was the only member of the group Keiko had taken into his confidence – but Keiko had not told him the outcome of his meeting with the German admirals that morning.

'The mission will proceed as planned,' Keiko said. 'But that the Nazis should obtain any propaganda profit from it is nauseating. I intend to write Admiral Yama-moto, so that he may tell the world of the obstacles being placed in our way after it is over. Well, gentlemen? Shall we see what are these pleasures we are to sample?'

There was a fleet of Mercedes automobiles waiting for them downstairs, lights hooded, as there were few lights to be seen on the street. Berlin was obviously more accustomed to enemy bombing raids than Tokyo. But there was no enemy to be seen or heard tonight. The automobiles drove them into a huge courtyard, surrounded on three sides by a magnificent building, in one wing of which there appeared to be a ball in progress. 'This is absurd,' Keiko grumbled. 'Is our visit not supposed to be secret?'

He was feeling disgruntled on every point. Quite apart from the German perfidy, and this ridiculous time-wasting when he and his men could already be in Kiel, there was the suggested contempt with which Raeder had referred to the suicide mission. Well, how could people like these Nazis understand about the honour of dying for one's country? And now they seemed to have no idea of security, either.

But once inside the building he was somewhat reassured to discover that the only other men present were German naval officers, who were doubtless sworn to secrecy. On the other hand, he was dismayed again to see a group of some thirty young women, wearing evening gowns and obviously also waiting to entertain them. 'These people,' he said, turning to the officer on his left and discovering him to be Admiral Doenitz himself. 'My apologies, honourable Admiral. But these girls . . .'

'Are all navy secretaries, Commander,' Doenitz assured him. 'There is no one in Berlin, outside these walls, and the Führer's own circle, of course, who has any idea what you are doing in Germany.'

'Hm,' Keiko said. 'In any event, none of my men speak German.'

'Ah,' Doenitz said. 'But here in Germany we endeavour to anticipate every eventuality. For the past month, my ladies have been learning Japanese. Now come, will you not hand over your swords?'

Keiko realised that the stewards to whom he and his men had handed their caps on entering the room were still hovering expectantly – and that the German officers were all unarmed. 'We Japanese officers are incorrectly dressed without our swords,' he pointed out.

'Nonetheless, my dear Commander, as you are in Germany . . . by all means retain your dirks.'

Keiko hesitated, then gave the necessary orders. It was his business to make the mission a success, no matter what might occur – and that could only be done with full German cooperation.

'You will certainly find it more comfortable for dancing,' Doenitz remarked, as Keiko unbuckled his sword belt. 'Now, come and meet my ladies.'

Keiko signalled his men, and the Japanese group crossed the floor to meet the girls, who had arranged themselves in a line. Keiko could not imagine what thoughts might be going through the minds of the pilots behind him, who were being treated to a shameless display of naked shoulders and breast tops such as he had never supposed possible in a public place. And these

German women were so large and pale-skinned; their white flesh gleamed to match their golden hair and their flashing teeth. They were positively awe-inspiring.

At the very end of the line, however, there was a sudden pleasing contrast. 'My personal secretary,' Doenitz explained. 'Fraülein Helga Staffel, may I present Commander Keiko Hatatsune, of the Imperial Japanese Navy.'

This girl, if no more modestly dressed than any of her companions, was actually an inch or two shorter than Keiko, and she had black hair, even if it was cut short in a most unfeminine fashion. Her complexion was as white as any of the others, but her midnight blue evening gown, while absolutely bare in the back, was at least fully concealing up to her neck in the front. 'I am gratified, honourable Commander,' she said in uncertain Japanese. Again, unlike her companions, her voice was low and musical.

'As am I, Fräulein,' he replied in German. 'Shall we not speak your language, as we are in your country?'

Helga glanced at Doenitz and received a reassuring nod. 'I should like that,' she said. 'Champagne?'

A waiter was hovering with a tray, while the five-piece orchestra struck up a tune.

'Would you like to dance, Commander?' Helga asked.

'I do not know how to dance, Fräulein.'

She raised her eyebrows, then smiled. 'Then shall we sit down? And you can tell me of your journey.'

Keiko glanced at the rest of the room. The evening was clearly setting up to be the most abject disaster. His men had formed a huddle, looking almost beleaguered, at one end of the room; the German girls had formed another huddle, some distance away. Then the German officers approached, one actually taking a girl into his arms and starting to whirl her about the room in a most indecent fashion.

'It is called a waltz,' Helga explained, smoothing her

skirt. 'It is an old-fashioned dance, but it retains its popularity. Perhaps because all the best waltzes have been written by Germans. Would you not like me to show you how it is done?'

'Later, perhaps.' He sat beside her, endeavouring to keep his body upright. But it really was very difficult to be comfortable in these deeply upholstered western chairs and sofas. The girl beside him had allowed herself to be absorbed by the softness around her, and sunk into the upholstery, while she had draped one blue-clad knee over the other to allow her foot to dangle an inch or two above the ground. It was quite impossible to envisage Akiko, or any Japanese woman, sitting like that.

'Well, then,' she said. 'Tell me of your voyage.'

'It was tedious. Yokohama to Cadiz.'

'As simple as that? Were you not troubled by the enemy?'

'We saw some British warships. But when they recognised the Spanish flag they did not interfere with us.'

'And you weren't frightened?'

For the first time since their introduction he looked directly at her, frowning.

'No,' she remarked. 'I don't suppose you were. Look, honourable Commander, I'm virtually in charge of this do, and it's not going very well, is it? I simply have to get you on that dance floor, then maybe some of the others will follow. Okay?'

'If that is what you wish, Fräulein.'

She stood up, held out her hand. 'I tell you what we'll do. I'll call you Keiko, right? And you'll try Helga.'

He bowed. 'It will be my pleasure . . . Helga.'

She nodded. 'Please take off your gloves.'

'My gloves are part of my uniform.'

'But you're the senior Japanese officer present,' she pointed out. 'You can make a new dress rule. I know it is more correct to dance with your gloves on, but it would be far nicer for me if you were to take them off. It is more' – her mouth gave a peculiar little twist – 'intimate, shall I say.'

Keiko hesitated, then drew off his gloves and placed them under his right epaulette.

'Now, put your left arm round my waist.'

He hesitated again.

'Don't you want to?' she asked.

'In Japan one does not do these things.'

'Ah, but you're in Rome now, are you not?'

'Rome? This is Berlin.'

A look almost of desperation crossed her face, but she kept smiling. 'Forget it. But I would like you to put your arm round my waist, Keiko.'

He obeyed, and to his consternation her body actually came against his.

'A little higher, I think,' Helga suggested.

His hand had settled on the waistband of her gown, because there was nothing above that but naked flesh. Very cautiously he slid his hand on to her skin. It felt delightful, and faintly moist.

'There,' she said. 'Now, please, I would like you to hold me firmly with that hand.'

Keiko was beginning to sweat as well, because the girl's crotch was firmly wedged against his.

'Now you take my left hand in your right. Good. Hold it as far away from our bodies as you wish; it helps to keep the balance. Now, listen to the music. It's a series of beats, right?'

'Yes,' Keiko said, although he couldn't make head or tail of it.

'So just count the beats. The waltz is to the count of three. Are you ready? Count with me. *One*, two, three, turn, *one* two three, turn, *one* two three.'

The room began to spin, and the girl seemed glued to him; he could feel her thighs moving against his.

'You're doing fine,' she smiled.

The music stopped, to his great relief. For a moment he lost his balance, but the girl still held his hand; reluctantly he moved his fingers from her back – his fellow officers were applauding.

'That calls for a drink,' Helga said, and signalled the waiter. The champagne continued to flow, and the music started again. The girl stayed in his arms. He was pleased to see that his fellow officers were equally enjoying themselves, more and more of them venturing into the dances, holding the big, busty German girls tightly, discovering the exciting indecencies of life as lived in the West. He had no desire to change places with any of them, even if his partner had the least voluptuous figure in the room; with every moment Helga became more and more fascinating, the touch of her hand, or of his hand on her naked, sweat-wet back, more erotic. Her perfume played around his nostrils like nectar from the gods themselves, her soft, throaty laughter filled his ears, and he became increasingly aware that he would never hold Akiko in his arms again. He had not, in fact, ever intended to hold any woman in his arms again. But were not the Germans right? Would it not be an act of stupidity to leave this world, filled with wonderful things, without sampling as many of those things as possible? And the most wonderful thing he had ever encountered was this girl. While in her size and the colour of her hair she could have been Japanese, she dressed and acted and spoke and drank and smelt in a way he had never known in a woman before – therefore she would do other things in a way he would find strange as well. All he had to do was regard her as the ultimate geisha, sent by his German hosts to entertain the warrior who was about to die.

The music stopped for the tenth time and this time, very daringly, he gave her a hug, holding her as close as he dared, feeling every contour of her body against his.

'Oh,' she said, her mouth giving that delightful twist of half pleasure, half distaste. 'You're learning very quickly, Keiko. Oh, bother, they're all drunk.'

The German officers had gathered at the far end of the room and were now raising their voices in song, a discordant but very loud noise which was accompanied by the breaking of their glasses as they hurled them to the floor.

'What do they celebrate?' Keiko asked in wonder.

'Nothing. Listen, let's go someplace else.'

He frowned at her, disturbed by the difficulty he found in focusing. 'Where?'

'I know a place. Do you like strip-tease?'

'Strip-tease?'

'It's a night-club. A place where one goes after a party like this, and has some more drinks, and watches a girl taking off her clothes.'

'I would rather be with you.'

'Of course you'll be with me, silly,' she said. 'We'll be together. We'll make up a party.'

'And this girl will take off her clothes for all of us?' He had heard there were geisha who would do that, but had always disapproved of the idea. Anyway, geisha only ever performed for men.

'It'll be fun,' Helga said. 'Don't go away.' She hurried across the room to collect three of the other German girls, and their escorts, amongst whom, he was relieved to see, was Tadatune Takanawa. 'It's all set, come on.'

'My men . . .'

'They'll be taken care of. Don't worry.'

'Yes, but if we are seen in public . . .'

'We're going to a private club,' she promised him. 'No one will question what you are doing there.' She held his hand and dragged him towards the door, where one of the waiters was holding his cap and sword. 'Oh,

160

you can't possibly bring that thing.' Helga gave one of her low laughs. 'Suppose it got stuck between your legs?'

'A Japanese officer cannot be separated from his sword,' he protested.

'Of course he can, for one night. Four of those great toothpicks will never fit in the car, anyway. Oh, Keiko, come on.'

He had never been commanded by a woman before. He simply did not know what to do, how to refuse her, save by actually striking her, as he would certainly have struck a Japanese woman, even Akiko, who sought to drag him about in public by the hand. But his instincts warned him that would be frowned on here, and besides, being led by the hand by Helga Staffel was a delightful experience.

The eight of them tumbled down the stairs, the girls laughing and excited, the officers as bewildered as he, but clearly enjoying themselves also, making grabs at their respective companions. He wondered if he dared make a grab at Helga, and as they debouched into the yard, closed his hands on her hips and drew her back against him for a moment.

'Oh,' she said, allowing her hair to nuzzle his cheek, and still further clouded his senses with perfume. 'I think I am going to have to put a ball and chain on you, honourable Keiko.'

Before he could decide what she meant, they were scrabbling into a big Mercedes, and Helga was giving instructions to the apparently disinterested chauffeur, but speaking so quickly Keiko could not understand her. She had got into the back seat first, and beckoned him to follow. He had barely sat down when another female body was wedged against his, pressing Helga against the outer door. She gave a little wriggle and rose; his body flowed into the vacated space, and before he knew what he was doing she sat on his lap. He was

161

quite petrified. Only one woman had ever sat on his lap before, and that had been Akiko for the purpose of sexual intercourse. He wondered if she was as drunk as she appeared. He felt sure she was only pretending, and was actually quite sober. But he couldn't understand why she should wish to do that. He put his arms round her waist, felt the valley where her thighs joined her trunk and slid his fingers to touch the breasts which had been so delineated against the bodice of her gown during the dancing.

'If you don't stop,' she whispered in his ear, 'I am going to slap your face.'

He didn't know what to make of that, especially as the other three officers were unashamedly exploring the giggling companions now sitting on their knees. But before he could decide whether or not to call her bluff, the car stopped.

He was aware of bright lights as the door opened, and of a drizzle of summer rain. But in fact the car ride and the headiness of the woman, far from sobering him up, had made him feel more drunk than earlier. Focusing was very difficult, and he was glad of Helga's hand holding him steady as they entered a darkened doorway, then went down a flight of even darker steps. He nearly fell, but was restrained by a laughing Helga. Now there were sounds in front of him – music, laughter, the clink of glasses and the hum of voices – and a moment later they went through a heavy curtain and emerged into a smoke-filled room. Here there was a bar along one wall, backed by a kaleidoscopic array of bottles and mirrors. In front there was a mass of tables, and chairs, and people, mostly men but some women, drinking beer and smoking cigarettes, talking, or watching a stage at the far end of the room, where a woman, to the accompaniment of a band which consisted of a drum and a piano, was slowly removing various articles of clothing, jerking and posturing her

162

body as she did so. Keiko was quite lost in staring at her; he was only vaguely aware that he was being pushed into a chair at a table very close to the stage, where there were some people already sitting, but these seemed to be friends of Helga, from the way they hugged and kissed her – on the mouth. One of the men actually squeezed her backside, and she didn't seem to object. He wanted to do that himself, but she was out of his reach, smiling at him.

'I just have to pee,' she said. 'Won't be long. Get my friends a drink, will you, Jan? Oh, Keiko, this is a friend of mine, Jan Anderssen. He's Swedish,' she added, and disappeared.

Keiko did his best to focus on the man he had just been introduced to. The fellow was very large. Even sitting down he looked like a giant, with a mass of yellow hair topping a big, handsome face. And he was smiling. 'My pleasure,' he said, and then changed to a frown. 'You do speak German?'

'Of course,' Keiko replied with dignity.

'That's great.' Jan snapped his fingers, managing to make sufficient noise, even above the racket in the room, to attract the waiter. 'Champagne.'

'That is very generous of you,' Keiko protested, feeling that he had been outmanoeuvred; he should have ordered the champagne.

'Not really,' Jan Anderssen confessed. 'I'll put it on expenses. Are you after Helga? Or do you prefer men?'

Keiko goggled at him. He had been told that to show interest in men, if one was a man, was tabu in the West.

'Because if you do,' Anderssen went on, 'there's a pretty number.'

He was looking at the stage, where Keiko now discovered to his amazement that the girl who had been slowly stripping had now removed her G-string . . . and was actually a very well-endowed young man. Yet his make-up was so perfect and his wig so lifelike that from the waist up he still looked like a woman – he had retained his brassière. The spectators certainly appreciated him; both men and women cheered and clapped as he waved his penis at them before fleeing the stage.

'If you nip round behind and have the ready, he'll give you a quick thrill, I imagine.' Anderssen grinned at him, but before Keiko could decide whether or not the Swede was trying to be rude, Helga returned, arriving at the same time as the waiter and the champagne. 'You missed the prick,' Anderssen said, attempting to do the pouring himself and depositing most of it on the table.

'I am choosy about pricks.' Helga sat between them.

'Your friend is offensive,' Keiko whispered in her ear, mainly as an excuse to put his lips against her.

'Don't worry about him,' Helga whispered back, turning her head so that her lips actually brushed his. 'He's drunk. He's always drunk.'

'He is not your lover?'

'Why, yes, sometimes. Does that bother you?'

'Very much,' Keiko said.

'Well, I'd forget it. He'd eat you alive. Look, this one's great.'

Keiko turned his head. The stage had once again been occupied, again by a very pretty . . . person? Like her predecessor, she was doing a series of bumps and grinds as she slowly pulled off her gloves, while again the audience clapped and cheered.

'Is she a man or a woman?' Keiko asked.

'Oh, she's a woman,' Helga assured him. 'Just wait until you see her tits.'

Which were at that moment slowly emerging from a slipping evening gown. 'Aren't they something?'

'I prefer yours,' Keiko said boldly.

Helga turned her head in surprise. Their faces were only inches apart, and Keiko seized his opportunity to kiss her again. She didn't move her head, but when he moved his, her lips were twisted. 'I would like to be your lover,' he said.

'I think you need another drink,' she suggested.

'I am going to kiss you again,' he announced.

'A toast,' Anderssen bellowed, making the rafters ring as he got to his feet, holding a champagne bottle. The orchestra promptly gave a drum roll, and the girl on the stage, undisturbed by the interruption of her number, although she was now down to pants, garter belt, stockings and shoes, stood to attention. 'I give you,' Anderssen shouted, 'Grand Admiral Tirpitz, the founder of the German Navy.'

The people in the room roared their applause, scrambling to their feet to drink, while Anderssen poured from the neck of the bottle on to his upturned face and down his neck.

'Grand Admiral Tirpitz!' Helga shouted, climbing on to her chair.

Keiko discovered that his face was on a level with her crotch, and put both arms round her thighs to kiss her there instead. She gave a little shriek and fell off the chair, on to his lap.

'More champagne,' Anderssen suggested, and poured some on to her head; it splashed on Keiko's face.

'You bastard,' she shouted, trying to stand up and subsiding again; Keiko wished he could be certain which of them she was referring to.

'Grand Admiral Raeder!' someone else was shouting, and again they struggled to their feet to drink. Then the toasting became general. 'The Führer!' 'Admiral von Scheer!' 'Admiral Hipper!' 'Admiral Graf von Spee!' 'Admiral Doenitz!' 'General Rommel!' There were apparently some army men present as well.

The noise slowly died, and Keiko discovered to his pleasure that he was still holding Helga in his arms.

The orchestra resumed its beat, and the girl on the stage began to unfasten her stockings.

'Why don't *you* give a toast, honourable little man,' Anderssen suggested, still standing above him.

'Of course.' Keiko got to his feet, still holding Helga against him; she appeared to have passed out. Anderssen waved his arms and the band gave another drum roll, while the stripper paused with her right stocking slipping about her ankle. 'I give you,' Keiko shouted, 'Admiral Isoroku Yamamoto.'

'Admiral Yamamoto!' shouted Takanawa. There was little response from the other two Japanese, who also seemed to have passed out, and none from the rest of the room.

'Admiral who?' Anderssen demanded.

'Yamamoto,' Keiko explained. 'Isoroku Yamamoto is the greatest of all living admirals.'

'I wouldn't say that too loudly in this company, if I were you,' Anderssen warned. 'Don't you know any German admirals?'

'Only those who have been named.'

'Well, there are other sea heroes. Think of a U-boat commander.'

Keiko frowned, while his brain seemed to be spinning. He had never heard of any U-boat captain, because they had never received any publicity in Japan. But he was aware that he might have insulted these men, his allies, by not knowing the name of any of their great heroes. And yet . . . he did know a name. He had been told it that very afternoon and, more, been told that it belonged to Germany's greatest current naval hero. Therefore it was surely a name they would all recognise. He regained his feet, losing control of Helga, who slipped through his arms and lay in a midnight blue and white hump on the floor beside the table. 'I give you,' he shouted, 'Hjalmar Koenig!'

He had scored a major success. The rafters rang as the company toasted Hjalmar Koenig.

And Anderssen was smiling at him. 'I approve of your choice, honourable little man.'

It was very odd, Keiko thought, how he had suddenly stopped slurring.

CHAPTER 7

The Command

Jennie Rhodes thought that of all the cities in the United States, New York must have changed least since the declaration of war. Grand Central Station was as crowded as ever, the trains as frequent as ever. The women as smartly dressed as ever, and if there were more men in uniform around, that meant the men were even more smartly dressed than ever. There were the same number of taxi cabs waiting outside, the same chat.

As she was on furlough she had left her uniform behind in Washington, and wore instead a pale blue rayon dress with a pattern of white spots, navy blue handbag and gloves, with a matching dark blue hat of velvet leaves, and black court shoes. 'Say,' her taxi driver remarked, inspecting her in his rear-view mirror. 'You an actress or something?'

'Just something,' Jennie replied.

'Going to the Plaza and all,' he commented.

She had never felt so wicked in her life. She had only been to bed with three men, and it had all been unheralded and spontaneous – but this was planned. And she wasn't even sure she liked the guy, even if she had enjoyed making love with him the first time.

Yet she had not really considered not taking this furlough. For one thing, as the admiral had pointed out, it was going to be her last for some time; Torch was getting ready to roll. And she certainly needed a break.

If she had always found her job a tense affair, the tension had been nearly unbearable over the past month. This last week had nearly driven her mad, because Friday had passed and there had been no message from Seven-Seven-Four. She kept telling herself that if Johnnie had pressed too hard and been arrested, Seven-Seven-Four would surely have informed head-quarters. Yet, although her furlough had officially commenced at six o'clock last night, and she had had time to catch a train to New York after leaving the office, she remained at her desk until nine, waiting for the signal that never came.

So now she was either going to have a good time with Clive Wharton, or she was going to turn this taxi-cab round and go back to Grand Central Station and thence Washington, and lie on her lonely bed and weep.

And think about Johnnie Anderson risking his life. If only she could know what he was doing.

Gongs banging to and fro. Getting drunk on champagne was probably the most hazardous part of his job, John Anderson thought. He rolled on his back, flung out his arms, touched nothing, frowned, and rolled on to his other side. The bed was empty. Yet her perfume hung on the air. But that could be stale from last night, before she had even gone out. So if she wasn't here . . . that Jap? He just couldn't believe it. Helga was his woman. His private double agent, even if she wasn't aware of it.

But as his private agent, if she *could* bring herself to dally with the fellow . . . now he knew he was on to something. He had played the admiral's hunch, and the Japanese had fallen for it. It was possible that Hatatsune had read of Koenig in a newspaper somewhere, but not likely. The Japanese had already left Tokyo before *Atlas* returned from her last cruise, and they had travelled in radio silence. By the time they reached Cadiz, Koenig's news value had ended; there had certainly been no reference to him in the German Press in the week Keiko Hatatsune had been in Europe. And the Japanese had only reached Berlin yesterday, after being hurried across Spain and France in secret. So, someone had mentioned Hjalmar Koenig to Keiko Hatatsune yesterday, and mentioned it so hard Keiko had remembered the name.

A noise alerted him, and he looked at the bathroom door. When not in full command of herself, Helga had a way of appearing to shrink, until she appeared as nothing more than a white wisp. She had certainly shrunk this morning, and looked even smaller because her champagne-soaked hair was still plastered to her head. 'Christalmighty!' she remarked. 'The things I do for you.'

She staggered across the room and fell across the bed. John got up, went to the bathroom himself and flushed both their vomits. Then he went into the kitchen, found a tin of tomato juice, split it between two glasses, added a raw egg to each, a heavy dose of Worcestershire sauce, a dash of red pepper and an even heavier dash of vodka, stirred them and took the glasses back to the bedroom.

'Forget it.' She had rolled on to her back and lay with arms and legs outstretched. She looked good enough to eat, let alone screw. But the thought of either eating or screwing made him feel sick again.

'It'll do you good.' He sipped his own and shuddered. Sitting on the bed, he passed the other glass to and fro beneath her nostrils.

She sat up, sipped and gave an even more convulsive shudder; tomato juice dribbled down her chin. 'I feel like fresh shit.'

'What time did you get in?'

She shrugged. More tomato juice appeared between her breasts. 'God damn, that stings.' She dried it with the sheet. 'Three. Maybe.'

'I was home at half-past two. You mean you didn't go off with your friend?'

'Friend? Christ! Oh, he wants to be my friend. Do you know what he said to me? "I would like to be your lover." Very formal. If he hadn't been sitting down he'd have bowed.'

'I remember. I was there. You mean you declined?'

'Me. With that creep? What do you take me for? Mind you, it wasn't easy. I had to see him home, you know. There we were, eight of us crammed in the back. The other three Japs had passed out; we had to shovel them into the car like sacks of cement. But not Mr Keiko. I was explored, and I mean explored, all the way home. He could've been a doctor looking for warts. And all the time he was just about buggering me through my dress. Then he wanted me to go inside with him. I had to run for my life. I did you one big favour, Jan, taking him to that club. You owe me a big one.'

'And I shall give you a big one,' John promised 'Again and again and again. When this medicine takes effect. But I'd hate you to go off the fellow too much.'

'Oh, yes?' She drank some more, shuddered some more, spilt some more; her hands were trembling. 'I have decided that I wish to get married.'

'He could be very useful to the story I'm trying to write.' John resolved to ignore her idle thoughts. 'Because his being in Germany has something to do with our friend Hjalmar Koenig.'

'And I have decided that I am going to marry you.' Helga announced.

'And that makes it something real big,' John went on. 'I've had the go-ahead from my editor, you know. He thinks it could be a terrific story.'

Helga gazed at him. 'When do you propose to propose?'

Perhaps he had put too much vodka in her pick-me-up, he realised. 'I thought marriage wasn't up your street?'

'It's a woman's privilege to change her mind.'

'When did you do that?'

'Last night. When I looked at all those druken bums . . . oh, German as well as Japanese.'

'I was as drunk as anyone there.'

'You did not show it as they did.'

'Well, it goes with my job. Getting other people's tongues working and then listening.' He wondered if she would ever know he was telling her the simple truth.

'I do not believe you ever get drunk at all, even if you do get sick.'

'And you regard that as an important qualification for marriage?'

She got out of bed, seeming to uncoil herself like a steel spring, and went to the bathroom. 'Do you not think marriage to me would be fun, my Jan?'

She did not wait for a reply, and a moment later he heard the splashing of the shower. But she was quite serious, he knew. Marriage to Helga – oh, it would certainly be fun . . . for as long as the Third Reich continued to career on its merry way. It would mean a round of parties, like last night. And eventually she would realise that when he went to parties like that he was indeed working.

But that was not the only reason marriage to Helga was impossible. How could he even pretend to love any woman as long as there was a chance of ever returning to the States and finding Jennie, somehow, miraculously, still waiting?

On the other hand, he could not take the risk of losing her, certainly not at this vitally important moment. So he must become even more of a heel than he had already been. For the admiral; he wondered if it had ever occurred to the admiral that he was playing God?

Helga stood in the doorway, towelling her hair. He

172

got up and held her in his arms, feeling her shower-cool body against his own liquor-warm one. 'You should shower too,' she told him. 'You will feel better.'

She was also a bossy woman, he thought. He showered, and she brewed ersatz coffee, to which she added the last of the bottle of Scotch. 'Today is Saturday,' she told him. 'And as a reward for entertaining those creeps I have been given the weekend off. What shall we do?'

'Let's take a trip. You and me.'

'I'd like that. Where?'

'Kiel-Holtenau.'

'What on earth for?'

'I want to see how work is progressing on *Graf Zeppelin*, and if Hjalmar Koenig is there.'

'If I thought you rated your shitting story above me I'd throw you out,' Helga remarked. 'And if the Gestapo find you snooping about Kiel, they will confiscate your notes.'

'But what if they find *us* snooping around Kiel? You can remind them of Uncle Adolf.'

'You really expect me to help you?'

'Honey doll, I'm not asking you to go and break into Doenitz's private files. I just want to see what we can see. And I want you along.'

'Why?'

'Because we're engaged to be married.'

She attempted to frown and failed. 'Are we?'

He leaned across the table and took her hand. 'I would like you to marry me, so very much.'

'Would you, Jan? Would you?'

'Yes,' he lied, staring into her eyes, where tears had suddenly appeared.

'Oh, Jan, I thought you didn't. Then I know where we shall go today. Down to Munich, and see papa.'

'You're right. After we've been to Kiel.'

'But *why*? For some stupid story you can't even print for at least a month?'

173

'I must get the story ready, Helga. Listen.' He held her hand tighter than ever. 'If I am right, it is very possible that Hjalmar Koenig is going to take your Japanese friend to sea in *Graf Zeppelin*. Once that is done, I won't have any idea if he has or not, if you follow me. They will both have disappeared, and no one will know if they went together. I tried to tell you just now, my editor has really gone for the idea of a feature on Koenig. He wants to make it big. I have never had a big feature article, front-page stuff, before. It'll mean promotion, and a bigger salary. I will need that, to marry you. But if I flunk it, either by not obtaining the necessary information, or by using guess-work which turns out incorrect . . . well, I could wind up out of a job.'

It sounded fairly thin to him, but as he had hoped, Helga had her mind on other things. 'It is ridiculous for you to worry about money,' she said. 'I have more than enough for both of us.'

'Do you really think I am going to live off my wife?'

She stared at him. 'No,' she said at last. 'I suppose that's what makes you different to those bums last night.'

'Then will you come with me to Kiel? You'll be able to take me places I might be barred from on my own. I just have to be sure about three things. If I can tie those up, then I'm home and dry. Hatatsune, Koenig and *Graf Zeppelin*. We know *Graf Zeppelin* is in Kiel. If Koenig and Hatatsune are there as well, then I'll have my story.' The amazing thing was that he was as usual telling the absolute truth – which was as good a reason as any for hating himself.

Helga was smiling, and reaching across the table, and placing her hand on his cheek. 'You'll get your story, you great silly oaf. If you swear to me nothing will be printed until I give you clearance.'

'I swear.'

'And when you have got the story, I'll expect you to screw me every night for the rest of your life.'

The orderly stood to attention. 'Commander Hatatsune,' he announced. 'Of the Imperial Japanese Navy.'

Koenig got up and walked round his desk. 'Commander,' he said. 'I was told by phone from Berlin that you were on your way.' He held out his hand.

Keiko bowed, then straightened and shook hands. 'It is my pleasure to be here, honourable Captain,' he lied, while his mind did another of its sags of disappointment. He had been a little reassured by the security checks he had had to undergo to get into the Germaniawerft yard at all, by the way it was totally concealed from any prying gaze by its high walls and its armed sentries. But the man standing in front of him was short, fat, too cheerful to be ruthless, and distinctly untidy: his tie was an inch to one side of his collar stud.

'Your men are with you?' Koenig inquired.

'No. Commander Takanawa has accompanied them to some place in Norway called Trondheim.'

'It is a Norwegian seaport, where *Graf Zeppelin* is undergoing sea trials. Your men are to use her for training.'

'Yes,' Keiko said, staring at him. 'She is the ship I had been promised.'

Koenig gave one of his easy smiles. 'Man proposes, and our leaders dispose. I also asked for *Graf Zeppelin*, when I was given command of this operation, and was refused. She is Raeder's pride and joy, all that is left of Plan Z.'

'Plan Z?' Keiko asked.

'Raeder's dream.' Koenig continued to smile. 'He was going to create a navy of eight *Bismarck*-class battleships, two aircraft-carriers, six heavy cruisers ... and take on the Royal Navy in the biggest naval battle in history. He was at Jutland, you know, and has never forgotten that. Well' – the smile died – 'so was I.'

Keiko began to realise there might be more to this man than he had suspected.

Koenig's smile was back. 'Trouble is, Plan Z wasn't due to be completed until 1946, and we were forced into war in 1939. And then last year *Bismarck*, the first ship to be completed, was squandered on a quite irrelevant commerce raid undertaken for propaganda purposes. So Raeder is down to one battleship, *Tirpitz*, one aircraft-carrier, *Graf Zeppelin*, neither quite completed, and the two battle-cruisers, *Scharnhorst* and *Gneisenau*. I don't believe he will ever let them go to sea again. Still, Commander, *Graf Zeppelin* will serve admirably for training your pilots. I am surprised you have not accompanied them. Or have you flown bombers off an aircraft-carrier before?'

Keiko shot him a glance. 'No, honourable Captain,' he said evenly. 'I will have to practise as hard as my men. However, as I am commander of the strike force, I felt it my duty to inspect the actual launch vehicle, if there is one.'

He was being rude, he knew; this man was his superior officer. But he was feeling even more angry than he had yesterday afternoon – and now it was not entirely to do with what he still considered Raeder's betrayal of his plans. For one thing, he had a raging headache; champagne was clearly something to be avoided for the future. For another, he felt that he had been indiscreet. He did not suppose the matter was serious. He had checked, and the girls at the party had indeed all been navy secretaries. In addition, the night-club had been reserved only for top-ranking navy and army officers. The man Anderssen should not have been there, but he had checked that also: the Swede was regarded as totally reliable by the Germans, and very valuable to their propaganda machine, by which they set so much store. Nonetheless, by getting drunk and then blurting out Koenig's name, he had let down his personal estimation of himself.

But far more than that, he was angry about Helga Staffel. This was less easy to determine. He had made a fool of himself, for a start, because he had allowed himself to get drunk. But it was more serious than that. Used to self-analysis, he was prepared to admit that he had fallen heavily for the German girl. It was not that she was more beautiful than Akiko; it was because she was unlike any woman he had ever met, in her independence of spirit, her assumption that she was the equal of any man, her use of language and alcohol, her total freedom from any conventions; her very shamelessness, in fact. He had never been so powerfully affected sexually before.

He knew it was at least partly the heady atmosphere of this country, this regime. He had felt it the moment he had stepped off the train in Berlin. These people were living the greatest adventure in history, but it was essentially an evil adventure, and thus it could not last. They knew this, and therefore they were living their adventure with all the gusto they could manage, knowing that the day of reckoning, when it came, would be terrible in the extreme.

How different, he thought, to the Japanese aim, which was, and always had been, simply the creation of that perimeter within which they could live at peace with the rest of the world; but at the same time, as had always been the aim of Japanese leaders since history began, independently of it.

Helga Staffel, unachieved, was a distraction, he decided. Therefore she should be achieved, if it were at all possible, in order that total concentration could be resumed. He had thought she could be achieved last night, and she had just slipped away, and therefore lingered on his mind, a hindrance to his task.

177

'Oh, there is a launch vehicle,' Koenig was saying. 'I am told you will not be returning to it.'

'It is not possible to carry enough fuel for that.'

Koenig nodded. 'That is our problem, certainly. I would take you up to the Ambrose Light at the entrance to New York harbour, if I could. But once I emerge from the ice and mist cover I will be immediately detected. So you too are determined on a suicide mission.'

Keiko frowned at him. 'Too?'

'I do not rate my own chances very much higher than yours,' Koenig told him.

'That is not the view they hold in Berlin,' Keiko said. 'Nor is it the view I hold myself. As you say, you can penetrate as far south as Newfoundland, especially in December, with a good chance of escaping detection. You have done this before, have you not?'

'Four times,' Koenig agreed. 'But every time, once through the Allied Patrols, I have raced for the wide Atlantic – not closed the American coast.'

'But having done so, briefly, you have only to return to Norway this time.' Keiko pointed out.

'If I can. The project is dated 7 December. We shall of course leave some days before. This is a good time, in many ways. At the beginning of December the weather is at its worst, not only from the viewpoint of wind and sea, but also of visibility. However, by the beginning of December, equally, the ice-packs will be forming. Now, I have arranged for an ice-breaker to accompany us on the outward journey, but she can only come as far as Iceland, of course. South of Iceland, where the British and American patrols operate, she would be a sitting duck. I have been promised that she will remain on station, north of Iceland, for my return.'

'What happens south of Iceland?'

'South of Iceland, in December, we should just about

make it through the ice floes. With fortune. But then, the whole enterprise depends on fortune, does it not?'

Keiko frowned at him. 'What are you trying to tell me?'

'Simply that the whole force is actually regarded in Berlin as expendable, no matter what they say.'

'Are you not their finest captain?'

'But I am not their *favourite* captain, I suspect. I am probably considered as being of more value to the Reich as a dead hero who implemented the bombing of New York than as a live veteran.'

Keiko regarded him for several seconds. 'So they do not care whether you live or not,' he said. 'But they will hardly sacrifice an entire aircraft-carrier.'

'You wished to inspect the launch vehicle,' Koenig remarked. 'Look out of the window.'

Keiko hesitated, then got up and went to the window, which overlooked the yard itself. His brows drew together. He was gazing at a hulk. A hull, and a deck. A flight-deck, certainly, but empty of any island.

'We are launching her the day after tomorrow,' Koenig said. 'Perhaps you can stay for the ceremony.'

'I do not understand,' Keiko said.

'That hull was ordered to be scrapped last April,' Koenig told him. 'In fact, as far as the records show, it *was* scrapped. The order was countermanded after the correspondence between your Admiral Yamamoto and Grand Admiral Raeder, but the fact that it has been countermanded has been kept a close secret. She was originally going to be used for a couple of submarines. However, the steel has deteriorated to such an extent through sitting on that slip for three years, waiting for work to be resumed, that Doenitz refused to use it for any of his precious *Unterseeboote*. So Raeder talked the Führer into allowing this project to proceed, in view of the possible propaganda profit – especially in view of the now worthless nature of the hull.'

'And we were never told,' Keiko muttered.

'Otherwise you might have abandoned the project,' Koenig agreed. 'But similarly, it was determined only to use personnel who were also due for scrapping. My career as a commerce raider is over, you see. I am regarded as too prone to take risks in order to ensure the safety of the men whose ships I destroy. The crew who will accompany us do not know this, of course, but they do know that they have volunteered for a mission from which they cannot expect to return.'

Keiko sat down again. 'Why are you telling me these things, Captain Koenig?'

'Because I do not wish you to be under any misapprehension as to what you are about. I am disobeying orders in placing the true facts before you, but I will lie to no man. It is for you to evaluate the chances of this mission being a success, and make your decision accordingly.'

'But if I decide to continue, you will take that ... ship to sea?'

'I am a German officer, Commander Hatatsune. Even if I abhor my masters, they are my country's masters and I will serve them, and thus my country, to the best of my ability. I am quite prepared to die for the Fatherland. But I do not intend to throw my life away to no purpose. I wish you to have no doubts about that. If you decide that the mission is still viable, I believe I can take that hulk to a position off Newfoundland. Once we put to sea, I will do that, or perish in the attempt. You must be clear on that. There can be no changing our minds. We go, you fly – regardless of the weather or the opposition. No false heroics, Commander Hatatsune. Just work to be done.'

'Do you not suppose my men also know they are going on a mission from which they will not return, Captain? They too are volunteers, and I may add that I have hand-picked them from amongst four times their

180

number of would-be volunteers. We did not come twelve thousand miles to be put off by weather, or discomfort, or ice, or internal German feuds. We came to inflect a morale-damaging blow on the enemy, and to die. If you can get my aircraft to within range of New York, we will do those things.'

Koenig gazed at him for several seconds. Then he said, 'In that case, Commander Hatatsune, welcome aboard.' He held out his hand, and Keiko grasped it. 'Now,' Koenig went on. 'Come with me, and I will show you our aircraft-carrier.'

'She is eight hundred and twenty feet long,' Koenig said, standing beside Keiko on the flight-deck. 'And as you will observe, that is also the length of this deck. *Graf Zeppelin*'s deck is some fifty feet shorter than this. So your men will have a little more space from which to take off.'

But Junkers were heavy machines. 'There is no catapult,' Keiko remarked.

'There will be one,' Koenig promised him. 'It is expected daily. It can be fitted afloat. I am not, of course, fitting retaining wires as you will not be landing. I have also limited us to a single elevator.' He led Keiko aft, past busy construction workers still painting and firing rivets. 'But the elevator has been especially enlarged and strengthened to lift the Junkers.' He signalled the waiting crewmen, and they stood on the wide platform and slowly descended into the ship, where again Keiko stared in amazement.

The entire interior, on this hangar level, was nothing but open space. 'It is the same on the next deck as well,' Koenig told him. 'Our masters have given us the least possible, and told us to do what we can with it.' He stepped off the elevator as it came to rest. 'But it is possible to do a great deal with the least possible, provided one approaches the problem from a positive

181

angle. This ship was designed to displace twenty-seven thousand tons.' He led Keiko to one of the few ladders leading downwards, and thence on to a catwalk, from which Keiko could look down at the enormous turbines, the sixteen mammoth boilers. 'However,' Koenig continued, 'empty shell as she is, she will actually displace something less than twenty thousand. I intend to maintain her close to that weight. There will be no bulkheads, except where required for lateral strength. There will be no cabins, and no mess decks. Even if we add her crew, which is going to be skeleton in any event, and twenty bombers, we are still not going to increase her displacement by more than a thousand tons. Now, those are Brown-Boveri geared turbines, capable of delivering two hundred thousand shaft horse-power; they are in fact, the original engines, and were designed to produce a speed, under full load, of thirty-five knots.'

Keiko scratched his head. 'That is as fast as most destroyers.'

'Exactly. But with the weight reduction, I am hoping for speeds in excess of forty knots. We will be able to outstrip any ship afloat capable of sinking us. And of course we are not going to carry our normal fuel capacity, just enough for ten days' steaming at full speed. Then, she was designed to carry over forty aircraft; we will be carrying twenty. Heavier machines, perhaps, but not significantly so. She was also designed for a crew of one thousand, seven hundred and sixty men, excluding flying personnel. We shall be carrying no more than six hundred. And you see, both the speed and the unconventional design will confuse the enemy. When we are picked up on their radar, travelling at more than forty knots, there is no way they can possibly suppose we are an aircraft-carrier. But again, should we be sighted visually, with our flush deck we look like a British escort carrier. By the time the interceptor has decided we are not one of theirs, we will be past him. Oh, we will do it, Commander, if the gods are on our side. Needless to say, I am carrying no guns whatsoever, and she was designed for sixteen six-inch, plus subsidiary armament. Do you know, if I had been able to start from scratch, I would even have abandoned all idea of armour?' He pointed upwards. 'That flight-deck is one and a half inches of steel. Well, that has to be, to take the weight of the aircraft. But we have belt armour of three and a half inches. That is no use to us, and it would have saved another couple of thousand tons.'

Keiko's brain was in a whirl. The ship was a simple delivery vehicle and nothing more. As such it was a brilliant concept. But she was also close to a floating coffin, if she *could* be intercepted – a fact that Hjalmar Koenig seemed prepared to accept. Keiko had never encountered a man, not even Yamamoto, who seemed able to devote himself so completely to the achievement of the task he had been given.

'But your men must eat and sleep,' he said. 'And mine also. Where will they do that?'

'They will sleep in hammocks slung from the deck-head, as they did in the old sailing ships,' Koenig told him, returning to the hangar deck and leading him forward, their shoes echoing in the great empty space. 'Food will be carried in specially prepared containers which can be jettisoned as they are used. Water will be kept to a minimum, and will be used for drinking purposes only. Oh, it will be uncomfortable, especially in winter conditions and rough seas. The noise from the engines will be enormous, as of course there can be no sound-proofing.' Koenig glanced at his companion. 'I am sorry to inflict such hardships upon your pilots, Commander, but it is necessary.'

'My men will bear whatever hardships are necessary,'

183

Keiko said, and allowed himself a smile. 'Providing you will promise to carry enough gasoline.'

'We will carry exactly enough gasoline to give each of your aircraft a full tank, Commander. You will see, therefore, that once you and your men, and your aircraft, and your gasoline, have taken off, we should be able to return even faster than we came out.'

'Indeed,' Keiko agreed, falling in with the German's mood of almost desperate gaiety. 'Providing you have the equipment to navigate.'

'Ah,' Koenig said. At the end of the huge empty seven-hundred-and-fifty-foot-long hangar deck there was at last a bulkhead, and a doorway. Koenig opened the door and several construction engineers stood to attention. 'I at least have a bridge.'

'Below the flight-deck?' Keiko murmured.

'As I said, this gives us a similar silhouette to several of the British merchant vessels which have been converted as auxiliary carriers. One of them you know – *Audacity* – was actually the German ship *Hannover*, which the British confiscated at the beginning of the war. There is audacity for you, eh? However, we sank her last year. Yet the same flush flight-deck had proved the most simple for conversion. You have found the same thing in Japan. *Ryujo*, for instance is . . . I beg your pardon, was, of this design.'

Keiko raised his eyebrows. 'Was?'

'*Ryujo* was sunk, just over a week ago, in the Eastern Solomons. You did not know this?'

Keiko inhaled sharply. He was beginning to wonder if Japan had any aircraft-carriers left at all. Oh, yes, there was still *Shikaku* and *Zuikaku*, sister ships which were as large and powerful as any afloat, excepting the American giants. Still, it must have meant that Japan had lost another naval battle.

'I am sorry to be the bearer of such bad news,' Koenig said.

'The fortunes of war,' Keiko told him. 'I was on *Akagi* when she went down.'

'That must have been an unpleasant experience. I have never been on a ship which was actually sunk. I was on *Seydlitz* at Jutland. She should have sunk, but didn't. We were fortunate.'

Keiko's heart warmed even more to this man, who could have phrased that sentence so very differently. 'We must endeavour to keep your watertight record intact, Herr Captain,' he commented.

Koenig smiled as readily as ever. 'I certainly intend to try. But here, you see, Commander, is a very fully equipped navigating bridge. We have even managed to install a radar set, which is very necessary when navigating the northern seas in winter, if only to avoid icebergs.'

'I would like to compliment you on your concept,' Keiko said. 'As you say, there is no limit to what a determined man may do with the smallest amount of materials, if he is at once determined and talented. May I ask the name of our vessel?'

'Why, do you know, she is known only as "B". *Graf Zeppelin* was "A", you see, and was christened at her launching. But a name has not been chosen for this one. Nor will there be one, as she is officially scrapped.'

'Then she shall have no name,' Keiko said. 'I like that. The ship with no name.'

'Except between you and me, Commander. *Nemo*.'

'*Nemo?*'

'That is what the word means: nameless.'

Keiko laughed. 'Then *Nemo* it shall be.'

'Well, then, Commander, will you lunch with me at the officers' club? It is the best place, as it would be a breach of security for you and me to be seen on the street together. But the club is perfectly secure. We shall meet no one but naval officers there.'

'It would be my great pleasure, sir,' Keiko said.

At last, he thought, as they drove away from the dockyard in the official Mercedes, with the curtains drawn over the rear windows. After all the disappointments and downright treachery of the past two days, here was a man prepared to risk as much as himself, prepared to do or die, to do *and* die, in fact. A man he felt instinctively he could trust, and like. He felt a peculiar warmth surging through his veins, a foretaste of success. Now he suddenly knew he would not fail. Not with a man like Hjalmar Koenig behind him.

They entered a courtyard and left the automobile. Sentries saluted, and a high fence shut them off from the world outside; as Koenig had promised, here was security. They were admitted by a marine orderly.

'A drink before we eat?' Koenig asked.

'I would like that,' Keiko agreed.

'The bar is this way. But you will bring us the menus, Claus,' Koenig told the orderly, and pushed open the swing doors to lead into a large and well-appointed bar. At half-past twelve in the morning there were very few people present, and Koenig took his guest straight to the counter, where a red-jacketed barman was waiting to serve them. 'Schnapps?'

'With pleasure,' Keiko said. He had no idea what schnapps was, but he was prepared to drink anything except champagne.

'Why, Commander Hatatsune,' said a soft voice, and he turned in alarm, to gaze at Helga Staffel. At her shoulder was the huge Swedish reporter, Jan Anderssen.

CHAPTER 8

The Suspicion

'Mrs Wharton?' The desk clerk smiled at Jennie. 'Would you fill in the register, please?'

Jennie frowned as she picked up the pen. 'Isn't Commander Wharton here yet?'

'No, madam. But he is expected.'

She wrote "Jennifer Wharton" in her clear, bold hand, and decided that it didn't look as good, or sound as good, as Jennifer Rhodes. On the other hand, phonetically, it was better then Jennifer Anderson.

A bellhop escorted her to her room, which was a prime double overlooking the park. Clive must be paying a fortune for it, she thought.

She undressed, unpacked, had a shower, put on a pair of lounging pyjamas she had bought especially for the occasion – in pale green and almost sheer – made up her face and brushed out her hair, leaving it loose, and inspected herself in the mirror. She could hardly look more seductively ready for a naughty weekend, she decided. She was determined to make a good job of it.

And then hate herself all over again? She refused to think about it, sat down, picked up the Raymond Chandler paperback novel she had bought in the station, read a few pages . . . and awoke with a start. That had been silly – she just hadn't realised how exhausted she was. And someone was knocking on the door.

'Just a moment.' She tossed hair from her eyes, dragged a brush through it and went to the door. 'Well,' she said. 'Late as ever . . .' It was the bellhop.

'Message for Mrs Wharton,' he said.

She took the envelope slowly, slit it with her nail and took out the slip of paper inside. 'SOMETHING ON STOP CAN'T MAKE IT STOP AM I BLANK OFF STOP I ADORE YOU STOP CLIVE'. She reckoned it had been censored; there had certainly been a word before 'Off'. Well, she thought, she felt pissed off as well.

The boy was still waiting patiently. 'Hang on,' she said, going to her handbag for a quarter.

'Would you like to check out this morning, Mrs Wharton?' he asked, clearly having read the telegram.

Check out, Jennie thought. Having checked out, what was she going to do? She could go up to Connecticut and visit with her parents, she supposed. If in the four years since Johnnie's disappearance they had not regained any of their former closeness, they were at least friends once more. Her mother would be terribly disappointed, Jennie knew, were she ever to learn that Jennie had managed to get as far as New York and not paid them at least a call.

But seeing the folks right this minute was the last thing she wanted to do. It would involve conversation, inevitably leading towards what might have been. Since the admiral's slip of the tongue six months ago, she had been afraid to see her parents at all. She wasn't sure she could sit through an evening of being told what a heel John Anderson was, and what a lucky escape she had had, without breaking security to show them just how wrong they had always been.

She couldn't avoid feeling that, had they been happy about her engagement instead of so obviously unhappy, Johnnie might have stayed. Except, if he had stayed, he might well have had his head shot off by now. What a

God-damned confusing world it is, she thought, to suppose that Johnnie might actually be safer as a spy in Germany.

'Madam?' the bellhop asked.

Or she could go back to Washington and stare at the walls of her apartment. Or she could stay right here, in a beautiful room, with a beautiful view, her whereabouts known to no one in the world save Clive Wharton, and just sleep, and eat, and drink, and try to shut off her mind. And, she was slowly realising, that was what she wanted to do – alone. She was enormously relieved that she would not, after all, have to spend the weekend with Clive Wharton.

'Isn't the room booked up to Monday morning?'

'That's right, madam. But . . . it's kind of expensive.'

'Do I look like a pauper to you?' Jennie asked. 'Listen, sonny, you go and get me the biggest and spiciest double Bloody Mary this hotel knows how to make, and then tell room service I want a luncheon menu. Move!'

John Anderson had been about to propose going to Munich that afternoon, because they had drawn a blank.

One of Helga's great assets was her enthusiasm. When she decided to do something there was no hanging about. She had even worn her smart blue uniform with its white blouse and neat black tie. Helga in uniform looked remarkably severe – but also close to beautiful.

Wearing uniform, she had gained entrance to the officers' club with the right to introduce a guest. She enjoyed showing off her handsome fiancé; even if it wasn't official yet – it would be by Monday. And having promised to find out what the *Graf Zeppelin* was doing, she had hurried up to the bar, ordered them drinks, and asked in the most straightforward fashion, 'Where is *Graf Zeppelin*? I have a message for someone on board.'

The barman had grinned at her. 'You've missed him, Fräulein Lieutenant. *Graf Zeppelin* sailed three weeks ago.'

'Three *weeks* ago?' John had asked, involuntarily.

'For where?' Helga had demanded.

'Ah, Fräulein, who can say?'

'Well really,' Helga had remarked, in not entirely simulated disgust. Then she had marched John to a secluded table where they could not be overheard. 'All this way for nothing. *Graf Zeppelin* left a fortnight before the Japanese arrived. Even if Koenig is in command, your theory is still wrong.'

'Jesus,' he had said. 'It just doesn't figure . . .' Then he had looked up and watched Koenig and Keiko Hatatsune entering the bar.

'Fräulein Helga!' Keiko exclaimed in obvious delight. 'I am sure you know Captain Koenig?'

'Of course. How are you, Herr Captain?'

Koenig's normal jolly smile was absent. 'I am very well indeed, Fräulein Lieutenant,' he said, and looked past her at Anderson.

'You know Jan, of course, Herr Captain?'

'Indeed.' Koenig shook hands. 'What brings you to Kiel?'

'Working,' John confessed. 'Hunting for trifles. I don't only spend my time in Wilhelmshaven, you know.'

'I have never thought about it,' Koenig said.

'And when I heard that Helga was taking a ride up here, I thought I'd tag along,' John continued. 'I never expected to run into you. Or Commander Hatatsune.'

'Then what brings *you* to Kiel, Lieutenant Staffel?' Koenig inquired.

Helga took refuge in feminine mystery. 'I have my reasons, sir.'

John could have hugged her because she could hardly

have chosen a better reply; Keiko was looking more and more pleased to see her.

'You'll join us for lunch?' John asked.

'Well . . .' Koenig looked doubtful.

'I should like that very much,' Keiko said.

'Then I'll just change the table.' John went to the bar. 'Drinks for everyone over there,' he said. 'And will you change my table to one for four, please.'

'Right away.'

'Before you go . . .' John let his hand drift across the counter, the corner of the hundred Mark note just peeping between his fingers. 'I wish to pay for the lunch,' he said. 'Regardless of what Captain Koenig may say. But I must get away early. Do you suppose, just before the dessert is served, that you could inform me that there is a telephone call? Then I can appear to take it and settle up at the same time.'

'Of course,' the bartender agreed, sliding the note expertly into his pocket.

'Thank you. And finally, can you lend me the use of a pad of paper and a pencil?'

'Of course, sir,' the barman said again, reaching beneath the counter.

John wrote:

'Darling doll, we obviously missed something some-where, and Koenig will never tell me. But Hatatsune may tell you. I am going to find an excuse and sidle off back to Berlin and wait for you there. See if you can snow Keiko into telling what he and Koenig are up to. Please do this, darling doll, and tomorrow we'll go down to Munich and see your dad. Then we'll be officially betrothed. Hoorah!'

He did not sign the note, but folded it into the palm of his hand and returned to the table. 'It's all arranged. Menus are on their way.'

191

'I so enjoyed last night,' Keiko was saying to Helga. 'But I feel I should apologise. I'm afraid I had too much to drink.'

'Didn't we all?' Helga smiled magnanimously.

'Last night?' Koenig inquired, looking grimmer than ever.

They were all looking at each other. John allowed his hand to droop between his chair and Helga's, found her handbag, unclipped it, slipped the note inside and clipped it shut again.

'We were required to entertain Commander Hatatsune and his officers,' Helga was explaining. 'I say required, but it was great fun.'

Koenig looked at John in bewilderment. 'You were there?'

'Good lord, no,' John said.

'We met Herr Anderssen at the night-club we went to afterwards,' Keiko explained. 'It was splendid. We toasted everyone we could think of. I toasted you, Herr Captain.'

Koenig looked ready to explode.

'Now, Hjalmar,' John said quietly. 'You know I never, see, or hear, anything I am not supposed to. Ah, the menus.' They ordered, and then, as John had anticipated, Helga went to the Ladies before going in to lunch.

Keiko watched her walk to the door, and then turned to John. 'I would like to ask you what you may consider an impertinent question, Herr Anderssen.'

'So shoot. I'll try to think of one to ask you back.'

'Is Lieutenant Staffel of importance to you?'

John frowned. 'In what sense?'

'Are you in love with her?'

'My dear fellow, of course not. She's a valuable contact, like Hjalmar here. They give me little bits of inside gossip about the working of the navy, which sometimes the Gestapo let me publish.'

'Ah,' Keiko said, looking greatly relieved.

'And what bits of gossip were you hoping to find in Kiel?' Koenig asked.

'Is there some?' John asked. 'I did hear a rumour that you are here, Commander, to train German pilots in the techniques of flying from carriers.'

'Why, that is quite true,' Keiko agreed. 'But it is very confidential.'

'Oh, I have no intention of publishing it. But of course, everyone knows *Graf Zeppelin* is on trials.' He looked at Koenig. 'I would have bet a million you were going to get her, Hjalmar.'

'Me?' Koenig smiled. 'My dear fellow, commanding an aircraft-carrier requires years of training and very special skills.'

'Then . . .' John frowned in bewilderment. 'Does that mean you're going back to *Atlas*?'

'No, my friend,' Koenig said. 'I am not going back to *Atlas*. I have been beached, as a worn-out old war-horse. It is sad, for me. Sad to think I will never again bask in the reflected glory of your brilliant pen.'

John returned his smile. 'I am sure I shall think of something to say about you, from time to time. Ah, our table is ready.'

And Helga was returning from the powder room, where she had most certainly opened her handbag. She had on one of her steely looks. John blew her a kiss.

'But what is *your* purpose in visiting Kiel, Commander Hatatsune?' he asked conversationally. 'I had supposed you also would be bound for *Graf Zeppelin*.'

'There is time,' Keiko said easily. 'As I am in Germany, I wish to look at things. And my good friend Captain Koenig has very kindly consented to show me what he can of the shipbuilding industry here in Kiel.'

'There's no better place,' John agreed, and changed the subject to the latest opera being performed in Berlin.

He felt around cautiously under the table and brushed Helga's knee with his own. She promptly moved her legs. She was annoyed with him. But she would do what he wanted, he felt sure.

Was he really sticking his neck out? Well, he was by being here at all, he supposed. Koenig was certainly not pleased to see him, even if the Japanese appeared blissfully content that all was well, lost as he was in his obviously erotic consideration of Helga. And Koenig had been even less pleased to hear that the Japanese had been at a night-club the previous evening. But *he* could hardly be blamed for security breaches and, as usual, he was being perfectly open about what he wanted to find out. He was an ambitious, pushing news-paperman, the image he had carefully built up over the past four years. And if Helga could be persuaded to do his dirty work for him, he was even more in the clear, however more dirty that might make him feel.

'Excuse me, please, Herr Anderssen,' said the barman, bending beside him. 'There is a telephone call for you. You may take it in the bar.'

'For me? Oh . . .' He smiled at his guests. 'You'll excuse me, please.' He hurried from the dining room. The barman had the bill waiting for him. He paid in cash, then returned to the table. 'Damnation,' he announced. 'There has been an accident in the naval dockyard in Malmö, and my editor wishes me to go up there immediately.'

'Malmo?' Helga cried. Malmö was in Sweden itself, just across the Sound from Denmark.

'Well, my dear, I *am* the paper's naval correspondent. Apparently a warship may have been damaged.' He winked at Koenig. 'Only a Swedish warship, but these things matter to us Swedes.' He held out his hand. 'It has been a great pleasure, Commander Hatatsune. Good fortune with your stay in Germany. Hjalmar, the meal has been taken care of. Helga, I will see you the next time I am in Berlin.'

'Oh, but . . .' Then she closed her mouth again; she realised this was the ploy he had mentioned in the note, and that he was on his way to Berlin now. She would do what he wanted, he knew, as he hurried from the room.

'Well,' Keiko remarked. 'Is he not a busy man?'

'I had no idea you knew Anderssen so very well, Lieutenant Staffel,' Koenig commented. 'I am not sure that he is a good security risk for someone in your position.'

'Oh, he has been vetted by the Gestapo,' Helga assured him. 'And Admiral Doenitz approves of him. Besides, we are engaged to be married.'

'Married?' Keiko cried in dismay.

Helga smiled at him. 'One day, Herr Commander.'

Keiko seemed visibly to relax. 'I am sure you will be very happy.'

'Well,' Koenig said. 'I must be getting back to work.' He smiled at Helga. 'I am still finding it difficult, becoming used to a desk job and office hours. Why do you not put in a word for me with Admiral Doenitz?'

She raised her eyebrows. 'You wish a submarine?'

'Anything to get away from the desk.'

He was watching her closely, she noticed. Trying to trap her into an admission? She wished Jan were still here, the louse. She didn't know why she was helping him at all – except that she loved him. 'Then I shall, Herr Captain.'

'I will arrange a flight for you to Trondheim,' Koenig told Keiko. 'This evening.'

'I would rather go tomorrow,' Keiko said. 'Can I not spend the night here? I understand the Junkers 88 we are to use will not be ready before tomorrow.'

Once again Koenig looked ready to explode. But he

controlled himself. 'Then you wish to come back to the office with me now?'

'Well, I thought perhaps Lieutenant Staffel would show me something of Kiel. Is that not permitted? I was told by Admiral Doenitz that the lieutenant is entirely trustworthy.'

'Do you know anything of Commander Hatatsune's mission, Lieutenant?' Koenig inquired.

'Of course I do, Herr Captain,' Helga said. Things were working out exactly as Jan had planned. But then, they always did. The *louse*.

'I see. Well, then, I think showing Commander Hatatsune something of Kiel is the best thing you can do,' Koenig said, and left the room.

'He thinks we are breaching security,' Helga said, wondering if he would do anything about it.

'I hope we are not,' Keiko said. 'I would like you to know that I am very gratified that you should have followed me like this, even though there are aspects of the situation I do not understand. Such as your relationship with Anderssen. You are to marry, but he told me, before we sat down to lunch, that he is not in love with you.'

'Well,' Helga said angrily, 'he was probably telling the truth. It is one of those arranged marriages, you know.'

'That is how things are done in Japan. But if you are betrothed, then you are already his.'

'I am neither officially betrothed to him yet, nor am I already his,' Helga snapped. 'I belong to no man.'

'This would not be possible in Japan. But I am glad it is possible here. Fräulein Staffel, I behaved very badly last night. I know this, and I wish to apologise. I am not used to this champagne, I think. But I wish you to know how much I admire you.'

'You were going to call me Helga,' she said. This funny little man, with his so perfect manners and his

196

tremendous interest in her, was really quite a treat. And as for Jan . . . of course she understood that he had told the Japanese he was not in love with her merely to make her "snow job" the easier to accomplish. But sometimes it was difficult to escape the impression that Jan was more interested in her as a naval secretary than as a woman. He was always using her, and taking her cooperation for granted. Well, she thought, suppose I did cooperate, all the way? She'd only be doing what he had asked her to. And whatever happened, he'd deserve it.

'I had forgotten,' Keiko said. 'And you were to call me Keiko.'

She held his gaze with her own. 'I can hardly do that, Herr Commander, while we are both in uniform.'

'Is there nowhere we can go, and not be in uniform?'

Helga allowed her tongue to come out and circle her lips. 'Have you ever seen the Kiel Canal?'

'No. Is it worth seeing?'

'Oh, very much so. It stretches right through the Jutland peninsula, and comes out at Brunsbüttel on the Elbe. It was built by Kaiser Wilhelm II in 1894, to facilitate the passage of German warships from the Baltic to the North Sea. It really is a masterpiece of engineering, and is also very dramatic, very beautiful. If you wish, I will show it to you.'

He continued to gaze at her.

'And there is a hostelry just below Holtenau. That is the suburb where the canal ends, you know. At that hostelry we could be . . . well, we could relax discipline.'

'Could we spend the night there?'

His directness was as exciting as it was disturbing. So Jan would be waiting for her in Berlin, to go down to Munich. But they could go down to Munich any time. And she would have done what he wanted. 'I don't see why not,' she said. 'I have an overnight bag in the locker room.'

'Why,' he said. 'So have I.'

They walked, because that was part of the ambiance she wanted to create. It was not far from the officers' club to the great lock gates, rising some thirty feet off the canal, big enough for the largest of warships. They stood on the concrete wall and looked down on several barges from Brunsbüttel moored inside the lock beneath them; out in the Kieler Bucht two destroyers waited to replace the barges and begin the journey down to the Elbe. Once the gates were shut to allow the water level to be lowered, they walked across the bridge to the northern side.

'Do you see those moorings over there?' Helga asked. 'In peacetime they are full of yachts. You know, sailing boats. Sailing is a very popular pastime in the Baltic.' She pointed up the harbour. Kiel itself was situated at the toe of a dogleg, and from the Germaniawerft yard, or the officers' club, one looked at apparently entirely enclosed water. But here at Holtenau it was possible to look straight up the Kieler Bucht at the open sea, several miles away. 'That is the Baltic,' she explained. 'Although we call this entire western arm the Kattegat, even south of Denmark. The Baltic proper is the East Sea. But it is all our sea, now.'

She led him along the stone verge of the neatly land-scaped canal bank, with the still water on their left, and the trees and green lawns and flower-beds rising on their right. They walked west now, towards the small hotel-restaurant which was situated about a quarter of a mile away. She glanced at him; he was saying very little. 'Are you married, Herr Commander?'

'Oh, yes Fräulein Lieutenant.'

'Ah,' she said thoughtfully.

'But I am twelve thousand miles away from my wife,' Keiko explained. 'And I shall never see her again.'

'Never? You mean you've split up?'

'I mean that the nature of my mission precludes the possibility,' Keiko told her. 'But you know that, of course. In any event, she would not be disturbed by what we are about to do.'

Helga had reached the door of the inn. But she would have stopped anyway. 'What are we about to do?'

'I am hoping,' Keiko said, 'that I am going to make you very happy.'

Suddenly Helga was breathless. His façade of total composure was more exciting than anything she had ever known. There was no problem in obtaining a room; the hotelier did not risk even raising his eyebrows at the appearance of two naval officers who wished to share a bed for the night – they were of different sexes. He gave them his best, looking out over the canal.

'Well, what do you know,' Helga remarked, looking at her watch as the door closed on them. 'It's only three o'clock. Would you like to take a walk down the canal? It's very beautiful.'

'I would like to stay here and make love to you,' Keiko said. 'Because you are very beautiful. Take off your clothes. I would like to look at you.'

She had never been quite so bluntly commanded to bed in her life. But that too was exciting. She took off her jacket and hung it on a hanger, then hung her skirt on another. She released her tie and unbuttoned her blouse, feeling very much like one the strippers in the night-club, because Keiko never took his gaze off her. She wore no brassière, and watched his nostrils dilate as she hung the blouse on a third hanger. She sat down to remove her shoes and stockings, deliberately half turning away from him. Without a word he moved to

199

the other side of the room, to watch her cross and uncross her legs from the front.

She knew she was blushing. Carefully she stood up. 'Do you mind if I use the bathroom?'

'Of course. Where is it?'

'Down the hall.' She opened her valise, took out her blood-red dressing gown, wrapped herself in it, and felt she could breathe again. 'I won't be five minutes,' she said, and frowned as he accompanied her into the corridor. 'Where are you going?'

'I am coming with you. I want to watch you.'

She didn't know what to say. She had never been concerned about sharing a bathroom with Jan, providing they were each doing something different, because they knew each other so very well. She didn't know this man at all. But she had walked into this situation with her eyes open. And her excitement was growing. 'Well,' she said. 'Come along, then.'

He leaned against the door, watched everything she did, while she prayed that the hotelier would not come upstairs right this minute.

'You are utterly beautiful,' Keiko remarked, as she washed her face and hands and cleaned her teeth.

'That's very nice of you.' She put on her gown.

He frowned. 'Do you not wash your genitals before having sex?'

'Do you?'

'Of course.'

'Oh,' she said. 'Well, we don't, necessarily. We wash them afterwards.'

'We do that as well.'

She hurried back to the bedroom. He followed, and undressed, simply and without embarrassment. If he was not a big man, he was perfectly proportioned, and in the very peak of physical condition, she estimated; his muscles simply rippled at thigh and belly and shoulder.

She got into bed and lay on her back, beneath the

covers, the sheet pulled to her throat, waiting for him to return from the bathroom. Which he did soon enough, having very obviously had a bath. She felt positively dirty. But she wasn't going to surrender to the extent he seemed to require.

He stood by the bed, looking down at her. 'Do you not wish to make love now?' he asked.

'Any time you feel the urge,' she said. He didn't seem to be feeling the urge at all at the moment, going on appearances.

'I am ready now.'

It dawned on her that he did not consider a woman lying on her back beneath a sheet in a proper position for making love. Slowly she peeled the sheet back and sat up. As she did so, to her consternation, he thrust a hand beneath each of her buttocks, and with an amazing display of physical power lifted her from the bed. She thought she was going to overbalance and threw both arms round his neck, a gesture he ignored as he lifted her straight up, using arms and shoulders and back only, so far as she could estimate, until her vagina was on a level with his mouth. Desperately she flopped her legs over his shoulders and clasped his head, while he kissed her to his satisfaction.

'Oh,' she gasped. 'Oh, my God. Oh!'

But she wasn't calling for help.

Hjalmar Koenig sat at his desk, the telephone in his hand.

'Admiral Doenitz's office,' said the girl.

'Is it possible to speak with Admiral Doenitz, please? This is Captain Koenig.'

'One moment, Herr Captain.'

Koenig supposed he was lucky to find the admiral in his office on a Saturday afternoon.

'Koenig?' Doenitz said. 'Are you in Berlin?'

'No, Herr Admiral. I am calling from Kiel, where I

have just encountered one of your secretaries. Helga Staffel.'

'Ah, yes, Staffel,' Doenitz commented.

'Did you send her to Kiel, Herr Admiral?'

'Send her to Kiel? Why should I do that, Koenig? Staffel has been given a weekend pass. She must have a private reason for visiting Kiel.'

'Yes,' Koenig said doubtfully. 'May I ask how much she knows about Operation Kong, Herr Admiral?'

'Kong? She knows nothing of Kong. Of course not.'

'There is no file on the matter to which she has access?'

'There is no file on Kong at all, Herr Captain. Operation Kong is known only to the grand admiral and myself, and the Führer's immediate circle. And to you, of course, and that fellow Hatatsune.'

'Lieutenant Staffel seemed to be acquainted with Hatatsune.'

'And that is disturbing you? We endeavoured to entertain our guests last night, and Helga was hostess. She is used to that sort of thing. Naturally, as Hatatsune was the senior Japanese officer present, she made herself responsible for him.'

'And took him to a night-club afterwards,' Koenig told him. 'Where they met the Swedish reporter, Anderssen. That does not disturb you, Herr Admiral?'

'That they should have met Anderssen? My dear Koenig, are you suggesting Anderssen is a security risk? I wish some of our officers were as enthusiastically supportive of government policy as he.'

'But still, Herr Admiral, in view of the extreme secrecy which is supposed to shroud the Japanese visit . . .'

'Good security is a matter of balance, Koenig,' Doenitz told him. 'There is no possibility of our concealing the fact that there is a group of Japanese pilots in our midst. Therefore the decision was taken to announce that they are here to train our pilots in the techniques of taking off from aircraft-carriers. That is logical and understandable. We would be very stupid to suppose the British are not aware that *Graf Zeppelin* is close to being commissioned. They are also aware that we have no pilots in the Reich with any experience of flying from carriers, an art at which our Japanese allies are very experienced indeed. In publicising this story, Anderssen will be very helpful. Fräulein Staffel is aware of the official reason for the Japanese presence. Nothing more. I may say, incidentally, that Staffel, whom I have known since she was a child, has my total confidence. Good day to you.'

The telephone went dead, and after a moment Koenig replaced the receiver. He wondered if the rebuke was justified. The truth was, he had never been so excited and enthusiastic about any command, so determined to make it a success.

His initial response to the slowly dawning under-standing that he had been appointed to lead a suicide mission had been anger; this was the reward his Nazi masters had chosen for him, after years of devoted service attended by success on a scale achieved by no one else. But then he had been overtaken by another mood. They were giving him nothing, and telling him to do the impossible. Then he would damned well *do* the impossible, and then tell them to fuck off.

In that mood he had attacked the project, and been satisfied with his progress. His last doubt – the quality of the Japanese pilots who would set the seal on what he proposed to accomplish – had disappeared when he encountered the dedicated determination of Keiko Hatatsune.

Now suddenly he was anxious again – because of the presence of Jan Anderssen in Kiel, asking questions? He liked Anderssen, and he was sure Doenitz was right in his appraisal of the man. If the Swede sometimes pushed too hard, well, he was an ambitious young man who clearly looked on this war as an opportunity to make his name on the next Mahan.

And Helga Staffel? Koenig was perfectly prepared to admit that he did not like Helga Staffel, or her father, or anything the pair of them represented. Partly this was because he knew Helga was born with a silver spoon in her mouth while Brigitte Koenig was dying of starvation. But equally it was because Helga Staffel clearly looked at both war and Nazism as the current "in" thing to be involved with. Koenig had no use for Nazism as an ideology, but he could respect those who genuinely felt it was the only hope of Germany; he could not convince himself that Helga Staffel was one of those dedicated souls. Nazism to her meant belonging to the current best in society, just as wearing a smart uniform and being Karl Doenitz's secretary merely gave her a cachet over the other bright young things of her group. And that she should be announcing with one voice that she was going to marry Jan Anderssen, and with the same voice accepting the most blatant invitation to an affair with Keiko Hatatsune . . . no doubt he was out of touch with modern morality. But he really felt that if Anderssen married that little bitch he would need his head examined.

None of that necessarily made her a security risk. Save that she was probably at this moment in bed with Hatatsune, who was in Germany on a mission of desperate secrecy. But she was Doenitz's secretary, and had his trust . . .

The telephone jangled, and he picked up the receiver again. 'Koenig.'

'I have a call for you from Wilhelmshaven, Herr Captain,' said the girl on the switchboard.

'Kurt? Put him on.'

'Father!'

'Kurt! How good to hear from you. How is your arm?'

'It is quite better, thank you, father.'

'Good. You will be able to come to Berlin for a few days?'

'No, father. I have only a moment. I am ringing to say goodbye.'

Koenig frowned. 'Goodbye?'

'We are sailing this evening.'

'But . . .' *Atlas* usually spent at least six weeks in port before setting off again. 'This is very sudden.'

'The orders came out of the blue. Captain Wiedermayer is very excited. So am I.'

'Of course,' Koenig agreed. 'Mind you do well.' He chewed his lip, his brain racing. *Atlas* usually went to sea for approximately six months. She would therefore not return before the spring of 1943. By which time . . . He had intended to obtain leave and go down to Wilhelmshaven at the beginning of October, sure she would still be there. Of course he would not have been able to tell Kurt what he was doing, but he could at least have taken a proper farewell of the boy.

'Father? Are you there?'

'Kurt, I may not be here when you return.'

'Oh, father! You have received a new command? I am so proud. Is she a proper warship?' He knew his father's ambitions.

'Yes,' Koenig said, looking through the window at the hulk on the slipway. 'A proper warship at last. However, Kurt . . .' To suggest that he might never be here again would not only distress the boy, but would also be a breach of security. 'When I do return, we will have a big celebration together, eh? Just take care of yourself.'

He replaced the receiver slowly. Of course he was coming back, no matter what. The only thing which could possibly stop him coming back would be a breach of security which would let the Royal Navy know the exact day he was going out. To allow any over-confidence or complacency on the part of others to put this mission at risk would be utterly stupid. He could not blame Keiko Hatatsune for falling for Staffel. She was an attractive little bitch, and the Japanese counted himself already dead, yet he was very much alive, and eager to live these last few weeks to the maximum. To a man in such a mood, who was in any event experiencing an alien society for the first time, a woman like Helga Staffel would appear as manna from heaven, especially as he had apparently been told he could trust her absolutely.

But what could he do about it, while she enjoyed Doenitz's confidence? Nothing, except . . . he reached into his inside breast pocket, took out his wallet, and from it extracted a slip of paper. Grand Admiral Raeder had given him that name and address personally. 'One cannot afford to be squeamish, Koenig,' the grand admiral had said. 'Nothing, nothing at all, must be allowed to hinder the success of your mission. If there is any member of your crew, or the construction force, or *anyone* else with whom you come into contact until this operation is completed, about whom you have the slightest doubts, I wish you, no, I command you, to call upon Colonel Doerner for assistance. The investigation, and any subsequent action that may be required, will be handled with the utmost discretion. One may not like the concept of the Gestapo, but there are times when a police able to act both secretly and without being hampered by civil laws can be greatly to our advantage. Remember these things, Koenig.'

Remember these things, Koenig thought. The Gestapo! The very word made him shudder. But only to be used in an investigative capacity – he would insist on that. And then he could return to his task, the success of the operation, with all the concentration that it required.

He picked up the telephone and asked for the number Raeder had written down. After a few seconds a man's voice said, 'Yes?'

Koenig took a deep breath. 'I would like to speak with Colonel Oskar Doerner,' he said.

CHAPTER 9

The Strike

'Well, Commander, you're looking very fresh this morning. Had a good furlough, eh?'

Jennie stood to attention before the desk. 'As a matter of fact, sir, yes.'

'Don't tell me,' the admiral remarked. 'I'll bet you spent ninety per cent of it lying on your back.'

'No, sir,' Jennie told him. 'I spent one hundred per cent of it lying on my back.' Alone, she thought.

'Yeah?' the admiral commented. 'Well, that's history now. There's been all kinds of flap going on down here. First of all there's been a false report of a German break-out . . .'

'Sir?' Jennie's heartbeat quickened. Was that the reason for Clive's cancellation?

'Sure. Some British agent reported *Atlas* due to leave Wilhelmshaven for another cruise. So we put the whole God-damned Atlantic Ocean on full alert. After all the publicity that guy Koenig had been getting, we want him.'

'You think Koenig is still in command, sir? That doesn't correlate with the information coming out of Sweden.'

'The information coming out of Sweden right this minute doesn't correlate with a God-damned thing,' the admiral grumbled.

'And did we get *Atlas*, sir?'

'We didn't get shit,' the admiral said. 'Because there

was nothing there. Well, hell, I could've told them that. *Atlas* had only been home just over a month. She never sails again so quick.'

Jennie didn't know whether to laugh or cry. Poor Clive, sitting up there at Goose Bay waiting for a summons that had never come. Poor Jennie, lying in an empty bed at the Plaza Hotel overlooking Central Park. But she *had* enjoyed her solitary weekend.

'Talking about Sweden,' the admiral was saying. 'There's not been a God-damned word from Anderssen this week. What the hell is he *doing*?'

'I'm sure you meant Seven-Twenty-One, sir,' Jennie said severely.

'It's between you and me and the wall, Jen. Listen, put a bomb under that character's ass. You make to Seven-Seven-Four that even if he has to go to Germany himself and shake that asshole by the balls, we have to have that information on Koenig's assignment. I want it before Torch sails. That is number one priority.'

'Don't you think, sir,' Jennie ventured, 'that Seven-Twenty-One is doing the best he can, and will deliver the information just as soon as he gets it?'

The admiral leaned back in his chair. 'Just what the hell is going on?' he inquired.

'Sir?'

'Every time I give an order about this shit Anderson you get uptight. For Christ's sake, you the guy's sister or something?' He waved his pencil at her. 'Girls can suffer from combat fatigue just like the guys in the front line, you know. Now you listen to me, Jen. To you, those guys are all numbers. That's how it has to be, or you can't function. And if you can't function, you're no God-damned use to me. You want to remember that. Now you go and get me whatever information Anderson is sitting on. And do it quick.'

Jennie saluted, and left the office.

*

'God-*damn!*' Clive Wharton remarked, for the fiftieth time in four days. He sat on the verandah of the officers' mess in Goose Bay, Labrador, and looked out at the Hamilton Inlet, while he drank his rapidly cooling coffee. Even in early September the days were getting short. At seven-thirty in the morning the dawn was still happening, but most of the birds had already left; there was as increasing chill in the air – he was wearing a fleece-lined flying jacket, and wishing he could follow the birds. He had hated this whole damned set-up from the moment he discovered he was going to be flying Brewster SB2A Buccaneers. The Buccaneer had come out over a year ago, intended as a reconnaissance bomber to fly off carriers, but it had never measured up for speed or performance.

'But what the hell, Wharton?' the Canadian wingco had remarked when he raised the point. 'You're not here to engage in aerial combat. You see a sub, drop a bomb on it. You've enough power for that.'

But Clive would have disliked Goose Bay even if he'd had his old Douglas Dauntless dive-bomber to fly. Not only was it cold, it lacked women. The wingco's wife was here with him, but she could have stepped straight out of an aspirin bottle without wriggling her hips. The only other females were Eskimos, which was all any man could ask for as long as he only wanted blubber oil and a lot of weight.

And the sea was like jumping into a tub filled with ice cubes. The scenery was great, he supposed, but it was cold, impersonal and depressing. Almost all summer long there had been persistent fog, penetrating the warmest garment to chill the bones, and also making it just about impossible to fly any worthwhile patrols, or to teach green pilots how to conduct themselves in combat. But most annoying of all, this was the world of the false alarm. He didn't doubt the alarms were real enough. Maybe some guy on radar watch did pick up an unidentified blip and start the bells jangling; that was his job. But the blip never seemed to have substance. That hadn't been anything more than a minor irritation until last Friday. He had even welcomed the jangling bells: the best possible training was the real thing, he knew, even if there is nothing on the end of it. He was here to teach his pilots how to get airborne in seconds, how to fly in formation where they had no idea where the other guy's wingtip was, how to maintain radio silence – close to impossible – and how to get back to base before their fuel ran out.

They were actually a great bunch of guys, he thought. They dreamed of high adventure and one day sinking *Tirpitz* as the giant battleship attempted to break out into the Atlantic. The wingco had apparently walked straight off the set of *The Dawn Patrol*, big moustache and all, only instead of flying Sopwith Camels he had flown Spitfires all through 1940, and wound up with a chestful of ribbons and a gammy leg. The young airmen worshipped him. But they rated their new flight commander a good second, even if he was a Yank and not a Canuck. He had been at Pearl, and then at Midway. He was the man they hoped to follow into blazing action, one day.

Friday was the first time he had had a furlough messed up because of a false alarm. 'God-*damn!*' he said again, and lit a cigar.

'She'll be there next time,' suggested Abe Bostwick, his deputy. Abe was from Georgia, and spoke slowly. Like Clive, he had been seconded to teach the Canucks what combat flying was all about, because he too had seen too much action; he'd been over the Coral Sea. They had to be friends, because they were the only two Americans on the base. But that didn't mean they had to agree on everything.

'She'll be there, shit,' Clive remarked disagreeably. Jennie Rhodes: all of that patrician beauty and self-confidence and poise and sheer woman . . . stood up in New York, all on her lonesome, while he was sitting on his ass here in the mist, waiting for some call that never came. 'God-*damn!*' he growled. 'Fucking Brits,' he remarked. 'They got nothing else to do but get excited? Fucking Brits.'

'Squadron alert,' came over the loudspeaker. /Squadron alert!'

Clive sat up, stubbed out his cigar and ran for the radio room, Abe Bostwick at his heels, while around him there came a tremendous hubbub of excitement as the message penetrated all the various stand-down activities.

'Ah, Commander.' The wing commander was already there. 'Hope springs eternal, eh?'

Clive had no idea what he was talking about, 'What's up?'

'Reykjavik is reporting an unidentified vessel in position sixty-five degrees twenty-eight minutes north, twenty-three degrees eighteen minutes west.'

Clive hurried to the huge wall map. 'There!' he said. 'Just west of Iceland. Has to be a Kraut.'

'Or a Swede,' Bostwick suggested.

'What's a Swede doing in the Denmark Strait. She'd come through by the Faroes.'

'Anyway, thirteen hundred miles is a bit far for us,' Bostwick commented.

'I'm afraid Lieutenant-Commander Bostwick is probably right on both counts,' the wingco said. 'She can't ever be our pigeon. Iceland Control is looking into it, and she'll either be stopped up there, or she'll be given a clean bill of health.'

'Okay, sir,' Clive agreed. 'So she gets a clean bill of health. But let's pretend she's a raider. Let's get the boys working, have them in here for a briefing.' He made rapid mental calculations. If she kept coming down the strait, she'd be within range in about four hundred miles from her present position. She would probably make about sixteen knots. Just over twenty-four hours. 'I'd like to scramble at dawn tomorrow, sir, and see if we can find her. Just an exercise.'

The wingco stroked his moustache. 'I suppose that might be useful. But, Commander, if she is a peaceful neutral, I want no buzzing.'

'Just an exercise,' Clive promised, knowing that if he didn't get airborne soon, but instead stayed here thinking about Jennie, he'd go stark raving mad and fuck the damned man's wife, aspirins and all.

Sub-Lieutenant Packe stood to attention. 'I'm afraid it looks like another false alarm, sir,' he said.

Lieutenant-Commander Rodney Bowen took the slip of paper. 'TARGET IDENTIFIED SWEDISH LINER *FREYA* STOP CHECKS PROCEEDING BUT NO FURTHER ACTION REQUIRED STOP REYKJAVIK CONTROL'.

'That makes sense,' Bowen commented. 'I think we can stand down the alert. Mr Winder, pipe the hands to breakfast.'

'Aye, aye, sir,' Winder acknowledged.

Bowen stared out of the bridge windows at the heaving grey seas through which *Erebus* was slowly ploughing her way. He thought that the southern exit of the Denmark Strait must be the most dismal spot on earth. He could thank God that in three days' time his ship would be turning her bows south for a refit in Plymouth, and that he personally would not be returning here on so small a ship.

The next three days would be his last in command of the destroyer. He regarded this prospect with a mixture of anticipation and regret. He was going to the cruiser *Bombast*, a ship possessing several times the size, strength and sea-going qualities of *Erebus*. He was also getting a fourth stripe, and moving into the higher echelons of naval society.

So, all ambitions were falling into place. Why, if this war lasted long enough, he might even wind up with a flag. That would so please Harriet. Flag rank carried all manner of additional possibilities such as knighthoods, if one happened to be in the right place at the right time. Rear-Admiral Sir Rodney and Lady Bowen. Nice.

But against the exhilaration of taking another step up the ladder, and of commanding a ship which actually could fight, would be the wrench of leaving *Erebus*, and Winder and Packe and the chief and all the men with whom he had shared every experience of the last year. *Bombast* was in full commission, and he would be stepping on board a fully functional ship, with a doubtless idiosyncratic crew. Well, they would have to get used to his own idiosyncrasies pretty damn quick, he thought.

'I'm going to turn in for a while,' he told Winder. He'd been up all night, because one never knew with unidentified ships in these waters. It could even have been *Atlas*, out once more. How he wished it could have been. When he left his chair and went down to his day cabin, he sat at his desk for a moment, then thrust out his hand and pulled down his reference book from the shelf, flicked the pages and found *Freya*. Sixteen thousand tons, five hundred feet overall length . . . she was almost a twin of *Atlas*. But she had been identified as *Freya*. So why did he suddenly feel uneasy?

He picked up the phone to the bridge. 'Anything on radar?'

'No, sir.'

'Visibility?'

'One and a half miles and closing, sir.'

Under two miles was officially classified as poor. Under a thousand yards was officially classified as fog. But what difference did it make? He would get a blip

214

on radar which would certainly be *Freya* before she was past him, but there was nothing he could do about it save call on her to stop for another inspection. That would be harrassment, as she had already been checked. It was better to forget about her and think about *Bombast*, with her eight six-inch guns, and her adequate armour, certainly when opposed to an AMC. If he *could* come across *Atlas* at some time this winter, with *Bombast* under his feet . . . but he knew how dangerous it was to make a fetish of a single ship, a single opponent. *Atlas* was nothing more than a pin-prick against the Allied war effort, because there was something very, very big in the offing. He knew this, even if he had no idea what it was; he had been informed that the day he stepped ashore from *Erebus* for the last time he was required to step on board *Bombast* for the first time – and stay there. There was no leave available, and he had to be at sea again in a week, as every ship in the Royal Navy, and in the American Navy, had to be at sea and on station by the beginning of October. Something very big.

The buzzer sounded. 'Captain,' Bowen said.

'Bridge here, sir. There is a target on radar, bearing thirty-five miles, approaching from the north at an estimated sixteen knots.'

'Thank you,' Bowen said. He put on his cap and went up the ladder. He looked into the screen for a few moments, then out at the morning. Visibility was now certainly less than a mile. Obviously there was a sun up there, because the mist had turned a dull yellow. But the colour combined with the glare it created only made seeing harder than ever.

'Raise her on radio, Mr Packe,' Bowen commanded. 'Ask her to identify herself.'

'Aye, aye, sir. Will we stop her?'

'Not if she's *Freya*, Mr Packe, and she can hardly be

215

anyone else. All we need is identification.' He returned to his cabin.

Freya replied correctly, and the British sailors watched the blip moving steadily across their radar screen. Bowen had an early lunch and retired to his bunk for an hour. He was dreaming of *Bombast* when he was awakened by the buzzer. 'Captain,' he said drowsily.

'Urgent message to all ships patrolling the Denmark Strait, sir.' Sub-Lieutenant Packe's voice was so excited his words were running into each other.

'Yes?'

'*Freya* reported still alongside in Gothenburg.'

Bowen sat up. 'Say that again.'

He heard Packe inhale. 'The Swedish liner *Freya* has been reported by a British agent to be still alongside in Gothenburg, sir. She is loading, and is not expected to depart until midnight. Reykjavik says contact is to be regained with the ship previously identified as *Freya*.'

Contact to be regained, he thought. 'I'm coming up.' He dragged on his clothes and ran to the bridge, still buttoning his jacket. 'Where is she?'

'She went off the radar screen three hours ago, sir.'

Forty-eight miles, at least, beyond radar range, he reckoned. Probably something like eighty miles away by now. She was through the patrols, and had the whole damned Atlantic in which to hide.

'Message from Goose Bay, sir,' said the radio operator. 'They are putting up that flight of Buccaneers again.'

'Oh, magnificent,' Bowen said sarcastically, staring into the murk. The rookie pilots had been up at dawn, filling the air with excited chatter despite repeated orders from their commander to maintain radio silence. Now they were coming rushing out again to take on someone like Hjalmar Koenig. 'What is the ceiling?'

'Estimated half a mile surface visibility, sir,' Winder said. 'Ceiling maybe four hundred feet.'

They'd never even see him, Bowen thought, and stared at the compass. *Atlas*, or whoever it was, could be steaming in any one of twenty odd directions. She was through, and she would know it. Due to poor intelligence, and a haphazard inspection by some US Navy lieutenant, junior grade. Now he was left trying to find a needle in an ocean. 'Alter course one-eight-zero,' he said.

'One-eight-zero,' the helmsman repeated, and the ship made an abrupt turn to port.

'Sir?' Winder asked.

'What the hell?' Bowen said. 'Due south is as good as anything. She could be zigzagging. She might just drift on to the radar screen. We'll make due south at full speed for six hours.'

'Jesus,' grumbled Clive Wharton, peering into the solid grey surrounding his aircraft. 'Have you got a fix on the target?'

'There isn't one, sir,' replied Lieutenant 'Happy' Smith, his navigator. 'Seems a British destroyer had her on radar, but has lost her.'

'God-damned Brits,' Clive commented.

She had previously been boarded and passed by a US ship,' Smith ventured. He was a Canadian and was determined to remain neutral in the coming recriminations. 'There's fifteen minutes of patrolling fuel left, sir,' he added. He was known as Happy because of his disposition, but he was also a competent navigator, which was why Clive had chosen him.

Clive glanced at the fuel gauge and switched on the VHF. Radio silence was a waste of time now. 'Red Leader to pack,' he said. 'Forget it. Home to base.' And that, he thought, was two wasted patrols in one day. The story of his God-damned life.

'Say, Clive,' Abe Bostwick protested. 'He could just be down there.'

'When I say home to base I God-damned well mean home to base,' Clive snapped.

'Okay, skipper,' Bostwick acknowledged.

'Course will be three-zero-seven, sir,' Smith said.

'Three-zero-seven . . . who the hell is that?' His earphones were crackling.

'Red Leader, this is His Majesty's Ship *Erebus*. Do you read me?'

'*Erebus*, Red Leader, I read you loud and clear. Say, where are you guys?'

'Our position is sixty-two degrees fourteen minutes north latitude, twenty-seven degrees nine minutes west longitude.'

'I read that, *Erebus*,' Clive said, glancing at the slip of paper Smith had thrust forward. 'We're sixty miles to your south. You got anything on radar?'

'Negative. Can you see anything where you are?'

'In this f'ing soup? What's your vis?'

'Under half a mile.'

'Yeah. Well, I'm sending my boys home. We don't have enough gas to hang around here. Good hunting. Christ, what the shits is that?'

'That is blue sky, sir,' Smith said.

'Say again, please, Red Leader,' *Erebus* requested. 'I didn't read that.'

'Ten minutes,' Happy observed.

'I'm gonna take a look anyway. We may never see such a thing again.' Clive swung the machine into the gap in the clouds and looked down seven thousand feet at choppy blue seas. 'Well, God give me strength.'

'You reckon that's her?' Happy asked, also staring down at the large white ship immediately beneath them.

'I aim to find out. *Erebus*, Goose Bay Red Leader.'

'Come in, Goose Bay Red Leader.'

'We have an unidentified vessel on visual,' Clive said. 'We're going to take a look at her.'

'Position please.'

'Give him the coordinates,' Clive told Happy, concentrating on the dive. The Buccaneer dropped from the sky almost to wave level, and he stared at the crew and passengers lining the ship's rails to wave at him, at the red ensign standing proud away from her stern. 'Fucking hell,' he commented, and pulled his aircraft into a climb again.

'Have you identified the vessel?' *Erebus* asked.

'*Alcoa Trader* out of Liverpool. I'm going home,' Clive said in disgust.

'Red Leader, *Erebus*. We would like you to take another look.'

'Seven minutes,' Happy droned.

'What the hell,' Clive said. 'I saw the name.'

'Name boards can be changed,' said a new voice. 'Red Leader, this is the captain of *Erebus* speaking. We have strong reasons for believing *Alcoa Trader* may be a German AMC. Can you hold her until we get there? We should catch her up in two hours.'

'Two hours,' Clive muttered. 'What's our maximum capacity, Happy?'

'A possible four hours, sir,' Happy replied. 'And we are four hours from base.'

'Red Leader.' The voice was faint, but it belonged to Abe Bostwick. 'You need assistance?'

'Where are you?'

'West of Greenland.'

There was no way any of the squadron could come back now without risking running out of gas. 'Keep going,' Clive said. 'We'll catch you up. Happy, suppose we hang about for two hours, where could we make after that?'

'Well . . . Greenland, I guess.'

'Can't be worse than Goose Bay.' He put the machine

219

into a steep dive and screamed down at the ship again. This time he aimed straight for it, as though about to strafe it, and certainly caused a commotion on deck. Clive kept going until he was just astern of the ship, then pulled up again. 'I think we may have something here, *Erebus*,' he said.

'Skipper.' Happy's voice was unhappy. 'If that ship is the *Alcoa Trader* . . .'

'She isn't,' Clive told him. 'She has VHF and she has to be listening to our chat. But she ain't said a word. Not even a "get away, you buggers". Now, why do you reckon that is?' He swung the plane again, banking steeply as he looked down at the ship. 'You see what I see, Happy?'

On the aftercasle of the ship a segment of deck was slowly rotating to uncover an anti-aircraft gun.

'Holy *cow*,' Happy commented.

'*Erebus*, Red Leader,' Clive said. 'We have your man.'

'Hold him,' *Erebus* replied.

'You guys think we have a long rope up here?'

There was a flash of light from the raider's after-deck, and a puff of black smoke appeared close to the aircraft.

'Well, that's it,' Happy said, watching the fuel gauge. 'It's Greenland or the fish.'

'We'll have one Nazi raider for starters,' Clive growled. 'There's only one way we're gonna hold on to this guy. Get your sights ready.'

Happy did not reply. Clive remembered that his navigator had never seen action before; taking on a well-armed warship single-handed was one hell of a way to begin.

The next shot from *Atlas* came even closer, as Clive was lining himself up. Now he could see men uncovering a battery of Bofors guns.

'Red Leader, *Erebus*. Please report your situation.'

'I am under fire,' Clive replied.

'Under fire?' The man seemed surprised.

'Sure. What did you expect? I am about to carry out a bombing run.'

'Any time, skipper.' The tremor had left Happy's voice.

'So here goes nothing.' He put the machine down, but this time into a shallower dive. He was only carrying hundred-pound bombs today, although he had two of them. But he still had to be accurate.

There was a violent explosion, and the Buccaneer trembled and was momentarily enveloped in black smoke.

'Ain't we kind of low, skipper?' Happy asked.

'I don't mean to miss. Watch your sights.'

He was immediately astern of the raider now, and as he had anticipated, she altered course violently to port, leaving a huge curving swathe of white wake. But Clive had been ready either way, and swung the plane to match the new course, roaring up to the stern of the ship at a height of a thousand feet. Now he could see the pinpoints of light as the Bofors opened fire, and he was again buffeted from left to right.

'Oh, Jesus,' Happy remarked.

'Concentrate,' Clive told him, pulling the nose up.

'Bombs gone,' Happy gasped.

As he spoke, the machine was picked up and tossed upside down, leaving them hanging in their belts. Then it rolled over and came out right side up. 'What the hell is all of that smoke?' Clive demanded.

'Us,' Happy told him.

'Oh, shit,' Clive commented. 'You hurt?'

'Some.'

'Well, cold water stops bleeding, so they say.' Clive twisted to look over his shoulder, but Happy's face was just a blur behind him. A smoke-shrouded blur. Time was running out. Then he looked down at the ship. 'Holy Christ!' he remarked.

Both bombs must have struck, one on the bridge

itself, the other just aft, and penetrated either a fuel or munitions store. The raider was turning round in aimless circles, smoke billowing high into the air.

'Red Leader, *Erebus*. Report your situation.'

'*Erebus*, Red Leader. I am about to ditch with one wounded crewman. Oh, by the way, your boy's in trouble too. But for Christ's sake hurry.'

'We're on our way,' *Erebus* replied. 'Well *done*, Red Leader.'

'Say, Happy,' Clive inquired. 'You with me?'

'Does cold water kill pain too?' Happy asked.

'Every time. Can you jump?'

'Aye aye, skipper.'

'Then it's time to go.' He had levelled out at two thousand feet, but the starboard engine was dead, and there were flames coming from the port engine as well. Thank God he'd got rid of those bombs, he thought. He looked over his shoulder again as the machine lurched and saw the parachute begin to billow. Only then did he wonder if Happy's Mae West was functioning, or if it had been torn up by shell fragments. He swung the machine back, but was blinded by smoke, which blew across his face and made him choke. Fucking hell, he thought, this was the first time he'd ever been shot down. He pushed his cover back, released his belts and rolled out, looking right and left as he plunged through the air; Happy's chute was some distance away. 'Hold on, boy,' he said. 'I'm on my way.'

'There, sir.' Winder lowered his binoculars and pointed. They had had the blip on radar for some time now, but it had been indistinct and inclined to dwindle. Now, looking at the smoke, Bowen could understand why: the raider was ablaze from stem to stern, and was very low in the water. She had clearly been abandoned.

'Boarding nets down,' he commanded. 'But I want those Yanks before *anyone*.'

222

'There's a boat, sir,' Sub-Lieutenant Packe stared through his binoculars.

'Put two of our own down, Mr Winder.'

'Here, sir?' This was submarine territory and, stopped, the destroyer was a sitting duck.

'I want those airmen, Mr Winder,' Bowen repeated. And I want Hjalmar Koenig too, he thought. He no longer had any doubts as to the identity of the sinking ship.

'Aye aye, sir.' Winder gave the necessary orders.

Men were waving from the first lifeboat; there was another astern, also crammed with men. *Erebus* reduced speed as she came up to them, while her own two diesel pinnaces were swung out. The destroyer lost way, and Bowen picked up the speaking trumpet and went on to the bridge wing as the noise of the engines died and *Erebus* began to roll in the long, low Atlantic swell. 'What was the name of your ship?' he called.

There was some hesitation. But the Germans realised that they could find themselves in serious trouble if they persisted in their attempt at subterfuge, and were caught out. 'The armed merchant cruiser *Atlas*,' came the answering call.

'We've got the blighter,' Packe shouted.

'*We* didn't, sub,' Bowen pointed out. Was he disappointed? he wondered. In a sense. But this was a team effort, and the important thing was that *Atlas* had been got. 'Who is your senior officer?' he shouted.

'I am,' came the reply. 'I am the ship's doctor.'

'Come alongside. Have you wounded men?'

'Many,' Dr Schenck told him.

'We'll cope. Have you seen the American airmen?'

'We have them here,' Schenck said. 'One of them is wounded too.'

'We'll cope,' Bowen repeated. 'Mr Winder, you can swing those boats in. Let's get these men on board and get ourselves under way.'

*

223

He waited on the bridge for Schenck to be brought up. The German clicked his heels. 'Otto Schenck.'

'Rod Bowen. You were unlucky.'

'The break in the clouds,' Schenck agreed. 'The fortunes of war. But the Americans were very bold.'

'Yes,' Bowen said. 'Your captain?'

'Went down with the ship. He was a brave man.'

'Agreed. I am sorry. He and I were old adversaries.'

'*Erebus*,' Schenck said. 'You were unlucky on the two previous occasions. But luck always turns, for most of us. Not for Hjalmar, at least personally. Captain Koenig was not on board, Herr Captain.'

'Eh?'

'He has been transferred to other duties. Our commander was Hans Wiedermayer. He had previously been first officer, so you may regard him as an old adversary as well.'

'Well, damn it,' Bowen commented. But hadn't he known all the time that Koenig hadn't been on board? Koenig would never have so lost his head as to open fire as long as there was any chance of getting away with his deception.

'However, it is sad,' Schenck said. 'Captain Koenig's son was on board. Lieutenant Kurt Koenig.'

'And he went down with the ship too?'

Schenck nodded. 'I have known that boy for years. As I have known his father for years.'

'I am truly sorry, Dr Schenck. Now, I know you'll want to get back to your men.'

Schenck saluted, went to the ladder, then paused. 'Have I permission to ask a question, Herr Captain?'

'Certainly.'

'We were listening to your radio transmissions. How could you be so sure we were not the *Alcoa Trader*, when you could not even see us?'

'In these waters, Herr Doctor, a British ship would have been in convoy.'

'Ah,' Schenck said. 'An elementary error.' He sighed. 'A mistake Hjalmar would not have made.'

'No, I don't think he would,' Bowen agreed.

'I would like, if I may, to make a comment on the action, Herr Captain. The American pilot: I would like to suggest that you recommend him for exceptional gallantry.'

'Explain.'

'He came in very low to make sure of hitting us. That itself was a bold act. He hit us, we hit him, and he went in. We fought the fire for an hour before abandoning ship, so only then did we have the opportunity to pick up him and his navigator. The navigator was unconscious and wounded; his life-jacket had been punctured and was useless. For that hour the pilot had held the other man's head clear of the extremely cold water. He is a very brave man, Herr Captain. A caring man.'

'I'd like you to sign an entry in the Log,' Bowen said. 'This evening, when you dine with me, Dr Schenck.'

It felt odd to be knocking on the door of his own cabin.

'Yeah?'

The two men gazed at each other. Bowen had told the orderly to give the pilot whatever he wanted, but obviously his clothes would hardly fit this bear of a man; Wharton still wore a blanket. And still shivered, although the bottle of brandy on the desk was half empty.

'Red Leader, I presume,' Bowen said.

Clive looked at the Englishman's insignia. 'Snap.' He grinned. 'You Limeys are civilised, Commander. On board one of our ships I'd have been drinking medicine.'

'It's not the done thing, to indulge at sea,' Bowen

agreed. 'But it's nice to know it's there.' He held out his hand. 'Rod Bowen.'

'Clive Wharton. We met on the air. How's my boy?'

'He's going to be all right.'

'Maybe I'll save some of this stuff for him.'

'There's another bottle.'

'Then maybe you'll join me, Commander.'

Bowen hesitated, then nodded. 'A very short one. We should drink a toast, Commander. I would say we have both been hunting *Atlas* for some time.'

'Wrong,' Clive said. 'I'm a new boy at this game. And I owe you guys an apology.'

'For sinking him?'

'For swearing when it seemed a false alarm. That cost me the best weekend of my life, I reckon.'

'I'm sorry about that. But it's odd the way things work out. I've been hunting *Atlas* for more than a year. You come along and sink him first time around.' He raised his glass. 'Anyway, congratulations.'

'You're a good loser.'

Bowen smiled. 'I haven't actually lost yet, Commander. The man I want is *Atlas*'s skipper, Hjalmar Koenig. But he wasn't along this time. So I'll keep looking.'

'Then I'll drink to your future good fortune. Where are you taking us?'

'I'm afraid we have to return to station. But I've called Reykjavik Control, and there'll be a ship out to pick you up. They'll fly you home from Iceland.'

'I've always wanted to see a geyser. You reckon I can make an official report?'

'Of course.'

'My rough log went with the machine,' Clive explained. 'You know, Commander, Happy Smith was green. All of my boys are green. I reckon Happy had never been under fire before. I also reckon he was hit by just about the second shot those guys put up. But

226

he never said a word, just kept aiming those bombs. That boy has a lot of guts. He has to get a medal.'

'What about yourself?' Bowen asked.

'Me?' Clive grinned. 'For Jesus' sake, Commander, I have a chestful. Whenever I walk in full dress, I lean to my left. Anyway, what's heroic about shooting up an old German tub playing hide-and-seek?'

Bowen gazed at him. 'Maybe not a lot, Commander. But if I have anything to do with it, you're about to overbalance altogether.'

CHAPTER 10

The Arrest

'Oh,' Jennie Rhodes cried. 'Isn't that just marvellous!'

Heads turned. Commander Rhodes was not given to showing emotion. 'You know this guy, ma'am?' asked Signalman Brown. Fortunately, Signalman Brown had a poor memory for names.

'We've met,' Jennie said, and hurried in to the admiral. 'They've got *Atlas*.'

The admiral raised his head. 'No kidding?'

'She's at the bottom, sir, Clive Wharton did it.'

'Wharton? Didn't he get a Cross for Pearl? You mean that guy Koenig is dead?'

'Koenig wasn't on board, sir.'

'He wasn't, eh?' The admiral frowned.

'But Clive . . . Commander Wharton, sir . . .'

'He's dead, eh?'

Of course he isn't, you old goat, she wanted to shout. 'The captain of the destroyer which picked him up . . .'

'You mean he went in? Jesus Christ, what this war is costing us in dumb pilots . . .'

Jennie took a long breath. 'The destroyer captain submitted a report, sir. And Commander Wharton has been recommended for the Medal of Honor.' So stuff that up your ass and sit on it, she thought.

'For sinking a Kraut AMC?'

'Single-handed, sir. And then for saving the life of his wounded navigator. May I put a call through to Goose Bay, sir? To congratulate him?'

'He a friend of yours?'

'In a manner of speaking.'

'Well, you can't call him, Jennie. Not until after the newspapers get hold of the story, or he may just start wondering where *you* got hold of it. Right?'

Jennie's shoulders sagged in disappointment. But the old goat was right, as usual. She'd been behaving like a schoolgirl. Why? Because Clive was getting another medal to add to his chestful, and this was the big one? She didn't think so. Because *Atlas* had been sunk? She wasn't that bloodthirsty. Or because he had survived a dangerous mission? Clive Wharton, big and loud, domineering and egotistical – not her sort of man. Yet her heart was pounding like a base drum. 'Yes, sir,' she said, and saluted.

The admiral let her get as far as the door, then he said, 'But this hero didn't get Koenig. You sent that chaser off to Stockholm?'

'Yes, sir,' Jennie said, and left the office. She wondered if anyone would ever think of giving Johnnie Anderson the Congressional Medal of Honor, for services above and beyond the call of duty.

Lieutenant Helga Staffel unlocked the door of her apartment, entered, closed the door behind herself and gave John a bright smile. She was no longer apprehensive of this meeting; it had been too long delayed. 'Where have you been?' she asked.

'Wilhelmshaven. Have you heard the news?'

'About *Atlas*? Koenig must be glad he wasn't still in command.'

'His son was on board.'

Helga took off her jacket, went to the cupboard, poured herself two fingers of vodka and added a splash of tonic water. 'The fortunes of war.'

'I doubt Hjalmar looks on it that way. I passed by

229

Kiel on my way here, to give him my condolences . . . and he refused to see me.'

'He'll get over it.' She sat beside him on the settee. 'You went away for a week, without even a note.'

'I didn't get a note from you last weekend, either, honey doll. And I was working. Kurt Koenig wasn't the only man to have gone with the ship, you know. There were families to be interviewed . . . everyone down there is a trifle unhappy.'

'It took you a week to discover that?'

'It took me a week to get the human-interest stories, yes. Don't tell me you missed me? What price last weekend?'

'I too was working,' she said. 'For you.'

'I'm glad to hear it. Interesting work?'

Suddenly she was angry. 'You are a God-damned fucking bastard,' she remarked. 'I spent the weekend in bed with Keiko, and you don't care.'

'You must tell me about it.'

'Oh, sure, I'll tell you about it. You ever had a girl sitting in your lap? You know how you go in and in, and the girl feels you coming in, until she can just about fee1 you in her mouth. Jesus.'

'Is this your way of telling me that our engagement is off?'

Helga gazed at him for several seconds, then got up and went to the bar for a refill. 'I would prefer it not to be.' She turned. 'Do you wish it to be?'

Being truly angry with her was of course impossible, at least until he had found out what she had discovered – if she had discovered anything. Yet he had to *be* angry, up to a point. The incredible thing was that he was actually jealous. 'You going to see him again?'

Helga shrugged. 'Would you object?'

'As a man? Or as your fiancé?'

'That has to be your decision,' Helga said.

John appeared to consider the matter, and then

allowed his body to sag with the despair of a hopeless lover. 'If it's what you want.'

'But it would make you angry? It shouldn't.' Helga smiled. 'Although I'm glad it does. Jan . . .' She came back across the room, put down the drink, sat beside him and held his hands. 'Keiko is like nothing I ever even suspected existed. I just have to go through with it. If I didn't, I'd never forgive myself. Please try to understand. But it won't be for long. In another couple of months he's going to be gone. That's what makes it all so irresistible, I suppose.'

John frowned at her. 'You mean he's going back to Japan? He'll have finished training German pilots in carrier techniques?'

'No. I mean that he is going to die.'

John's frown deepened. When he had got to Wilhelmshaven, there had been a message from Stockholm waiting for him, a message which had come so close to breaking his code – nothing in it had made sense, save for the selected words – that his hair had nearly turned white. And the message had apparently originated in Washington. Washington was sure there was a link between Keiko Hatatsune and Hjalmar Koenig and *Graf Zeppelin*, and wanted to know in a hurry. Well, he had felt that too. But what she was saying made nonsense of that probability. 'You mean he's got some kind of incurable disease?'

'I mean he's going on a mission from which he won't return.'

'A mission connected with Koenig?'

'I don't think so. I've discovered *Graf Zeppelin* is in Trondheim in Norway. But . . . I'm not sure Keiko has anything to do with her, either. He's here to fly Junkers 88s.'

John scratched his head. 'He's going to train German pilots to fly land-based bombers? That's nonsense.'

Helga shrugged. 'I don't think he was lying.'

'So what's Koenig doing now?'

'He has a desk job at the Germaniawerft Yard,' Helga said. 'To do with design. It's a job he doesn't like very much. He asked me to use my influence with Doenitz to get him a posting back at sea.'

John felt he was standing in the middle of a very thick fog, with absolutely no point of reference from which he could possibly obtain a direction in which to travel. But he was certain Helga was telling him the absolute truth, as she saw it. 'So when are you seeing Keiko again?'

'I don't know. He said he would come whenever he could.'

'Down from wherever it is he is teaching German pilots to fly a machine they have been brought up on.'

'Don't ask me to explain it.'

'I want you to ask your friend Keiko to explain it when next you meet. Which had better be soon.'

She pouted. 'Anyone would think you were a spy.'

'All newspapermen are spies,' John told her. 'I have to get my facts straight. What do you wish to happen when this Keiko character pushes off and commits hara-kiri or whatever it is he's planning?'

Another shrug. 'I was hoping well . . . that we could be friends again.'

'You mean you wish to marry me, after you have had your fill of Keiko.'

'There is no need to put it like that, but if you insist, yes. I would like to marry you when Keiko is gone. I love you. I really do.'

'But you also love Keiko.'

'He just turns me on. I've tried to explain. It's like nothing I've ever known before. And where's the harm in it, if he's going to die, anyway?'

He squeezed her fingers. 'I'll bet you don't ever go to confession, honey doll. But if that's what you really want, I guess I'll go along with it.'

'Oh, Jan, that would be just marvellous.'

'I love you, too.'

She kissed him, as slowly and adoringly as she could manage. 'Then make love to me now.'

He shook his head. 'I don't think I'm *that* broad-minded. I think I'll go back to Wilhelmshaven, and get on with some work.'

'Oh, Jan!'

'It has to be done. I'll be back in town in a couple of days, and I'll give you a ring. But if you don't mind, we won't go down to Munich to see your papa until Keiko has pushed off.'

'But you are going to come back?'

'I said I would. When you and Keiko have sorted yourselves out. But Helga, I really want to know what he's doing, and what Hjalmar is doing. That's all I'm asking in return for letting you enjoy yourself. I don't think it's very much, when you consider what I'm giving.'

'Of course it isn't,' she said, too pleased and relieved to quibble. 'I'll find out, Jan, I promise.'

'And the moment you do, you'll give me a ring?'

'Of course, my darling,' she said. 'I am going to be so happy married to you, Jan. You are so understanding.'

If Helga was representative of German morality as prac-tised by the Nazis, then it was a truly frightening world, John thought.

He stared out of the train window as it rumbled across the Lüneburger Heath. Think, concentrate, he told himself. Twenty pilots and twenty navigators, all serving officers in the Imperial Japanese Navy, had been smuggled round the world to reach Germany. Officially they had come to train German pilots in the techniques of flying from an aircraft-carrier. That was an entirely reasonable proposition. Germany had but one aircraft-carrier, therefore the training had to be done from that carrier. The commander of the Japanese, Hatatsune, not only knew the name of Hjalmar Koenig, but was found lunching with him at the officers' club in Kiel, when he should have been in Norway with his men: therefore they must have had a reason for meeting. It was a logical deduction that Koenig had been appointed to command *Graf Zeppelin*, the ship from which the Japanese would be operating.

Except for the fact that, in that case, Koenig should also have been in Trondheim. And that Keiko had told Helga he was to fly Junkers 88s. One just did not take off in a Junkers 88 from the deck of a carrier. Or at least, if it could be done, one certainly could not land it again.

But Keiko had also told Helga that he was soon to die – presumably for the very reason that he could not land again. So he had to be about to undertake a mission which required the use of a big bomber, flown from a carrier, and therefore certain to be lost. He and all his forty air crew. But all Germany's enemies, save of course for the United States, were within range of land-based bombers. So where could there be a target which required taking off in a land-based bomber from the flight-deck of a carrier – a feat which had only once before been attempted in all naval history?

John sat up, realised the two other occupants of the compartment were staring at him, and leaned back again, closing his eyes as if in sleep. It had been obvious for some time, and he hadn't seen it – because he couldn't accept the mentality that would risk so much? Hadn't Doolittle's pilots known what they were risking? It was all there . . . if only he could reconcile Koenig and *Graf Zeppelin*.

He realised he was simply starting from the wrong end of the puzzle. He was taking all the facts he had obtained, and trying to make Washington's suspicions fit those facts – and getting nowhere. Whereas what he had to do was take the suspicions, and make the facts fit *them*. So, Hatatsune was in Germany to carry out a suicide mission, which would be commanded by Koenig, and which could only be carried out by experienced carrier pilots; and it involved the use of land-based bombers because they could carry a much heavier bomb load than any navy plane and would also have a longer range. The Germans were giving the mission their best available skipper . . . but not, apparently, their only aircraft-carrier, because they knew it might not get back. Therefore there had to be another ship involved, and if Koenig was sitting at a desk in the Germaniawerft yard in Kiel, the other ship had to be behind the high walls and tight security at that yard – and the ship had to be another aircraft-carrier!

The whole scenario had suddenly dropped into his lap; save for the actual target – and the date. Helga would get him those, but he couldn't afford to wait to send the alarm.

But he couldn't convey a message of this nature by using his code. He was going to have to stick his neck out.

The realisation came as a considerable shock. Of course he had felt he was sticking his neck out when he first set foot in Germany. But his cover had been so immaculate there hadn't really been any danger of detection. And he had been careful. Now he had to abandon that caution. He had been given an emergency contact, should he ever need it, who could transmit messages direct to London, and thence Washington. The contact apparently used a code of his own which had not been broken by the Germans. He had to believe that.

He thought how much safer it would be to repeat he had found nothing relating visitors to Koenig or carrier. And that was true, if he just accepted the facts he possessed, and determined to wait for Helga to amplify them.

He wondered if he was afraid. It was not a problem he had considered before. He had always supposed he would have to conquer fear when first he faced an enemy in the air but that probability had become increasingly remote. Time and again he had been told that as long as he kept his head and his nerve, and thus maintained his cover, even detection by the Gestapo could only mean deportation to Sweden: the State Department's certainty that, no matter what happened, Sweden would maintain its traditional neutrality had caused him to be selected for this job in the first place, and sent him here as a Swedish newspaper reporter rather than an American naval attaché, even in the days when the possibility of war between America and Germany had seemed an absurdity. Nothing since then had changed, for him. There was no reason for fear.

Only for speedy action. And the train was slowing. John Anderson got up, swept his case from the rack, opened the door and stepped on to the rainswept platform, to wait for the next eastbound train.

Wilhelm Mundt was an antiquarian bookseller, and looked the part. His shoulders were hunched, and his hair receding. He peered out from behind horn-rimmed spectacles, face expressionless, manner subservient. 'May I be of assistance, sir?' he asked.

There was no one else to be seen in the little shop. But John was taking no risks. 'I am seeking a copy of the Gutenberg Bible,' he said. 'In Yiddish.'

Wilhelm Mundt stared at him for several seconds. Then he said, 'That is an unusual request, young sir, in this day and age. One might even say, damnable.'

John grinned at him. 'In that case, a pencil and paper will do.'

'No, sir. Just tell me what you wish to say.'

236

'Tell you? You'll send it immediately?'

'No, it will be sent tonight.'

'Without being written down?'

Mundt smiled; for a moment his face held pride. 'I am here principally because of my memory.'

'There can't be any mistakes,' John told him.

'There will be no mistakes.'

John hesitated, then spoke the message. Mundt listened, nodded and repeated it word for word. But could he suppose the old man would actually remember every word for perhaps several hours . . . ? 'When will it reach Washington?'

'It will be sent to my Swiss contact tonight. I often go from Berlin on the evening train to spend a night with my sister in Potsdam. This is well known to everyone. The message will be sent from her house.'

'Your sister must be a very brave woman,' John observed.

'Or a very desperate one, like myself. Your message will be in London by noon tomorrow. How soon London will relay it to Washington I cannot say. But in view of the time difference, I would expect the Americans to have it by noon, or shortly afterwards.'

'It is very urgent,' John reminded him.

Wilhelm Mundt inclined his head. 'Or you would not have come to me, young man. And now you must buy a book.' He gave another of his secret smiles. 'There is no such thing as a Gutenberg Bible outside of one or two libraries, of course. And certainly not one in Yiddish. But I can sell you a copy of Hakluyt's *Divers Voyages*, in Swedish.'

Jennie Rhodes placed the sheet of paper in front of the admiral. She was jubilant. Johnnie had delivered the goods, despite the hazards. Both the men in her life – and she was now prepared to accept that there were going to be two, when Clive came to town to collect his medal – had scored triumphs. She meant to capitalise on this one.

The admiral leaned back to study the words. 'JAPANESE FORCE COMMANDED KEIKO HATATSUNE TRAINING IN GERMANY TO FLY JUNKERS 88 BOMBERS FROM AIRCRAFT CARRIER STOP IMPROBABLE CARRIER WILL BE *GRAF ZEPPELIN* NOW LYING TRONDHEIM NORWAY STOP CONSIDER PROBABILITY GERMANS POSSESS ANOTHER UNDISCLOSED CARRIER STOP COMMANDER WILL BE KOENIG STOP DESTINATION OF MISSION UNKNOWN BUT STRONGLY SUSPECT TARGET TO BE NORTH AMERICA PROBABLY NEW YORK STOP WILL PROVIDE POSITIVE WHEN POSSIBLE STOP SEVEN TWENTY ONE'.

'Holy Mary Mother of God,' the admiral remarked. 'This came in from Sweden?'

'No, sir. From London via Switzerland. Seven-Twenty-One used the emergency route.'

'Well, he did right, even if he is more bananas than I thought. New York? The man's an idiot.'

'Do you think it's impossible, sir?' Jennie, as usual, found herself beginning to get annoyed.

'Nothing's impossible, Jennie. But apart from being a suicide job, what's the point in dropping a few bombs over New York? That's not going to stop us.'

'The Japanese put a lot of store by face, sir. We bombed Tokyo. They are under a moral obligation to retaliate.'

'Oh, balls to that oriental stuff. Hell, this is as plain as the tits on your chest, Jen. The Krauts know about Torch, and have brought in the Japs to give them a hand.'

'With respect, sir,' Jennie said patiently. 'We know the Japanese flyers left Japan before the end of July. It must have been arranged at least a month earlier. *We*

238

didn't know about Torch, back in June. And they've sent Hatatsune, their number one ace. They wouldn't waste him on something routine.'

'You think Torch is routine, eh? There are times when you have to look facts in the face, Jen. And all the facts we possess indicate that the Germans know about Torch. And they're getting ready to stop it. I have to get over to Admiral King immediately.'

The admiral straightened his tie and buttoned his jacket. Jennie obligingly held out his cap. 'I would like permission to inform Seven-Twenty-One, sir, through Stockholm, that he has done a great job and can now go back to straight ship observation.'

The admiral adjusted his cap. 'I want the date that carrier is going to sea.'

'We know the date, sir, if you are right. Either four or five days before the Torch armada sails. So surely there is no need for Seven-Twenty-One to risk his neck any further.'

The admiral considered a moment, then shrugged. 'I guess you're right. He *has* done a great job, at least of reporting, if not of deducing. Okay, Jennie, congratulate him and tell him to take things easy for a while.' He went to the door. 'Yes, sir. He's done a great job.'

'Colonel Doerner is here to see you, Herr Captain.'

Hjalmar Koenig stood up. Suddenly he was nervous. He had never, to his knowledge, met a Gestapo officer before.

The colonel was a small man hardly taller than Koenig himself, but thin and sharp-featured. He even looked like a policeman, although he was not wearing uniform. On the other hand, he was not wearing a belted raincoat or a slouch hat either, but a well-cut three-piece suit, and he carried a rolled umbrella. 'Heil Hitler!' he said.

'Heil Hitler,' Koenig agreed. 'Sit down, Colonel.'

'Thank you. I wish to begin by offering you my condolences on the death of your son.'

'Thank you, Colonel.' Sufficient time had elapsed for Koenig to be able to say that without tears springing to his eyes. Kurt's death had very nearly been too crushing a blow to be withstood. Now he recognised it as part of Fate's pattern; they would meet again sooner than he had expected. Now, only the mission mattered. 'You have discovered something?' he asked.

'There are straws in the wind,' Doerner said. 'You have heard the news from Africa?'

'I have heard rumours.'

'Unfortunately, there is considerable substance to the rumours,' Doerner remarked. 'It is incredible to me that the British and the Americans could have sent a vast armada across the Atlantic, and landed a vast army in North Africa, without us knowing anything about it until it happened, And without the invasion fleet being sighted by even a single submarine. It is a mixture of incompetence, imbecility, bad luck . . . and probably treachery.'

'Did you come here for a political discussion, Herr Colonel?'

Doerner allowed himself a brief smile. 'I came to discuss your suspicions with you, Herr Captain. But the situation in North Africa may have a bearing on this. It is a reasonable supposition that any enemy agent in our midst would have concluded that your relationship with the Japanese pilots was intended for use against the Torch fleet. But no action whatsoever was taken against the Torch fleet, because apparently no one knew it existed. Therefore the enemy agent will have to think again.'

'You have discovered such an agent?' Koenig's heart gave a curious lurch.

'Perhaps. In my business, one requires a great deal of patience. There are, as I have said, straws in the wind.

For example, the man Anderssen spends most of his time down in Wilhelmshaven and comes to Berlin twice a month – that is, four times in the last two months. When he comes to Berlin he takes Staffel out to dinner, and he afterwards sleeps in a hotel, where previously he lived with Staffel when in Berlin. It is my opinion that this is to enable Staffel to obtain information which is then passed on to him at their meetings.'

'Why do you think this?' Koenig asked.

'I have placed a hidden microphone in Staffel's apartment,' Doerner explained casually. 'The listening position is in the basement of the building, and my men have a recording machine down there.'

'My God! Is that legal?'

Doerner raised his eyebrows. 'I am not concerned with legalities. I am concerned with security, and with the answer to certain questions. The microphone has proved a great value, but it is also limited. The only place it could safely be situated was in Staffel's lounge, and it is therefore difficult to be sure what is said in her bedroom. This is a pity. However, as I say, while Anderssen visits her from time to time, Commander Hatatsune also visits her, from time to time. They also make love.' He gave a little smile. 'There is evidence to indicate that Staffel prefers to make love with Hatatsune than with Anderssen.'

'But no evidence that she is a spy,' Koenig said, with some relief. 'It has now been two months since I voiced my suspicions. Some concrete evidence would have turned up by now, Herr Colonel. It seems that I have wasted your time in unfounded fears.'

'I do not agree with you, Herr Captain. I have been explaining that we are encountering certain difficulties. But we have uncovered certain interesting facts.'

Koenig frowned. 'Such as?'

'Well, the relationship between Anderssen and Staffel is itself, as I have said, interesting. They are engaged to be married, yet she prefers Hatatsune, at least in bed. Anderssen knows this. She also told Anderssen about Hatatsune's visits. He was with her last night, which is why I have come to see you this morning.'

Koenig's frown had deepened. 'What was Anderssen's reaction to being told this?'

'Certainly not the jealous anger one might have expected. Shall I tell you why? Because he does not feel any jealous anger over Staffel.'

'So their ideas of morality and ours do not coincide,' Koenig observed.

'Morality has nothing to do with it. Staffel also told Anderssen that she had learned nothing of value from Hatatsune's visit.'

Koenig stared at him. 'My God!'

'Quite. Anderssen replied. "Well, maybe it doesn't matter now. But I'd still like to know".'

'You must arrest the woman. And Anderssen. My God, I would never have thought it of him.'

'I intend to act in due course,' Doerner told him. 'However, I would prefer not to as yet, providing a further brief delay will not jeopardise your operation in any way. There are things I need to learn. For example, it seems fairly clear that Staffel is attempting to obtain certain information from Hatatsune. You would agree with that?'

'That was my fear from the start, which is why I came to you,' Koenig reminded him.

'Quite. The point is, do you think she will succeed? You know Hatatsune.'

'I would say he is a dedicated man. But who can tell what a man will say in the throes of passion.'

'It is such a pity we could not have the microphone in the bedroom. However, it also seems clear that he has not told her what she wishes, yet. So we can wait a while longer. It is very necessary for us to be sure about Staffel, to have irrefutable proof of her treachery before we arrest her. This is both because of her high connections, and because at this moment a spy scandal connected with your mission might well tell the enemy things he does not yet know. But there are other things I wish to discover, as well. Why is Staffel doing this, for instance?'

'It would appear, to give the information to Anderssen.'

'Why?'

'Well . . .' Koenig frowned.

'You see? We need to find out, first, if Staffel is the spy, and is using Anderssen as her go-between; second, who Anderssen is working for – Sweden or the Allies; and third, if he himself is a spy. We have no evidence of Anderssen ever having done or written anything to the detriment of the Reich. His dispatches to Sweden are carefully studied, his friends and acquaintances have been watched. Whatever Staffel may have told him, I have been able to find no evidence that it has been used for any illicit purpose. There is only one possible inconsistency in anything Anderssen has done over the past two months.'

'Yes?'

'Well, as soon as I had spoken with you, I put a tail on him, of course. He went down to Wilhelmshaven on the Monday after leaving Kiel. This is way back at the beginning of September. The following Saturday he returned to Berlin and visited Staffel. Unfortunately, my people had not yet had the opportunity to enter the apartment and install the microphone, so I do know what was said on that occasion. I do know that Anderssen did not spend the night with her. In fact, he left early, returned to his hotel, and next morning caught the train to Wilhelmshaven. But then he did a very strange thing. Quite without warning, when the train reached Hanover, he got off. My agent was so surprised he did not follow.'

Koenig raised his eyes in disgust.

'Oh, indeed,' Doerner agreed. 'However, my man made amends for his slow-wittedness by leaving the train himself at the next station, and telephoning Berlin. One of my men met the next train in from Hanover, and Anderssen was on it.'

'You mean he doubled back to see Staffel again?'

'He did not go near Staffel. He went to the shop of an antiquarian bookseller named Mundt, made a purchase and went back to Wilhelmshaven the following morning.'

'And this man Mundt?'

'I have put him under surveillance as well. But nothing has turned up. He is an elderly recluse, whose only living relative is an equally elderly sister living outside Potsdam.'

'He could be a relay station,' Koenig suggested.

'Oh, indeed. And there is no doubt that on the evening of Anderssen's visit he went to see his sister in Potsdam. Unfortunately, at that short notice surveillance was not complete, and I do not know if he saw someone along the way. I could have raided both his shop and his sister's house, but I decided against that. When I pull in my net, I hope to have one or two fishes in it.'

'How often has Anderssen been back to see him?'

'That is the strangest thing of all. Anderssen has not been back to see him. It is exactly as if he did decide to return to Berlin that day especially to purchase an old book. That is why I think we must continue the investigation.'

'I am sure you are right. But, Herr Colonel, I must tell you that from my point of view, the situation will cease to be of interest within another fortnight. And frankly, while it would be a most serious matter were the enemy to learn anything of the mission, the vital factor is that they must not learn the *date*. If Staffel has

244

not yet managed to discover this, as I am sure she has not from what you have told me, then she ceases to be important to me. Commander Hatatsune and his men have just about completed their training, and will be returning here at the end of next week. I shall simply forbid Hatatsune to leave Kiel.'

'I would not do that,' Doerner said. 'Staffel may cease to be of importance to you, once you can carry out your mission. As a spy she is certainly of importance to *me*, Herr Captain. I think that should the Commander wish to go down to Berlin and bid farewell to his lady love, he should be allowed to do so.'

'But if it is farewell, she will then be in possession of the sailing date.'

'Of course. But she will not have the opportunity to use it. Because the moment she attempts to impart that information to a third party, I shall arrest her. We will then have positive evidence against her; we will pick up her contact – if it is Anderssen, so much the better – and at the same time we will not endanger your mission at all. You will sail on schedule, and we can keep Staffel and Anderssen, and indeed the whole affair, under wraps until you have completed the mission. We will both have everything we are looking for. No, no, Herr Captain. You will let Commander Hatatsune visit Berlin. We will all benefit.'

John Anderson lay on his hotel bed and smoked a cigarette. He had got in that morning and called Helga immediately – and been told she couldn't see him this evening. Which presumably meant that Hatatsune was there.

He wondered why he kept it up. Washington had seemed entirely satisfied with his information, such as it was, and had told him to go back to ship-spotting and gossip-collecting. He couldn't understand that. But as usual, Washington seemed to be right. It was now 2

December, getting on for three months since he had first been told to find the link between the Japanese and Koenig and a carrier, and Keiko Hatatsune was apparently still giving his men practice at flying Junkers 88s; Koenig was still sitting at his desk in Kiel; and there was no evidence there was any new carrier being readied for sea. John had managed to discover that a ship had certainly been launched at the Germaniawerft yard in early September, and he had even managed to have a look at her from the far side of the harbour. She was definitely going to be a carrier one day. But she was so obviously at least a year away from completion that he reckoned she was hardly worth worrying about in relation to Keiko.

And Washington had said to forget it – obviously because Hatatsune and his men had been linked to an attempt to halt the Torch invasion. But they had not been used for that. And, in fact, there had been no suggestion in the German Press that anything had been known about Torch in advance. The Press projected the official viewpoint that the invasion would amount to very little, even if there were disturbing rumours that Marshal Rommel had suffered a major defeat at the other end of Africa – Rommel had been forced to retreat before and had come storming back a couple of months later. The German people were being encouraged to be more incensed at the "treachery" of their French "allies" in not resisting the Americans to the death, and more excited about the German occupation of Vichy France in retaliation, than in the exploits of an unknown general named Eisenhower.

So, obviously, he realised he had been wrong in supposing that the Japanese were planning to do a Doolittle. His only sensible course was to obey orders and forget about how he had nearly blown his cover to send the information.

The telephone rang. He lifted the receiver. 'Yes?'

'Jan? Helga. Jan, come round and see me. Please.'

It was a strangely subdued-sounding Helga. 'Now?' It was just after midnight.

'Please. I am alone.'

'Give me ten minutes,' he told her, and leapt out of bed. Maybe she had something, after all, he thought. But what the hell could it be?

He wrapped himself in topcoat and scarf, and put on a soft hat. It was very cold outside. He walked, as her apartment wasn't very far, and felt a light, near freezing drizzle settling on his hat and coat. He went up the stairs, knocked, and a moment later was in her arms.

'Jan!' she cried. She wore her crimson dressing gown, and nothing else. He lifted her to the settee and she sat on his lap, without even removing his hat or his damp coat. She didn't even seem to notice. She was weeping.

'What's all this?' he asked.

'He's gone,' she said. 'Gone to die.'

'Who?'

'He came to say goodbye,' she sobbed. 'He told me I had been the most wonderful experience in his life. Then he left to return to Kiel, because he is sailing at midnight.' Another sob.

'Sailing? From Kiel? Tonight?'

'Not this night. But tonight, yes. "I go to my death," he said. Oh, Jan, the way he said it made me feel so proud. "We shall go down in history," he said. "Once more, we shall teach the Americans against whom they are fighting. Seventh December will be a date they will never forget, on either score. Kong will never be forgotten." Then we made love. Oh, Jan . . .'

John pushed his hat back on his head. His brain was doing handsprings. 'He told you he was sailing tonight, to teach the Americans a lesson on 7 December.'

'Yes. Oh, Jan . . .'

For God's sake shut up and let me think, he thought. The first anniversary of Pearl. Kong: what the hell could

Kong stand for? The only Kong he had ever heard of was that movie about the ape . . . who had wound up on top of the Empire State Building, being attacked by fighter planes. 'Holy Jesus!' he muttered. He had been absolutely right all the time, despite Washington's disinterest. And now he had the delivery date. Too close for comfort.

Helga, snuffling into his chest, raised her head. 'What is it?'

That meant the hulk lying off the Germaniawerft yard *had* to be the delivery vessel. Far from being a hulk, she must be ready for sea. He had been completely hoodwinked by Hjalmar Koenig. But for Helga, the mission would have sailed, and struck, in total secrecy.

A suicide mission. But with more than just prestige, or revenge, involved – because if they could do it once, at whatever cost to themselves, there would remain always the nagging fear that they might do it again, on an even larger and more effective scale. That fear would be sufficient for public opinion in America to put pressure on the President, and through him on the chiefs of staff, to keep more men and planes and ships at home than were being sent overseas – in effect, it could cripple the war effort, at the cost of one unfinished ship and a relative handful of men.

'Jan?' Helga was staring at him.

'I have to go out,' he said.

'But Jan! You've only just got here. Jan, I want you to stay. I want you to hold me in your arms.'

He held her wrists. 'Just for an hour. I'll be back, honey doll. For the rest of the night. For all tomorrow, if you wish. I'll be back in an hour.'

'Where are you going?' she asked suspiciously.

'There is someone I have to see. I was just leaving to see him when you called. But I'll cut my visit short.'

'Him?' she snorted. 'You mean *her*. You wouldn't be going to see a man after midnight.'

'It's a man,' he said. 'I swear it on my mother's grave. I'll be back in an hour.'

He closed the door behind him, adjusted his hat and hurried down the corridor. Washington had been right in feeling that Hatatsune's presence in Germany meant something big was on the way, he thought. And they should have been right in assuming it was linked with an effort to stop Torch, had the German intelligence system been up to scratch, and had the German Navy been commanded by anyone with the least tactical sense. But who was to say that, strategically, Hitler wasn't going to be proved right, as he had so often been proved right in the past, strategically. If he wasn't stopped.

He ran down the stairs, opened the street door, then checked as two men emerged from the shadows. 'Herr Anderssen. Police. We would like a word, please.'

John's reaction was immediate and instinctive. He swung his right arm backwards, using the elbow as a fist, into the midriff of the man who stood behind him. The suddenness of the movement took the detective unawares, and he gasped in pain. In almost the same movement, John was kicking, with all the force and accuracy of a man who had had a trial as a place kicker for the navy. His toe crashed into the other man's shin, and he too gasped and fell to his knees. John, twice his size, picked him up by the shoulders before he could hit the ground, swung him round, and used him as a weapon to fell the first man as he recovered his wind. Then he hurled the man against the wall with all of his force.

It was over in a second, and the deserted street contained two unconscious bodies. John turned away from them and hurried into the darkened drizzle, stepping into a doorway for concealment as a car came round the corner. Once it was past, he ran into the night.

*

The car stopped, the doors opened and Oskar Doerner got out, followed by two of his men.

'There has been a disaster, Herr Colonel,' one of the men remarked.

Doerner looked down at the two unconscious detectives. 'Wake them up,' he commanded. He looked left and right, but the street remained deserted.

One of his men knelt and passed an opened flask of brandy to and fro under the first detective's nostrils. The man's eyes opened slowly, and he blinked. 'Christ,' he muttered.

'What happened?' Doerner inquired.

'Anderssen,' the detective gasped. 'Just after we telephoned you, Herr Colonel, to tell you he was in the apartment receiving information from Staffel, he came down the stairs. Well, sir, you said to detain him until you arrived. So we attempted to arrest him, and . . .'

'He beat you up,' Doerner said disgustedly. 'Two armed men.'

'He was so quick, Herr Colonel. We had no chance to reach for our weapons. And he was so strong.'

'And now he has got away. Streseman, you had better put out a bulletin for him. Was he armed?'

'He did not show a weapon, Herr Colonel.'

'Well, still describe him as dangerous. But I want him taken alive. Understand that, Streseman. Where is the woman?'

'She did not come down, Herr Colonel.'

'Ah.' Doerner's face relaxed slightly. 'Then you will accompany me.' He entered the building and climbed the stairs. The tenants of the other apartments, although undoubtedly awakened by the noise, prudently kept their doors shut.

'Apartment three,' said the detective, hurrying at Doerner's side.

Doerner walked along the corridor, stood before the

door and knocked. After a moment there was movement inside, and the latch turned.

'Jan,' Helga said. 'You've come back already. Oh . . .' She stared at the man in front of her. 'Oh!' Her voice began to rise.

Doerner hit her in the stomach.

PART THREE

December 1942

CHAPTER 11

The Prison

'Jen,' said the admiral. 'You're going to have a drink with me tonight.'

'Sir?'

'Because I can tell you,' the admiral went on, 'that I am feeling happy. For the first time in one hell of a long time. I reckon I must've lost ten years of my life since last summer. Christ, worrying about Torch, worrying about those God-damned Japs in Germany, worrying about aircraft-carriers . . . and what the hell was it all about. You heard Tunis has fallen?'

'Yes, sir,' Jennie said. 'But there are still a lot of Germans in North Africa.'

'What the hell? They'll smoke them out. The important thing is that our boys are *there*, and nothing, not a whole fleet of aircraft-carriers suddenly appearing off Gibraltar, is gonna stop them now. And the U-boats are being licked. And the *Graf Zeppelin* has never sailed. As for this other aircraft-carrier the Germans are supposed to have . . . I reckon Seven-Twenty-One must have been eating too much borscht. Anyway, it's done, so far as I can see. Everything's falling into place. The right place. You realise that next Monday we'll have been at war a whole year?'

'Yes, sir.'

'It sure began bad, but now it's all falling into place. I think I am going to get *drunk*. And you're gonna get drunk too, Jen. And then, you know what I am going to do?'

'Yes, sir,' Jennie said unhappily.

'I am gonna fuck the pants right off you,' the admiral promised.

'Yes, sir,' Jennie sighed. 'But what do you think the Japanese were sent to Germany to do?'

'Search me. I reckon there was nothing fishy about it at all. I reckon they did go to Germany to train pilots, and that's all there was to it. I reckon we've been seeing shadows in the dark. Helped by our friends, of course.'

'Then you think the information Seven-Twenty-One relayed was incorrect, sir?'

'Incorrect? Shit, I reckon he made up the whole God-damned thing to get me off his back. You know something? I reckon he's had it. I thought that last summer, remember? I'm not knocking the guy. Four years doing what he's been doing is a hell of a job of work. Maybe we just left him there too long. But now that we just about have this U-boat problem sewn up, and now that *Atlas* is gone, and now that Koenig has been retired, and now that what's left of the German Fleet is tucked away up by the North Cape and staying there, he's redundant. I'm going to pull that asshole out.'

'Oh, sir,' Jennie gasped. Her knees suddenly felt weak.

'Yes, sir,' the admiral said. 'I'm going to pull him out, bring him home, give him a medal and that extra stripe I promised him, and put him back into uniform; then send him to sea and let the wind blow some of the cobwebs out of his brain. So you draft me a message for Seven-Seven-Four, instructing him to recall Anderssen to Stockholm – promotion within the newspaper or something like that – and then we'll see about getting him on a plane home. Hell, once he's here we could release his identity and what he's been doing and really twist old Adolf's tail, eh?'

'Yes, *sir*. Oh, yes, sir. And thank you, sir.'

The admiral raised his eyebrows. 'What're you thanking me for, Jen?'

'For everything,' Jennie said.

'Then you'll come along and have a drink with me? And maybe dinner after?'

Jennie hesitated. But suddenly she wanted to. He might be a lecherous old goat, but he had his good points, she thought. Besides, she also wanted to get drunk. Not just because of the stupendous news about Johnnie, either; Clive was due in Washington tomorrow, for his medal. That was going to be some celebration. As the admiral had said, everything was falling into place.

Everything? she wondered. Her problems were just beginning; in another couple of weeks both Johnnie and Clive would be in America. But that wasn't really a problem. There was only one decision she was going to make about that. So tomorrow would be a farewell as well as a celebration. Oh boy, she *needed* to get drunk.

'That would be very nice, sir,' she agreed.

The bookshop was dark and shuttered. John could only pray that Mundt wasn't down in Potsdam with his sister. He looked left and right while pausing to catch his breath, then frowned as he thought he heard a sound like a shoe scraping the pavement. But it was not repeated, and he could see no one; it must have been a cat, he decided. He had certainly got clear away from the Gestapo. He wondered if they would trouble Helga. He doubted it, because if they did, she had only to telephone her father, and Doenitz, and Hitler himself, to have them seen off.

But why the hell had Gestapo agents been there at all? It could only be because, despite his cover, they had been keeping him under surveillance. But why decide to arrest him tonight? Those were all things he did not know and could not now spare the time to think about. They all added up to just one fact . . . that he had no time to lose. He knocked on the door, and again, and heard movement within. Slowly the bolts were drawn, and Mundt peered at him. The old man frowned.

'I'd like to buy a Gutenberg Bible,' John said, keeping his voice low and even with an effort. 'In Yiddish.'

'That is a damnable request,' Mundt replied. His frown deepened. 'At two o'clock in the morning?'

'There's an emergency,' John told him. 'Will you please let me in.'

Mundt stood aside, closed the door behind him and slipped the bolt. 'There had better be. This is very irregular. The whole point about my operation is that it is foolproof, because people come here simply to buy books, and nothing is ever written down. If anyone had seen you coming here at two o'clock in the morning . . .'

'No one did,' John assured him. 'I have a message which must be sent tonight.'

'That is not possible.'

'Don't you have a transmitter here in the shop?'

'Well . . . I do,' Mundt confessed. 'But it is only to be used in the most serious circumstances.'

'This is such a circumstance. Will your Swiss station be listening?'

'They maintain a twenty-four-hour watch.'

'Okay. Then I want you to send, for immediate relay to Washington, the following message: "Have certain evidence Japanese air strike force using German aircraft-carrier intend to mount air raid on New York 7 December stop Ship will sail Kiel midnight 2 December and should enter Denmark Strait some time during night of 5 to 6 stop Commander will be Hjalmar Koenig stop Japanese strike force will be commanded by Keiko Hatatsune stop Seven-Twenty-One." '

Mundt frowned at him. 'Today is already the second of December.'

'That is why it is an urgent message, Herr Mundt.'

'I see. Well, it will be sent.'

'I'll wait, if you don't mind.' Quite apart from his determination to make sure the message *was* sent immediately, he needed time to decide what he was going to do next. Wherever he went, he was going to be arrested by the Gestapo, and whatever their suspicions, they now had a reason: he had assaulted two of their people. He had to brace himself for an unpleasant couple of hours – perhaps even longer. But he too had friends, and he was a neutral. He had to remember that.

'It will have to be coded,' Mundt was saying.

'So let's get started.'

Mundt hesitated, then led him behind the counter and up the stairs to the living quarters above the shop. Here there was a kitchen, a sitting room and a bedroom. The apartment had the untidy neatness of the confirmed bachelor; the flowers in the vase on the mantelpiece were nearly dead, and the mantelpiece itself needed dusting. In the bedroom, Mundt pulled a chest from beneath his iron bedstead, and from it took a very modern transmitting set; slowly he began extending the aerial.

'I thought you fellows kept things like that in false compartments under the floor or in the wall,' John remarked.

'Only when they are in constant use. I normally transmit from my sister's house. This set has never been used.'

'You think they'll trace the call?'

Mundt shrugged. 'I do not see why they should. They have never traced any of my calls before. Besides, I intend to make it as brief as possible. Now let me see . . .' He finished preparing the set, then sat at his desk with a pad of paper and a pencil. Obviously his remarkable memory enabled him to carry the code in

259

his head. John sat on the bed and waited, looking around the room. This too was the room of an old and confirmed bachelor. There was nothing here for anyone to get suspicious about, so long as no one thought of looking into the old chest under the bed. But that was the first place any searcher would look. Mundt's security had always been based upon never even coming under suspicion. He could understand the old man's concern. But once his message was sent he would just fade away and hopefully never trouble Mundt again.

Mundt wrote down the first word, started on the second, and checked, as there was a squealing of brakes from the road outside. The two men stared at each other, and a moment later there came a crashing summons on the door of the shop.

'You were followed,' Mundt accused. 'You said you were not followed.'

'I know I was not followed,' John snapped, and ran into the sitting room.

'Keep away from the window,' Mundt begged.

John hesitated. His stomach felt curiously light, while his brain seemed to have gone dead, refusing to accept that this was happening. 'Your house must have been under surveillance.' It might have been a stranger speaking. But he was remembering that sound he had heard and dismissed as imagination.

'My house?' Mundt demanded. 'It has never been under surveillance. Because I have been careful. I . . .'

'Break it down,' someone said on the street.

'Oh, God,' Mundt whispered. 'Oh, God.'

'Send the message,' John told him.

'I cannot. There is no time.'

'There is no time to code it. Send it in clear.'

'Clear? But . . .'

'We are finished, anyway,' John told him. 'Send it in clear.' Then the Germans might call off the mission, he thought. That would do as well.

Mundt stared at him, and then sighed. 'I curse you, young man,' he said, 'for bringing this upon us. I will send your message, but . . .' he pointed at the telephone. 'There is a number on the pad. Call it. You need only say one word. Eleven. Do it now.'

The wood below splintered as heavy bodies were hurled against it. Mundt's fingers began tapping out the words. John knew sufficient Morse to be able to tell he was relaying the message exactly as he had been told, his marvellous memory working even at this direst moment of his life. Thus he must play his part. He picked up the phone, gave the number, listened to the shattering sounds from downstairs, and to the steady tap tap of Mundt's Morse key. He was amazed at his calmness, even as his heart pounded and he broke out in a heavy sweat.

There was a click, and then a woman's voice said, 'Yes?'

John took a long breath. 'Eleven,' he said.

He waited for a reply, but heard only breathing for a moment, then the click of the receiver being replaced.

'Thank you,' Mundt said, listening now instead of sending.

John laid down the receiver. 'Will she get away?'

'No,' Mundt said. 'But she will know what to do.'

John felt an overwhelming sense of guilt that he had so suddenly and completely destroyed these people's lives. He stood in the doorway, listening to the sounds from downstairs. He didn't know what to do. He had no weapons, no means of escape. Besides, how could he escape and leave Mundt? But he could not help Mundt by staying, either – by doing anything. He could only help himself, by keeping his head and his nerves, by refusing to admit anything, by . . . . He heard the street door give; cold air drifted up the stairs, accompanied by thudding feet. He closed the door and turned back to the room as the key fell silent.

'It is sent, and acknowledged,' Mundt said.

'Thank you. Now . . .' His mouth sagged open as Mundt lifted his hand to his mouth, bit the capsule he was holding and stared at him. A moment later the old man gave a jerk and a gasp, his eyes rolled, and he fell across the radio, while the room became filled with the scent of almonds.

Then the door behind him burst open, and John plunged downwards into darkness.

Helga gasped and fell to her knees as the blow slammed into her belly. Great waves of pain and nausea swept up from her stomach to fill her throat. She had never been hit like that before; hers had indeed been a life singularly free from pain.

A shoe prodded her in the ribs, and she fell over and banged her head. The shoes stepped over her, and she saw other trousered legs around her.

'Search the place,' someone said.

A hand seized her hair and dragged her upwards. The pain started to recede from her body as it was replaced by the pain in her head, but this was more irritating than debilitating. She realised that her dressing gown had opened, and reached to pull it shut, but instead had her arms seized by another man, who had knelt behind her. Her wrists were pulled into the small of her back and snapped into handcuffs. She gasped, her face crimson with outrage, her mind exploding with vicious anger. 'You . . . I will have you hanged,' she screamed.

The man holding her hair smiled at her, and released her; she sagged against the settee. 'On the contrary, Lieutenant Staffel, I am going to have *you* hanged. In the course of time.'

'You . . .' She stared at him, still too angry to be afraid, although fear was beginning to hover. He was too confident. 'Who are you?'

'I am Colonel Oskar Doerner of the Gestapo,' he said. 'And I am placing you under arrest.'

She licked her lips and looked down at herself; the dressing gown had fallen open and her stomach was a mixture of blue and white discoloration against the pink flesh to either side, reaching all the way down to her pubic hair; and now it was hurting again. But it was the realisation that these louts were gazing at her nakedness that was most disturbing. 'Would you mind closing my gown, please?' She controlled her voice with an immense effort. She had to restore some sanity to what was happening.

Doerner sat down and crossed his legs. 'I rather approve of the view, Fräulein.'

Helga choked back an urgent desire to scream and shout and weep and beg. Her instincts told her that would only make matters worse – only calmness and confidence could help her now. She struggled to her knees cautiously; she did not know if she was going to be hit again. There was nothing she could do about the gown, which hung straight from her shoulders. One of her mules had come off as well, and she didn't think she would be able to get it back on without the use of her hands. She was a prisoner of the Gestapo . . . it was all too horrible to be true.

'Why have I been arrested?' she asked, as reasonably as she could. 'I have committed no crime. There has been a mistake. When Admiral Doenitz learns of this . . .'

'A full report will be made to Admiral Doenitz in the morning, Fräulein,' Doerner said. 'He will certainly endorse your arrest when he has read it.'

'But what have I done?' Helga shouted. 'What is my crime?'

'Your crime is espionage, the most serious crime of which anyone can be guilty, especially when he or she is a serving member of his country's armed services.

You are going to die, Fräulein. Nothing can prevent that happening. However, the manner in which you die, and what happens to you before then . . . these are things you should think about. Very quickly. It would pay you to cooperate with us.'

Helga wanted to get up. But to do that would involve moving her legs and further disarranging her dressing gown. Besides, she felt she had again been hit in the stomach. She sank back on to her heels. 'To die?' she whispered. 'Me? To die?' she screamed, her self-control snapping and tears bursting from her eyes. 'How can I die? I am twenty-five years old. I am Hans-Jurgen Staffel's daughter. I am a friend of the Führer's, I am . . .'

'Also a traitor, to the Führer. The Führer does not like traitors, Fräulein. He hates them.'

'But what have I *done*?' she shrieked, rising to her knees again and overbalancing, so that she fell over against the settee. 'What have I done?' Now she could hardly see for the tears.

Instead of replying, Doerner looked past her at another man who had appeared in the doorway. 'There is a message, Herr Colonel,' the newcomer said. 'From Sturmer.'

'Ah,' Doerner said. 'Now that is interesting. I will come at once. Streseman, you will take Fräulein Staffel down to headquarters.'

'Is she to be interrogated, Herr Colonel?'

Doerner gave another of his smiles. 'Not immediately. I would prefer to be present. And perhaps others. You may . . . prepare her for interrogation, Streseman. Amuse yourself, but do not mark her.' He thrust his fingers into Helga's hair again and pushed her head back again. She stared at him, mouth and eyes wide. 'I will see you later, Fräulein.'

The door closed behind him. Helga gazed at Streseman, who had moved round to stand in front of her. 'Come along, Fräulein,' he said. 'Get up.'

Helga inhaled, blinking the tears from her eyes. This man was an underling, she thought. At her father's house he would have to use the tradesman's entrance. 'Then help me,' she snapped. 'Take off these silly handcuffs and give me your hand, and then permit me to dress.' She spoke as imperiously as she could, wishing the tears hadn't escaped her eyes to stain her cheeks.

Streseman, copying Doerner, thrust his hand into her hair and pulled. She gasped and screamed as she scrambled to her feet. 'You . . .'

'Get outside,' Streseman said.

The tears were back. But surely he could see reason. 'You cannot take me out into the street without any clothes on,' she wailed.

'Why not, Fräulein?' He took her chin in his hand and turned her face to and fro. 'You must try to understand,' he said, 'that now we have sufficient proof to arrest you, we can do anything we like to you. Anything at all.'

Helga stared at him, suddenly having difficulty in breathing, while she felt sick all over again. This could not be happening.

Streseman grinned at her, and then thrust his hands inside the open dressing gown. He pulled her against him while he squeezed her buttocks; pushed her away to finger her pubes; brought his hands up to squeeze her breasts while she panted like a wild animal. 'What are you afraid of, Fräulein?' he asked. 'That the cold will tickle your tits? That is not important. Because we are going to tickle your tits too.' His voice hardened. 'Now walk.'

The entire world seemed to be spinning, with John Anderson in the centre of it. Round and round he went, at frightening velocity. When he opened his eyes there were only bright lights and indistinct sounds making a kaleidoscope, and again he was in the centre.

But the pace was slackening, even if the pain seemed to be increasing. He realised he was lying on the floor, and that a man was kneeling beside him, wiping his head with a wet towel. There were three other men in the room, one of them standing immediately above him. 'His eyes are open,' this man commented. 'That is a relief. I must apologise, Herr Anderssen, for your discomfort. My men had assumed that you would be armed and perhaps desperate.'

John blinked at him, then past him at Mundt, who was still slumped across his key.

'Yes,' the man said. 'He took the obvious way out. You did not. We shall be interested to discover why, of course.'

John had a mental picture of Mundt's sister also sitting at her desk, in Potsdam; also dead, having bitten her cyanide capsule without hesitation as a result of his one-word message. He wondered if he would ever possess such powers of decision.

Mundt had said, 'I curse you, young man, for bringing this upon us.' Yet the message had had to be sent; it was up to him to use it to the very maximum benefit, somehow to atone for the old man's death.

'However,' the man standing above him went on, 'it would be better if you answered our questions at Gestapo headquarters, while my men search this place. By the way, I am Colonel Oskar Doerner of the Gestapo.'

Cautiously John pushed himself up; the back of his head still felt as if it was inside a threshing machine, which made coherent thought extremely difficult. 'I am Jan Anderssen. I am a Swedish national.'

Doerner nodded. 'That I know. That is why I have not yet handcuffed you. But I will do so, if I have to. Please remember that.'

John reached his feet. The room swayed about him, and the waves of pain racing through his brain made him feel sick. Yet Doerner seemed to be accepting his cover. 'I have done nothing to be ashamed of,' he said. 'I came into possession of sensational information, which I felt I had to use. That is not a crime.'

Doerner appeared to consider. 'Possibly not,' he agreed. 'The crime will probably lie in how you obtained the information, and in what manner you decided to use it. Shall we go?'

'I learned,' John said, not moving, 'that the German Navy intends to carry out an air raid on the American mainland, using Japanese airmen. This struck me as being so sensational that I transmitted it.'

'To whom?'

'To my newspaper.'

'I see. This man Mundt also works for your newspaper?'

'I do not know, for certain,' John said. He could no longer harm a dead man. 'I was given his name and address as a means of transmitting material which it was felt would be censored through ordinary channels.'

'I see,' Doerner remarked, appearing to be genuinely interested. 'May I ask who gave you Mundt's name and address?'

'That is my business,' Jan said. 'I am a newspaper-man. No one can expect me to reveal all my sources of information.'

Doerner nodded. 'That is a valid point. But you have used Mundt before?'

'Why, yes,' John agreed; he had no idea for how long they had been keeping the bookshop under surveillance. 'Several times.'

'How convenient for you,' Doerner remarked. 'Well, come along, Herr Anderssen. I can see we shall have to discuss this matter at great length.'

John hesitated, but having established his position — so far with some success, he estimated — it was now time to be cooperative. He went down the stairs. Two detectives waited at the bottom; two more, and Doerner, came behind him. A large Mercedes was parked outside the front door, and one or two people had gathered on the far street corner, awakened and alarmed by the breaking down of the door.

'Sit in the back, Herr Anderssen,' Doerner invited, and got in beside him. 'Cigarette?'

'Thank you.' John discovered to his delight that his hand was not shaking.

Doerner flicked a gold-plated cigarette lighter and lit both cigarettes, then leaned back and inhaled. 'You are, of course, entirely within your rights to adopt this attitude, Herr Anderssen,' he said. 'However, I do wish you to understand that as the information you have obtained can be considered detrimental to the well-being and safety of the Reich, your presence in Germany can no longer be tolerated. Unless, of course, you do decide to cooperate.'

'So deport me,' John said.

'Oh, that will certainly be done, eventually. First, you may have to remain in custody for some time, to answer charges of having assaulted two policemen in the course of their duties.' He paused, but John merely continued to look at him, apparently unconcerned by the covert threat. 'However,' Doerner continued, 'I would also like you to consider what harm your silence may do to other people who are not as priviledged as yourself. The source of your information, for instance. Because we do know who it is.'

'Oh, yes?' John asked. 'Who, do you suppose?'

'Why, your mistress, Helga Staffel.'

John laughed, and winced. 'Do not be absurd, Herr Colonel.'

Doerner showed no offence. 'I do not think there can be any mistake about it, Herr Anderssen. And it is important for you to remember, as she is your mistress, that *she* can expect no privileges. She is not only a

268

German, but she is a member of the armed services. Regardless of why she gave you information, the mere fact of her having done so is treason. In time of war, treason carries the death penalty, as I am sure you appreciate.'

'You are wrong about Fräulein Staffel, Herr Colonel,' John said evenly. 'And I will swear to that in court. You should also remember that Helga Staffel is not some street urchin.'

Doerner smiled. 'How facilely you people from the democracies speak of courts. I am not concerned with courts, Herr Anderssen. I am concerned with facts. With truth.' His smile widened. 'And with consequences. I have had a listening device placed in Fräulein Staffel's apartment for the past several weeks. It has recorded every word spoken between her and anyone else, and these conversations have been tape-recorded for our own use. Now then, do you still feel that you can deny that she obtained information, specifically from the Japanese Commander Keiko Hatatsune, which she then passed on to you?'

John continued to look at him. His brain was spinning as he tried to recall everything that had been said between Helga and himself. He had certainly pressed her from time to time, but he had endeavoured to hoodwink her as to why he wanted the information – and, hopefully, he would also have hoodwinked any listeners. In fact, his treatment so far tonight suggested that was the case. So, all he had to do was stick to his story, and his cover ... but would that help Helga? She *was* a serving officer, and she *had* given secret information to an alien.

He wondered if anything he could do would help her. Confessing that he was an American spy? That would only make matters worse. If he wound up against a wall, she would be stood against the wall beside him for being his accomplice. What was more, as he would undoubtedly be tortured out of his mind first, he would equally undoubtedly blow the whole operation, revealing the identity of Seven-Seven-Four and everyone else with whom he had come into contact. That, in turn, might enable the Gestapo to pull in agents of whom he had no concept – he had no idea how many people Seven-Seven-Four controlled.

The one thing he had had drummed into his brain before leaving training school was that, no matter what happened, he must forget about heroics and any schoolboyish fantasies that it was possible for *any* man, or woman, to withstand the sort of physical pressure used by people who did not care how their victim appeared at the end of it; he would tell them everything they wished to know, simply because they would reduce him to a state where he would not know what he was saying. There were only two defences available to a spy. One was instant suicide on arrest. The other was never to be arrested – as a spy. And that was the defence he knew he must adopt. No matter what.

And no matter what happened to Helga? He simply had to help her, if he could.

'Well,' he said. 'Then I must make a confession, Herr Colonel. Of course Helga has given me certain information from time to time. We are lovers, and we are to be married. Perhaps you did not know this. And of course she knows my interest in naval matters. It is, after all, my profession. However, she has always made me promise most faithfully that I would never publish such information without her permission, until she obtained the necessary clearance from Admiral Doenitz. In this case, she knows that I intend to write a feature on Hjalmar Koenig and his magnificent exploits. I have long been sure that Commander Hatatsune's visit to Germany is somehow connected with Koenig, and now I have been proved right. But Helga again made me swear absolute secrecy. She has no more idea of being disloyal to the Reich than you have. Unfortunately . . . I'm afraid I lost my head. I knew that I was in possession of a real scoop – the first scoop I have ever had, Herr Colonel. I just could not resist the temptation. So I dashed out and sent the message to Stockholm. Helga will undoubtedly be very angry with me. But a scoop like this could make me famous.'

'Indeed,' Doerner agreed. 'And I am sure that Fräulein Staffel will be angry with you. It is even possible that I may be angry with you, Herr Anderssen, for attempting to defend your mistress with such a pack of lies.'

'Lies?' John demanded. 'My dear Colonel . . .'

'Do you seriously expect me to believe that Herr Mundt was a Swedish newspaper reporter who found it necessary to commit suicide on arrest by the Gestapo? No, no, Herr Anderssen. I think we have uncovered a very nasty spy ring here, originating with Fräulein Staffel, who used you as a messenger boy for relaying her information to her employers, whoever they may be.'

John stared at him. 'And I will swear that you are wrong, and that I have told the truth.'

'We will see,' Doerner said. 'We will see. Ah, we have arrived.'

The car drove through an enclosed courtyard. A uniformed policeman immediately opened the door and stood to attention.

'You will understand, Herr Anderssen,' Doerner reminded him, 'that the warning I uttered when leaving Mundt's bookshop still applies. I do strongly recommend that you do nothing but watch, and listen, and endeavour to answer my questions truthfully. That is by far the best course for you. It may even be the best course for Fräulein Staffel, although I will tell you frankly that I despair of finding a best course for her at all. Now, come with me, please.'

He got out of the car, and John followed. Once again

his stomach felt light, while his pain-shrouded brain seemed to be hovering, curiously in abeyance, knowing that something terrible was about to happen, and yet almost anticipating it.

The rain continued to settle on his head and shoulders – his hat had been forgotten in the bookshop – as he followed Doerner across the courtyard and into the doorway; but the damp was almost a relief. They entered a guardroom, where several policemen stood to attention. Doerner nodded to them and led the way along a corridor at the back, and thence down a flight of stairs, This was a cold, dank, odorous world but, amazingly, there was a gramophone playing very loudly. At three o'clock in the morning?

Doerner marched along another corridor, threw open a door and stepped into a large room. John followed, conscious that two policemen were at his elbow. It was a curiously furnished room. In the far corner there was a desk, with a comfortable chair behind it, and the room itself was heated; in comparison to the corridor outside the temperature was quite comfortable. But there was no carpet on the stone floor, and no other furniture at all, save for a stool in the very centre of the room. The object looked like an incidental table, some two feet from the floor, and about three feet long by one wide. But it was being used for another purpose. Helga Staffel's body had been placed on it. Even for Helga it was too small. She was face down, her legs on the floor and her head draped over the other end, with her arms. She looked extremely uncomfortable, but there was nothing she could do about it, for her wrists and ankles had been secured to bolts in the floor, pulled as tight as they could stand, so that she was spread-eagled in an extremely undignified, not to say obscene position; she was naked, her crimson dressing gown a crumpled heap on the floor.

Around her there stood four men. How tiny she seemed, and how large the men.

She was conscious. At the sound of the door opening, her head jerked, but she was facing away from the door. At least, John thought, there were no marks on her body as yet. But he did not doubt that there soon would be – just as he did not doubt that she had already been abused, if only for amusement. Her position, her nudity, the smiles on the faces of the men, the very odours hanging on the air, all told him that.

He discovered he was pouring sweat. If he had never loved this woman, he had made love to her often enough, and he had felt jealousy at the thought of her making love with Keiko Hatatsune. What should he feel now? But, sex apart, if he had attempted to use her, he had the protective feeling towards her of a benevolent employer towards a faithful employee. Just to see her stretched out like a cow awaiting slaughter or, worse, like a woman awaiting total destruction – as she was – horrified him. To understand that he could do nothing about it and must continue to act his role, no matter what horror was about to be perpetrated, made him angrier than he had ever been before in his life.

'We have prepared the prisoner for interrogation, Herr Colonel,' said one of the waiting men.

'I can see that, Streseman.' Doerner stood above and behind Helga, looking down on her, while he lit another cigarette with great care. 'Are you awake, Staffel?' he asked.

Helga's head twisted to and fro, endeavouring to see him. 'You bastard,' she said, her voice low. 'Your . . . your thugs have raped me. When my father hears of what you have done to me, you . . . aaagh!'

Doerner had leaned forward, gently parted the white buttocks and stubbed out his cigarette between them. Helga's body arched away from the table to the full extent of the straps holding her wrists and ankles, and then collapsed again with a curious slap. Breath exploded from her mouth and nostrils.

'Oh,' she gasped. 'Oh . . .' Tears rolled down her cheeks, and her hips moved from side to side with erotic helplessness. 'Oh, God!'

Doerner walked round in front of her, thrust his fingers into her hair and raised her head. 'I have brought someone to see you, Fräulein.'

Helga tried to focus as Doerner beckoned John round in front. 'Jan?' she whispered, 'Oh, Jan . . .' Slowly it dawned on her that he had clearly not been ill-treated at all. 'Jan!' she screamed. 'Tell them, Jan. Tell them that I was only doing what you wanted. Tell them, Jan. Tell them to release me.'

'I have told them everything, honey doll,' John said, amazed that he could speak at all, much less in quiet, well-modulated tones. 'I have told them. But they refuse to believe me.'

'I wish to believe you, Herr Anderssen,' Doerner pointed out. 'I just find it difficult to do so. However, now that you are together . . .' He released Helga's head and allowed it to drop forward. Helga panted, and her body gleamed with sweat. Doerner stooped beside her. 'Helga,' he said quietly, but with a sense of urgency. 'Do you remember what I told you at your apartment? You are going to die, Helga. There is no prospect of your living. But Anderssen is going to live, perhaps — unless you tell us the truth about him. He is going to live, and he is going to forget all about you. He will take some other girl, some nice plump, blonde Swedish bitch, and make her his mistress. One day he will probably even be married. And he will have forgotten all about you. Do you think that is fair, and just?'

Helga's head rose of its own accord, and she stared at him.

'I do not think that is fair at all,' Doerner went on.

'So I want you to listen to me very carefully. He claims to be nothing more than a Swedish newspaper reporter attempting to put together a feature on Hjalmar Koenig. He claims that is why he asked you for the information regarding Commander Hatatsune's reasons for being in Germany. This is what he claims, Helga. But you know, and I know, that he is lying, don't we? Why don't you tell me what he really is, and for whom he is working?'

Helga stared at him some more, while a faint frown gathered between her eyes. Then she turned to look up at John. He found himself holding his breath. But what could she tell them except the truth.

'He *is* a newspaper reporter,' she whispered. 'You must know that. He *is* doing a feature on Hjalmar Koenig. He has been compiling the material for some time. I was only trying to help him. That is the truth. I swear it. I swear it, on my mother's grave. That is the truth.'

'I think,' Doerner said, standing straight again and looking down at her, 'that you are both going to have to consider what you wish to tell me, very carefully. There is no hurry. We have several hours in front of us. And Staffel has a great deal of very delightful flesh for us to play with.' He stooped again, pulled Helga's body slightly sideways so that her left breast came off the table and drooped beside it. She gasped, as the table was now cutting into her. 'You must watch this carefully, Herr Anderssen,' Doerner said, as he lit another cigarette, and then leaned forward to stroke the glowing tip across Helga's nipple.

John exploded. Breaking every rule he had ever been taught, he grasped Doerner's shoulders and jerked him upwards, hurling him to one side as he did so. Instantly fists and gun butts crashed into his back and shoulders and head. He tried to turn to face them, and was sent to the ground. More and more blows thudded into him, and for the second time that night he felt consciousness slipping away.

In the far distance, Helga was screaming.

CHAPTER 12

The Decision

'What was it like, Clive?' asked one of the men crowding the bar.

Clive Wharton finished his champagne; the glass was immediately refilled. 'It was cold,' he said. 'Fucking cold.'

'I meant, shaking FDR's hand.'

Wharton grinned. 'That was cold, too.' His eyes searched the packed room, a faint frown gathering between them. She should've been here, he thought. Everyone else was. And if she didn't come soon he was going to be pissed right out of his mind. He was pretty well there already.

'They tell me you're getting another stripe,' remarked another man.

'Oh, sure,' Clive said. 'They're kicking me in the ass, all the way upstairs. What a way to run a navy. Run a war. Run a . . .' He gazed at her as she stood hesitantly at the back of the admiring group. 'You guys are gonna have to break it up,' he said.

Heads turned.

'Je*sus!*' someone remarked. 'She yours, Wharton?'

Clive eased himself off the bar stool, swayed slightly. 'You better believe it, sailor.'

'Some guys,' his friend commented. 'Some guys have all the luck that's going.'

'I make my own luck,' Clive told him, and held her hands. She had just taken off her gloves, and her fingers were cold; she still wore her topcoat – the dark blue flecked with traces of snow. 'Well, hell, lover,' he said. 'I thought you weren't going to make it.'

'So did I.' Jennie smiled at the other men, and especially at the lieutenant who was offering her a glass of champagne. 'Why, thank you. You going to introduce me, Clive?'

'Nope,' Clive said. 'They're a bunch of creeps. So long, you guys.' He tucked her arm under his and went to the door, followed by a barrage of shouted comment and laughter.

'That was unsociable,' Jennie remarked.

'I mean to be. When I'm with you.' He took his cap from the hook and placed it askew on his head.

'I think we'll take a cab,' Jennie decided. 'It's pretty miserable out there, and I don't figure you're up to walking on ice, right this minute.' But she was more relieved than angry that he was drunk. He might even be incapable tonight, and that was what she wanted most of all. That would give her time to think, to choose her words . . . besides, after a night spent coping with the admiral, she just did not feel she could spend tonight coping with Clive.

Yet she had felt she had to come. Because he was a hero? Because he had once given her the best screw of her life? Because he had the power to stop her thinking? Or just because she had given him her word?

Or just because?

He rested his head on her shoulder as the cab, occasionally slithering on the slippery road, drove them towards her apartment. 'I'm sorry about that weekend,' he said. 'Christ, I was burned up about that.'

'If you'd been with me, you wouldn't have bagged *Atlas*,' she reminded him.

'You want me to tell you which would have been more fun?'

'You wouldn't have got the medal, either.'

'Bugger that,' he said, and sat up. 'I'd have had you. Say, you got a drink?'

She hesitated. But she didn't want him falling asleep on her before they actually reached the apartment. She opened her handbag and took out her flask. 'It's Scotch, I'm afraid. Not champagne.'

'Thank God for that.' He uncorked it and raised it. 'A toast. To Rod Bowen.'

'Who?' But the name was certainly familiar.

'A Limey skipper. He's the one pulled me out of the drink. Or I wouldn't have been here at all.'

'Then I'll drink to him with pleasure.' The neck of the flask was warm from his lips.

'He was a nice guy,' Clive said thoughtfully. Then held her hands. 'Jen . . .'

'We're here,' she said, and paid the driver while Clive negotiated the door. 'You okay?'

'Nothing a cup of black coffee won't cure. You mad at me?'

'For getting drunk?' She held his arm and helped him up the stairs. 'If you hadn't got drunk tonight there would've been something wrong.'

'I mean for standing you up.'

'I needed the rest. And it sure was comfortable.'

'You mean you stayed?'

'Sure I stayed. Think you can just lean against that wall while I unlock this door? I stayed, in bed. All by myself. For forty-eight precious hours.'

'That's what I aim to do now,' he said. 'Only I'm not going to be alone. Right?'

'Wrong.' She opened the door. 'At least some of the time. Tomorrow is a working day, for most of us.'

'Well, you're just gonna have to get some leave.' Clive staggered across the doorway, moved directly if uncertainly towards the bedroom, and fell across the bed.

'I'll make that black coffee.' She went into the kitchen

and filled the percolater. As always, when she was in this man's company, she was beginning to feel randy. And it wasn't going to do her a lot of good. She should thank God for that.

She set the percolater to boil, then went back into the bedroom and looked down at him. He had rolled on to his back and his eyes were shut; he was breathing heavily. She took off his shoes and socks; she just could not contemplate sharing a bed with a man in his socks, even if he was unconscious. Then she pulled his tie free and sat him up to take off his jacket. He did have a lot of medal ribbons, she noticed. While she was hanging up his jacket he fell over again, still asleep. But what the hell, she thought. She'd never undressed a man before and was rather tickled by the idea.

She unbuckled his belt, pulled down his trousers, rolled him to and fro while she got off his shirt, sat him up to tug off his vest – and discovered she was exhausted; he was a big, heavy man. She laid him down again to pull off his shorts and realised that, although unconscious, he had an erection. Before she could make up her mind whether to remove the shorts or not, he suddenly sat up of his own accord, didn't seem to notice her and headed for the bathroom. His shorts caught around his knees and he all but fell, but recovered himself in time and stepped out of them. To her relief he apparently wanted a pee rather than a vomit.

She went into the kitchen, made coffee and brought back two cups. He was sitting on the bed, looking at himself in her dressing mirror across the room. 'Don't tell me I fucked you and didn't know it?' he asked.

She handed him a cup of coffee. 'Do I look like it?'

'How do I know if you have pants on? Jesus, lover . . .' He sipped, then put down the cup. He wasn't the least incapable; his hand was perfectly steady. 'I was just damned tired,' he explained. 'But, Jennie . . .'

She drank her own coffee and undressed, shocked at herself. She hadn't meant to do this.

'I didn't come here just to screw you, you know,' he remarked, watching her; his erection was back, to give the lie to his words.

'You came here to get a medal,' she agreed. Crisis was rushing at her like a runaway train. She knew that. The funny thing was that, but for the past, and her dream of the future, there would be no crisis. She could love this man, warts and all – and he had a lot of warts, at least on his character. But maybe it was *because* of those warts. And he could turn her on. The sight of his hard-on, sitting there on her bed, had her scrabbling in haste as she discarded bra and panties. She could say yes, and yes, and yes and know she was going to be happy, now and always.

And the dream was four years old. Four hard and bitter and often frightening years. She didn't know what it would be like, any more. But Johnnie was coming home, and she couldn't agree to anything until they had met, and found out what it would be like, after all.

'I came here to ask you to marry me,' Clive said. 'Really and truly. Jennie, I love you. Love you, love you, *love* you. And you know what, I'm not even going to be allowed to fly any more. So if that was eating you, forget it. I'm brass, as of next Monday. Pure fried egg as far as you can see. You're gonna have to call me sir, in public. How about that, eh? I'm even going to be nine to five, right here in this little old town. We could live in Arlington. I've always wanted to live in Arlington. I'll commute. And you'll retire from this women's navy and bring up the kids.'

Clive Wharton, sounding like any other man in the world – he *had* to be in love, she thought.

She sat beside him, held him in her arms and kissed him on the mouth. She was the biggest coward in all history, she knew. But right this moment he was happy.

He was the happiest man in all the world. And the most successful. She wasn't going to end that dream. Not right this minute.

She held his hand, placed it where it ought to be, then put her own hand down to touch him and hold him. 'You came here to make love to me, Clive Wharton,' she said. 'That's all I want you to do, right this minute.'

It was such a relief to be able to tell the truth.

Hjalmar Koenig watched the eighteen aircraft being craned on board the *Nemo*, each plane cocooned in a canvas cover; tonight, this was at least as necessary to prevent them from turning into solid blocks of ice as it was to hide the tell-tale red-on-white rising suns of Japan from the prying onlookers. Not that anyone was about at this moment; it was too cold – his breath was clouding almost solid before his mouth and eyes.

First Officer Meyer stood at his shoulder. 'Commander Hatatsune has returned, Herr Captain.'

'Where is he now?'

'He retired immediately.'

Koenig nodded. 'I am sure he is very tired,' he agreed.

'He does not know the aircraft are being loaded, Herr Captain,' Meyer went on. 'He knows they were in the dockyard, but believes they will not come aboard until daybreak.'

Koenig nodded again. 'He thinks he is in Japan, where news takes a long time to reach the outside world.'

'Still, I think he is a good man, Herr Captain,' Meyer observed. 'His record speaks for that. But, also I watched him training his men in Norway. He really put them through their paces, regardless of life or limb.'

'And lost two aircraft, with their crews,' Koenig observed.

Meyer shrugged. 'Perhaps this was necessary, Herr

Captain. Those who are left at least know their business.'

'Let us hope they do,' Koenig agreed. 'Have you seen the forecast?'

'There is a deep depression over the eastern United States,' Meyer said. 'Moving east. It contains very strong winds and sub-zero temperatures.'

'Exactly. I estimate it will reach the Denmark Strait about twenty-four hours before we do. That is good for us, Meyer. We could not ask for better concealment. There will even be a few early icebergs to confuse the enemy radar. But for those inexperienced pilots . . .'

'I understand they are very experienced pilots, Herr Captain.'

'At combat, and flying from carriers. But not in an Arctic storm. I wonder if all of their training can have prepared them for that?' He turned away; the last aircraft had been lowered, and was being wheeled to the elevator. 'Do you suppose any of the crew have an inkling of our mission?'

'I am sure they do not, Herr Captain.' Meyer walked beside him up the flight-deck, which was slippery with the frost gathering every minute and crunching beneath their feet. 'But they understand it will be dangerous.'

'I will address them once we put to sea. Poor devils, they will not be able to change their minds, then.'

Meyer frowned. 'Do you not think we will succeed, Herr Captain?'

'Oh, we will succeed, Meyer – in getting there and getting back. As for the raid . . .' He shrugged, and led the way down the forward companion ladder into the relative warmth of the ship – relative, because there was no heating. 'But it is going to be a damned uncomfortable trip. And, Meyer, I know that Commander Hatatsune is a good man, or I would not be going on this mission myself. He is the best Japan has. He is merely . . . different, eh? Yes, Albing?' He looked at his servant standing beside the signal rating in the doorway to the navigation complex; both men looked anxious.

'There is a message, Herr Captain.'

Koenig frowned as he took the paper. He regarded it as poor security for the Admiralty to be sending him last-minute messages, simply because this was not the last minute; there were still twelve hours to go before he cast off. That was too short a time to make any changes in the plan, and too great a time to risk a breach of security.

But his frown deepened as he scanned the words: 'IMPERATIVE YOU COME TO BERLIN IMMEDIATELY STOP BRING HATATSUNE STOP MATTER MOST URGENT STOP AIRCRAFT WILL ARRIVE KIEL ZERO SEVEN THREE ZERO STOP ACKNOWLEDGE STOP RAEDER'.

He looked at his watch; it was five forty-five. Then he handed the message to Meyer, who looked equally dumbfounded. 'They cannot mean to cancel the mission now?'

'Who knows what they will do, at any moment?' Koenig asked. Cancel the mission? That was impossible, he thought. He would not let them. His whole life, his whole concept of death – since Kurt's death – was bound up in this mission.

But his brain was whirring. Doerner had been waiting to arrest Helga Staffel the moment she tried to relay any information she might have obtained from Hatatsune. Thus she must have tried, after their last night together. But that should not involve the mission. Indeed, Doerner had guaranteed that it would not. So something had gone wrong. Either he had discovered something unknown to any of them previously – or, more likely, those oafs had bungled it. How he wished he had not involved them at all.

He became aware of a slow anger burning in his belly. They had given him a job to do; a suicidal job,

284

but he had accepted it, and would carry it out. To have those fools in Berlin start to interfere now . . . but he knew part of the blame must lie nearer home.

'You'll awaken Commander Hatatsune, Meyer,' he said. 'Tell him we leave for Berlin in one hour and a half.'

They breakfasted on coffee and black bread, both having donned their shore-going uniforms. 'Do you know what this is about, honourable Captain?' Keiko asked. 'It is very late to summon us to Berlin. I had hoped to spend the day preparing my men for the final stages of this mission.'

'It is about us,' Koenig told him. 'You and me. More precisely, I think, you.'

'Me, honourable Captain?'

'You requested, and were given, special embarkation leave to visit Berlin,' Koenig reminded him. 'And were granted that leave. No one else of my crew would have been allowed ashore last night. I did not go ashore myself.'

Keiko's face was stiff. 'You were very generous, honourable Captain. Do you believe me to be untrustworthy?'

'No, Commander, or you would not be here. I believe you to be too trusting of other people. May I ask where you spent the night?'

Keiko did not lower his gaze. 'With Lieutenant Staffel. You knew that, honourable Captain.'

'And of course you told her what we were going to do tonight?'

'I did not, sir,' Keiko said.

'But you told her goodbye,' Koenig said gently.

'Of course I did. We have been lovers.'

'And it did not occur to you that Lieutenant Staffel might be an Allied spy?'

Keiko stared at him in consternation.

285

'A spy who has already obtained sufficient information about our mission, but up to last night lacked only the date and perhaps the destination. Did you tell her the destination?'

Keiko opened his mouth and closed it again.

'Well,' Koenig said, 'we shall soon find out. It may interest you to know that you were only given leave last night to entrap Fräulein Staffel into an overt move. This has undoubtedly happened. What else has happened, we shall have to discover.' He pointed at the seaplane dipping low out of the still dark morning sky to land on the calm waters of Kiel harbour. 'We shall be in Berlin in an hour.'

'It is not possible,' Keiko said, for the fourth time, staring out of the window of the command car at the snow-streaked streets of Berlin; he seemed to be trying to convince himself. 'I was given to understand that she was absolutely trustworthy – by Admiral Doenitz himself.'

'Even admirals can make mistakes,' Koenig pointed out. He was keeping his anger under careful control: time to explode when he discovered that the mission was lost beyond recall. That had not happened yet, but it seemed that the whole world was trying to obstruct him. He leaned forward and tapped the driver on the shoulder as the car swung through an archway. 'This is not the Admiralty.'

'I was instructed to bring you here first, Herr Captain,' the driver explained.

Koenig frowned, watching the sentries come forward to open the doors for them. Oskar Doerner waited in the doorway behind. Now he saluted them. 'Herr Captain. Herr Commander.' He looked tired. But also triumphant.

Koenig returned his salute. 'Is this necessary, Herr Colonel?'

'I wish you to have no doubt about the situation, and also to obtain all the information we possess,' Doerner said. 'Because you will have to make the final evaluation. This way.'

They followed him inside. In the guardroom a man sat on one of the straight chairs facing the desk. At their entry he sprang up and seized Hjalmar's sleeve. 'Captain Koenig!' His voice was high. 'You have come to help us. You must help us.'

Koenig stared at him in consternation. Could this dishevelled, decrepit creature truly be Hans-Jurgen Staffel? There were even tear-stains on the man's cheeks.

'There has been a mistake, you see,' Staffel gabbled. 'A most serious mistake. Fortunately I was in Berlin, so I was able to come down here immediately. But these dolts . . . they will not even let me see her. You know my daughter, Captain Koenig? Of course you do. They say she is guilty of treason. Now really, Captain Koenig . . .'

'I should talk to Admiral Doenitz,' Koenig suggested, gently freeing himself.

'I have tried,' Staffel cried. 'I have tried. But he will not speak with me. I have tried to reach the Führer himself . . . but he is unavailable. Affairs of state. While my daughter lies in a cell. Please, Captain Koenig, explain to these people . . . vouch for her. She knows you well. She has often spoken of you. Please, Captain Koenig.'

'We are wasting time,' Doerner remarked.

'If your daughter is innocent, Herr Staffel, then she will undoubtedly be released,' Koenig told the toy manufacturer. 'Have you no faith in German justice?' He stepped past.

'She *is* innocent,' Staffel wailed. 'For God's sake, she is innocent. At least let me *see* her.' He made to follow Keiko, who had also stepped past him, and was checked

287

by a policeman. 'She is innocent,' he screamed after them.

The door closed, to Koenig's relief. Accompanied by two guards, Doerner led them down the stairs and along the corridor, past the interrogation room and into a world of cells; the gramophone played behind them ceaselessly, the same tune over and over again, doing something to disguise the moans and wails, the groans and the sighs, that came from behind the doors, but in itself a form of torture, he supposed – at least to anyone with an ear for music.

'Do you really work down here?' he asked.

'When I have to. Oh, it is not pleasant,' Doerner agreed. 'And is kept deliberately unpleasant, you understand. Our first object must be to depress the spirits of our suspects. Abandon hope all ye who enter here, and that sort of thing. That is psychologically important. Are you ready?'

He paused before one of the doors, and Hjalmar gave an involuntary shiver; his instincts warned him that he was about to see something unpleasant. He glanced at Keiko, wondering what the young Japanese thought of the interior of a Gestapo prison – or of the prospect of coming face to face with the mistress who had betrayed him. But Keiko's face remained impassive. 'We are ready,' Koenig said, tightening his stomach muscles.

Doerner opened the peephole and looked through for several seconds, then nodded to the guards. The bolt was slipped and the door pulled open. Koenig blinked at the sudden bright light emanating from the unshaded two-hundred-and-fifty-watt bulb in the ceiling. Then he focused on the single steel cot with its permanent mattress, and at the crumpled naked white figure which huddled there. There was no heating in the cell, and the woman shivered all the time. But perhaps she shivered from more than just the cold. Her body was a mass of little black scorch marks, and there were also red streaks across her buttocks – she was turned away from the door. But her head jerked as she heard them, and she half rose to her knees and pressed her body against the cell wall, still not looking at them.

'No,' she whispered. 'No.' Then, as no one spoke, her head moved cautiously. 'Father?' Slowly her head turned some more, and with it her body, to stare at them. But she saw only Doerner. She gave a moan and turned her face to the wall again. 'No,' she moaned.

'Was such treatment necessary?' Koenig asked. His mouth had filled with saliva. *Have you no faith in German justice?* he had asked Staffel. My God, he thought, suppose she *is* innocent.

Doerner shrugged. 'She has refused to tell us anything of value. Which is foolish of her, when we already know so much. And it is not even courage. She is still convinced that her father will manage to get her out of here.'

Koenig thought of the broken figure upstairs. He wondered how Staffel would react when he learned what had happened to his daughter in this cellar. 'There is no doubt that she is guilty?'

'Oh, none.'

'And the man?'

'We shall see him in a moment. His guilt or innocence, except as a tool, remains the one question I have yet to determine. But the woman is the more important. Would you like to ask her a question?'

Koenig stared at him.

'We do not know what information she actually obtained,' Doerner explained. 'We only know what the man has told us, because he, unlike her, has been anxious to tell us everything. That encourages me to suppose that he is actually innocent. Of course, he is a coward as well. That is obvious. But that again is not the mark of the professional spy. He is also something of a fool, I think. Despite everything that has happened, he still seems certain that this woman isn't a spy. Of course, that in itself may be a form of subterfuge. I shall find out. But I thought you might be able to discover what information she gave to him.'

'I know what she gave to him,' Koenig said. 'The date of our sailing. And probably our destination.'

'Oh, I know those,' Doerner said. 'I was thinking of anything else. Perhaps Commander Hatatsune may be able to remember what else he told her.'

'Bitch,' Keiko snapped. He stepped past the two Germans and seized Helga's hair to drag her head backwards and slap her twice across the face. Koenig made to stop him, but was checked by Doerner.

Helga moaned and whimpered. Her eyes flopped open, stared at Keiko, and then flopped shut again.

'I thought we were lovers,' Keiko said in Japanese. 'But you are a bitch.'

'What's that you say?' Doerner asked.

'I have been betrayed,' Keiko said in German. 'I had not believed such a thing was possible. I have been betrayed, and thus I have betrayed my command, and my mission.' His face was rigid, little balls of muscle jumping at the base of his jaw. 'With your permission, honourable Captain, honourable Colonel, I will withdraw.'

Doerner looked at Koenig, clearly mystified by the reaction. But Koenig knew just what thoughts were running through Keiko's mind. He had been watching them build all morning. Yet he couldn't just let him wander off and stick a knife into his belly – not while there remained any chance at all.

'Permission refused, Commander,' he said. 'Until we are in possession of all the facts. I wish to speak with the man.'

Keiko stared at him, then looked at Helga again. 'She should be flogged,' he said, his voice almost a snarl. His anger was quite the most disturbing thing Koenig had ever seen; it far transcended his own. But that was reassuring. It was an indication of how much store the Japanese had set by this mission, how much he realised the fault was his own, in setting the operation at risk.

Doerner grasped Helga's shoulder, much as he might have grasped a prime side of beef in order to display its points, and turned her round. She moved, on her knees, without protest. Doerner pushed her forward, sliding his hand up the nape of her neck to do so, forcing her head down so that her body arched and the red weals on her buttocks could be more clearly discerned. 'She has already been flogged,' the colonel said. 'Perhaps we shall flog her again. But it will no longer serve any purpose. She would have told us more already, had she been prepared to do so.'

Koenig wondered which was the more distasteful, the way he handled her as if she were already a corpse, or the way she made no protest, did not even tense her muscles, as if she too accepted the fact that she no longer existed.

'She seduced me,' Keiko said.

Doerner nodded. 'I can believe that. Well, would it make you feel better to whip her yourself?' He looked at Koenig.

'No,' Koenig said. 'We have not time for that. We must see the man.' He stepped forward, into the cell. He had never liked this girl. He had never liked her father. He liked none of the things she had always stood for. Now it was difficult to decide whether she was a total fool or one of the bravest women he had ever met. And perhaps she had just condemned him to death. But that was not true; he had been condemned to death some months ago, by his superiors.

Helga seemed able to feel his gaze. She lifted her head and stared at him, eyes wide. He was sure she was not actually seeing him, Hjalmar Koenig, but only identifying him as a man who would press burning cigarette

291

ends into her nipples and her armpits and between her legs, who would pull her about the room by her hair, who would whip her until she bled, and who would strip away her precious femininity until only a raw, terrified animal was left.

'I am sorry for you, Fräulein,' he said. 'Very sorry.' But then, he thought, I am sorry for all of us, who must support a system which can so mistreat one of its own.

He turned and left the room.

John Anderson listened to the scrape of the bolt and tried to remember where he was. The night had become one enormous painful nightmare, built entirely around the increasing agony in his head. He had been unconscious . . . for how long?

He touched his scalp. It had been bandaged, but felt soggy even through the layers of cloth. He sat up on his cot and curled his fingers into fists to stop them from shaking. It was the cold; he was sure of that. But there was a certain amount of apprehension as well, simply because nothing had happened yet, save for those two thumps on the head, and various other incidental thumps on his body. But every time he thought of Helga, trussed there like a chicken ready for carving . . .

The door swung inwards, and he looked at the two guards, instinctively tensing his muscles. But the men stepped aside, and instead he looked at Doerner, and Hjalmar Koenig, and Hatatsune. He rose to his feet, overbalanced as the cell started to sway, and sat down again. 'Hjalmar,' he said. 'I must apologise.'

'For what?' Koenig asked him, looking him up and down.

'This man has not been interrogated,' Keiko snapped.

'Indeed he has, Herr Commander,' Doerner said.

'He is not marked.'

'There has been no need to mark him, except in

292

self-defence. He has been most cooperative, but for a tendency to assault people.'

'Have you seen your mistress?' Koenig asked.

John licked his lips. 'They will not believe me,' he said plaintively. 'She is innocent.'

'She obtained vital information from Commander Hatatsune here, and passed it on to you. Is that not true?'

'She told me Hatatsune was going to bomb New York, yes,' John agreed. 'We are lovers. She tells me everything.'

'And you remitted this information to America?'

'America?' John shook his head. 'I sent it to Sweden.'

Koenig studied him. 'What exactly did you send?'

'Ah . . .' John closed his eyes and tried to remember exactly. 'I sent: "Have reason to believe Japanese air strike force flying from German carrier will bomb New York on morning 7 December. Carrier will be commanded by Hjalmar Koenig, strike force by Keiko Hatatsune. Expect carrier to penetrate Denmark Strait approximately night of 5/6 December." ' He opened his eyes again. 'That is what I sent.'

'This man must be shot,' Keiko shouted.

'That would be rather like shutting the stable door after the horse has bolted,' Doerner observed. 'But presumably that information is all accurate?'

Koenig continued to stare at John. 'Yes,' he said. 'Are you sure that is all you sent, Herr Anderssen?'

'Of course I am sure,' John said.

'Then would you repeat it to me, once again?'

John frowned at him.

'Please,' Koenig said.

John repeated the message, word for word.

'You have a good memory,' Koenig remarked.

'Do you suppose he is telling the truth?' Keiko asked scornfully.

'As a matter of fact, he is telling the truth,' Doerner

said. 'The message was sent in clear from Mundt's bookshop, presumably because my people were already at the door. One of our monitoring stations picked it up. That was what was sent, almost word for word. I told you, Herr Anderssen has been most cooperative.'

'Even if he is telling the truth . . .' Keiko spat the words. 'Are we fools? If that message was sent to Stockholm, will they not publicise it? He could as well have sent it direct to Washington.'

'Yes,' Koenig said. 'That is unfortunate. What is going to happen to Herr Anderssen, Herr Colonel?'

Doerner shrugged. 'That will be for a people's court to decide, in due course. Oh, I am certain he will be found guilty. But there may be mitigating factors, such as his being a neutral citizen, which may be of assistance to him. However, whatever happens to him, as his information will have turned out to be untrue, he will be quite discredited.'

'Yes,' Koenig said. 'It is a pity. All of this time, and effort . . . all for naught because of an over-zealous reporter and a silly little girl.'

'I do apologise, Hjalmar,' John said. 'I had no idea I was going to cause such a disturbance. But I think I have actually done you a good turn. You would never have got away with it. You would all have been killed.'

'Oh, quite,' Koenig agreed. 'I am sure you are right. We would most certainly all have been killed.' He turned to Hatatsune. 'I think the sooner we see Grand Admiral Raeder the better, don't you?'

It was daylight above ground. Keiko stared at the houses, at the streets only now filling with the bread queues and the repair squads; there had apparently been a recent raid by the RAF. 'You should also have said that this catastrophe was caused by a lovesick fool,' he muttered.

'Were you in love with her?' Koenig asked.

Keiko sighed. 'I was fascinated by her, honourable Captain. It is difficult to explain. Do you know that I was married in July? Not six months ago?'

'I didn't know,' Koenig said.

'I honeymooned, then left on this mission,' Keiko told him. 'I knew I was going to die. I volunteered knowing that. I thought only of the mission. But being in that mood I was prepared to live to the last moment. I thought of this girl as a geisha . . . but then I realised how different she was, not only to my Akiko, but to any woman I had ever known. I was fascinated, honourable Captain. Can you understand that?'

'Of course I can,' Koenig said.

Keiko's shoulders slumped. 'And thus I have ruined our mission. I have betrayed my country. Far more than that girl, I am the one who should be put against a wall and shot.'

'As you have said, you were given to understand that she was absolutely trustworthy.'

'That is irrelevant. However, honourable Captain, let me assure you that in Japan we know how to atone for our mistakes. I will withdraw as soon as you give me permission.'

'And kill yourself?'

'And atone for my mistake,' Keiko said carefully. 'I would only ask you to care for my men, and see that they are repatriated to Japan whenever it is possible. And to forgive me.'

'I am not going to forgive you, Herr Commander,' Koenig said. 'Not if you bustle off to some dark corner and cut your belly open. That is pointless. If you are so anxious to die, at least do it over New York.'

Keiko's head turned slowly.

Koenig smiled at him, and pointed at the flag flying on the building they were approaching. 'The Admiralty. Grand Admiral Raeder will be waiting.'

*

295

Doenitz was present, as well as the Japanese ambassador, and several other naval officers, and, of course, the grand admiral.

'Well, gentlemen,' Raeder said. 'A sad occasion. To think that wretched girl has been in our midst virtually since the war began, learning our secrets, passing them on to her associates . . . . The Führer is angry. I have never known him so angry.' He sighed. 'But that is by the by. The decision has been taken to abort the proposed Kong mission. I am making arrangements for you and your men, Commander Hatatsune, to be repatriated to Japan just as soon as it can be done. Believe me, I regret this decision more than anyone. To have come so close to success, and now to have to admit failure . . .'

Koenig wondered if any of these men, and Doenitz in particular, had any idea what had been done, and was being done, to that 'wretched girl'. Of course they did, however they might deny it. And not one of them, not even Doenitz, who had undoubtedly sat her on his knee as a child – and might have done a lot more than that in recent years, as she had been one of his secretaries – would lift a finger to help her. These were the men, the representatives of the regime they served, for whom he was committed to fighting . . . and dying. What absurdity.

And yet, in a perverse way, he was more than ever determined to fight, and die, for Germany. Because there was nothing else he could do, now, in honour. And because there was nothing else he *wanted* to do.

'With respect, Herr Admiral,' he said. 'But there is no necessity to abandon the mission.'

Raeder frowned at him. 'I do not understand you, Herr Captain.'

'I mean that to abandon this mission now would be to admit defeat, Herr Admiral,' Koenig said. 'But there is no good reason to admit defeat, yet. We can still succeed.'

'My dear Hjalmar, once that news breaks, as it will certainly do some time today, every warship the Allies possess will be waiting for you.'

'Where, do you suppose, sir?'

'Well . . . everywhere.'

'I do not think even the Allies have sufficient ships readily available to form a cordon from the Orkneys to Greenland, Herr Admiral. Besides, I am sure I know where they will be waiting: at the exit to the Denmark Strait.'

'That is the logical place, certainly. But I do not see how you can be sure of it.'

'Because I know the message relayed by the man Anderssen, Herr Admiral. It was picked up by one of our monitoring stations. He has sent that we shall be passing through the Denmark Strait on the night of 5/6 December. This was indeed my intention. But suppose we sail through the passage *south* of Iceland, between Iceland and the Faroes?'

'That is mined,' Doenitz objected.

'So are parts of the Denmark Strait, Herr Admiral. And, in any event, do not our submarines penetrate those waters? They have discovered the cleared passages. We can use those passages.'

'You would be under constant radar surveillance,' one of the other officers pointed out.

'Less so than in the Denmark Strait,' Koenig countered. 'It is a much broader area of water, between Iceland and Scotland.'

'But further south you would be within easy reach of the British Home Fleet.'

'Supposing they are in Scapa Flow, and not concentrated at the exit to the Denmark Strait,' Koenig reminded him. 'And supposing they can identify us in time. Gentlemen . . .' He walked to the map on the wall.

'According to the met reports, there is a considerable front moving out of the American Midwest and over New York and eastern Canada at this moment. This is a bad storm, with heavy falls of snow, very strong winds and poor visibility. The storm is expected to swing across Greenland and Iceland, and thence the North Sea, bringing Arctic conditions to all sea areas. Most important, visibility is expected to deteriorate further before it begins to improve. The storm will undoubtedly start movement amongst the early icebergs. In addition, we are sure that the whole area is going to be full of ships seeking us. Identifying any one vessel will be a problem to the British, even with radar. And do not forget that I will command more speed than any comparable vessel out there. However, it would greatly assist the success of the operation if there could be some diversionary movements. Would it be possible to send an AMC out through the northern passage, leaving tonight?'

Raeder stroked his chin. '*Coronel* is due to depart, certainly. I was going to keep her in port until after your mission, so as not to hamper you in any way.'

'She could be a great help.'

'It will mean sacrificing the ship,' someone objected.

Koenig gazed at him, and then at Raeder.

'Yes,' Raeder said. 'But it would be worthwhile.'

'It would also help if those U-boats already on station, Herr Admiral' – Hjalmar looked at Doenitz – 'would desist from attacking convoys for a day or two, and instead attack units of the British Fleet. This would be a most powerful distraction.'

Doenitz nodded. 'I will signal them to that effect. You really think you can pull it off?'

'I believe we have as good a chance of carrying this mission to a successful conclusion now as we did when it was first considered,' Koenig said, choosing his words

298

carefully. 'Perhaps an even better chance. I request permission to sail as planned, at midnight tonight.'

Raeder stared at him for several seconds, then looked at Keiko. 'You concur in this decision, Commander Hatatsune?'

Keiko's whole being swelled. 'Oh, indeed, honourable Admiral,' he said. 'Oh, indeed. We sai1 at midnight, as planned. Kong will not fail.'

CHAPTER 13

The Challenge

Clive Wharton opened his eyes and blinked, slowly taking in the fact that Jennie was fully dressed, in uniform, and was in fact adjusting her cap as she peered at herself in the mirror.

He sat up. 'Jesus! What are you doing?'

'Going to work,' she told him. 'Some of us have to, you know.'

'Isn't today Saturday?'

'No,' she said. 'It happens to be Wednesday.'

'But, say . . . I have a furlough. Until Monday.'

She turned towards him. 'What do you want to do with it?'

'Well, sleep, get drunk and make love to you.'

'All things are possible. There's Scotch in the cupboard. I may even bring some gin back with me this evening.'

'This *evening*?'

'That allows you all day to sleep.'

'You mean I can stay here?'

'Why not? I've never come home to a man before. It might be rather nice.'

'Well stone the fucking crows,' he remarked. 'About us getting married . . .'

'Forget it,' she advised. 'Until this evening.'

She pulled on her navy blue topcoat and closed the apartment door behind her. She would never have believed she was such a coward. But it was easy to rationalise: refusal would involve explanation, and explanation, right now, would involve a breach of security. She could say nothing until she knew Johnnie was safe and his cover could be blown. Blowing his cover had been the admiral's own idea; one of his better ideas.

The weather was grim. Snowflakes flecked her face as she struggled along the street, trying to keep her footing on the ice; all feeling left her nose. What it was like further north, in Goose Bay, for instance, did not bear consideration. And what it was soon going to be like out at sea did not bear consideration, either. She had never been at sea in a winter storm. That would be bad. But far worse was the knowledge that there might be a U-boat lurking just beneath the surface, waiting to send you plunging into that freezing sea, with only a few terrible minutes between you and eternity. She shuddered, and gratefully entered the Pentagon, and warmth, and a tremendous sense of security. This was the hub, the heart, of the mightiest military force the world had ever seen. Nobody could be afraid, inside the Pentagon.

'Messages.' She took off her coat and hat and gloves, stowed them, slapped her hands together and sat at her desk. Cautiously she touched the end of her nose. But circulation was fully restored, and one of the junior girls had placed a steaming cup of coffee in front of her.

'Two, Commander.' Signalman Brown placed them on her desk. 'They've bagged a sub off West Africa, and one of our freighters has gone down off Iceland.'

'Poor bastards,' she muttered. 'Nothing from Stockholm?'

'No, ma'am.'

She nodded. Seven-Seven-Four would only have received her instructions two days ago. He had acknowledged immediately, but it would take time for him to pull Johnnie out without arousing suspicions. That meant another night of stringing Clive along. Somehow that was a relief. Telling Clive she wasn't going to marry him would mean he walked out of the apartment into the misery of Washington in a snow storm, for four lonely days. She just couldn't do that.

Lies, lies, lies. She knew the fact was that she wanted him there. Last night had been even better than in July. He was everything she wanted in a man – only he was the wrong man. But he kept her from going mad worrying about the right one. She was being deceitful and lecherous and downright amoral. It would be for the very last time. And Clive would forgive her. He loved her.

That thought made her want to weep.

The admiral arrived late, and in a bad humour; he had a hangover. 'Thank Christ for the weather,' he muttered as he slumped into his chair and reached a trembling hand for the cup of black coffee Jennie had in turn thoughtfully produced. 'There shouldn't be any big ones today.'

'This weather hasn't reached Europe yet, sir,' Jennie said cruelly.

'It's on the way,' the admiral said. 'Thank Christ for that.'

She left him to suffer, sat at her desk and caught up with some of the routine business which had to be shelved whenever there was a crisis. But there hadn't been a crisis since the successful completion of Torch. In fact, the month since then had been almost total anti-climax. She could stand a little anti-climax, she thought, and wondered what Clive would be doing. Drinking, and lying about the place, and waiting for her to come home. Almost like a husband.

For lunch she had a hot dog in the canteen, together with a slice of apple pie and two cups of coffee. Time to eat properly tonight – maybe, she thought.

She had only just regained her desk when Signalman Brown stood beside her. 'Commander!' He was trembling.

Jennie studied the paper. Her heart seemed to stop for a moment and then redouble its activity; she could feel hot blood pounding through her arteries, filling her cheeks, even her eyes, making it difficult to see. 'Where did this come from?' Could that really be her voice speaking? 'From Stockholm?'

'That's just it.' Signalman Brown was certainly having difficulty in speaking. 'It's come from London. Relayed from Switzerland. Do you see that, ma'am?'

Jennie stared at the additional words: 'THIS MESSAGE APPARENTLY SENT CLEAR STOP REGARD IT AS MOST URGENT STOP HAVE DISPATCHED RECONNAISSANCE AIRCRAFT STOP WILL REPORT EARLIEST STOP LONDON'.

This message sent clear. She knew that only the direst catastrophe would make Johnnie Anderson, or any other agent, send a message in plain English. 'Oh, fuck,' she said. 'Oh, fuck.'

'Yes, ma'am,' Signalman Brown agreed.

Jennie pushed back her chair, picked up the sheet of paper and ran into the admiral's office.

The bolt, scraping again. John Anderson sat up and stared at the opening door. They had left him his watch, and the time was seven o'clock in the evening. He had been in this cell for at least twelve hours, alone, and unharmed, apart from the gonging in his brain. He had even been fed, twice. But no questions, nothing. No sound, even, had been able to penetrate the remorseless drone of the gramophone. But there would have been sound, out there. They had been concentrating on Helga – up to now.

Oskar Doerner stepped into the cell, as quietly and neatly dressed as ever. He was also freshly shaved and

303

obviously recently bathed. John wondered if he was ever going to bathe and shave again.

'How do you feel?' Doerner asked.

'Rotten,' John said. 'I am filthy and my head hurts. I wish to see someone from the Swedish Embassy. I am entitled to do so. I have asked for this several times, and been ignored.'

'Perhaps tomorrow,' Doerner said. 'Now, I wish you to hold out your wrists.'

John frowned at him.

'I am going to handcuff you,' Doerner explained. 'Only temporarily. But it is for your own good, in view of your homicidal tendencies. I am sure you do not wish to receive another bang on the head right now.'

'You have no right to ill-treat me,' John told him. 'No right at all.'

'My dear Herr Anderssen, I would not dream of ill-treating you, of harming you at all — except, of course, in self-defence. Heaven forbid! I merely wish you to come with me, to witness a ceremony. It will not take long.'

John looked past him at the waiting guards. There was nothing he could do but obey. There was nothing he wanted to do; this was his appointed role. He held out his wrists, and the cuffs were snapped into place. Then he walked out of his cell between the guards. Doerner followed. They went along the corridor, and passed the interrogation room. John's muscles began to relax.

At the end of the corridor there was an elevator. He had not noticed this last night. Or had it actually been this morning? The four men stepped into the elevator and rode swiftly upwards for four floors. Then the doors opened and they stepped out into a warm and clean and sweet-smelling corridor, with thick carpeting, into which their heels sank noiselessly; there was no gramophone up here, no sound at all. There was also no one else to be seen.

They walked along the corridor, and one of the guards opened a door to admit them into a large and remarkably high-ceilinged room, almost like a ball-room, John thought. This room was also strangely deserted . . . save for a single man, who was standing close to the far wall, fussing over erecting a camera on its tripod. John raised his eyebrows. They seemed to be going to absurd lengths to take a mug shot.

Then he noticed that it was a movie camera. Suddenly he was cold. Once again he instinctively knew that something terrible was about to happen.

There was a row of straight chairs against the wall beside the cameraman. He was led towards the chairs and made to sit down in the centre one. Another pair of cuffs was produced, much larger than those on his wrists, and his right ankle was secured to the corres-ponding front leg of his chair.

'I must apologise for this,' Doerner said. 'But we really cannot have you committing mayhem whenever you see something that you do not like.'

'Am I about to see something I do not like?' John asked.

Doerner shrugged. 'That is up to you.'

One guard sat on each side of John. Doerner himself remained standing, waiting.

John gazed at the room. A large, empty room . . . save for a beam, which ran across the very centre of the room, some two feet below the ceiling, but because of the height of the ceiling it was still some eight feet above the floor. A plain, unpainted beam, quite out of keeping with the cleanly painted décor of the rest of the room. An old beam, John thought, because of the many grooves in the wood. John's heart constricted as he looked beyond the beam at the far wall and saw a winch, to which was connected a block and pulley; the winch was bolted to the wall. And it was intended for hoisting things, not dropping them; in any event, there was no trapdoor anywhere in the floor.

Doerner had been watching him. 'Yes,' he said. 'It is an unpleasant way to die. But it has been so ordered, by the Führer personally. He hates traitors, especially personal friends of his who have betrayed him. He is a man of the most savage anger when aroused.'

John swallowed, and gazed at the door, knowing it would be opening again soon.

'However,' Doerner went on, 'it is possible for mistakes to occur; for something to happen which might cause one of my men to lose his head – or even myself – and over-react, and perhaps shoot the condemned person before the prescribed sentence can be carried out.'

John turned his head to look at him.

'I'm afraid I can offer nothing better than that, Herr Anderssen,' Doerner said. 'But believe me, to be shot dead is a quick and painless death, and I am a very good shot. The other . . . it is really too horrible, and too degrading, to contemplate. To be slowly strangled means a complete disintegration of all bodily functions. Nor will that be all, of course. And it is to be recorded on film, as you can see, in all its horror and degradation, to be shown to the Führer and his friends on a suitable occasion. Perhaps to be shown to others as well. It is an unpleasant thought, is it not? I can at least prevent that.'

'Why would you do this?' John asked. His voice was thick.

'I would do it, should you choose to add anything significant to what you have already told me,' Doerner explained. 'Remarkably enough, I believe your story. I believe that you are nothing more than a Swedish newspaper reporter who has become involved in affairs beyond his comprehension. I believe it because you have been thoroughly checked out several times since you came to Germany, and because all of your dispatches have also been carefully examined, and there has never been the slightest grounds for suspicion regarding you. Until now. I cannot believe that you were sent here to spy, for anyone, and never sent a dispatch before last night. Therefore I believe that you were used last night by Fräulein Staffel to deliver that message to Herr Mundt. I believe you were used by her once before. That time, perhaps, you had doubts. You did not immediately do as she asked; you went as far as Hanover on your way back to Wilhelmshaven, did you not? But then your love for her won out over your common sense, and so you returned to Berlin and went to Mundt the bookseller. Oh, yes, Herr Anderssen, we know about these things. And so last night you obeyed her again, with less reluctance.

'I do believe all of these things, Herr Anderssen, and I am sorry for you. But . . . there is always a chance that I could be wrong, that in reality you are a cold and cunning and ruthless spy, who used Helga Staffel, rather than the other way around. Some of the transcripts of your conversations with her almost make me think that you are such a man. But unfortunately, I will tell you frankly, our transcripts are not very distinct, and I also do not know what sort of a game she was playing with you. However, were you to be the spy and she but the assistant, it would be very regrettable. Therefore I am giving you this chance, as a man who perhaps believes in honour, and who perhaps has been in love, and may still be in love, to act the man. You cannot save your mistress from death. But you can save her from degradation.'

John stared at him. He had anticipated only physical pain, not anything quite so mentally severe as this. 'You cannot execute her,' he said. 'She has not been tried.'

'She was tried this afternoon, by a military court,'

307

Doerner told him. 'She is a member of the armed services caught extracting vital information from another officer. There could be no question of a public trial, which might reveal traces of treachery in the Admiralty itself. This too was ordered personally by the Führer. And I am afraid that she was found guilty. Her sentence, and it is a severe one, has to be carried out immediately. Again, as ordered by the Führer.'

John licked his lips.

'I am going to have to hurry you, Herr Anderssen,' Doerner said gently.

John turned to the door and watched it open. Four guards came in; Helga was in their midst. Her head drooped, and although she walked, she moved in a series of jerks; her wrists were handcuffed behind her back. But at least she was dressed, if only in a shapeless grey gown which seemed several sizes too large for her, and hung straight from her shoulders as if to disguise the fact that she was a woman. This almost suggested some feelings of decency on the part of her executioners. But Doerner's words, and the presence of the movie camera, gave the lie to that.

She was about to die; horribly, or quickly – that was his decision. He himself might be soon to die. Those were definitive and irrevocable events. It was what shock waves spread away from their deaths that mattered. He could save Helga a few seconds of shame and agony; he could not save her life. And to do that he would be forced to betray countless others, sending them one after the other to a similar room, to a similar fate.

A fifth man had entered the room, behind the group. This man carried a length of thin rope coiled round his arm. Helga and her guards stopped, and for the first time John realised that her eyes were closed. But they opened now, not to look at the spectators, but to watch the fifth man, who went past her and threw his rope

308

over the beam. It struck the wood and fell back, and again on the second throw. John wanted to scream in anguish.

At the third throw the rope passed over the beam and fell down; the end had a noose in it. The man walked across the room, carrying the standing part, and fed this through the block and round the winch, proceeding with great care.

The noose swung slowly to and fro, five feet from the floor.

'Bring the prisoner over here,' Doerner commanded.

The guards marched Helga towards them. John felt sick, and at the same time knew an overwhelming desire to do a Samson and burst free from his bonds in a gigantic muscular thrust, and bring the entire filthy building down on top of them all. But Samson was a legend, and he could do nothing with his wrists handcuffed together and his ankle secured to the heavy chair.

Helga stared at him, seeing him for the first time. 'Jan,' she whispered. 'Oh, Jan.'

'I think perhaps Herr Anderssen has something to say to you, Fräulein,' Doerner remarked. 'Perhaps he has something to say to all of us.'

John looked back at her. Only a few seconds, he thought. Only a few seconds. 'Forgive me,' he said.

'Jan . . .' Her lips trembled, and tears rolled out of her eyes.

Doerner waited.

'Jan . . .'

'Only a few seconds,' John said. 'That is all.' The words dripped from his mouth like vitriol.

Doerner raised his eyebrows. 'You are a very hard man, Herr Anderssen,' he commented. 'Do you know, I actually thought that, even if you are innocent, you might be prepared to sacrifice yourself for the sake of your mistress.'

309

'If I had done that, you would torture me,' John said. 'I should not like to be tortured.'

'Oh, undoubtedly we would have tortured you,' Doerner agreed. 'And it would have been a pleasure.' His voice twisted in contempt. 'You may proceed, Streseman.'

'Jan,' Helga said urgently. 'Jan,' she shouted, as she was dragged away to stand before the noose. 'Jan . . .' Her voice trailed away into a whisper as she saw the rope.

Did she really believe he could save her? he wondered. He wanted to shut his eyes, but they simply would not close.

Streseman dropped the noose over Helga's head and adjusted it to fit snugly around her neck, fluffing out her hair and slowly pulling the noose tight, but taking great care that the knot was nowhere near her right ear and the wad of tissue, the occidental process, which protected the medulla and thus all the vital forces of the human body. In a humane hanging, the knot was driven into the occidental process by careful positioning and the force of the drop, shattering the medulla and ending life instantaneously. But this was not intended to be a humane hanging.

Satisfied at last, Streseman did something to Helga's back. John did not know what it was, for a moment.

The man by the far wall began winching the rope through the block. It was a powerful winch and he could probably have lifted someone several times Helga's weight; she presented no problem at all. The rope tightened, and Helga's face constricted. She tried to open her mouth again, and had it forced shut by the pressure of the rope. She stood on tiptoe, and then swung from the floor, body twisting, legs kicking as the breath was slowly crushed from her lungs. And the grey gown, the buttons on the back released by Streseman, slowly and obscenely slipped from her shoulders, and

310

down her body with every kick, every convulsive jerk; she wore nothing underneath.

While the movie camera whirred.

'You believe all this crap?' the admiral asked.

'Yes, sir, I do,' Jennie said.

'You don't think this jerk Seven-Twenty-One has just flipped his lid one more time? Japanese? Aircraft-carrier? Jesus!'

'Well, sir,' Jennie said, as usual keeping a tight hold on her temper. 'We know there are Japanese airmen in Germany. They have to be there for some rational purpose. We know Koenig was pulled out of sea-going duties for some special assignment. And we know the Germans probably do have another carrier. And this message was sent in clear. That is very serious, sir. In fact . . .'

'And the British have sent out reconnaissance planes,' the admiral said, half to himself. 'So *they* must believe it. Jesus Christ! It's really happening. I'm going up to Admiral King right away. I want everything we have waiting at the bottom end of the Denmark Strait by Saturday morning. And I want every convoy held until this thing is sorted out, got that? You get back on to London, and tell them we urgently need those recce sightings. The carrier won't be alone. There's bound to be an escort. By God, a fucking task force. That's what it'll be. *Tirpitz. Hipper. Lützow.* Probably *Scharnhorst* and *Gneisenau* as well. Hell's bells. This could be the big one, Jen. The Midway of the North Atlantic. Christ-almighty!' He was working himself up into a fuss, pulling on his jacket, reaching for his cap.

'I would also like to get through to Stockholm, sir,' Jennie said.

'Oh, sure. Do that. Any confirmation we can get, the better.'

'I wish to ask them about Seven-Twenty-One, sir.'

'Eh?' He adjusted his cap.

'He sent the message in clear, sir. He would only have done that if there wasn't time to code.'

'So there wasn't time. You're damned right there wasn't time.'

'As regards the message, there was time, sir,' Jennie insisted, speaking as quietly and calmly as she could. 'If the German task force sailed last night, it cannot possibly reach the Denmark Strait for at least two, probably three, days. There was time to code the message and still allow us to concentrate our forces; an hour or two would not have mattered. If Seven-Twenty-One sent it in clear, it was because the Germans were breathing down his neck.' She was amazed at her control, when all she wanted to do was scream and shout with the best of them. Because she had always known this was going to happen, one day? But for it to happen now, when Johnnie was actually on his way home . . . only he hadn't ever been on his way home. Not really. That had only been part of the dream.

'Okay,' the admiral said. 'Okay, if it's bothering you that much. Only don't let it get in the way of the important stuff. Seven-Twenty-One had a job of work to do. He knew that when he went out there. So maybe he's done it at last. We'll give him a medal. Even if it's posthumous.'

'I would still like to find out . . . sir,' Jennie said, wondering if she was ever going to have the opportunity to kick this God-damned asshole right in the balls.

'I said okay.' He hurried from the office.

Jennie returned to her desk and drafted the message.

'All systems red alert, eh, ma'am?' asked Signalman Brown.

'Send the message, sailor,' Jennie said. 'Before I lose my temper.'

She went across to the receiving desk herself, nails eating into her palms as she clenched her fists. One broke. But she knew there couldn't be a reply for some time. She went back to her desk, trying to work and not to think ... not to imagine. Imagination was a disease, in a job like hers. She felt like a drink. But that wasn't allowed. She nearly jumped out of her skin when Signalman Brown appeared at her elbow. 'Not good, ma'am,' he remarked.

She snatched the paper, feeling she was about to vomit, gave a sigh of relief, and felt her lunch slowly settling back into its proper place.

'REGRET TO REPORT RECONNAISSANCE MISSIONS UNSUCCESSFUL STOP TOTAL CLOUD COVER EXTENDS ACROSS NORTH SEA AND DENMARK STOP WILL KEEP LOOKING BUT WEATHER OUTLOOK ON THEIR SIDE STOP THREE FOUR TWO'.

'I'd better take this up to the admiral,' she said, knowing she just had to keep moving, keep occupied, keep herself from that dreadful trap of wondering ... until Stockholm came through.

She took the elevator and wandered into another world of trim young women. 'You can't interrupt him now, Commander,' the lieutenant explained. 'There's a very high-level conference in there.'

'I'm to do with it,' Jennie told her. The girl made a telephone call, and a few minutes later Jennie was in the big room, gazing at more assorted brass than she had ever seen accumulated in one place before. Admiral King she recognised right off, because of his beak-like face. But there were a lot of faces she didn't recognise at all. On the other hand ... her jaw dropped; they'd even got General Marshall sitting in.

'What is it, Commander?' The admiral had never called her 'Commander' before. She nearly dropped her papers. 'Have we got a sighting?'

'No, sir. No sightings from the British,' she said. 'There are eight oktas cloud right across the area.'

'Oh, hell,' Admiral King said. 'You're Commander Rhodes, right?'

'Yes, sir.' Jennie stood to attention.

'I've heard a lot about you. Bill here thinks you're the best.'

'Thank you, sir.' At what, she wondered.

'So what do you think of this?' King asked.

'Sir?'

'Could it be a bluff, Commander Rhodes?' George Marshall's voice was quiet. 'A diversion, perhaps? An attempt to make us concentrate our forces in one area while the German Navy breaks out in another?'

'No, sir,' Jennie said.

'Why are you so sure?'

Jennie stared at him. 'Because . . . if the German Navy had been going to break out for any other reason, sir, they'd have done so last month, and hit Torch.'

'They didn't know about Torch,' Marshall pointed out.

'Yes, sir. So this is a counterstroke for them, as well as for the Japanese.'

'Hm.' Marshall looked at Admiral King. 'There's sound reasoning in that. They sure as hell know by now that they're not going to push us out of North Africa.'

'Thank you, Commander,' Admiral King said. 'Let's hope you're right. If they come down the Denmark Strait, we'll blow them right out of the water.'

'Yes, sir,' she agreed, saluted, and left the room. She didn't doubt the Germans would indeed be blown out of the water. As if that mattered.

She hurried down to the office again. Signalman Brown was waiting for her. 'Well?' she demanded, her heart thudding down to the pit of her stomach. He looked like death.

He didn't say a word, just handed her the paper.

She read: 'SEVEN TWENTY ONE ARRESTED GESTAPO YESTERDAY STOP NOTHING HEARD

SINCE STOP MUST REGARD CONTACT AS
TERMINATED STOP WILL TAKE STEPS TO
PROTECT AGENTS IN VIEW OF POSSIBLE
CORRECTION PROBABLE BREAKDOWN OF
SEVEN TWENTY ONE UNDER INTERROGATION
STOP HOLD FURTHER COMMUNICATIONS
UNTIL NOTICE FROM ME STOP SEVEN SEVEN
FOUR.'

'Guess what?' Clive opened the door of the apartment
for her. 'I've baked a pie. And I've made the bed. You
didn't know I could cook, I reckon. Or housewife. They
teach you all kinds of crap in the navy.'

Jennie walked across the little lounge, threw her cap
on the settee, kept on going into the bedroom, dropped
her topcoat on the floor and fell across the bed on to
her face.

'Been a hard day, eh?' Clive inquired.

She couldn't weep. That was the trouble. Something
had died, in there.

'You okay?' Clive asked, at last getting some sort of
vibration.

'Fuck off,' she suggested.

She heard indistinct sounds, which she presumed were
caused by his withdrawal. But then they came back
again. 'Scotch?' he asked.

'Oh . . .' She turned and sat up at the same time, then
took the glass from his hand and hurled it with all her
strength at the wall. It shattered, and liquid flew left
and right.

Clive gazed at her, his expression indeterminate.
'Anything I can do to help?'

'You are a bastard,' she said. 'A miserable, fucking
asshole.' She thought she might be going mad. The
room seemed to be growing steadily smaller. If she
didn't scream or burst into tears, she *was* going to go
mad. But she didn't know how to scream or burst into

315

tears. She had lost that facility the moment she had realised she and Johnnie weren't going to be married, after all. 'Fuck,' she said. 'Oh, fuck, fuck, fuck, fuck.'

Clive was frowning. Then he did a surprising thing. He reached out, grasped her by the lapels of her jacket, pulled her to her feet and slapped her face, very hard. She had never been slapped before. She gasped and half turned, tasted blood, and would have fallen over the bed to the floor if he hadn't caught her sleeve and turned her right round. She kept on falling; she discovered herself across his knees, and realised that he had flipped her skirt to her waist. She gave another gasp and tried to push herself up, but was forced flat by his left hand on her back, while his right hand slapped her backside with all the force he could transmit. At least, she hoped it was all the force he could transmit. Silk provided no protection, and the shock was almost paralysing; it was a good second before the pain started.

Then she screamed, but by then he had hit her three times more. The entire area between her navel and her knees seemed alive with agony, and the screams merged into a long wail, which forced the tears from her eyes, sending them cascading down her cheeks. She had lost control of her muscles, and when he rolled her off his knee she just fell, tumbling off the end of the bed to the floor, arms and legs scattered, staring at the ceiling, chest heaving and hurting as the tears fought their way up from her very gut.

Dimly she heard a banging on the front door, and Clive opening it. 'What's happening in there?' asked the landlord, who lived on the floor below.

'We're rearranging the bedroom,' Clive told him.

'Yeah? Just who the hell are you, fella?'

'Someone who doesn't much like the look of your face,' Clive said. 'You want me to rearrange that as well?'

There was a brief hesitation. Then the landlord called,

'Hey, Miss Rhodes, you all right? You all right, Miss Rhodes?'

'There's a guy here wants to know if you're all right, Jennie,' Clive said.

Slowly Jennie held on to the bed and pulled herself up, winced, and turned on to her knees. 'Yes,' she said. 'Yes, I'm all right.'

'You heard the lady,' Clive said, and closed the door.

Jennie rested her head on the sheet and panted, then heard his footsteps approaching.

'Scotch?' he asked.

She raised her head, and he put the glass in her hand. It shook, and some of the liquid spilled. He took it back, knelt beside her and held the glass to her lips. 'When you feel better,' he told her. 'You can hit me. With a hammer, if you like.'

She looked at him as she felt the liquid trickling down her throat.

'You were suffering from suppressed hysteria,' he explained. 'I've seen it in guys under fire. We have to snap them out of it pretty quick, or they're never good for anything, ever again. On the other hand, some of those guys turn into heroes, if you can get them going.'

She rose to her feet, took the glass from his hand and drank some more. The tears were drying.

'If you're not going to hit me,' he suggested. 'I reckon you should tell me about it.'

'Who the hell are you?' the admiral demanded.

'Captain Clive Wharton, sir.'

'How the hell did you get in here?'

'I walked. I had to push some guy out of the way first.'

'Wharton? Wharton? Commander Wharton?'

'Captain Wharton, with respect, sir,' Clive repeated.

'Oh, sure. I remember now. Congratulations, Captain. I've always wanted to meet a real-life hero.

317

Now would you mind getting the hell out of my office? We have a major emergency on, and I have problems.'

'Like being without your number two, sir,' Clive suggested.

The admiral glared at him. 'What the hell do you mean by that?'

'I have come to tell you, sir, that Commander Rhodes won't be in today.'

'Won't be in? Christalmighty, I know that. I mean, I know she's not here yet.' His frown deepened. 'What the shitting hell have you done with her?'

'Put her to bed, sir.'

'To . . . you her brother or something?'

'A friend,' Clive explained.

'Jesus! What's the matter with her?'

'Battle fatigue,' Clive said.

'You . . .' the admiral looked ready to have a fit. He pointed at Clive. 'I don't know what the God-damned hell you are playing at, Captain, but if you don't start talking sense, I am going to have you thrown in the can, Medal of Honor and all. Talk.'

Clive talked.

When he had finished, the admiral stared at him. 'You're putting me on?'

'I wish to God I was, sir,' Clive said.

'Why?'

'Because I want to marry her.'

'Jesus,' the admiral remarked. 'Oh, Jesus. Well, you may as well go ahead and do that thing, Captain. Judging by what Stockholm has to say, that guy is a dodobird.'

'I know that, sir. Trouble is, Jennie knows it too.'

The admiral was pointing again. 'You know she's guilty of one hell of a breach of security, telling you all of that? Hell, it could be treason.'

'Then what are you guilty of, sir?'

'Me?'

318

'You identified Seven-Twenty-One to her in the first place, sir.'

'Jesus Christ! How was I to know she'd ever met the guy, much less had a crush on him? She sure as hell never let on. Although . . .' His frown returned. 'She was always kind of more interested in him than in anyone else.'

'She didn't have a crush on him, sir,' Clive said. 'I'm trying to tell you that she was engaged to be married to him before your people got at him.'

'Yeah. Yeah. It's a tough world. He could've told us that, you know. But he didn't. So he's a fucking hero too. I'm surrounded by the bastards. So what the hell am I supposed to do about it now?'

'Pull strings to get him out.'

The admiral shook his head. 'That's not on, Captain, and you know it's not on. We can't endanger our entire set-up in Germany for the sake of one man. You know that, and believe me, John Anderson knows that as well. If he plays it cool, he has a chance. We gave him the best cover of any agent in the world. So long as he keeps his head, the Krauts aren't going to break that cover. But the ball has to be in his court.'

'And Jennie?'

'Keep her at home for a few days. Don't let her out of your sight. That can't be too much of a hardship. We'll miss her, with this flap going on, but I agree that she's had a tough deal, and she's no fucking use to me in her present condition.'

'And me?'

'You? What the hell do you have to do with it? I told you, stick with the doll.'

'Find yourself a nurse,' Clive told him. 'I'm stuck in the middle, and I want to do something about that. You sure this raider is coming down the Denmark Strait?'

'Seems so.' Once again the admiral pointed at him. 'But if you breathe a word of that to a soul, I am going

319

to have you cashiered and put in a cell. And you won't have Jennie Rhodes to keep you company, because she's going to be in the female wing.'

'If the enemy come down the Denmark Strait,' Clive said, 'you'll be using all the aircraft you have. That includes my boys at Goose Bay.'

'Your boys?'

'I still reckon they are. I want secondment up there.'

The admiral shook his head. 'Can't be done, Captain. They have a new skipper.'

'Sure, I know the guy: Abe Bostwick. He and I have been friends for years. He'll be happy to have me along. So send me up as a relief pilot.'

The admiral gazed at him for several seconds. 'What the hell do you think this war is being fought for, Captain? Your personal benefit? This war is being fought to make the world safe for democracy. That's what the boss says, and I believe him. So it has to be won. And there ain't a single God-damned one of us capable of doing that on his own. We win all together or we lose, all together. You're one hell of a fighting man. Thank God you're on our side. But you've done your bit, and you're still alive, and you've accumulated a chestful of medals. Now we want a little bit of responsibility out of you. We want thinking at executive, strategical levels, not tactical.

'So the first thing you have to learn is that up here the cookie doesn't always crumble just the way you'd like it to, and you can't put it back together by climbing into an aircraft and flying off into the sun, either. You try sitting here at this desk day after God-damned day, moving men and ships around as if they were bits of cardboard, and every so often tearing one up and saying, well, that's him gone, so, we'll just move this fellow over here into that position and see if he can't do better. You try that for a couple of weeks, Captain Wharton, and then come back and tell me what it's like. Or report to sick-bay with some battle fatigue of your own.

'You're out of this one. You have a furlough until Monday morning. And you've a battle-weary woman on your hands. I'm fond of that girl. She's worth ten of any man I've ever met, and that goes for you too, mister bloody hero. You get back to that apartment, keep her there and make her fit. And if you have any sense, talk her into marrying you and forgetting about Seven-Twenty-One. And get the hell off my back. I have a war to win.'

'Message from flagship, sir,' said the signal lieutenant.

Rod Bowen held out his hand, watching the young man stagger as a huge sea struck HMS *Bombast* on the port bow. It almost threw him out of his chair. He had been out in North Atlantic gales before, but this was one of the worst he had known; he could only thank God that he was not on board a destroyer like *Erebus*. She could well be endangered by waves this big. He stared through the screens. It was already almost dark, and visibility was in any event limited by flying spray; out of the gloom there came another mountainous wall of water, hardly less than thirty feet high, towering above the cruiser.

'Port your helm,' came the quiet command from the officer of the watch, Lieutenant Clarke.

The wheel spun, and the warship turned towards the onrushing force.

'Full speed,' Clarke commanded.

The telegraph jangled, and *Bombast* surged forward. Her bows rammed into the foaming green which topped the monster, and she shuddered. Water cascaded over the fighting top, and for a moment even the five hundred odd feet of the warship seemed totally submerged. Then the bows were through, hurling themselves at the sudden void beyond the wave, plunging down into a trough deeper than the last pit of hell.

'Reduce speed.' Clarke's voice remained quiet. He was a consummate officer who understood the last detail of handling a ship under such extreme conditions. He knew that it was only the weight of water on deck that posed any threat of damage to a well-found ship; therefore, when approaching such a wave, the rule was full speed ahead, to break through and throw the water off in the shortest space of time. But the moment the wave was negotiated, speed had to be reduced, both to stop the propellers tearing the engines apart by churning air as the bows went down, and to prevent the bows from going down too fast and burying themselves too deeply, which might hinder recovery in time to attack the next wave. Now the cruiser was skating quietly down the back side of the wave, but already another huge greybeard was rearing in front of her.

Bombast could handle this sort of thing, of course. She displaced eight thousand tons, and every man of her crew was an expert – after three years at sea, in this war, and in this worst of oceans. Only the chance of bursting through one of these waves and ramming at full speed into an iceberg presented any real danger; no submarine could possibly maintain periscope depths in such conditions. That was a relief – for during the thirty-six hours preceding the storm, the U-boats had been very active indeed. They had even attacked heavy units, which was not their usual game, lending credence to the supposition that a major German break-out was on the way.

But such a break-out would mean little to *Bombast* – unless the unthinkable happened, and the Germans managed to smash through the home fleet and its American reinforcements, and gain the open Atlantic. *Bombast* had been about to take up convoy duties when the alarm sounded; now she waited in reserve, some fifteen hundred miles south of the Denmark Strait. Part of the reason for the huge seas she was encountering was that she was close to the North American continental shelf, the area known as the Grand Banks, where the ocean floor suddenly rose from several thousand fathoms to less than a thousand. Here she was stuck — ostensibly to pick up stragglers, should there be any, but actually in a position to rendezvous with the convoy from Halifax the moment it was released.

Which couldn't happen a moment too soon, so far as Rod Bowen was concerned. And maybe there was something happening up north at last, he thought, scanning the message as the seas temporarily subsided at last. 'REGRET FALSE ALARM STOP ENEMY ARMED MERCHANT CRUISER SUNK NORTH ICELAND ATTEMPTING BREAKOUT STOP WEATHER NORTH SEA CLEARED STOP RECONNAISSANCE AIRCRAFT REPORT NO OTHER ENEMY UNITS AT SEA STOP FLEET WILL DISPERSE TO PREVIOUS DISPOSITIONS STOP THANK YOU FOR ASSISTANCE STOP GOOD LUCK AND GOOD HUNTING STOP COMMANDER IN CHIEF'.

Bowen raised his head slowly. Then he looked at his watch. It was eighteen hundred, and the day was . . . for a moment he couldn't think . . . Sunday, 6 December. They had been holding this position for two days. And now it was over.

Bowen scratched his head. All that flap, over a damned AMC. Suddenly the tension was gone, and he was deathly tired. He had sat in this chair for damned near two days as well, waiting to hear of a possible fleet action. *The* fleet action, which would make Jutland seem like a piece of cake. And it hadn't happened. The Yanks, as usual, had got themselves into a flap about nothing at all, or some agent in Germany or Norway had totally misread a piece of information.

'You'll alter course two-one-five, Mr Clarke,' he said.

Clarke, busily negotiating another huge wave, half turned his head. 'Sir?'

'The flap is over,' Bowen told him. 'The admiral has decided it's a false alarm.'

'Oh, *damn*,' Clarke said.

'Yes,' Bowen agreed. 'So we are to resume normal duties. That means for us, making that rendezvous with the Halifax convoy. They'll be releasing her now that things are back to square one. I want to be off Sable Island by oh six hundred tomorrow morning.'

'Aye aye, sir,' Clarke said with some relief. He could at last turn away from the waves. Steering the ship downwind would remain a difficult and tricky business, but the movement would be easier going with the seas, visibility would be improved, and with every mile they steamed south there was less chance of encountering an iceberg.

'Anything on radar?' Bowen asked the petty officer.

'Two ships to the north of us, sir. Previously identified and acknowledged. And also one or two bergs, I would say, sir. Almost stationary.'

'Yes. Well, let's get the hell out of here. Mr Clarke, I'm going to turn in for a couple of hours. You'll call me if anything crops up.'

'Aye aye, sir,' Clarke replied.

'Make to flagship,' Bowen told the still waiting lieutenant, ' "Message received and understood. *Bombast*." '

'Aye aye, sir.'

Slowly and painfully, Bowen eased himself out of his chair; every muscle was cramped, and he was suddenly aware of how full his bladder was from the endless cups of coffee he had consumed. But not all the coffee in Brazil was going to keep him awake tonight.

He washed his face and cleaned his teeth, rubbed his hand over his thirty-six-hour growth of beard and considered shaving, but decided against it until the seas abated; there seemed little point in risking cutting his throat at this stage.

His steward was waiting with a plate of sandwiches and a small glass of rum; anything like a sit-down meal was impossible while *Bombast* was repeatedly trying to stand on her head. But a sandwich was all he felt like. He stripped off and rolled into his bunk; down here the heating made the freezing temperatures outside irrelevant, and once he was in the cocoon of his blankets inside his bunk, held from falling out by the padded leeboards, he could relax utterly.

His eyes closed, and a succession of images rushed past his consciousness. He wondered where they *had* got the idea the Germans were breaking out. Of course, it could happen. It even *should* happen, one of these days. But where and how did the top brass get their information . . . which so often proved so very wrong?

Bowen slept, dropping down into the deepest of dreamless slumbers, and awakening suddenly, as any seaman would, because the motion of the ship had changed.

He groped in the darkness for his intercom while looking at his watch; it was just past midnight. 'Bridge?'

'Yes, sir. Morrison here, sir.'

'Conditions?'

'Easing all the time, sir. Seas estimated ten feet. But very low cloud, sir. Visibility poor and closing.'

'That'll be the cold front,' Bowen remarked. 'Thank you, Mr Morrison. The wind may well freshen again as the front passes through. Anything on radar?'

'One or two small, almost stationary blips, sir. Presumably growlers.'

'Try to miss them, Mr Morrison.'

Bowen replaced the phone and lay back again. He knew that growlers – very small icebergs, usually having flaked off from their larger parents – were often nearly submerged and difficult to see with the naked eye. They were not as dangerous as one of the monsters which had spawned them, but they could still put a nasty dent in the bow of a ship.

He dozed off again, then was awakened by the buzzing of the intercom. Looking at his watch, he could not believe it was only just after one – he had slept for less than an hour. 'Captain.'

'Hawthorne here, sir,' Hawthorne was his first lieutenant. He would have taken over the middle watch – from midnight to four – from Morrison just about the time of his last conversation with the bridge. 'I'm sorry to disturb you, sir, but there is an unusual blip on the radar.'

'Unusual?'

'It's very large, sir, almost like a berg. That's what I thought it was at first. But it's travelling very fast.'

'I'll be right up.' Bowen pulled on his clothes and hurried for the ladders. Hawthorne was standing beside the radar petty officer, peering into the screen. Both men stood aside respectfully as their captain joined them.

'Bearing one-four-seven, sir,' the petty officer said. 'Distance thirty-seven miles.'

Bowen looked at the extreme bottom left-hand corner of the set, the south-east, and watched the sweep come round. The blip glowed brightly for a moment, and retained some brightness as the sweep continued on its way. He thought he could almost see it move as he watched. 'How fast is that thing travelling?' he asked.

'Estimated thirty-five knots, sir,' the petty officer said.

'Thirty-five knots,' Rod repeated thoughtfully. 'No chance this machine is on the blink?'

'No, sir.' The petty officer was staring into the eyepiece again. 'The object is increasing speed, sir. She must have spotted us as well.'

'*Increasing* speed?' Hawthorne asked incredulously.

'From thirty-five knots?' He stared at his captain, who had straightened to peer through the screens.

As Lieutenant Morrison had said an hour ago, visibility was thick. The wind had certainly dropped, down to about force six, twenty-five to thirty knots, he estimated, but the seas remained big and confused, and now the cloud seemed determined to settle on the very surface of the sea. He could only guess how cold it might be out there; traces of ice were gathering in the outside corners of the screens.

'She seems far too large for a destroyer, sir,' Hawthorne commented. 'But what else would be travelling so fast? She's making near forty now. I say, you don't suppose she's the *Queen Elizabeth*? Isn't she doing unescorted troopship runs?'

'Someone could have told us.' Bowen chewed his lip. 'Send a call. Give her position and ask for identification. Do not give our position or name, number one.'

'Yes, sir.' Hawthorne hurried for the radio room. Bowen remained peering into the radar screen, the petty officer having surrendered the eyepiece. He knew there was no hope of a physical interception. He estimated they could just close to within ten miles of the intruder before she crossed their bows and began to open up a gap – and visibility was under a mile. Of course, ten miles was within range of his guns, and they would be directed by the radar . . . but it didn't seem credible to him that she could be an enemy, in that position, and travelling at that speed – and how the hell could she have got there, with the entire Home Fleet at sea?

'No reply, sir,' Hawthorne said. He was accompanied by the signals lieutenant, who was obviously expecting further work.

Bowen pulled his nose. The intruder was now almost due south of them, and she was within fifteen miles. In only a few minutes she would start to draw away again. 'Make a flagship,' he said. 'In clear. I don't want any mistakes. Say: "Large unidentified vessel making estimated forty repeat forty knots, position two hundred and fifty miles south-east Cape Race, making west by south stop Does not answer challenge stop Please inform of identity and intention stop *Bombast*".'

'Aye aye, sir,' said the signals lieutenant, and hurried off.

'Quite uncanny,' Hawthorne remarked. 'I've never seen anything like it.'

'Neither have I,' Bowen agreed. 'Sound action stations, number one.'

Hawthorne turned his head in surprise.

'She could be an enemy,' Bowen reminded him.

'Good God! If the Germans have something capable of penetrating our blockade and travelling at that speed . . .'

'I said, she *could* be. Well, sparks?'

'Message from flagship, sir.' His voice was excited.

Bowen scanned the paper. 'FLAGSHIP TO *BOMBAST* STOP NO REPEAT NO ALLIED VESSEL REPORTED OR INTENDED IN POSITION GIVEN STOP SUMMON INTRUDER TO HALT FOR INSPECTION STOP IF NO ACKNOWLEDGEMENT AND COMPLIANCE INTRUDER SHOULD BE SUNK STOP FLAGSHIP'.

CHAPTER 14

The Encounter

Clive Wharton awoke when Jennie left the bed. He had in fact only been catnapping, as he had catnapped most of the weekend. Sleeping beside her, almost as if they had been married.

But they were going to be married. Remarkably, this didn't fill him with quite the euphoria it should have done, and would have done only a week ago. Not that he was any the less in love with her. He had always loved her body; she had the kind of body, and hair, and face, which could keep a man awake. And for all of his life he had never wanted more from a woman. Of course, it was great if she was intelligent enough to hold a conversation with, and it was at least a bonus if she wasn't quite so dumb as to be embarrassing in company . . . but from where he stood only the ass and the tits and the face had really mattered. Jennie had all three of those in better shape and proportion than any girl he had ever met. So he had fallen in love – his way.

He hadn't expected anything to change. But then he had never looked at Jennie as a human being, as opposed to a lot of sex. She was a female, and that was all he had to know about her. That attitude went with being a hero. He was proud of both badges of manhood. It had never occurred to him really to inquire what she was doing in this man's navy, and what had driven her to enlist in the first place. And he would never have considered for a moment that she could be doing the job she had been doing for the past couple of years. That was man's stuff, and sufficiently wearing even for men.

But last Wednesday night he had watched her begin to fall apart, and had reached out and pulled her back together, his way. It was then he had realised that he was in love with her on a bigger scale than bed. Ordinarily, when a female started to cut loose, he cut and ran. He had more important things to do with his life than cope with hysterics. But Jennie ... and it had happened before she had told him about her job. That had only added total respect, even awe, to the feelings he already had.

She was not only doing a remarkable job, she had done it knowing about Johnnie ... and he had been content to dismiss Johnnie as a coward – a drop-out, one of life's failures. Because in the image Clive had so carefully cultivated, one wore one's courage up front. He had had no dealings with men who possessed that greater courage, that sublime courage, which enabled them to step back from the ranks of their buddies and fade into the shadows, and *endure*, in secrecy, and thus in loneliness ... and in fear. Johnnie had done that for four years. And Jennie had known about it for a year. And both had endured, Jennie at the least preserving her love. But hadn't Johnnie also? Clive didn't think he would like to choose which of the two of them was the braver. He certainly wasn't going to decide which of them he admired more.

Learning all that had been his cue to creep away into the darkness. He just didn't measure up, he felt. These people were way out of his class, and for him to come stealing into this bed looking for a piece of ass, ass which belonged to a far better man than he could ever be, made him the biggest shit since Judas. His sole idea had been to get into a plane and go flying out into the North Atlantic, there to prove his courage to himself

330

once again, or there to die. The admiral had scotched that. Jennie described the admiral as the biggest asshole in the world. Clive was just coming to realise there was no such thing. Everyone had something, and to get to be an admiral you had to have more than most. The admiral had had the sense to tell him to go away and grow up. And growing up began with Jennie.

So he would marry her, and would get to lie on those tits every night, and he would be the happiest man in all the world . . . save when he, or she, thought of Johnnie Anderson standing against a wall while the Gestapo marksmen loaded their weapons.

At least, they would have grown up together, he thought.

She was his baby now. His worry, his responsibility. Another new experience. The only responsibilities he had ever accepted in the past were the lives of the guys in his squadron, not those of the broads in his bed. But he had sure accumulated one now.

He thought he had done a good job. The hysteria of last Wednesday had hovered all day Thursday. Then it had been complicated by guilt, by her awareness that there was an almighty flap on, and that she should have been at her desk in the Pentagon. He had had to get the admiral himself to telephone her and give her the two days off, and the weekend as well – the admiral had been great. They had been able to relax on Saturday, and they had even gone out to dinner – he guessed she had been getting pretty tired of his cooking, which was of the boiled-egg variety, even if he did know how to bake a piecrust – and they had danced a bit, and come home and made love, and she had even smiled. Yesterday had been best of all. But at lunchtime the admiral, who had apparently not taken the weekend off, at least up to then, had telephoned to say the flap was over. It was a false alarm, stirred up by a single blockade-runner who had been duly brought to book.

That had been a tricky moment, and was still being tricky, so far as he could tell. Jennie had slowly been coming to terms with the fact that Johnnie was dead, but she had been able to take refuge in the knowledge that he had died a hero's death, remitting priceless information to his motherland. Now she had to face the fact that he had died for nothing, remitting worthless information. She had gone into a brood, and he hadn't been able to shake her out of it. Last night she had drunk better than half a bottle of Scotch. So maybe that was why she needed to use the john at two o'clock in the morning. On the other hand, that was also a good reason for her to have crashed out for twelve hours or more.

The light went off in the bathroom, and he heard the door open. He switched on his own light. 'Okay?'

'Sure,' she said. 'I didn't mean to wake you.'

'So who sleeps when there's a war on?' he asked, hoping he hadn't made a mistake.

Apparently he had. He watched her open her bureau drawer, pull out various articles of underclothing, and start to put them on.

'What's up?' he asked.

'Like you said, there's a war on. And I have spent four days in bed. I have to get to the office.'

'At two o'clock in the morning?'

She shrugged. 'We stay on the job twenty-four hours a day.'

'Jennie . . .' He got out of bed. 'The flap is over. Remember? There is no German task force coming down the Denmark Strait. Even the admiral has gone home to bed.'

'So what?' she asked. 'Because one flap is over doesn't mean there isn't going to be another. I should be there.'

Clive considered her. He was toying with the idea of using force. But he decided against it. She wasn't hysterical now, even if, in his opinion, she was still a

332

long way from being totally sane. But this was a kind of madness with which he would have to go along; it was called devotion to duty.

He sighed, and also began to dress.

'Where are *you* going?' she asked.

'It's Monday morning – just. I start work again today as well. Besides, the admiral gave me an order: not to let you out of my sight.'

Rod Bowen peered through the bridge screen at the night, across which the mist lay like a shroud. He had been doing this for so long his eyes felt like badly poached eggs. And it was so pointless; the radar was doing the watching for him. But old habits died hard – he had been a watchkeeping officer when radar was a dream inside some boffin's head.

Besides, the ocean was endlessly fascinating. The seas were still big, although they were not the monsters of a few hours before, and they were going down all the time. Yet it was still uncanny to watch the walls of water appearing out of the mist in continuous succession, as the cruiser raced through them, rising and falling, occasionally lurching and shuddering, but now with total safety. Even in December, Bowen reckoned they were far enough south to be beyond the range of icebergs.

In any case, there were more important things to worry about. He turned his head as Hawthorne returned from the radio cabin. 'Well?'

'He's ignored our demand to heave to, sir.'

'All right, number one. We have our orders. Sink him.'

'Yes, sir,' Hawthorne said, and departed for the gunnery control beneath the navigation bridge. His voice came up the intercom. 'Range?'

'Fourteen miles and gaining, sir,' the petty officer said.

'You'd better hurry,' Bowen muttered to himself, knowing a familiar sinking feeling in the pit of his stomach. But a curious relief as well; he hated the thought of firing blind at a ship which might just be suffering from a radio breakdown.

'Bearing?'

'Red eighteen.'

Hawthorne gave the necessary elevations to his gunners. 'Fire as you bear,' he said.

A moment later the forward turret exploded; the ship shook, seemed to check for a moment, and then surged forward again into the darkness and mist, following the two hundred pounds of explosive.

'Fifteen miles and gaining,' chanted the petty officer.

The forward turret exploded again, the shells disappearing into the night.

'Sixteen miles and gaining,' remarked the petty officer.

'Cease firing, Mr Hawthorne,' Bowen said into the intercom.

'Oh, damn,' Hawthorne said, but he gave the required orders, and a moment later reappeared on the bridge. 'What are we going to do, sir?'

'Follow him,' Bowen said. 'Clear into New York harbour, if we have to.' He turned to the hovering signals lieutenant. 'Make to flagship: "Intruder out of range stop Still making west by south stop Am following stop *Bombast*." '

'Aye aye, sir.'

'Seventeen miles and gaining.'

Bowen sat in his chair and stared at the darkness. The intruder was simply walking away from them as if they were hove to. He reckoned she must be the biggest ship afloat, to be capable of speeds like that. She was certainly larger than a destroyer; the blip, the way she was never lost behind a big sea, told him that. He presumed the *Queen Mary* and this secret new ship, the

Queen Elizabeth, were capable of making thirty-five knots, especially if they were crossing perhaps almost in ballast, east to west, to pick up troops . . . but *forty*? And anyway, if she was one of the Queens, why hadn't she acknowledged his signal? Fear of breaking radio silence and thus alerting a sub? But what U-boat was going to be capable of hitting something travelling that quickly?

Anyway, if she had been a British ship, or an American one, the flagship would have known about her and told him so. She must be an enemy, he decided. But that didn't make sense either. The only thing coming down the Denmark Strait had been an unfortunate AMC, and she was now at the bottom of the ocean.

He accepted a cup of coffee and listened to the chanting of the petty officer. The intruder was gaining on them at the rate of one mile every ten minutes. At three o'clock she was twenty-five miles away, and at four, over thirty. In another couple of hours she would be off the screen altogether. But he was surprised that, although she must have radar of her own and must therefore know that the ship which had challenged her was shadowing her, she was making no effort to throw her pursuer off by altering course. Either she was skippered by a very clever chap who knew he could do nothing unobserved until he was beyond radar range, or she had an urgent rendezvous on this course – or both. Either way, there was nothing he could do about it save follow.

'Message from flagship, sir,' said the signals lieutenant.

Bowen scanned the paper. 'CONTINUE PURSUIT STOP HAVE DISPATCHED ALL POSSIBLE AID AND ALERTED AMERICAN EAST COAST COMMANDS STOP PERSONAL TO CAPTAIN BOWEN STOP SHOULD INTRUDER PROVE TO BE ENEMY COMMANDER WILL PROBABLY BE OLD FRIEND

KOENIG STOP GOOD LUCK STOP COMMANDER IN CHIEF'.

Second Officer Clarke had replaced Hawthorne at four o'clock. 'You mean she's another AMC, sir?' he asked, having read the message. 'Doesn't quite make sense to me.'

'No,' Bowen agreed. 'It doesn't to me, either.' And yet, Hjalmar Koenig, he thought . . . a very clever chap indeed. But what the devil was Koenig doing making west, closing the coast of Newfoundland with every minute, when, having broken through and with that speed under his feet, he had the whole damned Atlantic Ocean to play with?

And exactly what was he commanding?

'Thirty-five miles and steady,' said the petty officer quietly.

Bowen put down his coffee cup. 'Say again,' he snapped.

'Thirty-five miles and now closing, sir. The intruder would appear to have stopped.'

'Engine breakdown, most likely,' Clarke commented. 'Had to happen, careering about in the middle of a storm at forty knots.'

'No, sir,' the petty officer said. 'Correction. Intruder has not stopped. She would appear to have turned. She is steaming north, but dead slow.'

'That makes sense,' Clarke said. 'One engine breakdown, so she's turned into the wind and sea while repairs are made.'

Bowen had left his chair and was standing behind the petty officer, watching the screen. 'Could be,' he said, half to himself. 'What is that?'

'That's very odd, sir,' agreed the petty officer, watching a tiny blip appear above the big one. 'And there's another. Almost as if . . .'

'Yes,' Bowen said, his heart starting to pound.

'We'll get her now, sir,' Clarke said enthusiastically. 'Shall I call the men back to action stations?'

'Yes,' Bowen said thoughtfully. 'But I don't think we're going to be in time.'

'Sir?'

Bowen turned to the signals lieutenant. 'Make to flagship, sparks, for relay to all stations. Send it in clear, there's no time to lose: "Suggest AMC was decoy stop Intruder identified as aircraft-carrier now engaged in launching strike stop Hope to engage in one hour but cannot prevent strike stop *Bombast*". And for God's sake, hurry.'

Albing pulled the cork, and poured. The champagne frothed into the glasses and swirled about as *Nemo* hit a larger than usual wave, shuddered and shook, went down and came back up; solid water splashed on to the bridge screens, undoubtedly went over the top and cascaded along the flight-deck. But the helmsman merely laughed, as did everyone on the bridge itself. Koenig realised that his men were close to hysteria.

But it was the hysteria of confidence, of looming success. They had succeeded. *They* had succeeded. They were through the blockade and out into the Atlantic, and now even the hunt for them was over; the message from the British flagship, just decoded, told them that. Now it was up to Keiko and his men.

He sipped champagne. He had not really expected to make it, he knew. And he had not cared. He had come on this mission to die, just as determinedly as the Japanese themselves. Yet he had also wanted to succeed, at least in launching the strike. And nothing was going to stop that now.

'My congratulations, honourable Captain.' Keiko himself appeared on the bridge. 'I have just heard the news. A fine performance.'

'Not ours alone,' Koenig reminded him. 'I wish us to

drink a toast to *Coronel*, and all who sailed in her, and sacrificed themselves, so gallantly, that we might succeed.'

'*Coronel!*' said the officers.

'*Coronel*,' Keiko agreed. But he was concerned with the future, not the past. 'Do you think these seas will abate?'

'No,' Koenig told him happily. 'The storm is moving east, and we are moving west, further into it. This lull is temporary as the cold front passes us; in another two or three hours the wind will return. But we do not want the weather to improve, eh, Herr Commander? This is the best weather for us. Can your men not take off in these seas?'

Keiko peered out at the huge waves. 'They will do so,' he said. 'It is only a matter of confidence.'

'Well, I am going to turn in for a while,' Koenig said. 'We are still several hours away from the launch point. Take command, Herr Lieutenant,' he told Meyer. 'Call me if anything shows. Anything at all.'

'Yes, Herr Captain.'

'I suggest you also get some sleep, Keiko,' Koenig said. 'You are going to need all of your strength this morning.'

'Strength comes from prayer,' Keiko told him. 'Not from rest. I shall lead my men in prayer to the gods, that our mission will be successful.'

Koenig hesitated, then changed his mind about saying anything. The trouble with prayer, he thought, was that the other fellows were probably also praying to their god, wherever they were. He went into the small cabin he had had constructed behind the navigation complex. Like every other man on board *Nemo*, he had allowed himself only a hammock, as in the old sail-training days before the First World War, but he also had a desk, which doubled as a table; here Albing had erected the fiddles, and a plate of sandwiches was sliding to and

338

fro with every lurch of the ship. Albing himself was also here, with another bottle of champagne.

'Are you trying to make me drunk?' Koenig inquired.

'It will make you sleep,' Albing told him. 'You need sleep, Herr Captain.'

That was true enough, Koenig thought, as he bit into the first sandwich and felt the saliva almost painfully seeping into his mouth. He had not slept, except for the odd doze in his chair, for four nights. He had stayed on the bridge all the time they had slipped up the Kattegat, then during the first day as, thanking fate for the mist and low cloud which had come in before the storm, they had steered across the North Sea for the Faroes. They had passed the islands at night, travelling at reduced speed so as not to excite any watcher on radar, listening to chatter all around them as the Royal Navy received orders to prepare for a major German break-out. Their enemies had been in a state of high excitement, too high an excitement to concentrate on one blip already in their midst, where they were expecting a task force. *Nemo* had certainly been requested to identify herself on more than one occasion, but she had replied in English, in the midst of a flurry of self-induced static to suggest she had a problem with her radio equipment, and thereby only increased the confusion and uncertainty. In addition, Doenitz's submarines had played a magnificent part in distracting the enemy.

Then they had been through, and into the North Atlantic. He had opened her up then, and they had actually made the crossing in under three days. But all the while they had been aware that only a few hundred miles to their north was the entire British Home Fleet, able to turn at a moment's notice and come racing down to blast them out of the water. Then they had relied on *Coronel*, as much as on the weather. Neither had let them down. The clouds had remained low, and although they had heard Sunderland flying boats over-head on the first day, and heard the conversations between their crews as they had asked about this blip and that, there was no way the Britishers could make any positive identification. And with so much going on, so many ships racing to and fro, there was equally no way they could start bombing without such identification.

Eventually, *Nemo* had reached beyond the range of even a Sunderland flying boat. Soon, now, she would come within the range of the American Catalinas. But by then she would already be launching her aircraft. And the great thing was, he thought, no one was looking for them any longer. The initiative was his.

Koenig turned into his hammock and slept soundly, until awakened by a call from the bridge. Under-Officer Schmidt was on watch, but Meyer soon joined them as well, and Keiko. Koenig showed them the radio signal, then peered into the radar screen. 'There,' he said. 'Thirty odd miles away, and north-west of us. Probably a cruiser.'

'That is bad fortune,' Keiko observed.

'That is no fortune, Herr Commander,' Koenig told him. 'It is an incident which was to be expected. There are Allied patrols scattered all over this ocean. It has been our fortune not to encounter one before now.'

'But what will we do?'

'Outrun him,' Koenig said. 'We will do it.'

He remained on the bridge. The seas were smaller now, but in the low navigating position essential for *Nemo*, and situated so far forward, clouds of spray constantly rose from the bows only a few feet in front of them and scattered across the screens. They were running across the face of the storm; the big ship was rolling like a dinghy in a wake. When they turned north there would be some really big seas, but that was not

340

for a couple of hours yet, and the deterioration he expected in the weather had not yet happened. Maybe Keiko's gods were answering his prayers, after all, he thought.

'We will pass within ten miles of her,' Meyer remarked.

'Far enough, in these conditions, unless he is very accurate. See what he is saying.'

Meyer went off to the radio room and returned a few minutes later. 'He has summoned us to stop. When we did not, he sent for information on us. He has now been ordered to sink us if we do not respond. Do you think we can bluff him?'

'No,' Koenig said. 'Not here, and after he has observed our speed. He will want at least to look at us. Increase speed to maximum, Herr Lieutenant.'

Meyer was looking into the screen. 'We are already past him.'

Koenig joined him. the blip was starting to fall astern, and with every second the engine revolutions beneath his feet were increasing. 'He had better hurry,' he remarked.

There was a huge sound, and the ship trembled. There was nothing to be seen, although the shell must have struck the sea only a few hundred feet away.

'God almighty, that was close,' Meyer snapped, and Keiko also came hurrying back from the pilots' quarters.

'That was good shooting,' Koenig agreed, smiling at their concerned faces. 'But not good enough. Lieutenant Schmidt, you will obtain a damage report. That shot was close enough to have started a seam. But she has not stopped us, gentlemen. She will have to do better than that, and quickly. We are drawing away all the time.'

He heard the second salvo as well, but again saw nothing. The mist was thick and the shot was less accurate: *Nemo* did not even tremble. And now the range was seventeen miles. He didn't know what sort of armament the cruiser carried, but she would hardly have anything larger than eight-inch. Seventeen miles was a long way for an eight-inch gun.

'We are through,' he told Keiko. 'Again.'

'The Americans have been alerted,' Meyer said, hurrying in from the radio room.

'About what, exactly?'

'That there is an unidentified vessel approaching their coastline at exceptional speed. They will send out ships to intercept us.'

'But they will not get to us in time, because we have not yet been identified as a carrier. We will make an adjustment to our programme. Commander Hatatsune, what is the maximum range you can extract from your aircraft?'

Keiko frowned at him.

'I know that the launch position was set at five hundred nautical miles north-east of New York,' Koenig said, 'but you were not expecting to run out of fuel as you reached your target, surely.'

'I have allowed an extra hour's flying time, honourable Captain,' Keiko said.

'That is, three hundred miles.'

'But we may well need that hour, sir,' Keiko said. 'If we have to engage any interceptors on the way . . .'

'Herr Commander,' Koenig said, 'if you have to engage any interceptors on the way, you are done. Your only hope of succeeding in this mission is to get to your target before anyone knows you are coming. I propose to launch you from a distance of seven hundred and fifty miles. That will give you ten minutes of fuel spare over your target.'

Keiko opened his mouth, and then closed it again, biting his lip as he did so.

'Such a course,' Koenig went on, 'will almost certainly pre-empt any American response. Now, I estimate that we will be in position at zero-four-one-five precisely.' He jabbed the chart. 'There. That is two hours from now. And that time will give us the opportunity to draw away from the British cruiser, and perhaps even out of radar range.'

'And if we do not succeed in shaking her off?' Keiko asked.

'Then we do not succeed. This is the best we can do in the circumstances. Herr Commander, you may alert your men. The success of the mission now depends entirely upon them.' He smiled. 'And upon you, of course, Keiko.'

The pilots were breakfasting, most of them already in their flying gear and highly excited. 'We have heard the shooting, honourable Commander,' said Lieutenant-Commander Takanawa.

'A British cruiser,' Keiko told him. 'But we are past her now, and out of range. There is nothing now between us and our targets. Nothing that can stop us, anyway. Now . . .' He looked over the eager faces. 'To confuse the enemy, we have decided to launch one hour earlier than originally planned. This means that we will be ditching our aircraft over New York itself, but this is all to the good. Each of you knows what he has to do. You have the course, distance, altitude and target. There will be no radio contact once we have taken off. Remember that the prescribed altitude is a guide, nothing more. The lower you can fly without actually hitting the water, the safer you will be, as you will not be revealed on the enemy radar. But keep a look-out for enemy vessels. There will be a screen, because our presence has been reported to the Americans. But they will be looking for a ship, not for us. Remember, our take-off must be perfect in every way. There is no fuel at all to be wasted in these revised circumstances, nor can we ask the carrier to remain virtually at a standstill for more than half an hour, with enemy forces closing around her. That will give us just eighty seconds per plane. You must all understand that any aircraft failing to get airborne in that time will be immediately jettisoned.'

The pilots gazed back at him.

'Well, then,' Keiko said, 'good fortune to you all. What we are about to do will ring for evermore through the pages of history. We are the immortals. We will never be forgotten. And remember that we serve the Emperor, and our ancestors, and the greater glory of Japan.' He raised his right hand, the fist clenched. 'Banzai!'

'Banzai!' they chorused in reply.

He led them to the hangar, where the great planes waited, gleaming dully in their grey paint, against which the flaming suns stood out in bold relief. Mechanics were making the finishing checks, and the last of the fuel was being added. The bombs were already in place. The Junkers 88s were forty-seven feet long, with a wing-span of nearly sixty feet. They would fly at very nearly three hundred miles an hour, and despite their weight and armament, they were also very nearly as manoeuvrable as fighters. Each was armed with two thirteen-millimetre cannon and four eight-millimetre machine-guns. And each carried two two-hundred-and-fifty-pound bombs. No incendiaries for New York. In those cavern-like streets it was the blast which would do the damage.

Keiko gazed at the scene of activity. He had watched it all so often before. But now he had a vision of a shell striking the elevator above his head, and penetrating in here; *Nemo* would explode with a bang which would probably be heard in New York itself. This was his personal nightmare; he had not flown in combat since the sinking of *Akagi*. Today would exorcise that fearful memory, and a great number of other things besides . . .

344

The memory of his own weaknesses, which had all but jeopardised the mission. The memory of the woman, that sliver of painstreaked whiteness? No, he had no memory of her now; he would have killed her himself, with his bare hands, had he been allowed to do so. Well, then, the memory of Akiko? But now was not the moment for remembering Akiko. He had thought of her during the night, when he had knelt in prayer to the great goddess Amaterasu, who took the form of the sun to oversee the affairs of men, and who was the fount of all things, and the goal to which all things had necessarily to return. Might she oversee him and his men today as well, he wished now.

His men. He surveyed them with pride. They had been handpicked, and they had been picked well. They had shown no suggestion of fear or even concern when he had told them the truth about their mission. They had known from the moment they first donned their uniforms, many years ago, that it would one day be their duty to die for their Emperor and their ancestors; to be able to do so in such a dramatic and, it was hoped, telling manner was more than they could have prayed for. They would follow him straight down the roadway to hell, he had no doubt. Well, he would instead lead them up the pathway to the sun.

The elevator was descending, bringing with it a huge gush of icy air. The first plane was loaded, and went up. Keiko went with it, even though he was not intending to take off first. He had put himself down as tenth, exactly in the centre, so that he could largely oversee what was going on. Takanawa would lead the flight, and he and their two crewmen were with him on the elevator. The Junkers normally carried a complement of four, but Keiko had halved that for this mission to conserve fuel – he would be his own navigator, and his crewman, Lieutenant Fushido, would be concerned solely with bomb aiming. It had never been Keiko's intention to do any fighting; as Koenig had said, if that happened the mission was a failure anyway. But he had hoped to have that extra hour up his sleeve . . . why, he had no clear idea. But truly, it did not matter.

They emerged on to the flight-deck, where the wind plucked at them with such force they could hardly stand still, while their breath formed almost solid clouds of mist before their eyes. They had difficulty in keeping their footing as, in addition to the wind, the ship rolled through some thirty degrees, lurching and shuddering from wave to wave; the Junkers had to be tied down to prevent any risk of its going overboard.

'I have never seen weather like this, honourable Commander,' Takanawa confided.

'It is on our side,' Keiko reminded him. 'And when we are airborne it will be a tail wind.'

The next plane emerged, and then the next and the next, until at the end of an hour and three quarters all eighteen were ready. The crews climbed on board, waiting for the order to start their engines. But that had to be delayed until the last possible moment; not a single drop of fuel could be wasted.

'Aircrew prepare for launching,' came the order over the tannoy.

Keiko shook hands with Takanawa. 'Until we meet again, Tadatune San,' he said.

Takanawa grinned. 'That will be soon, honourable Commander.'

Keiko waited for Lieutenant Fushido to get on board and settle himself, then took his own place behind the controls. 'Start engines,' he said into his mike.

The buzz rose even above the whine of the wind, the slapping of the seas and the immense growl of the carrier's turbines far beneath them. The lead planes began to tremble as their engine revolutions increased.

'Flight commander to bridge,' Keiko said. 'All planes ready for launching.'

346

'Stand by,' came Koenig's own voice in reply, and *Nemo* began to turn into the wind. The bows rose and fell through an arc of some thirty feet. The dreadful rolling had stopped, but the windspeed had of course increased. It had been blowing at some thirty knots in any event; now that the carrier's thirty-five was added to it, there was a hurricane sweeping over the flight-deck, tearing at the aircraft, causing them to rise from the deck even while stationary.

'Go,' Koenig said. 'And good fortune.'

'Go,' Keiko said.

The wires were slipped, and Takanawa's machine rolled along the deck. It seemed to move with agonising slowness, surely not sufficient speed ever to become airborne. *Nemo* rose to a big wave, and then crashed down into the following trough. Takanawa's wheels were hurled from the deck by the lurch, and then he was over the bow. Keiko caught his breath as the plane for a split second disappeared, then it soared into the night, rising higher and higher as the wind caught it, then vanishing almost immediately into the murk.

'One,' Keiko said, breath gushing from his nostrils in relief.

Two, three, four, five ... the Junkers rose into the sky, each turning to fly his prescribed course. Six ... but this plane was not quite straight. One wing-tip seemed to dip as the pilot tried to correct, and the whole machine slewed sideways across the deck. Once again Keiko caught his breath as a mass of German sailors ran from the side of the deck, throwing their shoulders against wings and fusilage. The aircraft slid sideways on the slippery surface.

'No,' came the voice over the radio. 'We can recover. No.' The voice rose. 'No!' it screamed, as the plane plunged over the side of the carrier, entering the snarling, icy seas with a gigantic hiss of whirling propellers. The radio made a choking sound.

Keiko had to swallow before he could speak. The pilot should not have cried out, he thought. That was a pity, and let the entire team down. But it was also symptomatic of the tension gripping them all.

'Seven . . . Eight . . .'

Then it was nine. His engines were racing, the machine threatening to take off vertically like a helicopter. 'Banzai!' he shouted, and the wires were released. The Junkers rolled forward, and instinctively he looked to his right. He had always judged his take-off less by his instruments than his relation to the island. But there was no island, only darkness through which foaming whitecaps loomed in steady succession. He opened the throttle wide and felt the deck fall away. For a moment he didn't know whether he was rising or the ship was falling. He stared at what seemed to be a mountain of water rushing at him, pulled back on the controls, pushed on the already wide-open throttles – and soared into the night.

'Ten,' said Lieutenant Fushido. His voice was steady.

Keiko looked over his shoulders as he wheeled his machine to the west; the carrier was already lost to sight.

'Jesus,' Clive Wharton remarked. 'Jesus, Jesus, Jesus.'

Signalman Brown looked at him, frowning. He didn't know what the big pilot was doing in the intelligence room, anyway.

'Who's that message from?' Jennie demanded.

'The same guy as earlier. A Limey cruiser, *Bombast*. Commanded by some character called Bowen. I looked him up.'

'Bowen!' Clive exclaimed. 'That's the fellow who picked me up, remember?'

'What earlier message?' Jennie asked.

'About tracking an unidentified intruder into coastal

waters. Don't bother, ma'am, it went up to the duty room.'

'And now . . .' She looked at the paper again, then at Clive. 'You think he knows what he's doing? Or seeing?'

'He's good,' Clive said. 'Believe me. Or I wouldn't be standing here.'

'Seventeen aircraft,' Jennie muttered. 'And they'll be led by Hatatsune.'

'What did you say?' Clive shouted. She had told him about Johnnie Anderson signalling a German break-out itself. And he hadn't thought to ask.

'It's a Japanese raid,' she said. 'According to Johnnie. It's being launched from a German carrier. This has to be it, just as he said it would happen. And those bastards thought it was a false alarm.'

'And you're trying to tell me it's commanded by Keiko Hatatsune?' Clive asked.

'He's their best.' She peered at the decoding machine. 'How many more?'

'That seems to be it, ma'am,' Brown said.

'Who is the duty admiral upstairs?'

'I don't think there is one, right this minute.'

'For Christ's sake,' Jennie snapped. 'There has to be.'

'It was all stand down for twelve hours after the flap was cancelled, ma'am. Some of those brass hats were working seventy-two straight.' His tone was reproachful; he knew she had spent those seventy-two hours in bed.

'Well,' she told him, 'get on the telephone. Get our admiral, anyway. Get somebody. Wake somebody up.'

'You realise those guys are only a couple of hours out?' Clive demanded. 'They'll be over New York with the sun. Christalmighty! That's when they mean to be there.'

'I'm going up to Operations,' Jennie told him. 'I'll see you later. And Clive, don't hang about. If the admiral finds you here when he comes in he'll flip his lid.'

'So what am I supposed to do?' he bawled. 'Sit on my ass while Keiko Hatatsune is blowing hell out of New York?'

'That's how it works,' she told him, and ran for the elevator.

The duty captain looked at her as if she were a beetle. 'There's a rumour you've had a bit of a breakdown, Commander,' he remarked.

Jennie stared at him. How the devil had that got started? she wondered. It had to be someone from the intelligence room . . . that God-damned Brown. She kept her temper. 'It was a rumour, sir. Have you seen the report from *Bombast*?'

'Sure I have. Both of them.'

'What do you intend to do about it . . . sir?'

'I'm not sure that's your business, Commander. Why don't you go back to bed?'

'I've called my admiral,' Jennie said.

'I'm not sure it's his business either. I've called Admiral King. He wasn't very amused. But he'll be down in a little while.'

'Sir,' Jennie said, with great patience, 'it is half-past four.'

'Don't remind me,' the captain said. 'My relief should've been here half an hour ago.'

'Sir, those planes will be here in less than three hours. There simply isn't any time to waste, if we're going to put anything up against them.'

'If they're really coming,' the captain pointed out. 'This whole business has been one balls-up from the start, thanks to that crazy agent your admiral planted in Germany. There's even a suggestion the whole God-damned caper has been a German plant, just to have us running around like chickens with our heads cut off. Now it's more than likely that this Limey skipper is trying to make something happen where there ain't

350

nothing going to happen. You want me to scramble our air defences? You looked outside your window recently, Commander? You can't see fifty feet. What if those boys go up, on my say so, and then can't get back down? Or bang a couple of wing-tips together, eh? You tell me that.'

'Sir,' Jennie said, resisting the temptation to scream very loudly, 'what if it isn't a false alarm, and that Japanese wing gets over New York? Can you tell me that?'

'We'll know for sure soon enough,' the captain said reassuringly. 'I've put out a call to all radar stations asking for a confirmation. Those Brits are working off the box too, you know. They haven't made any visual sightings, even of this carrier they're burbling about. It could all be clutter.'

Jennie glared at him, knowing she was about to explode, then ran back to the elevator and rode down to the intelligence room. 'Where's the admiral?'

'He's not at his apartment.' Signalman Brown said. 'We're trying our list of . . . ah . . .' He rolled his eyes. 'Known addresses where he might be.'

One of which was probably hers, Jennie thought. She chewed her lip. This was Johnnie's message, his last message, sent from beyond the grave – the message for which he had sacrificed his life. And still no one would believe it. Confirmation by radar! Of course there'd be no confirmation by radar; the Japs would fly below radar level.

She snapped her fingers. 'Open the key to all interceptor stations from here to Goose Bay. Send in clear, there's no time to code. Send: "Air attack on New York imminent repeat imminent stop All interceptor squadrons to be scrambled to meet seventeen intruder bombers approaching from Grand Banks area stop Repeat this is an emergency stop All interceptor units to meet intruder bombers approaching from Grand Banks." '

Signalman Brown, busy copying, raised his head and looked past her at Chief Markham, who'd just come on duty.

'Begging your pardon, Ma'am,' the chief said. 'An order like that can only be sent on the authority of a senior officer.'

'So send it on the authority of the admiral,' Jennie said.

'But . . .'

'I'll sign the order, chief. Per pro. Just send it.'

'Jesus Christ, ma'am,' Signalman Brown remarked. 'If this *is* a false alarm you are going to be hung up by the balls. Begging your pardon, ma'am.'

'So what have I got to lose?' Jennie demanded. 'Start sending.' She looked around the room. 'And where the hell has Captain Wharton got to?' Despite her earlier suggestion, she rather thought it would be nice to hold his hand about now.

'I don't know, ma'am,' Signalman Brown said. 'You told him to get lost, and I guess that's what he did?'

'Gee, that's a smart car, Commander,' the lieutenant remarked. He had been awakened from a deep sleep by the screeching of brakes, and peered through the office window as if wondering who else was going to invade his pre-dawn privacy.

'I just stole it,' Clive told him. 'You in command here?'

'I am the duty officer, sir.' The lieutenant stood to attention. Clearly he did not believe what Clive had said about the car.

'You and me ever met before?'

'I don't think so, sir.'

'The name's Wharton. Clive Wharton.'

352

'Clive Wharton! Gee! Gee whizz!' The lieutenant stood to attention again. 'It's my great pleasure, sir.'

'Mine too.' Clive walked across the little office and stared at the mist-shrouded runway of Bolling Field. He couldn't even see the houses on Washington Heights beyond, while the Potomac at the end of the runway was only a whisper of sound in the darkness; he hadn't even seen the river while racing across the bridge.

And beyond the river, and the bridge, was the Pentagon, where Jennie would still no doubt be desperately trying to get someone to listen to her.

It was no night to be flying anywhere. But Keiko Hatatsune, already up there, would be happy about that. Therefore he had to be happy too. He was reverting to type, he knew. The new-model, responsible, adult Clive Wharton who had nursed Jennie Rhodes back to sanity and strength was being jettisoned – for the last time, he told himself. Oh, certainly for the last time.

But there was no way he could sit on his ass while the war might be coming home, physically, for the first time. Or while Keiko Hatatsune was up there.

Or while Johnnie Anderson was standing against a wall.

Or while Jennie Rhodes needed help.

'What have you got here that flies?' he asked.

'You name it, sir, and we have it,' the lieutenant said enthusiastically.

'That!' Clive pointed at a hardly visible single-engined fighter.

'Oh, yes, sir.' The lieutenant's voice became almost reverent.

'What is it?' It certainly looked good, he thought.

'That is the Vought P4U-a1 Corsair, sir,' the lieutenant said. 'That is the ultimate answer to the Zero.'

In which case, Clive thought, she would have to be

353

more than the ultimate answer to a Junkers 88. Perhaps even to seventeen of them. 'Is she armed?'

'Well, no, sir.'

'Then get her armed, and while that's happening, you come along and show me how she works.'

'But . . . you don't mean to take her up, sir?'

'Sure I do. What's her range?'

'Well . . . eight hundred miles, maybe.'

'Hot potato. In a fighter? Lieutenant, you're making my day.'

'But sir, that machine hasn't been properly tested yet. She was brought in here for a display for the navy staff, but she's been grounded because of this poor visibility. Sir, we don't even *own* her yet.'

'So I'll test her out, and when I get back I'll tell you if she's worth having. Let's go.'

'Sir . . .' The lieutenant looked deeply distressed. '*Everything* has been grounded. I'm under orders to let nothing up. I am going to have to get authority.'

'Who the fucking hell is going to give you authority at four-thirty in the morning?' Clive shouted. 'I'm giving you authority, God-damn it. I'm your senior officer. I'm Clive Wharton, right? You've heard of me, right? When I say do it, you God-damn well do it, buddy boy. I want that aircraft airborne in half an hour, armed and fuelled to the maximum. Now let's go. And if you touch that telephone, I'm gonna knock your block right off.'

The lieutenant trembled as he showed Clive the controls. But that might have been the cold; if it had stopped snowing during the night, it was threatening to do so again at any moment. And he had stopped arguing. Armament belts were being fed to the cannon, fuel was being pumped into the tanks. Clive looked at his watch: five-fifteen. According to this boy the Corsair would fly at damned near four hundred miles an hour. If he could believe that, it meant he could be over New

York in about twenty minutes after take-off. But then what? He had no idea where the enemy was, and he didn't dare call Jennie because he didn't know who else he was going to get on the end of the line. He had no idea what he was doing. He only knew that if all hell was about to break loose over New York, he intended to be in the middle of it.

'Great,' he said. 'Great. I get it. How much longer?'

'Ten minutes, sir,' said the chief mechanic. 'I've sent for the accumulator trolley.'

'Hooray,' Clive said. 'Okay, Lieutenant, now find me some gear.'

They hurried back to the office. 'All planes *are* grounded, you know, Captain,' the lieutenant said. 'There is going to be one hell of a flap if you suddenly appear on radar. They could even shoot you down.'

'I'm not all they're gonna have to aim at,' Clive told him, and turned up the radio. Suddenly the room was filled with noise, with voices, chattering: Jennie had got some action, from someone. But that didn't alter his plans. 'Grounded, are they?' he asked. 'Everyone and his son is going to be up there in a little while, Lieutenant. I sure aim to be one of them.'

The chief mechanic's ten minutes proved to be somewhat optimistic, but Clive was airborne at five-fifty, soaring into the predawn murk, the ground disappearing seconds after his wheels came up. The Corsair was a beautiful machine, even if he didn't yet know everything about it. He would be over New York by six-fifteen, which was at least an hour before any of the Junkers could get there, he calculated. But he still didn't have a clue exactly where the enemy was; approaching from the Grand Banks area covered a lot of territory. Yet common sense told him they would be coming over the sea, flying as low as possible.

He switched on the radio and listened to the chat.

Some of it was about him – already. There was going to be the devil to pay, he thought, when he got back down. If he got back down. Right now he didn't give a damn, either way, if he could just get Hatatsune in his sights. He owed that bugger. And indirectly, at least, he owed him for Johnnie Anderson as well.

He sent the machine out to sea, climbing above the twenty-thousand-foot mark. He reasoned they'd have more trouble deciding which one was him, up here, and he would get better radio reception. And almost immediately he heard, 'Goose Bay Leader, Goose Bay Leader, I have something. Five o'clock.'

'I see them,' came the reply. 'All together now. And watch yourselves. Those boys are low.'

'Abe!' Clive shouted, having recognised the second voice. 'Where are you, boy?'

'Who the hell is that?'

'Clive Wharton.'

'Where are you?'

'Off the East Coast some place. Maybe Atlantic City. You?'

'Cape Sable's behind us. Stick around, Clive baby. We have a flock of Junkers below us. Would you believe it's suddenly cleared up here? Boy, are they pretty. Seventeen fat ducks. Going down.'

'Oh, God-damn,' Clive muttered. He wasn't going to make it. He listened to the conversations, to the sound of machine-gun fire, to exclamations, screams and curses and shouts. It was all happening only a few hundred miles away, and he wasn't there. He felt like snapping the wheel off and throwing it out of the cockpit.

'Goose Bay Squadron, Red Leader. Where are you guys?'

Replies came pouring in. 'I got one, skipper.'

'So did I.'

'Harry bought it.'

356

'Yeah, I saw that.'

'I got two.'

'You see that guy take a dive? Boy, that was pretty.'

'Say, skipper . . .'

As excited as ever, Clive thought bitterly.

'Goose Bay Leader, Goose Bay Leader,' came a quiet, controlled voice. 'We have no radar contact with the enemy. Please advise of position.'

'There ain't no position,' Abe Bostwick said. 'We've shot them to hell. But two of my boys have gone in. I want air-sea rescue out here, and make it quick. Vis is closing down again. I guess that break was just luck.'

'Will do, Goose Bay Leader,' the voice said. 'Can you estimate the number of intruders eliminated?'

'Now, let's see,' Abe said. 'Not all at once, boys.' He listened to the tallies over again. 'I make it fifteen or so. But they all sure have disappeared.'

'Thank you, Goose Bay Leader. Good shooting. Return to base now. Air-sea rescue is on its way. All interceptor squadrons return to base. Operation completed.'

'Now say, wait just one moment,' Clive said. 'There were seventeen of those guys.'

'Identify yourself, Captain Wharton,' said the control – no doubt grinning all over his fat face, the bastard, Clive thought.

'What do you want, my social security number? There's at least one Jap unaccounted for.'

'There are no enemy planes on radar, Captain Wharton, and none reported by Commander Bostwick.'

'They could've gone into cloud.'

'It is almost certain they have been destroyed, I have an order here for you to return to Bolling Field immediately and place yourself under arrest. Please acknowledge.'

'Fuck off,' Clive said, and put his Corsair into a steep dive, down towards the sea.

CHAPTER 15

The Battle

'Will somebody tell me what the shitting hell is going *on*?' demanded the admiral. He spoke quietly, but he sat at his desk with his arms extended and his hands resting flat on the blotter, one on either side of the pile of order slips, incoming messages and reports, a position which indicated to Jennie that he was not in the best of humours. Well, he never was in the best of humours at being awakened early in the morning. And this morning, after some seventy hours on duty with just the occasional catnap in his chair, he had obviously been letting his hair down. When he did find out just what had been going on . . .

Jennie stood to attention. 'That false alarm wasn't, sir. A false alarm, I mean.'

The admiral was staring at the first of the messages. Then he moved slowly, turned it over, looked at the next, and then the next. Jennie had been afraid he would do that.

'Whose God-damned signature is that?' he asked.

'Ah . . . mine, sir.'

'Yours?' He raised his head. 'You sent up those interceptor squadrons? *You*?'

'The order was confirmed, sir. If you will look . . .'

The admiral was looking, now turning over messages fairly fast. 'Forty-five minutes later.'

'Well, sir, the duty captain was trying to contact his

admiral as well, and he was waiting for confirmation . . .'

'And you had ants in your pants.'

'I knew the information relayed by *Bombast* was accurate, sir.'

'Yeah,' the admiral said. 'Yeah. Jesus Christ!' He was halfway through the pile.

'Yes, sir.' The immediate crisis was over, now he had reached the Goose Bay reports, although there was still plenty of trouble ahead.

'They got the lot? Those guys from Goose Bay?'

'Fifteen confirmed kills, sir. Out of seventeen.'

'So where are the other two?'

'Well, sir . . .'

The admiral was nearly at the bottom. 'Holy fucking cows,' he shouted. 'You sent that asshole up as well? From Bolling?'

'Ah . . .' Jennie knew it would be a mistake to lie. Each order slip had the time automatically printed on it, and it would be obvious to anyone checking up that Clive must have been airborne before she had issued that confirmation. 'I okayed his decision, sir.'

'In the name of God, why? What the hell was he going to do down here?'

'He took a Corsair, sir. He'll get there in a hurry.'

'A what? He can't do that,' the admiral bellowed, thumping his desk and causing heads to turn in the outer office. 'Those planes aren't operational yet. We don't even know if they *work*.'

'Yes, sir. This one seems to have. Well, so far.'

'Jesus Christ! Commander, heads are going to roll about this.'

'I have recalled him, sir,' Jennie pointed to the final message.

'There's no reply.'

'Well, sir, he didn't acknowledge.'

'Since when?' He peered at the time on the paper. 'Half an hour ago. Godalmighty!'

'Yes, sir. I'm having the message repeated, sir.'

'Oh, Christ! He's gone in. You know that, don't you? He's gone in. With that brand-new machine.'

'I think he would have radioed, sir, if he'd had trouble.'

'Then what the hell is he doing out there, all by himself? You tell me that, eh?'

Jennie sighed. 'I believe he's looking for those other two intruders, sir,' she said sadly.

'All planes away, Herr Captain,' Meyer reported.

'Then we have done our duty,' Koenig said. 'Alter course zero-three-five, and increase to full speed.' He winked. 'With the aircraft gone, we should be able to improve on forty knots, eh?'

Meyer blinked. 'You are going to steam straight back into the storm, Herr Captain?'

'That is correct. It is our best chance of getting home. And we are going back through the Denmark Strait, too. That is the one place no one will think of looking for us at this moment.'

'And the Britisher?'

'We will have to pass him,' Koenig said. 'Range?'

'Thirty miles and closing, Herr Captain,' said the operator. 'Bearing zero-six-seven. He can cut us off, Herr Captain.'

'He can. But he'll have to be quick.' Koenig listened to the surge of the turbines from beneath him, and *Nemo* began to buck and plunge into the big seas now foaming down on her out of the north.

'Let's hope we hold together,' Meyer muttered, clinging to the nearest grab rail as the aircraft-carrier's bows went up until she seemed to be pointing at the sky, and then came down again with a crash which seemed likely to tear every rivet loose.

Koenig laughed. 'This is what the sea is all about, Meyer. Oh, she will claim us, one day. That is her right. But perhaps not yet. And we will make that Britisher *work*.'

'Signal acknowledged by Halifax, sir,' reported Lieutenant Morrison, 'and relayed to Washington. They are awaiting confirmation from down there, but intend to put up everything they have. And they're sending help out here, too. Should be along in about an hour.'

'Let's hope they hit the right target,' Bowen commented. It seemed thicker than ever.

'Range twenty-eight miles and closing,' chanted the petty officer. 'Intruder underway.' He gazed into the screen for several seconds, while Rod Bowen stared at him, waiting for the calculation to be completed. 'Speed estimated forty knots, course zero-three-five.'

'He's running for it,' Hawthorne snapped. 'Forty knots!'

Every officer was on the bridge.

'So we'll have to cut the corner,' Bowen snapped back. 'Give me an interception course. Full speed, Mr Clarke. Alter course three-four-zero to begin with.'

'Three-four-zero should take us some ten miles north of him, sir,' Hawthorne said, busy with pencil and parallel rule on the chart table.

'That's where I want to be,' Bowen said. 'Come on, now, chief. Give her everything you've got.' He rang the engine-room telegraph himself, repeating the full-speed order. *Bombast* surged ahead, crashing through the waves, smashing through the troughs, water foaming over her decks.

'You don't think she'll shake herself to pieces?' Hawthorne asked, somewhat nervously. The wind was back now, rising to gale force and beyond, and the seas were starting to build again.

'Koenig will do it first,' Bowen promised, staring out

at the slowly lightening sky. But that couldn't be sunrise; it still wanted two hours to dawn.

'The mist is lifting, sir,' Lieutenant Clarke remarked.

'By God,' Bowen said, 'so it is.'

'Range twenty miles and closing,' said the petty officer. The two ships were on a converging course, approaching each other at combined speeds.

'Odd he's not trying to turn away,' Lieutenant Morrison commented.

'We're dealing with the best, Mr Morrison,' Bowen said. 'He knows he can't hang about, because we have help on the way. And he knows he's a dead duck if he's still on our radar when it gets here. His only hope is to burst straight past us and escape out to sea.'

'Message from Halifax Control, sir.' The signals lieutenant joined them. 'Fifteen out of seventeen enemy raiders have been intercepted and destroyed.'

'Oh, that's marvellous,' Hawthorne cried.

'Yes, indeed, number one,' Bowen agreed. 'Well, all we have to do is wrap it up. Gentlemen, will you take action stations.'

Hawthorne hurried for the gunnery control; Clarke and Morrison also departed, one for the forward turrets, one aft. The bridge seemed suddenly empty, save for the coxswains and the radar operator, the signals lieutenant and two highly excited midshipmen. And the captain.

'Halifax also reports they are refuelling and rearming a Buccaneer flight to send to us,' the signals lieutenant said.

'Tell them to forget it,' Bowen said. 'They won't get here in time.'

'Range seventeen miles and closing,' the petty officer said.

'Bearing?'

'Green ten, sir.'

Bowen spoke into the intercom. 'Fire whenever you have a target, Mr Hawthorne.'

'Aye aye, sir.'

'Make to Halifax, with repeat to flagship, sparks,' Bowen said. ' "Am engaging intruder. Give them our position." '

'Aye aye, sir.' He too hurried from the bridge.

'Range sixteen miles, bearing green seven,' said the petty officer.

They were almost directly in front of the enemy.

'Shoot,' Hawthorne said, and the forward guns belched smoke. The cruiser recoiled from the blast, came upright again, was struck by a big wave and went the other way.

'Oh, damnation.' Hawthorne's voice came over the intercom. 'These seas are a pain in the . . .'

'Keep at her, number one.'

'Range fourteen miles, bearing green three,' said the petty officer.

'Alter course one point to port, cox,' Bowen said.

'Aye aye, sir. One point to port. Steering three-three-zero.'

'Shoot,' Hawthorne commanded. 'There's no damned way of telling how close we're coming,' he complained.

'Well, you haven't hit him yet,' Bowen told him. 'At least, you haven't stopped him yet.'

'Range twelve miles, bearing red two.'

'I'm coming about, number one,' Bowen said. 'Hold your fire till she bears. Steer one-nine-zero, cox.'

'One-nine-zero, sir.' The helm spun, and the cruiser came round so steeply she heeled almost scuppers under, while the following wave broke right over the super-structure. But she was now steering straight for the enemy.

'Strange he doesn't shoot back,' Hawthorne commented.

'He doesn't have it,' Bowen said. 'Fire as you can, number one.'

The guns exploded again.

'Range ten miles, bearing red seventeen.'

'He's altering course,' Hawthorne groaned.

'Steer two-zero-five, cox,' Bowen said. 'Keep at him.'

Once again the big ship was thrown over like a toy as she went back the other way.

'Excuse me, sir,' said Midshipman Annesley. 'I can see the enemy.'

Bowen's head jerked. He hadn't realised the clouds had lifted to that extent. But there she was, huge and long and featureless, not nine miles away – an immense dark hulk. 'There's your target, number one,' he said.

'Shoot,' Hawthorne said.

Smoke swept across the bridge screens, but as it cleared away they saw plumes of water spouting only a few yards to the left of the carrier.

'Oh, good shooting, number one,' Bowen said.

'Wait for the next one,' Hawthorne promised.

'She's altering course, sir,' Annesley said.

The carrier was turning, churning white water.

'She's coming straight at us,' the coxswain gasped. 'She means to ram.'

'Hit her, number one,' Bowen said. But he had no intention of altering course himself. This would be Koenig's only chance, now that he was a visual target. But he wasn't going to be pushed out of the way even by twenty thousand tons of hurtling steel. 'Hit the bastard.'

The guns belched again, now at virtually point-blank range and depressed as far as they could be. Flame and smoke erupted from *Nemo's* forward deck, and a burst of cheering rose from the cruiser.

'She's turning away again, sir,' Annesley gasped unnecessarily. This was his first action.

Bowen stared at the carrier as she yawed to port.

Hawthorne's voice came up the intercom, quiet and decisive. 'Shoot!'

This time the shells ripped into the exposed hull of the carrier as she swung back on course again. She rolled in a big sea, and seemed to keep on going, then came up again, yawing back the other way, moving as if she were alive, a dying, desperate creature furiously trying to reach the throat of its enemy. And she was not more than five miles away now.

'Shoot!'

The entire carrier became enveloped in flaming explosion. Bowen watched the rivers of red running along the flight-deck, racing aft to the elevator leading to the hangars, and the gases and fuel residue which would still be there. 'Hold your breath,' he muttered.

Noise belched skywards, accompanied by flying steel and flying men. The entire flight-deck seemed to have been torn off, and the carrier turned away again, for the last time. Bowen snatched up his binoculars and was nearly thrown from his chair as the blast reached the cruiser; she rolled heavily and one of the bridge screens shattered, letting in a gust of freezing air.

'Patch that,' he snapped. 'Cease firing, number one. All hands stand by to rescue survivors. Put down boarding nets.'

He could do no more than that; no launch was going to survive in these seas. He levelled the binoculars, staring at the carrier rent almost in two by the explosion; he was sure he could actually see into the engine-room by the glare of the flames – all the electrics had gone. By that glowing light he watched the seas pouring into the hull, watched the carrier rolling wildly, now completely out of control, watched men desperately throwing themselves into the water, as if *they* had any chance of surviving for more than a few seconds.

'Take her close, cox,' he said. 'Take her close.'

He went on to the wing, ignoring the wind which

tore at him like icy fingers, and stared down. He couldn't even stop engines, because he had to keep steerage-way to head into the seas, but he had rung down for slow ahead. The carrier was going now, with a vast sigh which hung across the surface of the sea. For a moment her bows pointed skywards, and then they too went back, sucked under by the water which was still surging into the hull.

There would be few survivors, he thought. And yet, always one or two were stronger than the rest. Hands were already clutching at the boarding nets, uttering screams of despair as even the slow forward thrust of the cruiser, combined with the roll, proved too great for exhausted muscles. But the eager British sailors were climbing down the nets themselves, being soaked with each wave, but determined to lend a hand to their recent enemies. And one or two were being brought out.

Bowen felt sick. This was a natural reaction to the stomach-churning tension of battle. Now there was no trace of the sunken carrier; even the explosive bubbles sent up by the air trapped in the hull were lost in the maelstrom of the sea. Now there were only the cries of drowning men . . . and one closer at hand. 'Help! Help me, for God's sake.'

The man was supporting an inert figure. But he was already aft of the beam, and too far away to reach the ladder as the cruiser forged slowly ahead.

'Help me,' the man screamed again. 'I have the captain.'

'Port your helm,' Bowen snapped over his shoulder.

'Port . . .' The coxswain hesitated. To turn to port would mean going broadside to the waves; at dead slow that promised a real buffeting. 'Port it is, sir.'

The cruiser turned, and immediately was sent almost on to her beam ends by a big sea. But she came up again, and her bulk for a moment left an area of calm in her lee. 'Those men!' Bowen shouted, himself sliding down the ladder to the main deck.

'We see them, sir,' called one of the seamen, and three of them went down on to the nets again. Bowen stood above them at the rail, strongly tempted to join them, whatever the dereliction of duty. The ship rolled again, seemed to shake herself, and came up; water splashed on Bowen's face.

Hands reached down to Albing's; the British sailors were forming a human chain, each man grasping the man beneath. Freezing fingers locked in Hjalmar Koenig's jacket and pulled him half clear of the water. Midshipman Annesley had followed his captain down and already rigged a block and tackle; a bowline was dropped round Koenig's shoulders, and he was slowly winched up to the deck.

'Now for you, mate,' said the first seaman.

But Albing's strength was gone. He reached up, and the cruiser rolled yet again, soaking the sailor, and seemed about to come down on Albing's head. When the ship came up again, the steward had disappeared.

Surgeon Commander King met his captain in the doorway to the sickbay.

'Well?' Bowen asked.

'I can save five. Maybe two more.'

Seven, Bowen thought. Out of the eleven they had managed to pull on board. But out of several hundred, really.

'The captain?'

King shook his head. 'He's not gone yet. Would you like to see him?'

'Yes,' Bowen said.

King led him across the cabin to the far bunk. Hjalmar Koenig was wrapped in blankets; beneath them his naked body was swathed in bandages – both bandages and blankets were slowly turning red.

'He must have been on the bridge when that first shell struck the fore deck,' King explained. 'He's been literally cut to pieces by flying splinters. Add that to the temperature of the sea . . . it really is a miracle he's survived so long.'

'He had a faithful friend,' Bowen said, staring down at his enemy. No strong, aquiline features, no goatee beard . . . just a rather ordinary little man. He did not even have piercing blue eyes, he realised, as they opened.

'My steward,' Koenig said.

'He didn't make it,' Bowen answered. 'He was a brave man.'

'They were all brave men,' Koenig said. 'And you . . .' His mouth twisted as he identified Bowen's rank. 'My apologies, sir. We have not met.'

'We have, you know, in a manner of speaking,' Bowen told him. 'My name is Rod Bowen. I was once in command of HMS *Erebus*.'

'Bowen? *Erebus*? Ah . . .' This time the smile was genuine. 'Old friends. Old friends. I congratulate you on your victory, Captain Bowen.'

'As I congratulate you, Captain Koenig. That was a fine and daring mission, and a remarkable feat of seamanship. To get so close . . .'

'I launched my aircraft, Captain,' Koenig said. Once again his face twisted. As his body warmed up, the pain was clearly growing more severe, penetrating past even King's analgesic injections. 'I may yet have won a victory myself.'

Bowen hesitated, wondering whether to tell him the strike had been destroyed. But the man was dying, and he had been a gallant enemy. 'Yes,' he agreed. 'You may still have won a victory, Captain Koenig.' He stepped back, and saluted. 'Your people, your government, your family, will know of this action, Captain, and of your gallantry. I will see to that.'

Koenig sighed. 'I have no family, Captain Bowen. I

368

have no government.' His eyes closed. 'But I do have a people. Yes, Captain. Tell them of this. They will be proud of me, and they will need pride in the years to come.' He gave another sigh.

King shrugged. 'Not much longer, I'm afraid.'

Bowen nodded, and returned to the bridge. He wondered about those last words. Wheels within wheels, the truth of which he would never discover. But Koenig was dying happy, as happy as he could be, believing that his aircraft were bombing New York.

He leaned on the bridge wing and looked out at the morning. The first fingers of daylight were just starting to creep across the sea, revealing the waves in all their terrifying majesty. And who could be sure, he thought, that there were not bombs falling on New York, at this very moment? Only fifteen of the seventeen aircraft had definitely been accounted for.

'Can you see anything?' Keiko asked.

There was a brief silence while Fushido clearly peered this way and that. 'No, honourable Commander. We are alone.'

Alone, Keiko thought. Out of seventeen. He would not have thought that possible. The American defences were just too strong. And their pilots had thrown themselves out of the sky like hawks after chickens. It made his blood boil to think that his men had not been able properly to defend themselves. As it made his blood boil at the way he had fled away from the dog-fight. But those were his own orders. Only New York mattered. And yet. . . . Perhaps they would have lost the battle anyway, but to have been picked off like that, simply because they lacked the fuel to stop and engage the enemy, and thus had tried to maintain their courses towards their target . . . simply because they had encountered that cruiser . . . simply because . . . the Allied defences were too strong.

But also simply because the clouds had opened for those precious five minutes and allowed the Americans to see them. Then they had closed again, enabling him to escape. But those five minutes had destroyed his wing. Could it be that the gods were not, after all, on his side?

Or could it be that they were simply reserving him for the greater glory of success?

'But the clouds are still very low, honourable Commander,' Fushido said. 'It is possible that there are other aircraft up there. Shall I put out a call?'

Keiko hesitated. Each pilot had his orders, and they had maintained strict radio silence since leaving the carrier. On the other hand, he was now close to the target. His instruments showed him that, and he could tell by looking down at the surface of the sea, only two hundred feet below him. The darkness was slowly turning to grey, and it was at last possible to see more than just the whitecaps. The waves were smaller here, although no less tumultuous, and the colour of the water was changing from deep blue to deep green. He calculated he was not more than seventy miles off the coast. Fifteen minutes, and the Americans had been recalled to base. They would never get airborne again in time.

'Yes,' he said. 'See if there is anyone there.'

'Strike Force Nemo, Strike Force Nemo,' Fushido said into the radio. 'This is Strike Force Leader. Strike Force Leader calling Strike Force Nemo. Come in, please.'

There was a moment of almost painful silence, then Keiko's heart leapt as a voice replied. 'Strike Force Leader, Strike Force Leader, this is Strike Force Two. Strike Force Two.'

'Takanawa!' Keiko shouted in joy. 'Is it really you?'

'It is I, honourable Commander. Where are you?'

'What is your altitude?' Keiko asked.

'Five hundred feet. I am in cloud.'

370

'Come down,' Keiko told him. 'Come down to two hundred.'

'Obeying, Strike Force Leader.'

They looked left and right.

'There,' Fushido said, and Keiko watched the Junkers dipping out of the clouds.

'Tadatune San,' he said. 'I am happy to see you. Together, we will complete the mission, eh?'

'Together, honourable Commander,' Takanawa said.

'There,' Fushido said again, his breath catching in his throat as he saw the third plane.

'Captain Wharton,' the admiral said into the mike, speaking very slowly and distinctly. 'This is the admiral speaking. I don't know what the God-damned hell you are playing at, but you had better get that aircraft back to this field, and in a hurry.' He thumbed the switch, gazing at Jennie and the control lieutenant, and beyond them at the suddenly crowded control tower at Bolling Field. Not many of the men who had come hurrying up knew exactly what was happening, but they knew it was something big, with an admiral in their midst personally talking to a pilot.

'He's not replying, sir,' the lieutenant said helpfully.

'I fucking well know he's not replying,' the admiral shouted, thumbing the switch as he did so.

Visibility was lifting all the time, and Jennie could even make out the sharp contours of the Pentagon across the river. 'With respect, sir, but it is incorrect procedure to use blasphemy on the air. Or obscenity.'

'Are you trying to tell me my shitting business?' the admiral bawled. 'Where the hell is that dumb bastard?' He thumbed the mike some more. 'Wharton? Wharton? Where the hell are you?'

Here, you great ox, Clive thought. He was low now, as low as he dared, dipping in and out of the clouds, watching the curling whitecaps only two hundred feet beneath him. This was one magnificent aircraft. He had never flown anything like it. He thought he could stay out here forever. She had just one fault, and it was common to all machines – she needed gas to fly forever. And he was down to less than one hour.

There was nothing. He had flown up and down from Atlantic City to Block Island three times, and seen and heard nothing, save from the ground. The cloud cover, however much it might have cleared further north, was still total down here. But whether he could see or not, he no longer believed there was anything there. He had goofed. Bostwick and the Goose Bay boys must have got the lot, after all. So he would have to go back and take what was coming to him. God-*damn*, he thought.

'Wharton,' the admiral said. 'You can't sucker me. None of you can do that. The boys have you all on radar, out there beyond Long Island, low as you are. We can see you, God-damn it. All three of you. So just call up your buddies and tell them to stop assing about and come on in. This is an order.'

Clive sat up straight. 'Would you repeat that signal, please,' he said.

'Wharton? That's you! I know that's you. Now you listen to me . . .'

'What buddies?' Clive shouted.

'Those guys fifty miles out to sea. Ain't they with you?'

'Holy Jesus Christ,' Clive said. 'Oh, boy. Hang about, admiral. I may have news for you.' He twisted off the wavelength then went through all the others. Fifty miles, closing at a combined speed of some seven hundred miles an hour . . . four minutes . . . and there they were, two Junkers 88s racing straight towards him at virtually wavetop height. And as he saw them, he heard a voice speaking Japanese. He had already turned past the wavelength, but came back to it. Someone was giving orders, and the two planes were separating, one climbing, and the other maintaining course and speed. He pulled back the stick and shot upwards himself, deciding the upper guy had to be the more dangerous. 'Hatatsune,' he shouted. 'Hey, Hatatsune.'

'Who is that, please?' Keiko asked politely, in English.

'Wharton's the name,' Clive said, soaring above the higher of the two Junkers, knowing there was no way they could match his rate of climb. 'I'm your old buddy boy from Pearl, remember?'

'And *Akagi*,' Keiko muttered.

'Come again? Say, were you on board her? Well, hooray! This makes it the best of three.'

The Junkers was spitting fire as it rushed past beneath him, and the pilot was throwing her over into a desperate roll. But she didn't stand a chance. 'Say hello to the sun,' Clive growled, and squeezed the triggers. Cannon shot ripped into the grey fusilage.

But the Japanese wasn't done yet. He had completed his roll, and once again his wings belched fire – and once again he was too slow. If the enemy didn't have an answer to the Corsair, Clive thought, then they were done, done, done. He pulled back the stick and felt the blood draining from his scalp as the plane screamed skywards and came right over in a loop, once again behind the stricken enemy. Smoke was issuing from the Junkers' port engine, but Clive came down, shaking his head from side to side to clear the grey mist behind his eyes, aware of the gonging headache which always accompanied the G-force. Again he squeezed the trigger, determined to make absolutely sure. This time there was no mistake; he could see the shots slamming into the belly of the bomber, and he could see the crewman in the midships turret staring at him in impotence, vainly trying to depress his machine-gun, shouting into his intercom. His pilot had been throwing the aircraft about so violently he hadn't been able to get in a shot as yet.

Nor would he now. The whole plane was in flames. A voice said something in Japanese, urgently, breathlessly. But it wasn't Keiko's voice.

Clive watched his victim go down and enter the water with a *whoosh;* he was so low himself the splash almost reached him. He raised his head and saw the other bomber already a long way away, screaming across the wavetops. 'You won't make it, buddy boy,' he said, hurtling in pursuit, staring into the distance, expecting to see the skyscrapers of Manhattan appearing out of the mist at any moment. Behind him the first rays of the rising sun were creeping across the ocean. And Keiko suddenly turned away.

'You, Wharton!' he screamed. 'You!'

'Geronimo!' Clive shouted back. Man to man, he thought. But there was no contest. There couldn't be, between a Corsair and a Junkers.

Then he was surprised, as Keiko came round in a far tighter turn than he would have thought possible, arriving underneath him, of course. But Keiko remembered what Takanawa had forgotten: that he had a gunner. Bullets ripped through the fusilage only inches behind Clive, and the machine shuddered as if a giant hand was squeezing it. Desperately he slipped sideways, down almost to sea level, before pulling her back. He had more speed, more acceleration . . . but Keiko had the position, and more firepower. Now thirteen-millimetre cannon shot tore by, slicing into the starboard wing. There went his fuel reserve. That God-damned Jap.

He spun his aircraft again, losing consciousness for a moment as he rolled, but at last coming up behind the bomber, wondering how the hell he had missed hitting the sea; it seemed only a few feet beneath him.

And once again he was under fire from Fushido's

machine-gun. He gritted his teeth and levelled off, feeling the Corsair jerking as the bullets thudded into it, then squeezed the trigger. Fushido stared at him, eyes wide; suddenly his head jerked back and he crashed into the glass bubble and disappeared. The Junkers dipped and Clive soared above it, immediately throwing the Corsair into another tight turn. Looking down as soon as his eyes cleared, he saw the Junkers also attempting to turn and rise. But Keiko had insufficient experience of flying a machine with a sixty-foot wingspan in these conditions, and misjudged. The end of his port wing touched a larger than usual wave, and the plane cartwheeled.

'Banzai!' Keiko screamed, as his nose went in. The aircraft, still being gunned at two hundred and ninety-three miles per hour, broke up as it smashed into the water.

'Oh, God-damn,' Clive muttered. 'God-*damn*!' He'd never know if he would have beaten the guy. And he suspected that he wouldn't have, had Keiko also been flying a Corsair.

'Wharton? Wharton!' The admiral had at last found the right wavelength. 'What the Christ are you doing? Wharton, let me tell you, if that aircraft is damaged, by God . . .'

Clive pulled the stick back, looked at his fuel gauge and wondered just where New York *was*. He didn't think he was going to make it, anyway. And he didn't really care. He'd never felt so tired in his life.

'I'm afraid I have some bad news for you, Admiral,' he said. 'The machine is a little damaged. Just a little. As a matter of fact, I reckon she's about to fall apart. But then . . .' He watched blood welling out of his pants leg and accumulating on the cockpit floor. 'Well, stone the fucking crows.' He hadn't felt a thing. Still didn't feel anything. 'So am I.'

'Wharton? Wharton! Now listen to me, boy, you're

only ten miles out. Bring her in, boy. At least find a beach. Bring her in, Wharton. You can do it.'

'Sure I can, Admiral,' Clive said. 'Oh, by the way, sir. I have to report that the Nemo Strike Force has now been eliminated; all seventeen aircraft are accounted for.' His eyes drooped shut. 'Wharton over and out.'

EPILOGUE

'There,' said Margaret Rhodes, adjusting the final flower. 'You look simply superb, my dear. I'm so glad you've stopped being foolish, Jennie. I was so *afraid* you would one day get married in a town hall . . . and wearing that terrible uniform.'

Jennie often wondered if her mother had ever truly been aware there was a war on at all. But she was right about some things. She did look simply superb. She stared at herself in the wall mirror, the longish face perfectly set off by the white headdress and veil, the tall, slim figure equally perfect in the ivory satin gown, which clung to her bodice and waist before flaring over her hips.

Then she stared into her eyes. Those eyes should be laughing. In less than an hour she'd be married, and would have nothing to look forward to but domesticity and kids. And then grand-kids. And then great-grand-kids. The eyes *would* be laughing, in an hour's time, she knew. Just for this moment, for the last time, they could be serious, to mask the memories in her mind.

But she wasn't going to weep. She was the luckiest woman in the world, because she was out of it, at last, and because she was marrying the one man in the world who could share those secret memories . . . and because he was out of it too, at last. They had both been retired on medical grounds; both, in the last instance, were unsung heroes. But of course they had both been aware of the reasons.

Clive's were the more genuine; that he had survived at all, both the crash and his immersion in the icy waters off Long Island, was a miracle, and he had indeed only recently regained the use of the leg which had been so badly shot up. He would never play tennis again, so he was taking up golf. Equally, he would never fly again. He could, of course, have been given a desk job. But even a recovered Clive, wearing the Congressional Medal of Honor, the Distinguished Service Cross, the Purple Heart and several other decorations besides, was a bit much for the navy; he had broken too many rules, and the thought of him giving orders from behind a desk had turned too many heads in the Pentagon grey with apprehension. So now he was going to be a stock-broker. With daddy's firm. Daddy actually liked Clive. But daddy would have liked any man with the Congressional Medal of Honor, the Distinguished Service Cross and a Purple Heart.

While she . . . . The admiral had been sorry to see her go. But he had recognised that he couldn't have an assistant who would send up the entire United States Air Force on her own authority, if pushed. Besides, she *had* been under a strain. Her discharge had been as honourable as Clive's.

And she regretted nothing of it. Except . . .

'Time to go, I guess, honey.' Her father stood in the doorway. 'And I want to tell you that you are the most beautiful little girl I have laid eyes on since the day I walked down the aisle with your mother.'

She lifted her skirt and went down the stairs, followed by her mother and the bridesmaids. The photographer was waiting at the foot to begin his collection, and she paused, and turned this way and that to suit him, first with them all, then with daddy and mummy, then with daddy, and then by herself. But at last the flashbulbs stopped exploding, and the photographer hurried off to be at the church when she arrived, followed immediately by mummy and the bridesmaids.

Alone at last, her father was licking his lips nervously; he wasn't at all sure that this tall, beautiful, experienced and incredibly self-possessed young woman was actually his daughter.

'There's some character here, asking to see you.'

Jennie raised her eyebrows. 'Some character?'

'Says he's an old friend. I would've sent him off. Hells bells, we'll be late for the church. But he really was insistent. So I told him he could wait in the library.'

'Does he have a name?'

'He wouldn't give a name. But he said he used to know you once, at Pearl.'

Jennie never remembered getting through the library door. The maid closed it behind her, and they were alone, separated by fifteen feet of floor space and a desk.

He wore a beard.

'Johnnie?' she asked. 'Johnnie?'

And it was Johnnie, even with the beard. But he was thinner than she remembered. And both beard and hair had streaks of grey.

'Oh, Johnnie!'

'There's quite a crowd at the church,' he said.

'Seven hundred and fifty, remember?' Her lips widened in an uncertain smile. 'Oh, Johnnie. They told me you were dead.'

'Well . . .' He was uncertain too – of what to say, how much to say.

She had to tell him. 'I know about what you were doing,' she said. 'I was in the service, too. In the Waves. I . . . I found out what you were doing. So I knew you'd been taken by the Gestapo . . . and we thought . . .'

He nodded. 'That I'd been executed? I should've been. But hell, the Nazis weren't sure what to do with me. They want to stay friends with the Swedes, you see. So they tried me and condemned me to death, and then kicked me out. I will be executed if I ever go back.'

'But when did you get back?'

379

'Oh . . . six months ago.'

'Six months? But . . .'

'I had to be debriefed, and sworn to eternal secrecy . . . and retired.' His mouth twisted. 'They gave me the stripe they promised. I'm a retired commander.'

'Oh, Johnnie.' She took a few steps closer.

'I didn't want to butt in,' he said. 'But when I read of the marriage, I, well, I guess I wanted to congratulate you. And maybe . . . Jennie, will you answer me a question?'

'Anything,' she gasped.

'If you were in the Waves, maybe you know . . . did anything, well, odd, happen over here last December? Early? Around the seventh.'

She frowned. 'Didn't they tell you?'

'Nobody has told me anything. And nobody I've spoken to since coming back seems to have noticed anything.'

'Well, it was never released. It was felt it might scare too many people if they knew how close those Japanese actually came to pulling it off. The whole thing is buried in the archives. And I guess the Germans and the Japs weren't going to talk about it either, because it was such a total disaster from their point of view. But they got here, Johnnie. They got here. And we wouldn't have stopped them, but for your warning.'

'I'm glad of that,' he said. And sighed. 'Maybe . . . maybe it was all worthwhile, after all. But nobody saw or heard anything?'

'Of course they did. But at that time the Nazi U-boats were very active up and down the coast. The official story was that one tried to land agents on the New England coast, and was shot up by navy planes. Simple as that. People believed it. People believe what they're told, in war time.'

'I guess they do. Well . . .' He came round the desk and held out his hand. 'You'll be late for the wedding.'

380

'Johnnie . . .' She was close to him now, close enough to touch. She held his hand. 'Oh, Johnnie.'

Just ask, she thought, and I'll throw everything away and come with you. That was crazy; she didn't know what he had become, what he had had to do, during his five years in Germany. And she did know the true worth, the true love, of Clive Wharton. Yet she would do it.

'Knowing you was the best thing that ever happened to me,' he said.

She gazed into his eyes. They hid secrets too, like hers. But as she looked into them, she knew that his secrets would make hers seem like a schoolgirl's. And suddenly she knew too that there was no hope for him, even with her at his side. And that she didn't want to go with him, any more . . . she loved Clive.

Perhaps he could see that.

'I've killed people, Jennie,' he said. 'Sure, there's a war on, and people get killed in wars. But I did my killing without even a gun. Without even touching my victims. I just did nothing, and watched them die. It went with the job.' He released her hand and turned away. 'But it didn't do much for me, I guess.'

'Oh, Johnnie . . .'

'Be happy, Jennie.' He went to the door. 'Oh, be happy. And give Clive a big hug for me. Now, there's a real *hero*.'

The full facts about Operation Kong have never been released. But there are some known facts which have a bearing on the story:

On 31 January 1943, just on two months after *Nemo* sailed on the remarkable voyage from which she never returned, Grand Admiral Raeder resigned and was succeeded as grand admiral and commander-in-chief

381

by Admiral Doenitz, hitherto commander-in-chief U-boats.

Doenitz's first allegiance remained to the submarine, and German surface activities dwindled steadily throughout the remainder of the war – but Doenitz clearly never forgot the possibilities of Operation Kong. When the collapse of Germany was imminent, he remembered it again. The records reveal that on 14 April 1945, Operation Teardrop began, with two Allied carrier task groups committed to an urgent search in the North Atlantic for a Seewolf U-boat pack reported to be armed with V-2 rockets for launching against New York. Once again, full details of this operation, and the eventual outcome, were never released – but once again the mission clearly failed.

Graf Zeppelin was never completed, and was scuttled by the Germans in January 1945 at Stettin. She was raised by the Russians and taken in tow for Leningrad in 1947, but sank *en route*, probably after striking a mine.

A second, smaller carrier, *Seydlitz*, was also scuttled, incomplete, at Königsberg in East Prussia, on 10 April 1945. She too was raised by the Russians, and eventually scrapped at Leningrad.

The third carrier, and the second designed for Force Z, remains recorded to this day as having been broken up on the slipway at the Germaniawerft shipyard, Kiel, by 1942.

THE CHARACTERS
Isoroku Yamamoto remained commander-in-chief of the Japanese Navy until his death, which occurred on

18 April 1943, when his aircraft was shot down north of Guadalcanal by American Lightning fighters.

Erich Raeder was sentenced in 1946 to life imprisonment for war crimes; he died in prison in 1960.

Karl Doenitz remained commander-in-chief of the German Navy until the end of the war, when he became the surprise successor to Adolf Hitler as Führer of Germany. In this capacity he surrendered the armed forces of the Third Reich to the Allies, and was sentenced to ten years' imprisonment for war crimes. Released in 1955, he did not die until 1980, aged eighty-eight.

Akiko Hatatsune gave birth to a son, named Keiko after the father he never knew, on 16 April 1943. For the next year she continued to live in Tokyo with her mother-in-law, hoping for the return of her husband, who was simply listed as missing. In 1944, she and Mrs Hatatsune and the baby moved from Tokyo because of the increasing American bomber raids, and went to live in the south of Kyushu with Mrs Hatatsune's family. Akiko and young Keiko were in Nagasaki shopping on the morning of 9 August 1945 when the second atomic bomb was dropped over the city. No trace of them was ever found.

Oskar Doerner was captured by the Russians when they took Berlin in 1945; in 1946 he was executed for war crimes.

Rodney Bowen received a bar to his DSC for his action against *Nemo*. He was promoted to rear-admiral in 1945 and fought in the Pacific against the Japanese. Knighted in 1948, he retired in 1963 with the rank of vice-admiral.

*

The admiral retired soon after the war and caused a controversy by publishing his memoirs. He later became president of an automobile company.

Jennie Rhodes is a grandmother, twice by each of her three children. Her husband still plays golf.

Agent Seven-Twenty-One disappeared, and has never been heard of again.